Madison's Song

Kay Plowman

UPFRONT PUBLISHING
LEICESTERSHIRE

Madison's Song
Copyright © Kay Plowman 2004

ISBN 1-84426-280-4

First published 2004 by
UPFRONT PUBLISHING LTD
Leicestershire

Printed by Lightning Source

AUTHOR BIOGRAPHY

Kay Plowman lives in London, where she sings, teaches, writes and marks hundreds of examination papers, in varying proportions depending on the time of year. She is a lyric coloratura mezzo, and, under another name, has written several GCSE and A level textbooks. She loves singing Mozart, Rossini, Bellini and Donizetti, the seaside, Australian wines and anything with pasta.

ACKNOWLEDGEMENTS

My influences are too numerous to mention and, since they were not aware that they were influencing me, need not learn of it here. In any case, I blame no one but myself for errors and infelicities in this story of love, betrayal, passion, and opera. I have allowed convenience to dictate some details of the plot: I am aware that the genies are likely to be double cast at Glyndebourne, but as Mr Ockham said, why multiply entities without necessity? There are no villains in this story, only flawed heroes and an imperfect heroine, and if you recognise yourself in these pages, I was there first.

Come tutte le cose che faccio per te, anche questo e per il maestro chi possede il mio cuore.

CHAPTER 1

I knew that something had changed as soon as I woke up. Something in the very texture of the morning was different. I pressed my face hard against the pillow in an attempt to dispel this unexpected, yet undeniable feeling. Why today of all days? Sighing, I shifted position better to see Andy, still lost in sleep on the other side of the bed. I studied him intently, waiting for the feeling to disappear as I reaccustomed myself to reality. It didn't.

'It's the wrong day for this, Madison' I chided myself as I pulled back the duvet.

Andy grunted, disturbed by my mutterings.

'It's okay. Going to do my hair.'

I needed to be alone if I was going to get back to reality.

The shower was hot and comforting, and I drank tea whilst drying my hair into its usual casual elegance; well, that's the intention, anyway. By the time I had addressed the question of my attire for the day – black jeans, old rose top, a soft pink scarf with darker pink embroidery, my trademark dangly earrings, black suede ankle boots – and reconsidered my options for the evening (the black and gold confirmed as the right decision) – I had to face today's revelation with some kind of temporary acceptance.

On the very day I was to sing *Gerontius* at my Albert Hall debut, I had fallen passionately, irrevocably in love. No, that wasn't quite correct: I had *realised* that I had fallen passionately,

1

irrevocably in love. The offence had already been committed; my mind – unable to bear too much reality – had blocked it out till now.

'Gerry,' I breathed, practising speaking his name aloud in the light of this devastating new information.

'Gerry.'

How could such an unremarkable, unromantic name be suddenly filled with such promise?

I buried my head in the fluffy, sweet scented bath towel.

It had begun.

I need to go back a little here, don't I? I've launched in rather abruptly on that day that it hit me like a thunderbolt. And what a day for it to happen – one of the most important days in my tentatively blossoming career. At thirty-eight I was old to be edging out there into the cut-throat world of classical music, but as a mezzo, I still had a chance. For the uninitiated among you, that means I'm a singer – the kind who sings *Carmen* and *He was Despised,* or dresses up as a man and pretends to be a lovesick page boy, or a heroic soldier who's usually lovesick, too. I was a very late starter. After an averagely competent school career, I suddenly discovered philosophy and all my early dreams of being a professional singer – which tended to revolve around Gilbert and Sullivan – went by the wayside. To the surprise of everyone, I rejected at place at the Royal College of Music, and went to UCL to read for a philosophy degree, and then took a PhD in moral philosophy. After that I taught, wrote, and spoke at learned gatherings, and, I suppose, began to carve out a respectable academic career. I'd kept on singing, and sang solos in oratorios and recitals, and put together rather jolly and slick shows with like-minded people to enthusiastic audiences, but it wasn't a big deal.

I married Andy in the middle of all this. Andy was a writer of sorts – meaning he sort of wrote when he sort of felt like it, and very occasionally, people published what he wrote:

poems, short stories, articles, scripts. He was actually very good, but… I won't go into all that now; it will emerge as my story unfolds. I suppose I had a very satisfactory life. I sang when I wanted to, I earned a reasonable salary, lived in a beautiful flat in an attractive part of south London; I was secure and I was married to a man whose worst fault was lack of self-discipline.

But then I discovered opera. The day I sang Cherubino in *Le Nozze di Figaro* for English Opera in Country Houses I was hooked. I came back from that little summer tour, resigned my teaching contract, took on private students in anything I could tutor just to keep the roof over our heads, and I went all out to sing. I had found my vocation, fourteen years after turning my back on it. At thirty-two it was a huge risk – but I was hungry and keen and I looked younger (I still do). I could pass for late twenties then (early thirties now) and I had more confidence than I'd had at eighteen. On the day I woke up to the knowledge that I was in love with Gerry McFall, after six years of hard graft, I had come a long way, and I was enjoying every minute of it. All this, and I had my Glyndebourne debut in three months' time: Second Lady in *Die Zauberflöte* – no arias, but good clean fun and, after all, it was Glyndebourne! I couldn't believe that I'd finally made it, but I had, and I loved it.

But for now, I had to focus on the day ahead. With a determined effort I pushed the image of Gerry's sweet face from my mind; Andy was moving about in the background – familiar sounds of drawers opening and closing, the wardrobe door swinging back, footsteps moving across the hallway. I stayed in the bathroom a little longer, drawing patterns in the steamed up mirror – treble clefs and initials – MB (that's me) and GM – in swirling italics. The smell of brewing coffee wafted under the door, followed by the soft sounds of the radio. I reluctantly unlocked the bathroom to face the day ahead.

CHAPTER 2

'Madison Brylmer, as the Angel, cut an impressive figure,' Andy read. 'She has a warm, charismatic presence, combined with richness of tone in the lower register and a ringing top. Ideally suited for Elgar's romantic score, Brylmer brought a theatrical flair to the performance and the Angel's genuine concern for Gerontius' fate moved me deeply.'

He beamed at me over the top of the paper.

'*Oh mezzo melissimo... oh bella suprema.*' He kissed his fingertips extravagantly, flourishing the paper over the kitchen counter.

'Cool. What does the *Telegraph* say?'

He rummaged amongst the papers we'd ordered especially for the day.

'Um... nothing... no review.'

'*Guardian*?'

'Hang on a mo. Here it is... "Tempi variable... Radin's Gerontius at its ringing best" – that's good for Pete – ah yes... here we are... "Madison Brylmer's Angel is a dramatic one indeed, and her intensely personal presentation is perhaps a matter of taste" – what a cheek! – "However, none can doubt that we will be hearing more of this fine mezzo."'

'Is that it?'

'"Fraid so.'

'What does he mean? "A matter of taste?" He means I was over the top, doesn't he?'

'He says you are a fine mezzo – as if we didn't know already, O Great One.'

I let it rest; I had to admit to being more than satisfied with the previous night's triumph and Andy was beaming.

'Wait for the phone calls now, Mads, but don't get out of bed for less than £10,000.'

I shook my head, laughing. Andy was proud, and never begrudged me a minute of my small success.

We were still chuckling complacently when the phone rang.

'Remember, no less than ten grand!' joked Andy as I leaned over to pick it up.

'Hello, Madison. Gerry McFall here. Pete Radin's just called me – I hear you've both got great reviews this morning. I had no idea you were doing *Gerontius* last night. We would have been there like a shot if I'd known.'

My hands were shaking so much I almost dropped the phone. To say I'd forgotten about the previous morning's revelation wouldn't be entirely true, but it had gone to the back of my mind in all the excitement.

'Hi, Gerry.' My mind was racing as I attempted to sound casual. Suddenly even the simplest conversation with him seemed impossible.

'Did you enjoy it?' he asked

'Yes. Absolutely terrifying, but wonderful.'

'Pete said it went really well, and that you were terrific.'

'Gosh! High praise indeed! It barely needs saying that he was awesome.'

'So are we still good enough for you to be associating with? Can we expect you at the weekend?'

'Of course. How's my mate Ben?'

'Cross this morning, I'm afraid. He can't play hockey today – he's rehearsing at the Coli.'

'It's tough at the top.'

'You should know!'

'I don't think so, Gerry, I'm just one of the girls.'

'Anyway, well done. See you on Saturday.'

I struggled out a cheery farewell, my hands still shaking as I replaced the receiver.

'Was that Gerry?' Andy enquired unnecessarily, still leafing through the paper.

'Uh huh.' I couldn't trust myself to answer properly.

'He's read the reviews?'

'Pete rang him.'

To my relief, Andy lost interest in pursuing the conversation and began folding up the newspaper briskly.

'I'd better be going if I'm going to get to the library before the crowds. What's your plan today?'

'Practising with Liz this morning. Student this afternoon; meeting Ellen this evening.'

'See you tonight then. Well done, Madsy. "Oh, she is the greatest thing!"' This last was fulsomely busked in mock Handel fashion and I laughed appreciatively as Andy gathered his kit and left the house.

If you're confused by all this, I don't blame you. So was I. But I'm leaving out essential background again, I know. Now I've told you something of me – and there's a lot more of that to come – I need to tell you about Gerry. As you have no doubt correctly assumed, Gerry was an integral part of my life as a singer and, quite clearly, about to become an integral part of my life in every other respect. On the day when my story starts I had known Gerry for about a year. As an extremely long shot I had been called for an audition for a production of *Butterfly*. I was already up for *Nabucco* and my efforts had been entirely concentrated on Verdi when my agent suggested I try out for *Butterfly*, too. It's almost a natural law in singing that when you try desperately hard for something you end up not getting it, and when you don't try at all it lands in your lap, and the law didn't fail this time! After weeks of work on Fenena's minuscule aria I was promptly passed over, and after less than an hour of practice I landed the role of Suzuki in *Madama Butterfly*.

I knew Gerry by reputation only. He was allegedly one of the most difficult operatic conductors on the circuit: rude, partisan, abrupt, and uncompromising. I remember little of him, except that he asked me to sing *Parto, Parto* when I'd been banking on singing *Faites-lui mes aveux*! No matter: I knew I had them captivated from the moment I opened my mouth – sometimes it just happens like that and you just have to grasp the moment and milk it for all it's worth. Six months later, I was standing on the stage of the most amazing open air theatre in England – waves crashing behind me, blue sky and beating sun overhead, rapturous audiences – what more could I want?

At that point, nothing. But something had been happening – so subtly that I barely noticed. As my initial awe of Gerry began to fade, I discovered that the reputation which had preceded him was quite wrong. He was a sweetie – to me, anyway. He was pleased with my work on the Puccini, said nice things, never shouted at me, smiled sweetly, I smiled back, and that was that. I had a wonderful time and hoped that I would be invited to sing something for him again.

With *Butterfly* over I was to start work on *Don Giovanni*. I had another terrific role – I loved flouncing around as Zerlina, hoping that I was even halfway as good as Cecilia Bartoli. Dennis Watkins had been due to conduct, but ill health had forced him out. Only now could I analyse my pleasure at hearing that Gerry was taking over from him. We rehearsed in the autumn, and took performances around the country from November to February, drawing good reviews for an opera that's almost guaranteed to bring in the punters.

I enjoyed getting to know Gerry better during that time, and meeting Ben, his eleven-year-old son. Ben was just fabulous – a proper little star, with a choral scholarship to a prestigious

7

school, and having just enjoyed his first season with the English National Opera children's chorus. I grew to look forward to our meetings, chatting about music and school, this and that, pouring nostalgically over photographs of our summer triumph. Gerry would remain quietly in the background, but occasionally we'd speak together on our own, and I realised that he viewed me differently from the rest of the cast. We had a history, having worked together already that year; he had not found me wanting as a singer and fellow professional and, in an otherwise unfamiliar environment, I was familiar. The other singers had loved Dennis Watkins with a passionate devotion, and Gerry was an unwelcome outsider. After the fey charm of Watkins, they baulked at Gerry's directness and impatience, failing to see that he was just as wary of them and the mantle that had fallen upon him. In any field it's hard to replace someone who has been universally loved, but in the emotional world of singing, it's harder than ever.

I discovered more about Gerry's family, and things that I'd heard on the grapevine began to fit into place. His wife had died of cancer three years earlier and he brought up two boys alone. Josh, at fourteen, faced GCSEs the following year, and was, in Gerry's words 'different'. Ben was loving and charming, precocious beyond his years, and completely at home in the adult world in which he moved.

One day towards the end of the run, I thumbed through a classical music magazine and found an article about an Italian boy, an eleven year old, who had just sung Miles in *The Turn of the Screw,* and was preparing to sing Yniold in *Pelleas* at the Arena in Verona. I clipped the article and gave it to Gerry with a note for Ben. As I penned the innocuous note – *Ben – I thought this might be of interest to you. Love, Madison* – my mind wandered over rather less innocuous thoughts. Always a great fantasist, I now conjured up a touching little scene.

'Gerry, could you give this to Ben? I thought he might be interested in it.'

Gerry would casually peruse the article.

'Yes, of course. You know this means he'll think you're even more wonderful than he does already.'

'Well, that's nice. As long as his dad thinks I'm wonderful too.'

'That goes without saying.'

The scene stumbled to a halt there, but I knew, when on the final night of *Don Giovanni* I daringly kissed Gerry on the cheek and said 'Thanks for everything', that I had a general idea about where I would have liked that scene to lead. I had to admit, I'd enjoyed catching Gerry's eye when he was conducting, and when he sent a deputy it just hadn't been the same. I'd even wondered whether to send him and Ben tickets for *Gerontius,* but had dismissed it, fearing the embarrassment of rejection.

So here I was three weeks later, weighed down with the knowledge of what all that was about. I'd been falling in love with Gerry McFall, and the slow release effect had reached its culmination. Now I desperately wanted to see him again, and I had to wait all of two days. I was singing in an opera gala concert; Gerry was conducting, Pete Radin, who'd sung in *Gerontius,* would be there too, along with Ellen, a good soprano pal (something of a contradiction in terms), and Graham Fellowes, a rather sexy baritone who'd sung Don Giovanni to my Zerlina just a few weeks previously. The rehearsal and the performance were my only chance of seeing Gerry again until the autumn – after that I was not booked to sing for him again until I sang Sesto in *La clemenza di Tito* in November and that just would not do!

CHAPTER 3

I took special care as I dressed and made up on the following Saturday. I put on a new light blue top, having recently discovered that it was a colour which particularly suited my pale complexion. I smoothed my trousers over my hips, wishing that I was a stone lighter, but not too dissatisfied with the image in the mirror. My hair gleamed, and had dried pleasingly into natural curls. I used blue mascara and ran bronzer over my cheeks. My stomach churned, and several times I had to steady my shaking hands. This was ridiculous, I chided myself, but I couldn't quench my excitement at the prospect of seeing Gerry.

I left Andy fiddling with the computer. He looked up briefly as I left.

'Have a good time,' he said.

'You, too. See you tonight.'

'You look nice,' he added, looking at me closely.

'Thanks,' I replied briefly, feeling oddly wrong-footed. 'Bye.'

As I headed over to Maida Vale, I considered the prospect that once I saw Gerry again, I would probably realise that I had simply been indulging a ridiculous fantasy. After all, it was pretty adolescent to wake up one morning and decide that I was in love with an influential colleague who hadn't shown the slightest romantic interest in me. The queasy feeling in my stomach and the hammering of my heart were surely not befitting a PhD three months off her Glyndebourne debut! By the time I emerged from the tube station at Warwick Avenue I was convinced that by the end of the day I would be laughing at the foolish thoughts I had been having.

Gerry was talking to Pete Radin as I wandered into the rehearsal room. He was in an expansive mood, laughing heartily at some yarn he was spinning. His fingers were laced together behind his head as he leaned back in his chair, his long legs stretched out before him. I did a quick inventory of my emotions. Was my heartbeat settling as I watched him? Did the rock and roll of my stomach steady as my nerves calmed? No. As Gerry saw me closing the door and standing motionless, staring at him, I melted. His eyes twinkled as he smiled broadly and got up energetically.

'Here comes the diva!' he joked, and Pete laughed as they broke off their conversation.

I checked Gerry over from head to foot, reluctant to believe that my emotions were, after all, not deceiving me. I appreciated afresh every delicious feature. Tall and spare, not an excess pound of flesh on him, but not too skinny either. Being in his arms would feel just right. Not a full head of hair, I had to admit, but it simply made Gerry look cute and vulnerable. (The sexiest tenor I knew was as hairless as a billiard ball and he had women dropping at his feet.) And I had remembered perfectly accurately Gerry's total lack of dress sense. To say that his clothes were uncoordinated would be kind; it was like an explosion in a paint factory: green jumper, wildly patterned tie, dun coloured trousers. My heart expanded with love. How beautiful he was. I was tongue-tied. Gerry, who didn't know my predicament, was not.

'What good timing. You and Pete can do your duet.'

He began to rummage through the scores which covered the top of the piano, pulling out *Carmen*.

'Oh, splendid.' I unloosed my tongue, reminding myself to be normal. 'I hope this is going to be at the beginning of the programme. If I'm worn out, I can't do it.'

'Surely not, Madison, a star of your calibre!'

'Stop it, Gerry,' I laughed, 'I am frail and fallible, and need handling carefully.'

'Oh yes, like an armoured tank needs careful handling.'

I slapped his hand.

'Just watch, it buster. Do what you're paid to do, and play!'

I was delighted at my bravura performance and it gave me an adrenaline buzz which carried into our duet. I enjoyed singing with Peter; he was an exceptionally talented young man, who was going places fast and would soon eclipse the rest of us. I made the most of singing with him while I could.

As we were toiling away, Ellen and Graham arrived and we quickly settled in to a businesslike rehearsal. My feelings for Gerry not withstanding, I was enormously looking forward to this concert. We were the star turns in a sparking gala in aid of cancer charities, which was being hosted in the banqueting hall in Whitehall. Gerry had useful contacts for whom he regularly provided singers at galas, prestigious corporate events, outdoor extravaganzas and so forth, and this was my first gig of the kind for him. It was an indication that Gerry thought well of me, and that seemed a pretty good basis on which to move forward.

We romped though an excellent programme of ensembles, duets, and arias, ending with *Un di se ben rammentomi* from *Rigoletto;* if I had a desert island list of my favourite pieces, the delicious pleasure of singing *Aha, rido ben di core che ta bai constan poco* put it close to the number one slot. So Pete and I flirted and flounced, and Ellen and Graham wept and stormed and we all resolved beautifully, and stood back and beamed at one another in appreciation.

'I think that just about covers it,' Gerry said, closing his score, as he reminded us of times and dates and arrangement for the concert. The following week we would have no more rehearsals, just a warm up on the day, and I knew that if I wanted a decent conversation with Gerry I had to take my opportunity now.

'What's Ben up to?' I asked as we packed our things away.

'He's in fine form,' Gerry told me. 'We've had some very good news, actually.'

'Oh yes?'

'After three or four different auditions, one of which was based purely on height, for goodness sake, we've been told that he's got First Genie in *Flute* at Glyndebourne this summer.'

If I'd any reason to doubt my hearing, I certainly would have done so at receiving this particular piece of intelligence. As it was, I gaped fish-like for several seconds.

'But Gerry,' I gasped when I finally found my voice again, 'I'm doing it, too. I'm Second Lady, remember.' We had discussed this often over the last year.

Gerry opened his eyes wide, a characteristic gesture, which, I was to learn, indicated amusement or pleasure.

'Oh, Madison, of course!' he exclaimed, 'I thought something about it all rang a bell.'

I knew there was no point wasting emotional energy being insulted that Gerry hadn't made the connection with me, and the whole prospect was so exciting I just kept grinning like a maniac.

'Of course, they cast the children virtually at the last minute, don't they? Not like us old troopers who've been fixed up for years.'

Obviously, if you're casting roles which require unbroken voices you can't make any assumptions too early. A boy's voice may only demonstrate its suitability for the handful of attractive and competitive operatic roles for trebles at the age of ten or eleven. With the prospect of that same voice breaking after as little as two years, there's no point in an opera house booking lads too far in advance of a production. At eleven, Ben had enjoyed a year in the ENO children's chorus, and was now, it appeared, about to undertake his first solo role in an international house. He could possibly have three years ahead of him as a principal artiste, but it was no good counting on it. Every opportunity had to be grasped and enjoyed as if it were the last.

'Oh, Gerry, that's just marvellous. I'm so pleased for him.' I paused, acknowledging Gerry's proud and happy smile. 'I can chaperone some days, if that's helpful,' I suggested, already foreseeing the opportunities that might unfold here.

'Well, obviously all the boys will have an official chaperone, but it will be great having you there, too. I'm sure we'll be prevailing upon your good nature soon enough. If you really don't mind, that is,' he added quickly.

'I'll be delighted,' I assured him. 'Oh, I'm so pleased, it'll be such fun having Ben there, too.'

We made our way to Gerry's car, carrying his pile of music between us. As we stacked them in the boot Gerry asked, 'Can I give you a lift anywhere?'

'Where are you going?'

'Victoria. Does that help?'

I felt nervous and excited as we drove through the streets of Maida Vale and onto the Edgware Road, but I barely got a word in edgeways as Gerry gave me a blow by blow account of all the hoops Ben had been obliged to jump through before he was finally offered his role. I smiled and laughed and nodded in the right places and, as we pulled up outside Victoria station, he smiled broadly at me.

'Well done you, too, Madison. A Glyndebourne debut is special at any age, and very important for you. It's going to make our *Tito* in the autumn a bit of a comedown.'

'Oh, Gerry, of course not! It'll be wonderful. I've wanted to sing Sesto forever, and it'll be years before I can expect to be offered it in a big house.'

'Well, I shouldn't be too sure of that,' he said.

I basked in his approval as we said our farewells, and stood on the pavement glowing as Gerry drove away.

CHAPTER 4

Andy was still at the computer when I got home. It wasn't usual for him to demonstrate such commitment to a task, and I wondered what had precipitated it. He soon told me.

'Madison! Joe Budzynski called from The Restless Dragon. They want *Lethal Desires* there in September.'

'Oh, Andy,' I breathed, my foolish distractions swept aside at the enormity of this news. The Restless Dragon was perhaps the most important fringe theatre venue in South London and plays worked there often transferred to the West End, or at least took a provincial tour. To have a play accepted for production there was the most tremendous accolade. I stared at Andy in awe.

'I don't believe it.'

'Neither did I, but it's true, Madsy. I'm meeting him at ten o'clock on Monday morning. Now I'm just working through the whole script, tidying up some awkward corners.'

Andy's eyes shone with happiness and I thought how handsome he was when he was fired up with enthusiasm. Andy was a big man: six foot one, broad chest and shoulders, powerful legs, a thick mop of dark curly hair, and rich brown eyes to match. Physically, he was as different to Gerry as two men could be, but this thought didn't distract me at the moment. I hurried over to hug him warmly.

'Andy, it's brilliant. What can I say?'

'It was you who bullied me to send the play to them, Mads. It's me who should be grateful to you.'

I remembered that we'd sent it six months ago, after I'd read what I thought was Andy's best work so far. Evidently Joe Budzynski had agreed. After years of struggling, not only to be recognised as a writer of quality, but against his own lack of motivation and repeated failure to follow through on a project – things which had so often made me angry and despairing – it looked as if Andy was about to make the break.

'Shall I look at what you've been doing?' I asked, knowing that Andy would welcome my input.

'Please, yes.'

So I brought a bottle of wine from the kitchen, along with a bag of tortilla chips and dip, and we settled before the computer in companionable industry.

Andy and I had married ten years previously. We'd met at a party he'd attended after a performance of *Guys and Dolls* in which I'd sung Adelaide. Andy, an outgoing, gregarious American, originally from New York, was a friend of Mick, who'd played my opposite number, Nathan Detroit. Mick introduced us, we got chatting and we'd hit it off that first night. Inevitably, it was a long while before I realised that for all Andy's talent it wasn't just because he hadn't yet been in the right place, or even in the right country, at the right time that he had not become a conspicuous commercial success. Gradually, I learned that Andy was incapable of working under anyone else's direction. Things had to happen his way, or simply not at all, and deadlines meant nothing to him, responsibility even less; Andy got on by dominating and bluffing as long as he could get away with it. When he was eventually rumbled by people who'd put a lot of faith in him, they were naturally cross and disappointed, and told him where to go, but as far as Andy was concerned, it was always their fault. So over ten years we'd had some pretty grim episodes, fuelled by my own inability to understand why anyone with talent and intelligence should invest less than one hundred per cent commitment and discipline in their art.

I knew that Andy was quite capable of blowing this wonderful opportunity even now, and thought I'd risk a word of caution.

'Budzynski may want more changes,' I said casually.

'As long as he doesn't forget whose play it is. If he wants it, then he wants it as it is,' Andy responded with predictable defensiveness.

'I expect he'll be prepared to negotiate,' I said calmly.

'Umm.' Andy was non-committal for a moment. 'Oh, but another thing!' he said excitedly. 'He asked me to be involved with the rehearsals.'

'Goodness,' I exclaimed, 'this is getting better and better.'

Andy had dabbled in directing at university and had longed to become seriously involved ever since. I was tempted to utter further words of warning to remind Andy that the success of this project would be contingent on his playing by the rules of those with the cheque book, but I couldn't bring myself to mar his happiness. There would be time enough for realities as the project unfolded.

We continued working until well after dark, then took the remains of the wine into the lounge to curl up in front of the Saturday night movie. I didn't think of Gerry and Ben again until I climbed into bed. I waited till Andy had fallen asleep and cautiously slipped out again. In my desk I found a little card: gold cherubs hanging decorously from staves.

Dear Ben, I wrote, *I was pleased to hear of your latest success, and look forward to our joint Glyndebourne debut. We'll show them how to do it! Love, Madison.*

Andy's meeting with Budzynski went like a dream and the contract was signed two days later. Andy had amicably agreed to a number of minor revisions, doubtless considerably sweetened by the prospect of acting as assistant director. We were both stunned and incredulous. The play would go into its initial production stages at the beginning of July and open in the first week of September, five days after my final Glyndebourne show. What a summer lay ahead for us both! We celebrated with our closest friends, Steve and Danielle, who genuinely rejoiced in our good fortune.

'Is there a part in it for me?' Steve asked.

'Yes, there is actually,' Andy enthused. 'The lead, Mort Williams, is ideal for you. I'll ask Joe about auditions; he says I can sit in on them.'

'The director may be going with people he's already worked with,' I said quietly.

'There's no harm in asking,' Andy snapped. 'I'll do it tomorrow, mate,' he told Steve.

Danielle smiled at me.

'Madsy, it's so good, especially with you doing Glyndebourne.'

We nodded at each other with understanding. Danielle was aware that I was deeply conscious of how my success had long since outstripped Andy's.

'Yes,' I concurred. 'It's time for a bit of levelling out, I think.'

As we spent a happy evening together I wondered what Danielle would say if I told her about Gerry. Something wise but firm, I thought, along the lines of, 'Look, but don't touch, and preferably, don't even look.'

Well, that would be impossible, since he was the man with the white stick, and besides, I knew it would be hard to resist taking a good, long look whenever the opportunity presented.

CHAPTER 5

There was a buzz in the air on Saturday when we trooped along for the charity gala in Westminster. The orchestra contained many familiar faces, and we greeted one another cheerfully. As ever, there was a very special pleasure in putting what we had rehearsed together with the orchestra. However many times you did it, the transition from piano accompaniment to the varied sounds of the different instruments was exciting. The afternoon rehearsal was a time of real musical sharing. Gerry blossomed in front of the orchestra, joking with the players, beaming from ear to ear, clearly enjoying it as much as we singers did. Ellen and I played around at out diva-ing each other in the full knowledge that in the evening we would be working to support and complement each other. There were some wonderful moments in the programme and the high paying punters were in for a treat, especially, I thought, with the Rosina/Figaro duet from *Barber* that drew applause even from the orchestra as Graham and I rehearsed. It was a lovely self-indulgent afternoon, and we broke for tea (Musicians' Union tea break, of course) in high spirits. Gerry was fiddling with orchestra parts, and I wandered over casually.

'Can I get you anything?' I asked.

'I've got a Sainsbury's bag somewhere.' He looked around vacantly.

I found it with his coat and baton case.

'Excellent.' He peered in. 'I've got bananas and crisps, and, oh, lots of stuff here,' he grinned. 'Do you want to share? Where are the others?'

'Gone to get a pizza I think. I couldn't eat one now – afterwards, perhaps!'

'I could eat one before and after, but shall we make do with what I've got?' he asked.

We adjourned to the green room and pooled our resources. I picked and sipped, whilst Gerry ate voraciously, and I made a conscious effort not to be overwhelmed by my fast beating heart, and to talk to him like a normal, sane person. By the time Ellen, Peter, and Graham returned we were thoroughly relaxed, idly picking grapes off a stalk and mulling over opera experiences we had known and loved.

'Madsy, where did you get to?' boomed Graham. 'We thought you were behind us.' He cast his eyes appraisingly over Gerry and me. 'You two look cosy. Having a picnic?'

'Yes,' Gerry declared appreciatively, stretching out his long legs luxuriously, 'and very nice it was, too.'

'Did you miss me then, Graham?' I teased holding out my hands.

'I certainly did, gorgeous,' he laughed, pulling me to my feet for a cuddle. He hugged me warmly for a moment as I remembered some very pleasant stage embraces in *Don Giovanni* and hoped that Gerry was taking note.

'Shall we get dressed, Mads?' Ellen suggested, and I reluctantly trotted after her to change and to focus on the evening's work.

Which was, as I'd anticipated, enormously enjoyed by a beautifully dressed and bejewelled audience. We looked pretty spectacular ourselves, I thought, admiring my dress in the mirror during the interval. It was made in a smooth, satiny fabric, jet black with tiny black sequins on a delicate but tastefully plunging bodice. I only wore simple styles in concert, and the line of the dress pleased me – straight up and down, touching lightly over bosom and hips. I wasn't tall enough to get away with some of the dramatic, diaphanous creations my colleagues wore, but after some trial and error I had found a style which suited me.

So we were puffed up with our own success as we sat down to dinner after our stint was over. I quickly slid into a seat between Graham and Gerry, making an attempt to appear casual about it. I made a point of talking to Graham all through the first course, leaving Gerry to chat with Ellen, Peter, and the leader of the orchestra (the token orchestra member who'd been invited to share the feast). By the time the main course arrived, conversation had spread out around the table, and Gerry turned quite naturally to me to draw me in. I felt flushed as we ate and shared bottles of far better quality wine than I would ever buy from Sainsbury's. I tested my reactions now and then, touching Gerry's hand to ask him to pass the water jug, or the condiments. It felt cool under my hot palm and I enjoyed studying his deft handling of the cutlery, and the idle drumming of his fingers on the cloth.

As the meal drew to a close, I was increasingly aware that I wouldn't be seeing him for a while unless I was very clever about it. I rapidly calculated how things were likely to pan out over the next few months. *Flute* went up at the beginning of July; music rehearsals started in the first week of May. Today was March 10th. Two blank months loomed and I couldn't see a solution. Ah, well, perhaps it was a good thing. My imaginings might wither on their youthful vine.

As we filed out into the cool night, I laid my hand on Gerry's arm.

'I'll let you know when I start *Flute* calls. If they coincide with Ben's, we can travel together perhaps.'

'Absolutely,' he agreed. 'We'll not be strangers over the summer, I'm sure. Don't forget to learn Sesto in the midst of all the excitement!'

We chuckled and I stood on tiptoe to kiss his cheek.

'Bye,' I said, deliberately looking him straight in the eye. He looked squarely back, clearly amused and faintly arrogant.

'Goodbye,' he drawled, raising his eyebrows ironically. 'See you soon.'

I squeezed his arm and turned a sharp left to walk towards Westminster tube. I wanted to look back at him and smile, but managed to keep my face firmly forward and my back ramrod straight. Whether he watched me or not, I don't know, but I'd sown the seeds and now I just had to wait and see if anything flourished. I pondered over the distinctly amused expression on Gerry's face as we'd parted. It was a 'This might be interesting and I'm in control' look, with a distinct touch of 'I've been here so many times don't think you can catch me off guard.' That was a bit disconcerting and unexpected, I had to admit. Perhaps it *was* better if I talked myself out of my ardour right now. I'd see how I felt in the morning.

CHAPTER 6

S ix days later, my favourite accompanist phoned me.
        'Madison,' she cried, 'I'm so sorry.'

'What about, Lizzie?' I asked, mystified.

'I'm in hospital.'

'Oh, goodness, darling, what's up?' I asked in concern, knowing that Lizzie was nearly seven months pregnant.

'I've had a miscarriage scare. The obstetrician has told me to cancel everything till after the baby's born.'

'That sounds sensible,' I concurred.

'But Madsy, our concert!' she cried. 'I'll have to pull out.'

Lizzie and I were due to appear together at the Solent Music Club at the end of April, just before *Flute* took over for the summer.

'Oh, Lizzie,' I consoled her, 'don't worry. I'll miss you, but I can get a deputy. And we'll have lots more opportunities to work together. You and the baby are far more important now.'

We chatted for a little longer, mulling over Lizzie's enforced confinement. Hanging up, I drew breath and let my brain slow down for a moment. Barely was Lizzie's first sentence out of her mouth and I had begun to imagine a monumentally appealing solution to her unexpected absence. Before I could lose my nerve I rapidly dialled Gerry's phone number. I was pleased to hear the answering machine click into action – they were such a marvellous invention for nervous callers who feared rejection.

'Hi, it's Madison Brylmer. I've lost my pianist for a gig on April 28th. I wondered if you might be free. Give me a call and I can let you know more details.'

I left various phone numbers and, working on the assumption that he would turn me down, flicked through my contacts, mentally noting whom else I could ask. There would be no problem coming up with an alternative if I had to do so.

Andy stuck his head around the study door.

'Who was that?' he asked.

'Lizzie. She can't do the Solent gig. Doctor's orders till she gives birth.'

'Oh. Can you get someone else?'

'Of course.' I waved my Filofax at him. 'About forty-five other options here!'

'Good-oh,' Andy smiled. 'I'm off now.' Andy taught a creative writing class once a week, something that he had managed to keep going for nearly a year now.

As he left, I wondered how long I should give Gerry to get back to me before following up other leads. There were less than six weeks to the recital and the promoters would need to know about personnel changes. Today was Thursday. I'd give him till Sunday night before abandoning hope.

He phoned on Sunday afternoon.

'It's Gerry McFall,' he announced formally. 'Sorry to take so long to get back to you, but, yes, that's fine. If you haven't got anyone else by now, that is.'

I wondered if he might think it odd that I had indeed waited three days to hear from him; in this business you are expected to return calls yesterday. I kept it light.

'Oh, yes, I'd put it to the back of my mind. Good, if you're free that would be splendid.'

I quoted him the fee, which was acceptable, and we talked about the programme: song cycles by Verdi and Schumann, and several arias he knew well.

'When shall we get together?' he asked.

We scrutinised our diaries and arranged a date for ten days hence, and pencilled in two other good long sessions prior to the gig. I hung up in such a state of excitement that it took several attempts to replace the receiver without the whole thing crashing to the floor.

'Fighting with the phone, Mads?' Andy called out from the kitchen.

'It's got a life of its own all of a sudden,' I laughed, glad of an outlet for my bubbling hysteria.

'Who was that?' he asked genially, ambling down the hall.

'Gerry McFall. He's going to play for the Solent concert.'

'Oh.' Andy sounded surprised. 'I didn't realise you'd asked him. He hasn't played for you before, has he? Not in concert, I mean?'

'No. I thought I'd try someone new for a change.'

'Right.' Andy still looked surprised. 'I didn't know he did that kind of thing.'

'Well, obviously he does,' I replied shortly.

'Okay, okay,' Andy held up his hands in mock surrender. 'You know best.'

I realised that Andy hadn't been suspicious about my choice of pianist, just concerned for me, and I felt guilty both for my sharpness and for my machinations.

'Sorry,' I apologised. 'He'll be fine. We've booked the rehearsals and he knows the stuff.' I smiled conciliatorily at Andy.

Perhaps I didn't have the stomach for this, after all.

CHAPTER 7

M y mother, Megan Matthews, was a new woman before the term had been invented but, typically of her, she had gone about becoming so in her own inimitable way. She had married my father at twenty, had me at twenty-two and, from what I could gather, spent the next eight years concentrating on trying to provide a sibling. I had vague memories of that time: my father, easy going and kindly, not particularly ambitious for himself or his loved ones, everyone's friend in a gentle and genial way. My mother, louder, faster, and, I suspect, burning with frustrated ambition even then, was by far the dominant force. She taught me to read long before my first day at school, and encouraged me to be the most precocious performer in every theatrical and musical event open to me.

My father died when I was eight and, to the amazement of everyone other than herself, Megan applied to King's College, London, was accepted to read law, and began her campaign to become the fastest of fast track corporate lawyers in the history of man or, in her case, woman. So as I entered senior school, Megan was graduating with first class honours; as I sat O levels, she began articles with a top city firm, doubtless beating down several thrusting young Cambridge graduates in the process and, as I began my PhD research, Megan was virtually established as one of the most powerful lawyers in the Square Mile.

She terrified me. Even though I knew I was her intellectual equal, I always felt that I was playing catch up in an unequal race since Megan would always have the advantage of having done it alone. She was desperately proud of reaching her position of considerable legal power not by having gone to St Paul's and Newnham, but from being a single mother with no one but herself to push, encourage and persuade her in her quest. Even whilst she applauded and delighted in my successes, there was always an undercurrent of patronage. She'd done it the hard way, whilst I'd had a silver spoon. When I made the life changing decision to abandon academia for music, it was her reaction I'd feared the most. Until I won my first tiny solo role at the Coli, I faced a barrage of questions, opinions, sighs and tight lips, but by the time my story begins she was pleased as punch. She would proudly tell her colleagues and clients of her daughter who was not only a PhD, but a burgeoning opera star, and her office walls were hung not only with her hard won diplomas, but with photos of my Maddalena at ENO, Rosina at Holland Park, and Pitti Sing at the Savoy (I don't admit to that one very often).

Megan was my greatest fan and my harshest critic. Not musically, since for all Megan's arrogance she wouldn't claim expertise she didn't have, but as an arbiter of my personal life there was no avoiding Megan's probing analysis. She had little time for Andy before we married, sharply appraising him as a lazy hanger-on but, once married, she would hear no word against him, and considered my commitment to him to be inviolate. She expected me to be utterly without reproach in all matters, my relationship with her and with Andy above all.

But ultimately, we were friends. I didn't confide in her, for that would open up avenues of argument and debate that I was simply not prepared to pursue, but as long as things went well, we got on. She faithfully attended as many of my performances as her schedule allowed, buzzing around the country in her customised Morgan, she was generous to me and charming to my friends. If she even got a whiff of my embryonic feelings for Gerry she would hit the roof. But whilst she was prepared to cut me no slack, leading inevitably to some pretty distressing exchanges over the years, I knew that to a considerable degree it was my disciplined upbringing that gave me strength as a professional in a tough world. I was more like Megan that I cared to admit.

I thought a lot about my mother that week after we'd all met for yet another celebration of Andy's good fortune. She was delighted, as befitted one almost as obsessed with Andy's success, or lack of it, as she was with mine. Even after the whole thing had been endlessly thrashed over in public, she still cornered me privately.

'Is Andy happy about the play?'

I groaned inwardly. It was a question typical of Megan's inability to accept anything at face value. Perhaps it came of being a lawyer, not just a control freak.

'Of course he is. It's a wonderful opportunity.'

'You'll both be very busy over the summer,' she observed. 'You'll need to find time to take a holiday together, just the two of you.'

A holiday! I couldn't think of anything less desirable or relevant, but I'd learned from experience that the best course of action was not to react to Megan's apparently innocent, but heavily loaded, comments.

'Yes, I'm sure we will,' I said smoothly.

'Andy will need your support in this project,' she observed. 'I know you'll be very tied up with Glyndebourne, but you mustn't neglect him.'

I gritted my teeth.

'Doubtless it will all work out,' I reassured her. 'His opening night is a week after *Flute* comes down, which is very convenient.'

Megan managed to make several comments along similar lines over the next week when we spoke on the phone, whilst I concentrated on keeping my temper. She was never clear about what she feared, I could only assume it was that one day

Andy and I would separate, forced apart by the demanding lover that was my musical career. Why it bothered her so much I couldn't work out, but ultimately I think it was about discipline, and being reliable and respectable. There was probably more than a trace of anxiety about what she would tell others if I was inconsiderate enough to bring shame on her with a divorce, but perhaps that was unfair of me.

All this hovered at the back of my mind as I looked forward to seeing Gerry for our first rehearsal. How ridiculous! I was mildly attracted to a colleague, would definitely not refuse his advances in the unlikely event he made any, but essentially there was nothing seriously at stake here, surely. That I should be tentatively anticipating my mother's inevitable and instantaneous reaction should I even contemplate leaving Andy for Gerry was ludicrous. And yet I was. Even more so when Megan announced that she planned to attend the Solent Music Club recital.

'It's nothing special,' I tried to dissuade her.

'I'd like to come, Madison,' she said firmly, brooking no argument. 'I can't see that it will inconvenience you in any way.'

'Of course not.' True to form, I backed down immediately.

'I can drive you down there if that's helpful.'

'Mum, I haven't sorted all that out yet. I'll probably drive down with the pianist. We haven't got that far with the arrangements.'

'That's Lizzie, I presume?' she asked.

'No. She's not working till she's had her baby. The guy who conducted *Butterfly* and *Don Giovanni* is going to play for me.' I was pleased that I could sound so matter of fact.

'I see.' Megan looked curious. 'I remember a chap who looked as if he thinks a lot of himself.'

I laughed, having to acknowledge the truth of Megan's apt description.

'Indeed. He'll be very reliable though.'

'How interesting,' said Megan cryptically and, not for the first time, I really did wonder if she was a mind reader.

CHAPTER 8

On the day of my first rehearsal with Gerry I'd spent the morning working on *Flute* with Robert, my splendid coach. He was a refined English gentleman of the old school; white haired and plummy toned. He had been a conductor in small European houses of some note in the seventies and he brought a wealth of experience and inspiration to his work with me. I never left his studio without feeling as if I could do anything. He was a hard taskmaster, never one to throw bouquets, but I enjoyed being bullied by him, knowing that he would not work me so hard unless he believed I was capable of achieving ever higher standards.

Although the Ladies in *Flute* have no arias, the ensemble work is rigorous and there would be no excuse for turning up at the first music call without being note and word perfect. My fellow Ladies, Clarissa Grainger and Anastasia Winkworth, were well established and highly respected singers, and my concern as I worked that morning was to ensure that I wouldn't let myself, and them, down. We toiled away for nearly two hours before Robert decided I'd sung enough.

'You'll get there in time, I think,' he said, with an ironic lift of an eyebrow.

'That's a relief,' I joked. 'Can I see you next week?'

Robert got out his diary and we compared dates.

'Could you do next Wednesday morning?' he asked.

I shook my head. 'I'm rehearsing for a concert at the Solent Music Club.'

Robert's interest was piqued and he asked me about the programme and the venue.

'I've never played there,' he mused. 'Who's your pianist? Lizzie Swallow?'

'No. She's out of action at the moment. Gerry McFall's playing for me.'

Robert smirked. 'That will be interesting.'

I had sensed some rivalry between Robert and Gerry when I'd spoken of him before, and I laughed now.

'What do you mean by 'interesting', in that tone of voice?'

'He's not exactly refined,' Robert said waspishly, 'and his dynamic range goes from loud through louder to very loud.'

I had to admit that there was some truth in this, but I wasn't going to let Robert have the last word.

'Well, I like him, and I'm sure we'll have a good time.'

He wasn't going to let me get away with it either.

'If that's your priority, Madison,' he said patronisingly.

I chuckled as I packed away my score, but I knew Robert was right. I did have another agenda and I feared it was rather too transparent.

I met Danielle for a quick lunch on the way to Gerry's studio in Maida Vale and, with some trepidation, pressed the entry phone just before three o'clock. A glamorous soprano who I vaguely knew was coming out as I entered. She nodded briefly, not inclined to chat, and I bristled with irritation. Why did some of these girls manage to make me feel five inches tall? I watched as she sashayed her way over to an expensive looking station wagon, before I disconsolately climbed the stairs to Gerry's studio. A medley of musical sounds accosted me as I passed busy practice rooms. I checked my reflection in the glass door, passing my hand through my hair yet again, and straightening my shoulders confidently.

Gerry was playing the opening to Act Two of *La Bohème* as I pushed open the door.

'Hello. Am I premature?' I asked.

Gerry closed his score, getting up from the piano energetically.

Of course not. Good to see you,' he greeted me expansively. 'I've been having a wonderful time. Did I tell you I'm conducting *Bohème* in September? I've just started renewing my acquaintance with it, and Caroline Lind has been here doing some preliminary work on Mimi.'

I realised now who the intimidating woman was who I'd seen as I'd arrived. The knowledge that she was singing Mimi was depressing. It was such a luminous, romantic role, barred from even the sweetest voiced lyric mezzo, but I certainly didn't relish the prospect of anyone other than me beguiling Gerry with its delights. Most of all not Caroline Lind. She was barracuda; I wouldn't even try to compete with her. I must have looked subdued as Gerry demonstrated some particularly delicious passages from Puccini's score, for he stopped abruptly.

'I'm sorry, I'm boring you,' he apologised.

'Oh, Gerry, of course not. It's beautiful,' I said. 'I was actually bemoaning the fact that I'll never get to sing *Bohème*.'

'It is a shame,' he agreed. 'I enjoy myself immensely conducting it. I've done thirty-six performances so far. This run will take it almost to the half century. But let's concentrate on you now,' he said kindly. 'This is a lovely programme. I particularly like the Verdi.'

I had chosen an early song cycle, called simply *Six Romances*. Each piece was a miniature of perfection, encompassing so many musical and emotional themes.

We worked on the songs for over an hour before Gerry suggested we broke for tea. It was interesting to compare his style with Robert's, especially after our conversation in the morning. We worked faster, but with less depth. It wouldn't help me in the long term; I needed someone like Robert to push me more aggressively, but I enjoyed Gerry's sense of purpose. His patience surprised me. He'd been brisk when we'd worked together before, and I appreciated now that his approach was quite different when we worked alone. He was unexpectedly gentle and generous, laughing when I looked dissatisfied with what I was doing.

'Don't pull that face,' he said. 'It's fine. Let's just do it again.'

Several times he was complimentary.

'That's good... a nice tone there... excellent.'

I wasn't used to such encouragement. Praise usually came only from biased audience members and insincere colleagues, not from those who had any real power!

It was the first time I had been alone with Gerry for any length of time and I tried hard to be objective. We were both focussed on our task, but once we'd stopped for tea I allowed myself to study him closely again. He positively pulsated with energy, enthusiasm for the music and the pleasure of sharing his expertise charged the atmosphere. But kind as he was to me, he nevertheless remained in control, talking non-stop about his plans and activities, about Ben's school and musical progress. He was used to engaging the attention of others, and I sensed that if our relationship were to develop beyond the professional, I would have to work hard at holding my own. Gerry liked to dominate every situation, not just musical ones, and I wondered how I felt about that when I was so used to taking the lead myself.

After we had our tea we resumed work: Schumann's *Frauenliebe und Leben* flowed easily from us both. The programme would conclude with three arias, all with a common link: each was sung by a trouser character, a mezzo playing a man. I loved these roles and the florid music which so often went with them. We decided to leave them till our next rehearsal, though, since I had virtually sung myself out by then, but we happily anticipated the pleasures of *Parto, Parto, Che Faro*, and the lovely violin aria from *Hoffmann*.

'You are going to give the audience a treat, Gerry said. 'Can you sustain all this in one programme?'

I shook back my curls. 'Am I or am I not a diva?' I laughed.

'Without a doubt,' he agreed. 'Can I drop you at Victoria?'

I didn't need asking twice, and in the car I decided it was time to take some initiative, so I regaled him with the latest news of an opera being written for me and colleagues with whom I'd worked closely over the years.

'When's all this going to happen?' Gerry asked, looking amused.

'I'll show you some of the music,' I told him. 'I can see you're not convinced.'

We laughed companionably as he stopped to let me out of the car.

'I've really enjoyed this afternoon. Thank you,' I said.

'Good.' Gerry seemed to find even this amusing. 'We must do it again.'

CHAPTER 9

In those very early days, a week without seeing Gerry didn't feel like an eternity in a timeless universe. Later, it did, and looking back I marvelled that it had once been so painless. Normal life continued between our first rehearsal at the studio and the second at Gerry's house, albeit punctuated by tremors of excitement and anticipation. I conjured up several versions of broadly the same scene, the pertinent details of which involved Gerry and I ending up in bed, and as I sat on the train bound for West Dulwich I felt sick with nerves. But I hadn't cried over him yet; that was still to come.

Gerry and his sons lived in Thurlow Park Road, a short step from Dulwich Park and West Dulwich station. It was a prestigious area; the roads were lined with beautiful houses, tall, impressive Victorian three-storey buildings with enormous rear gardens and garaging for several cars. The rising sun filtered through the newly budding trees and the air was fresh and fragrant. I strode out with happy steps. Outside Gerry's house I paused, noticing that there were serious signs of neglect around the front door: a long abandoned hanging basket, sprouting crisply dead vegetation; grass determinedly forcing its way between the paving slabs, and Gerry's utilitarian estate car, awash with music, clothing and food wrappings, was parked at a careless angle across the drive. The doorbell was not immediately apparent, and eventually I used the letterbox, flipping it back and forth to announce my arrival. Ben opened the door, hands and mouth busily occupied with toast and marmalade.

'Hi.'

He walked straight back into the house, leaving me to follow. The place looked like a demolition site. The enormous hall – full of potential – was a dumping ground. A bicycle took up residence alongside a cello, hockey sticks, several coats, ancient bags and their contents spilling over the floor, a brace of footballs, and a catering sack of potatoes. As I absorbed this horror, Ben called from the kitchen.

'I'm in here. Dad's gone to get some milk.'

I followed the voice into a room of equally palatial proportions, taking in the abandoned crockery, jars, packets and the morning's post, cast aside randomly among the crumbs on the huge dining table. I'd kill for a kitchen like this, I though covetously, itching to get to work with Mr Muscle and a scourer.

I took a place at the table. Ben was poring over a car magazine, and promptly started to draw my attention to vehicles that were apparently of a peculiarly superior nature.

'If you say so, Ben,' I agreed. 'They all look the same to me.'

He proceeded to launch into a detailed description of their respective merits and I listened as best I could, quite overwhelmed by the sheer pleasure of being in Gerry's house. He didn't take long to return, finding our heads bent over a picture of a glistening red Porsche.

'Hello.'

Gerry somehow always managed to invest the simple greeting with enormous promise, dragging out two syllables far longer than their worth, and raising his eyebrows speculatively.

'Hello. You were expecting me, weren't you?' I grinned happily at him.

'Of course. That's why I went for this.' He held up the milk carton. 'You're not boring Madison with that are you, young man?'

'No,' Ben replied innocently, 'how could she find it boring?'

'Very easily, I should imagine,' Gerry retorted, 'unless sports cars are one of your particular interests?' he asked, turning to me.

'Not as yet, but I'm prepared to be educated,' I answered, not entirely in jest.

'See,' Ben said with emphasis.

'I think Madison's being polite,' Gerry laughed, 'and she has much more important things to do this morning, so I suggest you decide how you're going to entertain yourself whilst we work.'

'Okay,' Ben agreed easily, immediately grabbing his magazine and making for the door. 'See you later.'

Gerry shook his head in wry amusement.

'School holidays,' he said as if that explained everything.

'Where's Josh?' I asked, curious to meet him.

'Staying with his grandmother,' Gerry replied without elaboration. 'Sugar?'

I shook my head, taking the mug gratefully. I would have liked to linger longer over tea, engaging Gerry in conversation about his sons, but he motioned with his free hand towards the hall.

'The piano's just been tuned. I'm looking forward to giving it a good work out today.'

Gerry's music room was even more wonderfully appointed than the kitchen. French windows lead straight out onto an enormous garden – an expanse of unadorned grass – and the sun poured into the room, dust motes dancing a jig in its beams. A grand piano took up less than half the space, leaving room for a deep sofa, computer desk and chair, and bookshelves on every wall. Nevertheless, music spilled out from boxes and crates, stacked on every available surface, and I had to pick my way carefully towards the piano.

'A mess, as usual,' Gerry said without apology, slurping his tea. 'I've got your music somewhere.'

I gazed out onto the garden as Gerry rummaged around, and eventually he was ready to start.

Working with Gerry was even more satisfying than our first rehearsal had been. He was diligent and totally engaged in what we were doing, encouraging me to be more daring, and to find deeper levels of meaning in both text and score. Time passed quickly, and it was only the arrival of Ben two hours later that brought us to a halt.

'Have you finished?' he asked, bursting into the room.

Gerry looked at his watch.

'Nearly, I think.'

I sighed inwardly. I longed to stay, but there was no reason to linger once the books were closed.

'Let's just run this bit again, Madsy, and then we'll call it a day, shall we?'

I smiled, pleased to hear him use my name with casual familiarity. Ben hung on his father's shoulder as we finished working on the last pages of *Che Faro*. As Gerry played the final notes, Ben nodded in approval.

'I like that,' he said.

'Good,' Gerry replied briskly. 'So you should. It's one of the greatest arias ever written and Madison sings it beautifully.'

'Hmm.' Ben looked at me appraisingly, a junior version of his dad. My heart expanded happily; I was going to spend the whole summer working with this beautiful boy.

'We're driving into town now. Can we give you a lift anywhere?' Gerry asked, rising from the piano.

We established that he was going close to Waterloo, so I rapidly opted to take that route home.

As I sat on the train later, I tried to analyse my teeming emotions, to think clearly and sharply, and to put into words the feelings that had been so suddenly thrust upon me and which spiralled with every hour spent in Gerry's company. I couldn't. All I knew was that I hadn't wanted to leave that crazy house and, given my obsessive predilection for order and tidiness, that must mean that I was very much in love indeed.

CHAPTER 10

Two weeks before our Solent gig, Megan confirmed her intention to attend; Andy, to my relief, did not. Mean spirited as it was, I didn't want Andy there. The day would be a test of how I really felt. An afternoon and evening in Gerry's company, driving there and back, sharing a mutual passion for our work, would serve well to show whether I was merely infatuated.

Meanwhile, Andy took me to see The Restless Dragon, and I met Joe Budzynski, the autocratic Polish manager of the highly successful fringe venue. We toured the excellent facilities, pored over reams of publicity and information about the theatre and its productions, and met Ron Stryker, who was to be the Director on *Lethal Desires*. He was younger than Andy, and I wondered if Andy would be insulted by this but, to my surprise and pleasure, they took to each other immediately. Andy was full of praise for Ron's initial ideas for the play and I was happy to hear him agreeing in the most amiable manner to some key adaptations Ron suggested. Ron and Joe were charming to me, fascinated to learn that I was a singer, and keen to hear of the forthcoming Glyndebourne season. Andy beamed proudly as I told them about it and I felt a heel. Nevertheless, I thought of Gerry and Ben several times every day, falling deep into reverie as I wondered what I wanted from him and how I would truly respond if he offered it to me, whatever it was.

But I really did try to put Gerry to the back of my mind after my visit to The Restless Dragon. I sang a Verdi *Requiem* in York and a Mozart programme in Norwich, and Andy came with me on both occasions, responding enthusiastically to my suggestion that he did so. And when Gerry and I met at his studio for our third and final rehearsal I made an enormous effort not to be seduced by his self-confident banter, his thoughtful attention to our work, his wry humour and his sensuous fingers drumming on the glossy finish of the piano lid, moving energetically over the keys, and gesticulating as he made a point. It didn't work. I was entranced, leaning as close to him as I dared and letting our hands touch as we studied a score. It took a serious effort of will on my part not to lay my head on his shoulder and put my arms around him, but I succeeded.

I felt mildly virtuous, though. Andy and I had enjoyed my concert trips, I had tried not to think about Gerry more than ten times a day, and since Andy showed no interest in coming to Portsmouth, I felt justified in not pursuing it.

'When do you think you'll be home?' he asked me on as the day of the gig dawned bright and clear.

'Midnightish, I should guess,' I calculated. 'Depends largely on the roads coming back.'

I smoothed my dress carefully, folding it flat into my bag, on top of shoes, jewellery, and make-up for the evening.

'Are you coming back with Megan?'

I wasn't sure I had a sufficiently good reason not to be doing so, but I tried it out anyway.

'No. I've told her that it would be ungracious just to abandon Gerry after the concert. After all, he's put so much time and effort into it. I'll travel back with him and be sociable.'

'Fair enough,' said Andy easily, and I breathed freely again. Even Megan had accepted my reasoning, so it was obviously just my guilty conscience that was bothering me.

...ood on the pavement outside Exeter House waiting for Gerry to collect me, my stomach was doing double backflips, and not just because I had a concert in less than six hours time. The prospect of the whole day had become so exciting that I was acutely conscious that the Solent Music Club were getting something rather less than the cool professional they were expecting. But Gerry inspired me to great things and I was confident that we would be putting on a good show for them. I just hoped there were no mind readers in the audience.

Gerry was inordinately cheerful when he appeared.

'I've tidied the car,' he said proudly, and indeed he had. The back seat was clear of everything except a music bag and suit carrier, and I could get into the front seat without clearing away the detritus of several takeaways and breakfasts eaten on the run.

'How are you?' he grinned as we set off.

'Not as nervous as I should be, but I'm sure it'll all catch up with me by tonight,' I replied. It was true; my nerves were, at the moment, quite unrelated to the evening's forthcoming musical events. But Gerry made things beautifully easy for me. He spun a long yarn about *La Bohème* casting, another about Ben's latest contretemps at school, and then told me about a conversation he'd had with the educational psychologist about Josh's attention deficit disorder, and his refusal to take Ritalin. By the time we were sailing down the A3, looking down on Guildford cathedral in the distance, I was thoroughly relaxed and glad that I could contribute intelligently to the conversation.

'If you can reach behind your seat, there's coffee in the flask, and some grapes and chocolate if you fancy them,' Gerry told me.

I turned around, boldly taking the opportunity to rest my hand on Gerry's shoulder, ostensibly to secure my balance as I leant behind my seat. He didn't flinch and, encouraged, I settled back, looking casual. Gerry's provisions amused me. I travelled all over the country to concerts but it had rarely occurred to me to take food and drink with me. I usually bought polystyrene cups of coffee, ready-made sandwiches, muffins and scones, and expensive bottles of mineral water and fruit juice, rather than packing my own supplies. It was sweetly endearing to discover that such a clever man had homely and unpretentious tastes and habits, and sharing it with him was friendly and intimate.

Gerry quizzed me about various things I'd been doing recently, and the conversation drifted back to the boys. When I compared Josh to a student I remembered from my teaching days, he asked me about my former career, and I realised that Gerry knew even less about me than I did about him. Encouraged by his obvious interest, I began to tell him about my academic life, and he still hadn't fallen asleep over the wheel with boredom by the time we were driving into Portsmouth.

It was lovely introducing Gerry to the chairman of the Music Club, giving our programme a bit of spit and polish in the venue, and then being swept away to have tea with the chairman and his wife. It felt as if we were a real partnership, which I supposed, of course, we were. But in my heart it was overlaid with so much more. Gerry was engaging and entertaining at tea, offering interesting and informed, but quite random, opinions on all manner of subjects, and dominating the proceedings so much that you'd have been forgiven for forgetting that I was supposed to be the leading artiste that night! But I loved him all the more for it, daring to sit close enough to him on the settee so that his thigh brushed against mine, and I could rest my hand briefly on his knee as I leant over to replace my tea cup. If he noticed, he said nothing, and I was so overexcited, I probably wouldn't have been able to take it in if he did. I made a concerted effort to appear distinguished and sophisticated, but inevitably once the conversation turned to Glyndebourne, Gerry leapt in to pronounce on the wonders of Ben and I sat back with pleasure and pride and let him take over again.

We changed at the chairman's house, arriving back at the venue through a rear door to avoid our audience. Gerry looked delicious in his tuxedo, complete with brightly coloured bow tie and cummerbund. Not quite as delicious as he did in white tie and tails, I thought, which suited his lanky frame to perfection, but sufficiently gorgeous to cause me to catch my breath as I came down the stairs to meet him. I saw appreciation in his eyes, too, as he watched me. I had chosen a sea green gown, full length, but simply cut as usual, skimming the top of my shoulders and cut stylishly under the bust to create shapely contours.

'Very nice, Dr Brylmer,' Gerry beamed.

'A bit less of that, thank you,' I joked. Gerry had been enormously impressed when I'd told him about my PhD, and I guessed that as a form of address, Dr Brylmer would now be a regular joke; I thought it was rather sweet.

We couldn't avoid Megan, of course. She appeared in the green room about two minutes after us, determined to see me before the concert. I was warming up quietly, but she soon put a stop to that.

'Madison, darling, you look lovely. So beautiful, so young.'

I hoped Gerry had noticed.

'Good!' I laughed, hugging her in welcome. 'Did you get down here okay?'

'Like the wind.'

I turned to Gerry. 'Mum's got a customised Morgan. It's seriously cool. Ben would love it.'

Gesturing to Megan to come forward, I continued. 'Gerry, this is my mother. She's seen you conduct me in *Butterfly* and *Don Giovanni*, but I don't think you've actually met before.'

'No, we haven't.' Megan held out her hand briskly. 'It was very handy that you could play for Madison tonight. She has a lovely regular accompanist, of course, but it will be very interesting to hear her singing with you,'

Gerry looked taken aback by this ambiguous greeting, but recovered quickly.

'Hello. It's nice to meet you too,' he said with some irony, which fortunately went completely over Megan's head. 'I'm sure it's a great honour to play for Madison. I'm looking forward to it immensely.'

I spluttered with laughter, and Gerry caught my eye and grinned. Megan looked faintly annoyed, and I thought it wise to backtrack.

'Thank you so much for coming all the way here. There are lots of your favourites on the programme: *Che Faro*, the Verdi songs.'

'Lovely, darling.' She took the programme I handed to her. 'See you in the interval. And afterwards. I've got some things in the car for you, so don't forget to fetch them before you go.' I saw her give Gerry a sharp and appraising look as she said this; they were a real Megan Matthews speciality.

'Of course. See you later.'

I kissed Megan and she trotted off to take her front row seat.

'*O Dio!*' I raised my eyebrows at Gerry.

'She's a serious mother,' Gerry said. 'Sussing out exactly who her daughter's hanging around with and whether she approves or not.'

'Exactly!'

'Dads can be like that too, you know,' he told me, 'and I expect I'll find out for myself that you never stop wanting to be sure that your offspring are doing okay.'

'There's always an agenda with my mum though,' I said, 'although it's such an inscrutable one I'm not sure that she even knows what it is.'

'She's very proud of you, that's obvious,' Gerry observed, 'and I recognise that too, being an inordinately proud dad myself.'

'Yes. That is true. Once she got used to the fact that I had given up a secure career for an insecure one, she's been my most loyal fan.'

We were prevented from continuing along these interesting lines by the arrival of our host. We were on.

CHAPTER 11

I was terribly pleased with myself by the time the friendly audience signalled their appreciation at the end of the evening. As soon as we had walked onto the small platform, I forgot everything except the job I was there to do. I enjoyed knowing that Gerry was there, supporting me, leading where necessary, concentrating as hard as I was, but I was not distracted by unprofessional concerns, and that was exactly as it should be. Only as we shared a glass of wine and mingled with the audience did I allow them to filter back. Still in our concert finery, we chatted and smiled, Megan at my shoulder whilst I worked one half of the room and Gerry, still looking heartbreakingly gorgeous, the other. Megan ensured that everyone knew she was my mother, and we graciously accepted the usual cries of 'You look like more like sisters!' Glancing away from a kind patron, I caught Gerry's eye as he scanned the room. As we smiled broadly in happy unison, I trembled with desire; he held my gaze just a fraction longer than necessary, just long enough for Megan to realise that my attention was elsewhere. I averted my eyes from Gerry's just as she pulled on my arm.

'Madison,' she said sharply.

I turned quickly, hearing the warning tone in her voice, but kept my expression neutral. She softened as I smiled.

'He played well for you tonight,' she said with unexpected warmth.

I nodded simply.

'Shall I get changed and come out to the car?' I asked, and I was glad that she also seemed to think it was time to make a move.

But I was nervous as we eventually said our farewells to Megan. She'd loaded me up with delicacies to take home – wine, chocolate, cheese and peaches – which Gerry eyed with envy.

'Oh, marvellous,' he said enthusiastically. 'Do we get to eat this lot on the way home?'

'Some of it perhaps,' I laughed. 'I don't think it would be sensible to open the wine, though. We could settle for the chocolate and peaches.'

'The intention is for you to take it home,' Megan interjected, looking distinctly unamused. 'I'm sure that Andy would like to enjoy it, too.'

I said nothing as I stowed the bag on the back seat, intending to rescue it once we were under way.

'I just have no self-discipline when it comes to food,' said Gerry charmingly.

I winced. There was no one Megan distrusted more than a man who tried to smooth things over by turning on the charm.

'Really?' she said coldly, as I tried to silence Gerry with a nudge.

'I'll ring tomorrow,' I told Megan, giving Gerry a chance to trundle round to the driver's seat and out of harm's way. She relented.

'All right, darling. Whenever is convenient. You were lovely tonight.'

We hugged farewell and she watched me like a hovering eagle as I climbed into the car. She tapped on the window after I'd closed the door. I wound it down.

'Don't eat it now,' she said, gesticulating towards the food bag.

I laughed, refusing to be drawn.

'Speak to you tomorrow.'

I stuck my hand out of the window and waved until we were out of sight.

'Just keep driving, Gerry. Don't look back, don't hesitate.'

He chuckled appreciatively.

'You two are a scream,' he said.

'Thanks a lot. That really helps,' I chided. 'Now, if I can escape this seat belt, I'll lay claim to our luxury hamper.'

I have to confess that the chocolate and peaches were entirely consumed by the time we drew up outside Exeter House just after midnight.

'I hope your mum doesn't pay you a surprise visit in the early hours of the morning to check up on you now,' Gerry teased.

'I don't think even she'd go to those lengths,' I replied. 'But I wouldn't put it past her to ask Andy if he'd enjoyed the food she'd sent back.'

'Then you'd better prime him to cover for you,' he said.

'Oh, goodness, that would get far too complicated. I'll just risk it.'

I smiled at Gerry, enormously reluctant to leave the car. He looked amused and pleased with himself.

'Thank you for a lovely day,' I said, suddenly shy. 'It's been such fun, and you played brilliantly for me. Thank you very much for doing it.'

'I've had a great time,' Gerry said warmly. 'Thank you for asking me.'

There wasn't really anything else to say short of my suggesting that I stayed in the car, and he took me home to bed. Since I was ninety-nine percent certain that he would not respond positively to that idea, I reached over to hug him instead. He hugged me warmly in return.

'See you soon,' he murmured, as we drew back, and then, to my utter amazement he kissed me. It was a friendly, good-natured kiss, but it was firmly on my astonished mouth and it was the most wonderful kiss I had ever received. Without hesitation I kissed him back in the same easy way, but not trusting myself to spoil such a lovely moment with an unwarranted display of emotion, I quickly opened the door and climbed out. We grinned at each other as I reached back into the car to rescue my bags.

'Bye,' he said with a smile in his voice too.

'Bye.'

I closed the door and my heart beat a rapid tattoo against my ribs as he drove immediately away.

CHAPTER 12

I was so excited that I could barely swallow my chocolate muffin as I sat on the train bound for Lewes on the first day of *Flute* music calls. The train journey was so easy it was a pleasure: a little over an hour from Clapham Junction, and then the cast bus met us at Lewes station to trundle us all over to Glynde. I looked around the carriage trying to guess if any of my fellow travellers were bound for the opera house too, but everyone was engrossed in books and newspapers or gazing pensively out of the window, and offered no clues. I was sick with nerves, but desperately happy. If only Ben was with me on this first day, my cup would be full.

There was so much to take in, however, that perhaps it was just as well that I wasn't distracted by his overstimulating presence. After all, we had the whole summer before us, and on this first awe inspiring day it took all my resources to concentrate on getting the notes out of my mouth in the right order. Not to mention the German! That was seriously frightening for an Italian lover who avoided German at all costs. But it was a small price to pay, I thought, as Colin Davis took us through our paces, and my initial fear was soon overcome when I heard how beautifully the three Ladies blended together and how wonderfully compatible we were.

My fellow Ladies were awesome. Clarissa Grainger, tall, slim, and fearfully elegant, was singing the First Lady in limpid soprano tones that would surely melt the serpent's heart. She looked intimidating, but smiled sweetly and I thought we'd get on fine. But Anastasia Winkworth, the Third Lady, singing out boldly in a strong, husky contralto, won my heart as soon as I set eyes on her. Our paths had not previously crossed, although we knew of each other and shared a broadly common repertoire.

'Hello,' she said directly, as we took a coffee break. 'I'm Annie. I've heard so much about you from Graham Fellows. He thinks you're fantastic.'

'Goodness, that's nice. He was my Don earlier this year.'

'So I heard,' she laughed loudly, throwing her head back in amusement. 'How did you stand it? He's such a lounge lizard.'

'He's gorgeous,' I protested. 'He gave me bags of confidence.'

'I'm so glad we've finally met,' she said warmly. 'I think we're going to have lots of fun here.'

I knew instinctively that I had discovered a soul mate. Over the years I had met some ghastly fellow mezzos with serious attitude problems, but I could see that Annie would have no truck with that. She was confident without being arrogant and sufficiently self-assured not to need to put down every other mezzo who crossed her path. She had a good career and was highly respected. I smiled at her with real pleasure.

'You're singing Carmen for ENO next spring, aren't you?' I asked.

'And you're Mercedes,' she added, nodding in agreement. She held out a small, capable hand. 'Here's to a long and happy association,' she grinned.

We shook hands cheerfully as we gathered our belongings to return to the rehearsal room.

'Do you know anyone in this cast?' I asked her.

'I've sung with Clarissa at Welsh, in *Flute* and *Falstaff*. But other than that, no. What about you?'

I smiled happily, unable to think of Ben without beaming.

'I know the First Genie.'

'That'll be a kid, surely,' she said in surprise.

'Yes, of course. He's eleven, and wonderful.'

'How do you know him? From the Coli?'

'I've been singing with his dad quite a bit. He's a conductor.'

'Who?' Annie was intrigued.

'Gerry McFall. I've sung Suzuki and Zerlina for him.'

'Oh, God, yes, I've heard of him. He's got an awful reputation.'

'It's not deserved,' I said quietly. 'He's very good to me.'

'How interesting,' said Annie. 'He's doing *Tito* in the autumn, am I right?'

'Yes. I'm singing Sesto.'

'That's great,' she enthused. 'I've sung Annio twice, but Sesto's too florid for me.'

I filed this away. If she was as nice as she appeared, perhaps Annie might be the answer to Gerry's dilemma: he had lost his original choice for the role and, as yet, had chosen no replacement.

'Well, I'm most intrigued,' she continued, her eyes twinkling with amusement. 'What's his son like? Good?'

'As far as I can tell,' I concurred. 'I find it hard to judge boy trebles; it's so different, isn't it? But he's a great little musician, and enormous fun. I must admit, having him around has made the prospect of this summer even more delightful.'

Annie shivered with distaste.

'Oh, Madison, you've obviously got more patience than I have. I'm afraid I don't have much time for kids, especially on stage!'

'When you meet Ben you'll know what I mean.'

'I wait to be convinced,' she laughed.

Later we wandered around the grounds and checked into everything with enormous interest. Although Annie had been singing on the circuit far longer than I had, it was her Glyndebourne debut as a soloist, too, and she was just as excited, albeit less effusively. We drooled over our photos and biographies in the programme, had a quick peep at the stage, and chatted in every free moment we had. As I trooped off to board the cast bus to Lewes I felt as if I had just spent the day in a magic world. Doubtless a great deal of hard work lay ahead of us during the summer, but I knew already that it was going to be marvellous.

It got even more marvellous at the end of the week when at last we had a music call which coincided with the genies. I had discovered that Annie generally preferred to drive to Sussex, but on that day she took the train and we happily met in the middle of the carriage between Clapham Junction and Gatwick. We studied our scores together for a while; I'd discovered that Annie spoke fluent German, and she had quickly proved to be a willing and able coach – far less intimidating that the official one Glyndebourne provided. In turn, she had started quizzing me about aspects of my vocal technique which she thought superior to hers, all in a far more genial and uncompetitive manner than I had ever previously experienced.

After a while, however, we closed our music and sat back to gossip as the last few miles passed.

'Are you married, Madison?' she asked tentatively. So far we had said little about our personal circumstances and I sensed that Annie was inclined to reveal little.

'Yes,' I nodded. 'I've been married for more than ten years now. Andy is a writer. He's got a big project on at the moment, the biggest he's ever had, actually. It's very exciting.'

So I filled Annie in on *Lethal Desires* and The Restless Dragon, but said nothing about our relationship itself. It made me realise that I'd already started to separate into two different personas, and the one I was presenting at Glyndebourne was not the Madison of Madison and Andy, but simply me, alone, far more independent and gregarious than I would have been even three months earlier. I knew it had something to do with what I felt for Gerry and Ben, but I hadn't put it into words yet. Maybe I was starting to free myself, to make myself available for them, at least in mind and spirit, if not in the physical world.

'What about you?' I asked Annie.

She told me that she had been divorced for some years, and enjoyed various on and off relationships. 'But I won't let anything get in the way of my singing again,' she said firmly. 'That's why my marriage ended. I wasn't prepared for him to have precedence over my career, and he wasn't prepared to take second place to a voice, so he had to go.' Annie laughed, but I sensed an underlying pain. I wondered if I could tell her about Gerry, but realised there wasn't really anything to tell. 'Oh by the way, the guy we were talking about the other day, Gerry McFall, I really like him.' So what?

'I'm so looking forward to seeing Ben today,' I offered instead.

'Never work with children and animals,' Annie countered.

'I promise, Annie, he'll win you over.'

'He'll be precocious, loud and demanding.'

'Of course, but that's the attraction,'

'I think you're in love with him, Madison,' she laughed. 'Get your hands out of that cradle.'

I felt my face redden. Was I that transparent? Clearly so.

The boys arrived mid-morning in the company of a cheerful chaperone. As they watched us rehearsing I caught Ben's eye and he grinned and waved. I winked and saw Annie look at us with amusement. As soon as the opportunity presented itself I sauntered casually over to Ben.

'Hello, darling.'

'Hiya, Mads. This is Gemma.' He indicated the chaperone who held her hand out with a smile.

'Hello, Madison,' she said. 'Ben tells me that you thoroughly enjoy his company and will be spending a lot of time with us.'

'Oh, really?' I laughed. 'I'm sure that will be an enormous pleasure for us all.'

'And this is Oli and Dusan, pronounced Dooshan. He's Serbian,' Ben told me.

I studied the other two lads with deep prejudice in my heart. How could they possibly be as wonderful as my lovely Ben? They both looked cool and super-confident. I wished I'd been like that at eleven. Gemma looked promising, in her early twenties, with masses of curly red hair and a mischievous smile. She clearly loved children and knew how to keep order whilst staying friendly.

'You've got a wonderful job,' I said to her enviously.

She laughed. 'I hardly think so, compared to you. You're up on that stage every night. I only get as far as the wings.'

'Maybe, but you get to be with this little one all the time.' I indicated Ben who was deep in conversation with his new colleagues.

'And I get the feeling I'm going to hit levels of exhaustion I never knew existed,' she said with a smile. 'Does he ever stop?'

'Only when he sleeps, I think.'

I longed to hug Ben, and stroke his soft blond hair, but it would so obviously bring his reputation with his new friends crashing to the ground before he'd even started that I refrained. I wished I could listen to the lads rehearse, but we were ushered off for our break whilst they got going. Annie came over to us before we parted.

'Hello,' she greeted Gemma. 'I'm Annie, another one of the Ladies. Madison has already bored me to death about this young man, and we've only known each other four days.'

'Ben, this is my new friend, Annie,' I told him.

'Hello, Annie. Are you the First Lady?' He greeted her with enormous charm.

'Not likely,' she laughed. 'Third is good enough for me. Madison tells me you are her very good friend.'

Ben smiled at me so sweetly that quick tears came to my eyes. I blinked them away, hoping no one had seen.

'Have a good rehearsal, darling. Which train are you getting later?'

Ben looked enquiringly at Gemma.

'Five o'clock, hopefully.'

'I'll see you on the bus, then,' I said with faintly concealed delight.

'Oh, no,' I heard Annie breathe behind me, and I poked her with my elbow, as she propelled me firmly out of the studio.

'So far this week, Madison, I had reached the conclusion that you and I are going to be enormously good mates, but let's get one thing straight here. I have no intention of entertaining small boys in our dressing room, on the bus, on the train, or anywhere else. I think you are seriously off your rocker.'

'But it makes me happy, Annie,' I said.

'That much is clear,' she responded. 'Just keep me out of it.'

Although Annie insisted on sitting several seats away from us on the return journey, she couldn't help but watch with horrified fascination as Ben talked at me non-stop all the way home. Gemma, too, was clearly amused and I realised that I couldn't hide my special affection for him, even from these virtual strangers. If someone told me a year earlier that I would actually want to be part of a conversation that revolved around *Star Wars*, Ferraris, Harry Potter and computers I would have seriously doubted their sanity, but I was delighted to be educated in these matters. Oli and Dusan were sweet kids, too, and I was pleased to see how easily the boys had gelled on their first day. By the time we had reached Victoria, Gemma had gone to sit with Annie in relative peace and I was thoroughly enjoying being entertained by three precocious eleven-year-olds.

'Is Gemma taking you home now?' I asked Ben as the train pulled in.

'Dad's meeting me,' he replied, retrieving his bag from the luggage rack.

Gerry was leaning lazily against a vending machine as we straggled onto the platform. There was a confusing moment as Annie turned to find me, and we bumped into each other as I stared at Gerry, suddenly unaware of anything else around me. It was two weeks since I'd seen him, and the painful rush of love and longing took me by surprise.

'Sorry, Madison,' Annie said. 'Are you coming on the tube now?'

I felt flustered and awkward.

'Not just yet, Annie. I'll see you on Monday.'

My confusion was clear and she looked around to see what was its cause. Gerry was moving easily forward, smiling broadly as Ben bowled into him.

'Hello,' he drawled as I drew level with them.

I saw Annie's eyes open wider with interest, but she covered it quickly.

'Sure. Have a good weekend.' She wheeled off towards the tube.

I waited whilst Gerry chatted with Gemma and the other boys, glad that I could still contribute intelligently despite my burning cheeks. Dusan's mother collected him from Gemma, and once he was safely despatched, Gemma headed towards the underground with Oli.

'Have you had fun today?' Gerry asked us both.

'It was cool,' Ben said casually.

I smiled happily at Gerry. 'I am having the most wonderful time of my life, and it's even better now Ben's here, too.'

Gerry raised his eyebrows mockingly. 'Oh, I'm sure,' he said sceptically. 'Can we give you a lift anywhere?' he asked.

I knew that Gerry and Ben would be heading in precisely the opposite direction to me, and I didn't think I could get away with pretending that I was unaccountably going to Lewisham or Peckham, so with some regret I shook my head.

'Thanks, but I'm heading home.'

We started to wander towards the exit, Ben pronouncing to Gerry about his first music call.

As we reached Gerry's car, he turned to me warmly.

'Madison, I'm taking the little one in the car next Tuesday. He's got an afternoon call. Can we bring you home if you're needed, too?'

I had already committed our schedules to memory, and didn't need asking twice.

'Yes, I'm there all day on Tuesday, and that would be lovely.'

I didn't want to leave them. I watched Ben scramble into the car, and Gerry kept talking to me as he started up the engine. I partly took in what he was saying, wishing I could simply climb into the car and go home with them.

'Bye, Mads,' Ben called cheerfully, as they pulled away.

I blew a kiss after his disappearing form. It felt so horribly unfair that I was left alone when I so longed to be with them; so much love left to dissipate into the cooling evening air, when I should be caring for them, making them feel cherished and adored. How was I going to get through to Gerry? I knew he liked me; he had to. We'd had so much fun in Portsmouth. He'd kissed me – briefly and in nothing more than the spirit of friendship maybe – but it was the most precious kiss I had ever exchanged. We'd laughed and chatted and eaten together. He knew I was easy-going and affectionate, and he brought out the best in me – without even trying, he made me blossom as no one before had done. But I longed so much for more. I wanted to be his alone, and every day that longing grew, as each moment in his presence made me love him more.

I shook myself out of my reverie. I had to give him time. His life was so full – of people, work and responsibilities, things that demanded his attention every hour and every day. I would have to find a way to work myself into his life, until I was indispensable to him. And perhaps I hadn't made a bad start. After all, I was the one who would be spending the summer with Ben, and already I could look forward to travelling back with them on Tuesday. Gerry had asked me, when he knew that I could easily take the train. Clearly my company was not something he wanted to avoid. That would have to satisfy me for now.

CHAPTER 13

I marvelled that despite my emotional upheavals Andy had clearly discerned nothing of what was happening.

'It must have been a laugh seeing Ben yesterday,' he said easily the next day. 'You're like another mum to him now.'

'I hardly think so,' I replied rather too vehemently. 'I'm not that close to him.'

'It's going to enhance your reputation nicely with Gerry,' Andy continued innocently. 'How can he not give you good roles in the future?' he laughed.

This seemed an excellent cue to make a joke of it all.

'Well, they're driving me home on Tuesday; I'll suggest a list of operas he can consider in the future, especially with me in mind!'

'Good plan!'

I didn't think that Gerry had registered what felt to me like earth quaking vibrations either. When I was alone with him, every sense quivered and I felt charged with electricity, but never had I met anyone so apparently oblivious to atmosphere as Gerry. Whatever I was feeling, he carried on in exactly the same uncomplicated manner, and yet I knew he was not an insensitive man. He was no different as we travelled back from Lewes the following Tuesday.

On the basis that Gerry was allegedly Ben's chaperone, he sat in on some of the music call that afternoon. I flourished under his amused and speculative eye, and exchanged pleased smiles with him as the Ladies sang with Tamino and Papageno. Gerry was clearly fascinated, absorbing everything for dissection and discussion later.

'I see your friend is here,' Annie said with a grin.

'He's chaperoning Ben, I think. At least they're in the car today, anyway. I'm going home with them after the boys are finished here.'

'Put in a good word for me, then,' she continued. 'I hear on the grapevine that he's lost his Annio for *Tito*.'

I turned to her in pleasure.

'Oh, Annie, would you like to do it? I thought of it last Monday when we met, but it was too soon to say anything. Shall mention you on the way home? It's not a big house production, though, just three London performances and a short provincial tour.'

'I think it might be fun, and I know the role already. It wouldn't take long to brush it up.'

'Okay. I'll sound him out tonight.'

'I'm still not convinced he's the good guy you claim, Madison,' she said, 'but you're obviously fond of them both.'

'Um.' I felt suddenly awkward, suspecting that if anyone was going to pick up on my emotional chaos it was going to be Annie. 'They're cool.'

After the Ladies had been despatched, Gerry stayed to listen to the boys. They were working on their quartet with Pamina, and sounding wonderful. I had to admit to not being a great fan of treble voices. I had sung Third Genie some years previously in a production that had used women for all the genies, and personally I would always favour that option, and not simply for the reason that it was another role for me to sing. But Ben was another matter, of course, and I was utterly biased. Gerry looked enormously proud, even whilst he whispered critical comments to me about all three lads, Ben included. Technically, I shouldn't have been there listening to them rehearse, but evidently Gerry's presence legitimised my own, and I sat back to savour the pleasure of it. I studied

Gerry's hands as they twitched restlessly, impatient to be involved in the rehearsal. They were long and beautiful, the sexiest hands I had ever seen, clearly made for conducting, playing the piano, and making love to me, I thought. This latter option was clearly the furthest from his mind at the moment, however, as he mentally conducted and coached each note. It was lovely to see him enjoying every minute of Ben's rehearsal, and I anticipated a most engaging return journey as he analysed it all.

It was Gerry's first visit to Glyndebourne in the company of insiders, so Ben and I took great pleasure in giving him the grand tour. I let Ben take a lively lead, until we collapsed on the grass by the lake for a few minutes before leaving.

'Gerry, this is so fabulous for Ben,' I said as we watched him wander to the water's edge.

Gerry nodded reflectively.

'It's come at a good time too,' he said quietly. 'He needs something important now. Both boys dealt as well as could be expected with Susan's death, but they need to find their feet away from me now.'

'But Gerry, he's only eleven,' I objected mildly. 'Does it matter if he depends on you? You're his security. Independence grows out of attachment.'

'It's never too early for him to learn to be independent, especially if he's going to be part of this business when he's older,' he replied. 'I worry more about Josh though, I must admit. He was older than Ben is now when Susan died, but it was especially hard on him. We're not always the best of friends at the moment, I'm afraid. He hates school, seems to have very few friends, and resents anything I do or say. It makes life very difficult,' he concluded with a sigh.

'He sounds fed up with everything,' I suggested. 'What does he enjoy doing?'

'At the moment, nothing,' Gerry said gloomily, 'but, when pushed, acting, art; he writes a lot of secret things in little books – he doesn't show them to me. But everything seems to have gone on hold whilst he indulges in a great deal of adolescent angst.'

'I'd like to meet him,' I said.

'Not at the moment, you wouldn't. He's started dressing in what I am told is gothic style.'

I laughed at the prospect. 'Oh Gerry, that's marvellous. All in black, I take it, with or without make up?'

'I'm glad you think it's funny.' Gerry looked cross. 'But since you ask, I have noticed that his eyelashes have been looking rather longer and darker of late.'

'He sounds great. If he hates school, have you talked to him about alternatives?'

'What alternatives, for goodness sake? He's got a part-scholarship at St George's, though he's not doing much to keep it at the moment. Why should he want to go anywhere else?' Gerry said with irritation.

'Well, I worked for several years with kids who needed a change of scene to kick-start their academic careers again, so if you ever want any ideas…' I petered out.

Gerry shook his head. 'I'm sure it will all come out in the wash. I think we ought to go,' he said, getting to his feet. 'Ben, we're off.'

Ben, who had been examining the lake at extremely close quarters trooped rather damply over to join us.

'Don't get me all wet now, buster,' Gerry said, backing away in mock horror.

'That's okay,' Ben teased, 'I'll dry myself off on Madison.'

To my surprise, Ben flung his arms around me, grinning broadly. Never one to miss an opportunity, I hugged him tightly, my heart fit to burst with happiness.

'Oh, Madison, don't encourage him,' Gerry laughed, but he looked at me with a new warmth, and for a moment we held each other's gaze. I trembled, and Ben looked up at me with a grin.

'You're shaking, Madsy. I've made you wet and cold now.'

I didn't take my eyes off Gerry. 'No, it's not that, Ben, I'm fine,' I said as I released him gently, and Gerry turned away smiling his quirky smile, and raising his eyebrows ironically. I wasn't sure what it all meant, but I enjoyed it.

True to form, on the way home, Gerry analysed the afternoon's rehearsal minutely, interrupted frequently by Ben. As I relished being part of their happy exchanges, I suddenly remembered my promise to Annie.

'Oh, Gerry!' I exclaimed.

'Madison!'

'Have you got any further with an Annio?'

'No. I must admit I've neglected it this week. I'd hoped that Julia Lethbridge might come through but she gave me a definite no, and since then I've been lazy, I'm afraid. Did you think of someone?'

'Annie Winkworth, my Third Lady. She's so cool and competent, and she's doing Carmen with ENO in the spring, so she'd be a real heavyweight to have in the cast list. Please think about her, Gerry, I really like her.'

Gerry laughed. 'So what you mean is that you want a friend to gossip with.'

'Well, that would be nice,' I smiled, 'but she's a serious player and she's done the role before.'

Gerry nodded thoughtfully. 'Have you got her number then? I'll ask her to sing for me this week if she can. Do you think she'd take it if it were offered?'

'Definitely.'

'Okay. That sounds fairly promising. Thank you.' Gerry turned to me smiling inscrutably again. 'You are very kind and helpful, Madison,' he said, and patted me on the knee.

'I am here to serve,' I joked.

'I had noticed. I do appreciate it.'

While I absorbed this, Gerry picked up the threads of a previous conversation with Ben. I was still pondering Gerry's words when he spoke to me again.

'I think there may be some Smarties under your seat.'

I rummaged and found a battered bag of confectionery.

'Help yourself,' Gerry instructed, holding out his hand. I passed some over to the back-seat to Ben, and then dropped a handful into Gerry's palm. The second time I did so I let my fingers brush across his. He didn't react, but when I daringly did it again a little later, he caught my eye and smiled. I looked innocent, longing to rest my head on his shoulder. With enormous restraint, I didn't, but I kissed him firmly on the mouth before I climbed out of the car outside Exeter House. He didn't respond, but he didn't back away either; soon I would discover that this was Gerry's standard approach, but that day it didn't matter, I was so happy.

'See you soon,' he drawled looking amused as usual.

'Absolutely. See you later in the week, Ben.'

Ben's pale hand waved vaguely from the back seat as I watched the car disappear along the heath, and I felt tears closing my throat. The closer I got to these two, the more I wanted to be with them, and if I had ever doubted that my affections were more than a passing attraction I could doubt it no more. I wanted this man and his sons in my life permanently (even without meeting Josh I knew I would love him, too), but with or without them, I would never be the same again.

CHAPTER 14

By the last week in May when we started production calls on *Flute* we were firmly into the routine of a Glyndebourne season and Annie and I were determined to make the most of it. Three other productions – *Simon Boccanegra*, *Peter Grimes* and *Manon Lescaut* – had opened ahead of us and we took the opportunity to avail ourselves of cast tickets to see them all. Each time we bought delicacies for a picnic we shared in our favourite spot by the lake, and drove back to town in Annie's car after the show, spurning public transport on the nights we were audience members.

I enjoyed getting to know Annie, although she still maintained a reserve that held us both back from exchanging personal confidences in those early weeks. But she and I were instant friends, drawn together by a shared love of what we were doing, and by a real complementarity of personalities. She was far more outspoken than I was, but her outrageous observations were a constant source of entertainment. In turn, she seemed to enjoy more serious moments with me than I noticed her exchanging with others in the cast, and I found her to be surprisingly perceptive as we lounged in the Courtyard Café between calls.

'Oh, gee whizz,' she groaned, looking out beyond the entrance to the courtyard.

I glanced over my shoulder to see what she was moaning about: Gemma and the boys were heading towards us. The genies were called for a full company rehearsal in the afternoon and I knew that Gemma had planned to bring them on a midday train, but the sight of Ben had its usual effect; my face wreathed in smiles and my heart lifted. He arrived at our table first.

'Put your phone on, Mads,' he ordered.

'Why? Is it off?' I rummaged in my bag and saw indeed that the display was blank.

'Have you been trying to call me?' I asked.

'Dad has. He says you're to ring him.'

I tried to look casual and suspected that I succeeded so well I actually looked bored.

'Okay. Shall I ring him now?'

'He says it's urgent. Can I get a hot chocolate with cream on top?'

I gave Ben my purse, suggesting that Dusan and Oli might also like to have something, and as the boys scrambled to order their drinks I dialled Gerry's number, catching Annie's eye as I did.

'How high?' she said.

'Pardon?'

'When he asks you to jump.'

'What are you talking about?'

If she intended to elaborate she didn't get a chance as Gerry answered his mobile.

'Hi. It's Madison. Ben told me to call you.'

I felt Annie's eyes on me, and the blush rose to my cheeks.

'Hello.' Gerry drawled out the greeting with such apparent pleasure that my stomach performed several somersaults. 'Are you having a good day?'

'Yes, thank you. His lordship is just buying up the whole café with the contents of my purse, I think,' I said, hearing much youthful laughter at the counter.

'Splendid,' Gerry chuckled. 'What's your schedule next Wednesday? Are you called for *Flute*?'

'Hold on.' I grappled in my bag for my diary, and flicked through the pages.

'No, that's my day off, and I finish at 1.30 on Monday. Why do you ask?'

'Would you do me a huge favour? I could do with you for a very high profile funeral.'

He named some dignitary of whom I'd never heard. 'They want the Mozart *Requiem*, for goodness sake – all of it! It's at Canterbury Cathedral. Can I tempt you?'

Tempt me!

'I'd love to.'

'Oh, good. The service is in the afternoon, so we can rehearse with the orchestra in the morning, have lunch, do the job, and be home for supper. Pete and Graham are coming too.'

'It sounds wonderful. I'll speak to you about what time I should get there and so on later, shall I?' I asked.

'Oh, come with me in the car,' he offered casually.

By this point Ben was pulling on my arm, trying to take the phone away from me.

'Ben wants to speak to you now. Thanks for asking me, Gerry. Oh, hold on, I wanted to say thank you too for bringing Annie into *Tito*.' Annie beamed at me across the table and I winked back.

'Thank you for suggesting her to me,' he said. 'She'll be ideal.'

I surrendered the phone to Ben with some reluctance, who proceeded to issue orders about a pair of trainers that he wanted Gerry to purchase for him immediately. I listened in a happy daze.

After Gemma had taken her charges off to prepare for the rehearsal Annie said quietly.

'I know I've joked with you about it, but you are very fond of Ben and Gerry, aren't you?'

'Yes, they're lovely,' I answered lightly.

'Be careful, Madison,' she said.

'In what way?' I wasn't sure if I was ready for this conversation.

'In any way that's relevant. Shall we make a move?'

Annie rose from her chair, moving away quickly enough to preclude further conversation. When I caught her up she had started leafing through her score.

'We're still not as confident on this section as we should be,' she said, showing me a tricky corner we were working to consolidate now we had ridiculously large swords to manipulate in the scene. I was grateful that she had smoothly changed the subject, but I was interested that she had started to draw conclusions about my relationship with Gerry on the basis of what seemed to me to be very little evidence. I hoped that if things got difficult that I would be able to talk to her. I was not used to confiding in others, but I felt that my feelings for Gerry might need confiding at some future date. In the meantime, I hugged them to myself, waiting to see how events would unfold.

CHAPTER 15

A ndy was still unfazed by my relationship with Gerry and
Ben and I took this as a good sign. I had pegged Annie as
unusually perceptive, and if she was speculating about my
feelings for Gerry she was not likely to do so to others, but if
Andy, or, God forbid, Megan, began to suspect, it would be
another matter altogether. So I was relieved when Andy
greeted the news of my Mozart job with equanimity.

'How interesting. I saw in the paper that Lord Metcalfe had
died.'

'I'd never even heard of him,' I said, 'but then I'm just an
ill-informed singer.'

'Who just happens to be first choice mezzo for his funeral,'
Andy quipped.

'That's only because Gerry's conducting. I doubt I would
have been asked if it were anyone else.' I enjoyed introducing
his name into the conversation, even if it were ill-advised.

'Don't underestimate yourself,' he chided me.

And that was the end of that. Andy even seemed to approve
of the fact that Gerry was driving me to Canterbury although,
to be honest, by the time I'd flogged over to Dulwich to meet
him, it would probably have been as quick to take the train,
but I certainly wasn't going to suggest it.

So I left the flat on the following Wednesday morning
exceptionally pleased with myself, and gratified to be greeted

enthusiastically by Gerry. There was no sign of the boys, who had already departed for school.

'Good morning!' he beamed. 'There's time for coffee before we leave. Pete's not here yet.'

'Pete?' I repeated stupidly.

'Pete Radin. I told you he was singing today, didn't I?'

'Yes, you did. I just didn't realise he was driving down with us.'

I was utterly crushed. Full of hope and expectations for a day spent in Gerry's company, I had blithely assumed that we would be alone in the car. Even as I fought against betraying my disappointment I tried to rationalise things. Why should Gerry have thought it necessary to clarify whether we were travelling alone or with Pete? There was no reason whatsoever. It was only because I so desperately wanted to be alone with him that it was a consideration, and Gerry didn't even know I wanted him to myself. If he did, he might not have offered me a lift anyway and so surely I was better off being with him, even in the company of Pete, than not at all.

Gerry had continued chatting as these thoughts raced through my befuddled brain, laughing heartily about Ben's frank descriptions of everyone's performance in *Flute*. I recovered quickly.

'Goodness, I dread to think what he says about me,' I said with some trepidation.

'Oh, don't worry, you come out of it very well. Ben's rather taken with you. I can't imagine why.'

Gerry gave me a mischievous look as he handed me a coffee mug.

'I'm very taken with him,' I said. 'And I'm sorry not to meet Josh this morning.'

'Oh, God,' Gerry said wearily, 'he was less than impressed about being forcibly detained at school yesterday for sporting an earring, yet again.'

I was most intrigued by the sound of Josh, who, it appeared, couldn't be more different to Ben; I said so to Gerry.

72

'Perhaps he'll be back in later if you really do want to submit yourself to the sight of him,' he said.

Pete's arrival prompted us to move, and by the time we hit the road I was rather more resigned to his unavoidable presence. One compromise I was not prepared to make, however, was sitting in the back seat. As we prepared to get into the car, there was an awkward moment as Pete and I jostled for the front passenger door. It wasn't an unseemly scuffle, more an odd shuffling dance, as I moved squarely in front of him and he hovered deliberately behind me. I grasped the handle, refusing to release it until Gerry had leaned over and opened the door from inside the car. I slipped in, leaving Pete no choice but to take the back seat. I could sense his displeasure, but my need was greater than his.

Nonetheless, it was a jolly ride to Canterbury. Gerry was in fine form, regaling Pete with tales of Glyndebourne as seen through the eyes of young Benjamin McFall, and he encouraged me to contribute material from my own store of anecdotes. Pete was a quiet young man, who had little to say about anything that didn't revolve around his singing, so once he had pronounced on his latest achievements and forthcoming plans he fell silent, leaving Gerry and I to chat. I found room to even feel sympathetic – a little! He and Gerry were old friends and Pete probably saw me as the interloper. If Gerry was bothered, he didn't show it, throwing the odd question or comment back to Pete, who replied stoically enough, but I could see he hadn't yet forgiven me the front seat battle. Magnanimous in victory, I tried to draw him out a little and when I made both men laugh, I thought that maybe some good would come out of the day after all.

It doesn't sound quite appropriate to say that I enjoyed the funeral, but it was very special to stand before a congregation of luminaries in the beautiful setting of the cathedral and sing Mozart's sublime *Requiem*. Hearing Graham's resonant voice declaiming *Tuba Miram Spagens Sonum* was spine chillingly awesome, and as Pete's ringing tenor cut across the final bass notes it was as if a bolt of electricity had shot through the building. Kate, the young soprano, smiled at me with delight as we listened to them and it inspired us to do glorious things with our own lines. It was thrilling, too, to be under Gerry's baton again and I felt myself blossom as I sang, full of joy, despite the solemnity of the occasion.

'You are sounding fabulous,' Graham Fellowes enthused as we changed to leave after the service. I looked at him in surprise.

'Thank you. So are you.'

'I mean it, Madison. Something's really taken off in your voice. It's like a switch has been flicked and it's flooded with light. You've always been great, but there's something special there now. Hold on to it, darling.'

'I'll try,' I laughed.

I thought back to the lunch we had all shared in the Weatherspoon's in town: simple, cheap fare, in enormously good-natured company. It had been easy to slide into a seat next to Gerry, and whilst he and Graham dominated the conversation I sat as close to him as I dared, until my thigh was pressed against his. I didn't change my expression, managing to continue an exchange with Kate at the same time, but warmth flooded my body and Kate's voice seemed to come from somewhere several feet away rather than just across the table. As Gerry kept talking I moved my hand cautiously until it rested on his knee. My breath caught high in my chest as I waited to see if he would respond and, without missing a beat, he laid his hand over mine, stroking it with his long fingers, letting them rest there for a few breathtaking moments. The room definitely moved and I gave up any attempt to finish my lunch. With the arrival of coffee, Gerry took his hand away, but he didn't shift position, and I sat with the warmth of his leg against mine, generating quite unprecedented feelings in my trembling little body.

CHAPTER 16

As we drove back to London, Pete lolling quietly in the rear (no battle this time – he had clearly got the message), it took enormous restraint not to reach out to touch Gerry as he drove, to rest my hand on his leg, or entwine my fingers with his. It was as if the moment over lunch hadn't happened. Gerry was absolutely as normal, not in the slightest embarrassed or awkward, but neither did he repeat the gesture or give me any reason to think he might do so when we were alone again. I watched him carefully for a sign that things had changed between, but could see nothing.

As we drew near to home, Gerry asked Pete where was convenient to drop him off, and he suggested East Croydon.

'Do you want to get out there, too, Madison?' Gerry asked.

It would have been perfectly sensible for me to do so, but I wasn't inclined to take the easy route home.

'No, I'll be fine if I go back to Dulwich and get the train from there.'

If Pete was as calculating as me he would doubtless have worked out that I must have had my own reasons for not leaving the car with him, and I wondered if he would say anything as he left, but he didn't even look interested as he scuttled off into the station.

Gerry was suddenly quiet as we drove on, and I felt certain he was thinking about the unexpected moment over lunch. I longed to touch him but sensed it would not be prudent. I had made the first move, he had responded, and now it was up to him to pursue things further if he wanted to do so. I pretended that I hadn't noticed his uncharacteristic introspection and covered it with some fairly unsubstantiated opinions about Süssmayer's contribution to the *Requiem* and about the day in general. I wondered if Gerry would pull up outside West Dulwich station, leaving me no option but to take the train then and there, but he drove past it without hesitation, continuing along Thurlow Park Road and into his driveway before stopping the car. In turn, I made as if to head straight off, gathering my bags and getting out of the vehicle quickly.

'Thank you for today, Gerry, the lift, and the job.'

I hoisted my bag onto my shoulder, lingering just a fraction.

'Do you want a cup of tea or something?' he asked abruptly. Suddenly, Gerry seemed as nervous as I did.

'That would be lovely,' I smiled in relief.

The house already buzzed with life as we entered, the television competing loudly with sounds of rock music, and Gerry was barely through the front door as Ben burst from the lounge, a flurry of long arms and legs and boyish energy.

'Hiya Dad, hiya Mads.'

He didn't appear surprised to see me, but I was aware that this said very little about me and a good deal about how many singers passed in and out of Gerry's house.

'Is all that noise really necessary?' Gerry enquired.

'It's Josh, not me,' Ben said defensively, kicking the lounge door shut behind him, and marginally muffling the sounds of the television. Music continued to blare out from upstairs.

'It's fit to drive a grown man to tears,' Gerry sighed. 'Come on, Madison, it's show time at the zoo.'

Ben followed us into the kitchen, his attention largely on a hand-held computer game, and sat at the table as Gerry filled the kettle.

'Can I help?' I asked, looking around the bomb site that masqueraded as a kitchen.

'You could start with cleaning the cooker if you like,' he joked. 'No, it's fine. Just sit there and look serene.'

I would willingly have cleaned the whole house for him, never mind the cooker, but I did as I was told. Ben demonstrated his game to me and we ignored Gerry as I tried to grasp the basics.

'Dad's crap at this,' Ben pronounced disparagingly as Gerry put mugs in front of us.

'I don't think it's a vital life skill,' I said in Gerry's defence. 'I suspect he'll cope without it.'

As I spoke we heard movement above us. The music stopped abruptly, a door slammed, and feet sounded heavily on the stairs. I was taking a sip of tea as the door opened and my hand froze, mug suspended, as I stared in fascination. Before me stood the most beautiful young man I had ever seen. Jet black hair gelled into a gleaming cap crowned a pale, intelligent face. Dark eyes glowered suspiciously at me, eyebrows faintly, but definitely, extended and darkened with kohl, and lashes just a fraction longer and blacker than nature intended. I smiled, recognising that Josh was evidently working within the parameters he could just get away with at school. He was slim, like Ben and Gerry, but he wore his leanness differently, mysteriously hollow-cheeked and bony armed, a refugee from the Haight-Ashbury deposited in Dulwich thirty years later. He was stunning, and completely unaware of it.

'Hello,' Gerry greeted him. 'I'd never have known that you were in the house.'

Josh ignored his father's sarcasm, sitting down gloomily at the table and taking the Nintendo from Ben's hands.

'This is so puerile,' he sneered.

Ben snatched it back.

'That's why you want it, then?' he crowed.

'Josh, this is Madison,' Gerry interjected, passing Josh a mug of tea. 'She's been singing with me in Canterbury today.'

'Hi,' Josh grunted with absolutely no interest.

'Hi, Josh,' I said quietly. 'I'm very pleased to meet you today. I've heard so much about you from Ben and your dad.'

'That must have been fascinating,' he mocked, smirking at Gerry.

'Madison's in *Flute* with me,' Ben told him, glued once more to the Nintendo.

'Oh yeah.' Josh looked at me under his incredible eyelashes. 'Cosmic.'

I laughed out loud, enjoying Josh's laconic manner. He clearly didn't allow either his brother or his dad an inch to manoeuvre. Gerry caught my eye and shrugged helplessly.

'What's for supper?' Ben asked him.

'Whatever we can find.'

Ben scrambled up to look in the fridge.

'Nothing,' he announced, closing it firmly. 'I think we need to order in a pizza.'

'Oh, sure,' Gerry replied disbelievingly. 'I distinctly remember seeing several pork chops there this morning.'

Josh remained aloof from their banter, tracing patterns in the breadcrumbs on the tabletop. I itched to get a cloth.

'Is Madison staying?' Ben asked.

Gerry looked at me with eyebrows raised.

'I don't know if she wants to stay in this madhouse.'

'Is that an invitation?' I asked lightly.

'Hmm. Something like that.'

'Thank you.' I grinned at him. 'If you let me make myself useful.'

So Gerry allowed me to prepare vegetables and I took the opportunity to do some surreptitious cleaning of the work surfaces. Ben and Gerry kept up a running commentary on this and that and Josh sat at the table looking bored, but obviously listening despite his show of utter detachment.

I was ridiculously happy as I sat at supper with Gerry and his boys. Josh remained monosyllabic, but the fragments of conversation he contributed were telling. I gathered he hated school, had little time for his father's career, even less for Ben's youthful foray into the operatic world, and a nihilistic view on the world, people, and life in general. Gerry was patient with him, even though Josh's negativity was so utterly opposed to Gerry's outgoing nature and, even more interestingly, I could see that there was an undercurrent of subtle, but obvious, affection between Josh and Ben. I sensed that the older boy was protective of his brother, and guessed that it to be a concern borne out of having lost their mother so young.

I held my own well enough in their forceful company, loving every minute of it, but once they'd demolished a tin of rice pudding each I reached the reluctant conclusion that it was time to leave. How I longed to stay, to spend longer in their heart-warming presence, to grow closer to Gerry, to let him take me to bed and to wake at his side in the morning... I called time on my feverish imagination, pushing my chair back slowly.

'I ought to make a move. Can I wash up before I go?' I asked.

'Of course not!' Gerry declared cheerfully. 'We just bung it all in the dishwasher and turn it on when we run out of crockery.'

I shuddered. Perhaps I obsessive-compulsive. I imagined they would quickly find my constant clearing up as irritating as I found their chaos, but we didn't need to cross that bridge just yet.

'Thank you for a lovely day, Gerry,' I said.

'Thank you for coming, and for joining us tonight.'

We grinned at each other across the table. I squeezed Ben's hand briefly and kissed his soft cheek.

'Bye, darling. See you tomorrow.'

'Yeah. Bye, Mads.' He smiled sweetly and I had to restrain myself from clutching him to my aching breast.

As Gerry led me to the front door, I told him, 'Josh is seriously cool.'

'If you say so,' he smiled, rolling his eyes. 'I guess you're more on the cutting edge of these things than I am.'

We hesitated, uncertain of what the next move was, or who should make it. I followed my instinct and reached up to hug him, and he put his arms round me as I buried my face in his shoulder.

'It's been really nice today,' he murmured.

'Umm.' I lifted my head to look him in the eye and he kissed me, firmly but briefly.

'See you soon,' he said.

I wanted more than this, but I knew it wasn't the time to press it.

'Absolutely,' I replied, kissing him back in a businesslike fashion as I stepped away and reached for the doorknob.

I didn't look back as I walked down the drive and onto Thurlow Park Road, but as I turned into West Dulwich station, I was crying and I didn't stop until I reached Victoria.

CHAPTER 17

Something happened to my appetite after that wonderful day. I could barely swallow a piece of toast in the morning, and the prospect of eating a full meal was horrendous. I felt tremulous and sick, my limbs aching and heavy, and I slept little, waking early to find thoughts of Gerry still where I'd left them the previous night, continually whirling through my head. I was desperately in love, with the ardour and despair of a teenager, but even as that thought materialised, I realised how foolish we were to think such love the province of the impetuous young. With the wisdom of thirty-eight years, I could rationalise exactly why my love for Gerry was foolish, hopeless, ill-advised, misdirected and just plain wrong, but every day I awoke feeling the same overwhelming longing for him. I told myself it was a crush, infatuation, lust, yet still my heart told me that I was falling more deeply in love that I had ever done before.

As I wrestled with my emotions, I waited painfully for Gerry to contact me. The days crawled by, and in his silence I feared that he was deliberately avoiding speaking to me after the beautiful, strange day in Canterbury. I had no illusions that those brief moments of closeness had meant as much to him as to me, but I longed to see him again, however little he wanted from our fragile relationship.

I was quiet at home, glad to be in Sussex for most of the week, and that Andy was already going to The Restless Dragon on a regular basis, seeing Joe Budzynski and Ron Stryker about casting, sets, and costumes. The Dragon management seemed to be allowing Andy room to make a real contribution to the preparatory stages of the play, and it certainly boded well for the rehearsal period. It was one of life's little ironies that Andy's long awaited big break had coincided with my emotional crisis. I was oddly detached from his tales of Joe, Ron, the audition process (Steve had landed the part of Mort with the unanimous agreement of all concerned), and the preliminary meetings of the production team. But he was happy, and remarked only occasionally on my unusually subdued demeanour.

He did so almost a week after I'd been to Canterbury. I was toying disconsolately with my Sainsbury's chicken tikka, finally pushing it away with a sigh.

'Are you okay, Mads?' he asked solicitously. 'You don't seem very happy tonight.'

'I'm just weary,' I said. 'Not much appetite tonight.'

'Nor for the last few days,' he observed, 'unless you've been tucking in during rehearsals.'

I grasped at this straw.

'Yes, I guess I've been snacking between meals too much.'

I fiddled with my fork, nibbling at the fragrant rice.

'Is everything all right?' Andy asked again. 'You're not having problems with *Flute* are you? I've been concentrating so hard on *Lethal Desires* that I've neglected you, haven't I? Sorry, Mads.'

He looked at me anxiously and I willed myself not to cry.

'*Flute's* fine, Andy. Everything's fine. I'm just a bit overtired. Do you mind if I leave this and get to bed? I'll wash up tomorrow.'

'Of course not. I'll clear up now, you get to bed and I'll bring you a hot toddy, shall I?'

I thought I wouldn't want the hot concoction of whisky, ginger wine and honey that Andy brought to me in bed, but I enjoyed its comforting warmth and I slipped into an easier sleep than I'd had all week.

The next day Ben and I, Gemma, and the other boys returned to London on the train. Things with Ben were just the same, for which I was deeply grateful. He was my link to the absent Gerry, and it felt almost as if I was with him as we laughed our way back into town. Gemma was proving a cheerful and interesting companion, too, and I was interested to note that other members of the cast (Annie obviously excluded) were evidently puzzled by my growing friendship with her and my association with Ben. I got the impression that the more elevated members of the company considered the children and their chaperones no more than a necessary evil, and I was definitely slumming it. It amused Gemma.

'Madison, you make my job so much easier,' she laughed as we sat on the train. 'Are you sure you don't want to take it over full-time?'

Ben was talking to Dusan and I didn't think he would overhear us.

'I'd like to take him on full-time,' I said, casting my eyes in Ben's direction.

'I thought so,' Gemma smiled. 'You're absolutely besotted with him. It's very sweet.'

I looked at Ben with love.

I said quietly, 'It's all a very new feeling for me, but I am enjoying it.'

But I grew increasingly nervous as we got closer to home. Ben had told me casually that Gerry was going to be at Victoria to collect him and I felt sick with apprehension. Ben was first off the train, up the platform, and accosting his father well before I sauntered up behind, trying to look unconcerned.

'Hello,' I said shyly.

'Hello.' Gerry looked me squarely in the eye and smiled confidently. 'Have you been all right?'

If it seemed an unusual greeting, I took it as some fragmentary evidence that he had been thinking of me.

'Umm, yes. And you?'

I studied him closely. He nodded, raising his eyebrows comically.

'Good day?' he asked Ben as we walked across the concourse.

'Okay.' Ben appeared blasé about his high-flying career, but I knew it was all an act, and Gerry winked at me over Ben's head.

'Madison, I've got a cheque for you for last week, but it's not with me. I'll give it to Ben on Friday.'

'Thanks.'

We had already arrived at Gerry's car, illegally parked outside the station, and I feared that he would be gone before we could say anything more important.

'Actually, Madison, can I be really cheeky?' Gerry said as we drew to a halt.

'What about?' I laughed.

He shuffled his feet for a moment.

'Well, come on then,' I urged.

'I've got a problem on Friday. I'm away in Worcester and I thought Josh would be at home and I could break the law and leave him in charge of a minor overnight. But I'd completely forgotten that he's got a geography field trip. Not that he wants to go, but it's compulsory. So, I was wondering...' He trailed off, looking at me helplessly.

My heart soared with joy.

'Whether I could take Ben back to Dulwich?' I finished for him.

'Actually, I hoped you might be able to take him home with you.' Gerry made an apologetic face.

'Of course.' I had to make a real effort not to look ridiculously overjoyed.

'Are you sure? It's a huge favour to ask of you?'

'Definitely sure. It would be a pleasure.'

And of course, it was, but finally, the pleasure had its price. I gave Andy twenty-four hours warning of our visitor and it clearly set an alarm bell ringing.

'Staying overnight? Here?' he asked in surprise. 'Why *here*?'

'I guess it's convenient. We'll both be at the rehearsal, so we can trundle back here together. Nobody else has to meet Ben at Victoria. It cuts out a third party.'

Andy shook his head in bewilderment.

'It seems rather sudden,' he mused.

'In what respect?'

'I didn't realise that you were all on such good terms. It's one thing singing together, staying over here is quite another.'

'It's what friends do, Andy,' I retorted defensively, 'you know, help each other out.'

'He must surely have other people he could stay with. Why doesn't he go home with the chaperone?'

This was a reasonable question, but I thought I had a reasonable answer to it.

'Because the chaperone doesn't get paid to do that.'

'And you do?'

'Of course not.'

I was stuck now as Andy looked at me questioningly.

'So you give up a rare free Friday night to babysit? I think this is way beyond the call of duty, Mads.'

'I want to do it,' I blurted out. 'It's no problem to me at all.'

'The decision is obviously made,' said Andy finally, 'but I'd be glad of more notice another time. In fact, I'd appreciate it if we didn't have all your new friends camping out here at all.'

'Andy, that's such an exaggeration,' I protested.

'Which I hope it stays,' he concluded. 'Leave it, Mads, you've got your own way – again.'

CHAPTER 18

Andy didn't get home until after nine o'clock on Friday night. Ben and I had been installed for almost two hours, and we were eating dessert as we sat at the computer when he eventually materialised. Ben had brought a game which he had put onto my system whilst I cooked and I was trying to learn fast. Things were getting lively when Andy put his head around the study door. He looked puzzled and put out.

'Hi,' I said lightly, and Ben turned to smile in greeting. 'Ben, do you remember Andy from Cornwall last year?'

'Yeah, hi,' he said briefly, focussing quickly again on the game.

'Hello.' Andy was subdued. 'What on earth are you doing?'

'*Death Raiders in Outer Space #1*,' Ben told him cheerfully. 'Madison's getting quite good, but she'll never beat me.'

'How did that get on the computer?' Andy asked coolly.

'I installed it,' Ben replied, oblivious to the mounting tension.

'Oh, great,' Andy said wryly, 'just what we wanted on there.'

I glared at him and fortunately he retreated before Ben realised that he was irritated.

After a while I left Ben to investigate the contents of my hard drive and went in search of Andy. He was slouched in front of the television, looking sulky.

'Come on, Andy, please,' I wheedled.

'Please what?' he snapped. 'You two are obviously having a great time, you don't need me around.'

I was torn. I wanted to keep Ben to myself, but I hated the possibility that Andy's anger would spill over and become apparent to him. Andy saw me hesitate in the doorway.

'Oh, for goodness sake, Mads, get back to him, I can see you can't bear being separated for five minutes. What is there to eat?'

I took advantage of the diversion Andy provided and bustled into the kitchen, Andy close behind. I warmed up leftover pasta I had made for Ben and me earlier whilst Andy leaned against the worktop, still aggrieved but quieter now.

'I don't get it, Mads,' he said eventually. 'It's just not you. You've never shown any interest in kids, not personal interest like this.'

'But he's a great lad, don't you think?'

'Maybe, but I'm just not happy about it.' He took his plate and opened the drawer for cutlery.

'What are you not happy about?' I asked, wondering what the real agenda was here.

'I don't know, Madison,' he said grimly, 'but I'm sure I shall find out eventually.'

I persuaded Ben into bed at ten, after we'd phoned Gerry and left a message on his voicemail, but he was reluctant to settle.

'Mads, you've got to hear this,' he laughed, brandishing the latest Harry Potter at me. So I sat on the bed, plumping up cushions against the wall, leaned back, and sipped tea whilst Ben read sections to me. I listened with one ear whilst I drank in the pleasure of sharing this time with him, feeling close to Gerry as I poured out my love for him into my care for Ben. Eventually, Ben flagged.

'I think I'll go to sleep now.'

He snuggled down under the covers and I climbed off the bed.

'Goodnight, darling. You know where I am if you want anything.'

I leant over to kiss his cheek, but as I stood up he put his arms round me and pulled me back down for a hug.

'Night, Mads,' he murmured, releasing me. We smiled fondly at each other, and after I'd left him to sleep, it was quite some time before I could face Andy again. My eyes, sparkling and smudged with tears, would take some explaining.

CHAPTER 19

I was at a loss at what to do in the morning. Gerry had arranged to collect Ben at ten o'clock and, as luck would have it, Andy was not going to The Restless Dragon over the weekend. He kept out of the way whilst I got Ben up, made him breakfast and endured a ridiculously energetic early morning game of charades. But when the entry phone buzzed, he appeared as if by magic, watching me closely as I spoke into it.

'Hello.' I knew my voice had softened even as I anticipated Gerry's tones at the other end.

'It's me.'

'Come on up.' I pressed the door release.

'Is that Dad?' Ben shouted along the hall.

'Yes.' I avoided Andy's eye as I saw him set up sentry guard between the front door and the kitchen.

Gerry bounded up the stairs two at a time, full of smiles and energy as he reached the top. We grinned at each other for a moment and I longed to hold out my arms to him.

'Hi, Gerry,' I said warmly as Ben materialised at my side, and we all beamed stupidly.

'I'm Andy. You probably don't remember me, but I'm Madison's husband.' Andy sounded like a death knell on our happy scene, his voice laden with sarcasm. I closed my eyes briefly, sighing with irritation, but Gerry moved in smoothly as if Andy had greeted him with the utmost courtesy.

'Yes, of course. Hello again. Thank you for putting up with his lordship.' He held out his hand easily, and Andy took it with an air of condescension.

'Oh, it didn't bother me. He and Madison were perfectly happy on their own.'

Ignoring Andy's rudeness, Gerry smiled with great congeniality.

'Jolly good. Come on then, young man, get your things. I'm sure Madison's had about as much of you as she can bear for the time being.'

I walked down to the car with them both, hot with embarrassment.

'Gerry, I can't apologise enough for Andy's behaviour.'

'It doesn't bother me,' he replied. 'What about you, though? Have we made things difficult?'

'Absolutely not,' I assured him quickly. 'You make things wonderful.'

The words were out of my mouth before I could censor them and I was embarrassed afresh, hearing the unmistakable note of love in my voice.

'We don't want to cause trouble for you, Madison,' he said seriously as he stowed Ben's bag in the rear seat.

'Gerry, you don't make trouble for me. I'm a big girl and I can look after myself. I'm doing what I want to do.'

We were silent, looking at one another for moment, then Gerry leant forward to kiss me.

'Umm.' He gave me a knowing look, though I had no idea what he was thinking. 'Thank you for last night. You really bailed us out.'

'It was lovely.'

I reached up to hug him, then put my arms tightly around Ben's bony shoulders, horribly sad that in a moment, they would be driving away again, leaving me to miss them desperately.

There was no reason for them to linger and too soon I was heading up the stairs to the flat. Andy was staring out of the kitchen window looking grim.

'Very cosy,' he sneered as I entered.

'What's that supposed to mean?' I sighed.

'I'm sure you all have a wonderful time together, Madison. Just count me out of it. Oh, but of course, you already have.'

'I think this is a gross overreaction,' I said calmly.

'Just tell me, Madison, are you having an affair with him?'

'No.' I hoped that Andy hadn't heard the irony in my voice. I spoke the truth, wishing it were a lie; that's how far I'd fallen from grace.

'I guess I'll have to believe you,' he replied, 'but you can't blame me for wondering, and don't try to deny you like him. It was written all over your face just now.'

'He's my friend, Andy.'

'I have gathered that. I hope he's no more. I'm going out,' he said finally.

'Where? I didn't think you were going to The Dragon today?' I asked.

'You don't tell me everything, Madison, so I don't see any need to explain myself to you.'

Andy's mood had softened by the evening, but I knew that a corner had been turned. No longer would I be able to tell him that simple version of the truth when I was seeing Ben or Gerry. If it was for *Flute* or *Tito*, he could hardly question it, but if I saw them for any other reason, it would have to be explained, excused and justified, or simply not revealed.

In the short term, I needn't have worried. Although I saw Ben regularly at *Flute* rehearsals as we neared the opening, I neither saw nor heard from Gerry, and yet again my sleep was interrupted, my appetite waned, and it was difficult to concentrate. I wondered what Gerry was thinking throughout all this. Had he an inkling of the agony I suffered between our sporadic, confusing, but wonderful meetings? I assumed not, thinking that there was little likelihood that he thought of me

91

at all. But then again… I was glad of the busyness of the last two weeks before *Flute* opened, and as Andy and I put some distance between the unpleasant scene after Ben's visit, he said no more about it, reassured perhaps, by my own silence.

A week before we opened, I asked Ben who was using his dress rehearsal tickets.

'Dad and Grandma,' he responded.

Andy and Megan were using mine and I hoped there would be no awkwardness. But in some strange corner of my mind, I wanted Megan to meet Gerry, to see that there was a spark between us, however intermittently Gerry allowed it to be fanned. What suicidal thoughts, I mused, as I shied away from the prospect of everyone coming face to face at the stage door, whilst at the same time wondering how I could wangle it.

As we entered the final week of rehearsals I sat by the lake with Gemma and the three boys as we ate lunch. Ben was quieter than usual, tired by the succession of long days we were enduring. Uncharacteristically, he largely ignored Dusan and Oli and, folding up my top into a cushion, placed it on my lap and rested his head there.

'Are you okay, darling?' I asked, stroking his cheek.

'I'm tired,' he complained.

'We've got half an hour before we have to get back. Have a sleep if you want,' I suggested.

Ben relaxed his long limbs and his head lay heavily on my knee. As he closed his eyes I sang softly: *You are my heart's delight, and where you are I long to be. You make my darkness bright, when like a star you shine on me…*

I saw Gemma smile even as she continued to chat with Oli and Dusan, and Ben murmured indistinctly as I ran my fingers through his soft hair. After a while he shifted position, looking up at me with soulful eyes.

'I love you,' I said softly, and he smiled inscrutably, just like his dad, and settled down to doze again.

CHAPTER 20

I thought little more about it, glad to have enjoyed the gentle moment with Ben, but sad and discouraged still not to have heard from Gerry. But early next morning, when I was installed on the Lewes bound train, drinking coffee and trying to read a novel, my phone rang, and at last it was Gerry.

'Ben was talking about you last night, and I'm conscious that I haven't rung you. I'm sorry.'

I was taken aback, unsure of how to respond.

'That's okay,' I said feebly. 'Is Ben all right today? He was very tired yesterday.'

'Yes, I know. He seems fine. He's gone to school today rather reluctantly, an activity he considers somewhat beneath him of late.'

I laughed, happy to hear Gerry's voice again.

'I was wondering if you'd like to come to the restaurant tomorrow night,' he continued. 'If you like a bit of light relief and a free meal, that is.'

I closed my eyes with pleasure and leaned back in my seat.

'Yes, why not?' I said. 'I won't be able to get there till after eight, if that's okay.'

'Of course. We don't kick off till around then anyway. Bring some music with you.'

He rang off.

The restaurant was a beautiful Italian diner based in a prestigious hotel in the West End. Twice a week patrons could eat to the accompaniment of opera selections, sung by an ever changing cast of singers, most of whom were chorus members from ENO or the Opera House. Gerry played there a couple of times a month and I had sung with him once at the back end of the previous year. To be fair, as nice as it was, it was a gig that I'd long outgrown, but I hoped I wasn't too far from the truth in thinking that Gerry's invitation was based on personal rather than professional motivations. I pondered what to say to Andy, deciding that it was easiest just to tell him I'd been asked to do a last minute cover at the hotel. I would leave Gerry's name out of it entirely, working on the assumption that Andy wouldn't recall that the last time I had sung there had been with him.

So the next day I packed a dress for the evening, plus a selection of arias, and drifted through the *Flute* rehearsal in a state of high excitement. Annie saw me hanging up my dress on a convenient hook, pulling it free of creases.

'Off somewhere nice tonight?' she asked.

'Il Frappocelli,' I said briefly.

'Good grief, I haven't sung there for years,' she said with surprise. 'Why are you going there?'

'Gerry McFall asked me yesterday. It's just a last minute thing.'

'I see,' Annie said with emphasis, and I turned away, blushing.

It was really rather silly to volunteer for a late night in the last week of *Flute* rehearsals, but I hoped that the adrenaline buzz would see me through. I changed at the restaurant whilst Gerry was working with two singers who appeared regularly at Il Frappocelli, a tenor named Richard, from the ROH chorus, and Emily Banks, a soprano from the Coli. They were busily engaged in singing *Soave Fanciulla* as I slipped into the seat at the table reserved for the performers. Gerry caught my eye and winked and I sat there happily drinking in the sight of him until the duet was over. He rose from the piano stool to introduce me to the others who I knew only vaguely by sight.

'Madison's come hotfoot from Glyndebourne this evening,' he said cheerfully. 'She opens in *Flute* next week in the company of young Benjamin McFall.' He beamed with pride.

As I held out my hand, first to Richard, who smiled and greeted me pleasantly, and then to Emily, I was astonished to see her stare at me with ill-concealed hostility. She was a beautiful girl, who I'd heard singing wonderfully well as I'd entered the restaurant; what on earth could she be so cross about? I didn't see myself as a threat to anyone, let alone a glamorous soprano ten years my junior.

'Hi, Emily,' I said enthusiastically, 'you sounded lovely.'

She smiled with disdain and promptly turned her back. The men typically pretended not to notice, and I felt stranded.

'Do you want to sing now, Madison?' Gerry asked me, 'or recover from your journey first?'

'Oh, I'm fine. Let's do *Chacun a son gout*, that'll get me going.'

Emily made a great show of ignoring me as I sang, though the punters clearly enjoyed it, which possibly added fuel to her fire. It was going to be an interesting evening.

As I was a guest I didn't sing as often as the others, which didn't worry me in the slightest. The pleasure of the evening was quite unashamedly to be with Gerry, and I ensconced myself next to him at the piano to turn the pages and hand him music for each piece. Every five or six numbers I would slip in an item and I covered some eclectic repertoire – Novello, Rossini and Lehar – until our dinner break arrived. I had become increasingly conscious of Emily's mood. Evidently my presence cramped her style, though she was far more the focus of the diners' attention than I was. It was only when she leaned straight across me, practically elbowing me in the mouth, to put her music on the stand, that I realised why she was so angry. She was furious that she had to compete with me for Gerry's attention. As she placed her hand on his shoulder, leaning closer, ostensibly to indicate some detail in the music, I felt a spasm of fear and misery. Thus far, I had been so obsessed with trying to inveigle my way into Gerry's life that I had no chance to be jealous. Focussed only on building a relationship with him and Ben, I hadn't looked around to see what the competition might comprise.

So, as we ate dinner, I watched Gerry surreptitiously. He treated Emily with friendly ease, joking mildly with her, smiling in his inscrutable way as she leaned all over him and flirted outrageously. Every so often she checked to see if I was watching her and I tried to look as if I noticed nothing of interest, but my happy mood had deserted me. Gerry sat diagonally opposite, separated by only twelve inches of table, but it may as well have been a chasm, and I retreated into silence, toying listlessly with my food.

Emily kept up her bizarre performance after dinner, to the extent that Richard clearly took pity on me.

'Madison, shall we do the *Trovatore* duet?' he asked kindly, looking over the piano with a smile.

Emily looked daggers at him, but Gerry was already finding the page in his score and she had no chance to intervene. It was enormous fun to sing Auzucena to Richard's Manrico. It was role I was unlikely to be offered in a big house – my voice wasn't a dark Verdi contralto like Annie's, although I could bluff it now and then – so it was a treat to sing such a wonderful duet to an uncritical audience.

'Well done,' said Gerry appreciatively when we were done. 'That's good going after singing Second Lady all day!'

I glowed proudly. Never mind Carl Davis, it was Gerry's pleasure and approval I craved.

'But you're not really an Auzucena,' Emily drawled from Gerry's side, where she'd quickly moved in to turn pages.

'No,' I said lightly. 'That's why it's so nice to sing it here.'

I wasn't sure I would be able to come back with another quick retort if she pursued the subject, but mercifully she flounced out to the front to sing the Laughing Song. I sighed.

'Are you all right?' whispered Gerry as he played. 'You're rather quiet tonight.'

'I'm fine,' I said shortly, resisting the temptation to bury my face in his shoulder. He looked me sideways, but I kept my eyes on the music.

CHAPTER 21

Our stint finally over, Gerry and I packed up his music, putting into a crate to transport it to the car, whilst Emily made a great display of going round the diners to collect compliments.

'I think I ought to take you home,' Gerry said to me. 'It's after midnight, and you don't want to pay for a taxi after coming down here for nothing.'

I shrugged.

'I don't mind Gerry. You'll be going out of your way again. I don't expect you to be my personal car service.'

Gerry laughed.

'And I don't expect you to go home on your own.'

'Okay. I won't argue.' I grinned at him across the piano. 'I don't need to change then if I'm being chauffeured, but I'll just pop to the loo, and then I'll be with you.'

I was happier as I trotted off, hoping I wouldn't get a nasty surprise and find Emily in the car when I returned, although I should have learnt from the Canterbury trip not to assume anything. But the surprise came earlier than I had anticipated. Emily was brushing her hair at the mirror in the ladies as I entered. I smiled, determined not to suggest any animosity on my part.

'That was fun, wasn't it?' I said cheerfully.

'Depends on your definition of fun,' Emily replied sourly.

I didn't see any future in pursuing that line, and racked my brain to think of something neutral and uncontroversial to say. I needn't have bothered.

'You think you've really got it made, don't you?' she said bitterly.

I looked at her in amazement.

'What do you mean?'

'You love swanning down here, the great Glyndebourne artist, slumming it with the plebs for the night.'

'Emily, I don't think that at all,' I gasped. 'I'm no prima donna, and I think it's lovely singing here.'

She didn't appear to have heard me as she ploughed on in her tirade.

'Because you're Gerry's latest woman, you think you can sit there looking bloody pleased with yourself all night. Well, let me tell you, Ms Fancy Name, Fancy Attitude, he'll screw you and dump you. You're nothing special to him at all, just another good-looking singer he can notch on his baton.'

Incredibly, I stayed calm.

'I'm not sleeping with Gerry,' I said quietly.

My failure to match her rage with a display of my own seemed to take the wind out of her sails.

'Whatever you say, but you were cosying up to him pretty well tonight. I'm not stupid.'

'It didn't occur to me that you were,' I replied coolly. 'But I do think this is a particularly pointless conversation, and I'd rather we abandoned it now.'

'I'm sure you would. You don't like the truth, do you?' she snapped.

I could feel my resolve diminishing by the second, but I was determined not to cry in front of her. Leaving my hair unbrushed and my make up untouched, I grabbed my bag and headed for the door, hating to appear a coward in the face of her wrath, but hating more the prospect of breaking down in her presence.

Gerry looked bewildered as I threw my bags into the back of his car and myself into the passenger seat with rather more force than was necessary.

'What's the matter? You look furious,' he asked.

I took a deep breath, and closed my eyes for a moment.

'I'm fine.'

I gripped my hands into fists and banged them lightly on my knees. Gerry put his hand over mine.

'Madison, what is it? Has someone upset you?'

'No, Gerry, please. Just leave it.' There was no way I could repeat to him what Emily had said.

Gerry sighed, unconvinced, and started the engine. I rested my head against the window as he manoeuvred into the traffic. Emily's harsh words ricocheted around my brain. I'd got the gist of it all right. Gerry had casual relationships with singers who fell for his charm and charisma, Emily presumably among them. She was now offended, if not actually hurt, and jealous of what appeared to be his new relationship with me. If only! The fact that I still had no idea what Gerry felt for me made it no easier. I visualised him in bed with Emily, with a full parade of glamorous, extrovert, talented and beautifully proportioned sopranos. It didn't occur to me for a moment that Emily may not have spoken the truth and I had no intention of asking Gerry to confirm or deny it.

The tears I had successfully held back in the restaurant finally betrayed me and I scrabbled for my handkerchief. Gerry caught the movement and turned briefly towards me, still looking puzzled.

'Madison, you're crying! Don't tell me now that nothing's wrong.'

I blew my nose and wiped my eyes, at a loss at what to tell him.

'Look,' he said firmly, 'just let me park somewhere safe and then you're going to tell me what this is all about.'

I gave up the fight as Gerry pulled into a side road and turned off the engine.

'Please, Madison,' he said kindly, taking my hand. I tried to resist, but I sobbed harder, and it was all hopeless. Gerry unfastened my seat belt and his, and pulled me round to face him.

'Are you going to tell me what's the matter or am I going to have to beat it out of you?' he teased.

I shook my head, but moved closer to him.

'Come here,' he said, putting his arms round me, and I wept unashamedly on his shoulder. After enduring a substantial dose of wordless misery, he pushed me away gently and looked me squarely in the eye. I averted my gaze, looking down at my hands nervously plucking at my damp handkerchief.

'You're obviously not inclined to tell me what's made you so upset so I have no way of knowing how to make it better, if indeed, I can,' he said seriously.

I shook my head again.

'Does that mean no, you're not going to tell me, or no, there's nothing I can do, or both?'

'Both,' I muttered, as I wept afresh.

'Is it me?' he asked. 'Have I done something awful?'

'No,' I said sadly.

Suddenly a light dawned behind Gerry's eyes.

'Was it Emily?'

I was silent.

'Ah.'

'It's all right, Gerry, please. I'm just oversensitive.'

'I think you made her feel rather insecure tonight,' he observed.

'Well, she did her very best to return the compliment,' I retorted. 'All I did was sing a couple of arias and say absolutely nothing to offend anyone, but she launched into a nuclear attack in the loo.' I was gathering my wits again, feeling more angry than upset.

'What about?' Gerry asked curiously. 'You hadn't pinched any of her arias, surely?'

He laughed and I looked crossly at him.

'Of course not. It was, well, personal.' Nothing would induce me to be more specific. 'She evidently took a monumental dislike to me.'

I longed to rest my head on Gerry's chest and feel his arms around me again. If he reached for me at that moment, I think I would have told him that I loved him. So it was just as well that he didn't, but rather straightened up and smiled cautiously.

'I'm sure you were able to handle it in your own inimitable way,' he said.

'Actually, no,' I told him, feeling the pain of Emily's words again. 'It was pretty hurtful and rather a shock, but that's the way it goes, I guess. I'm sorry to collapse all over you. I should have got a taxi, shouldn't I? I've delayed you horribly now.'

Gerry patted my knee.

'Don't be silly. I haven't been much help. Sorry.'

'It's okay. I'm fine now. Let's go.'

To Gerry's enormous credit he was marvellous as we drove to south London. Without the slightest awkwardness he launched into a long and amusing tale about a conductor of our mutual acquaintance, and soon had me laughing. He timed it perfectly to conclude just as we reached Putney Heath, by which time I was looking less bedraggled.

'Madison?' he said tentatively as we sat for a moment in the quiet car.

'Gerry?'

'If I did upset you tonight, I'm sorry.'

For once I overcame my natural instinct to smooth things over. Although Emily had been the instrument, it was her words about Gerry that had caused me pain, so perhaps he did bear some responsibility. But since he didn't know how I felt about him, I couldn't expect him to shoulder it. I smiled.

'I think I've got to grow up and learn to roll with the punches,' I said.

'I don't imagine there's many punches you don't roll with,' he chuckled.

'I'm not in full fighting form at the moment, Gerry,' I said quietly.

'Well, I know how that feels,' he replied wryly, switching on the engine again.

I marvelled at his obtuseness. Surely he must have picked up on the implications of my words, but evidently I was being too subtle if I wanted a reaction from him.

'So I guess I'll see you on the big day, then,' he said cheerfully.

I gulped comically. 'Five days and counting.'

'Marvellous.' Gerry grinned and leaned over to kiss me briefly.

'Bye then.' I got out of the car slowly.

'Bye.' His voice was lost as I closed the door, unable to stay any longer if I wasn't going to make a fool of myself again.

I turned quickly up the drive, hearing the engine rev and the car pull onto the road. I had travelled lightly thus far, I realised. Carrying the weight of my love for Gerry had been a happy burden until tonight, but from now on it would be tinged with sadness. Given my circumstances, that was perhaps inevitable, but I had not expected it to come in the form it had arrived. I felt cheated, but aware that I was robbed only of a dream. Reality was that Gerry had no interest in pursuing a deeper relationship with me, and so Emily's harsh words should have had no effect. But whoever said that mankind cannot bear too much reality was dead right.

I remembered who it was as I dozed off later. It was T S Eliot.

CHAPTER 22

The day of the public dress rehearsal dawned bright and clear. The summer was proving to be a glorious one as day after day of sunshine bathed the Sussex countryside, and our exposed limbs and faces began to glow and freckle. I went down to the theatre well ahead of Megan and Andy, excitement and fear driving me out of the flat earlier in the day. I wanted to sit quietly by the lake before I dressed, drinking in the magical atmosphere and focussing on the day's work. I was glad that I could lay aside my confused emotions on this day, of all days. Waking in the morning after the restaurant gig I had made a conscious decision not to dwell on Emily's verbal attack. I admitted and accepted that there was doubtless at least some truth in what she had told me, but if there was, I could do nothing about it. It was the future I could be concerned about, and if I hoped for a relationship with Gerry, moping about the past wouldn't help it. I was mortified as I remembered my tearful scene in the car, and I quickly wanted to restore Gerry's image of me as unflappable, in control, and dignified. At least, I hoped that was how he saw me. I contemplated sending him a card, apologising for my emotional outburst, but feared it would simply draw attention to it, so I stayed silent, deciding that the best policy was to keep at a distance until the dress was over. Instead, I bought an amusing card for Ben and composed myself sufficiently to compose an innocuous message to him.

Darling Ben

What a wonderful adventure this is proving to be! I'm sure you will remember your first Flute *years after you have been singing Tamino, Papageno, or Sarastro, whatever God and your vocal chords decree! Thank you for all your wonderful company. It is a pleasure always to work with you and to enjoy your friendship.*

With every good wish and lots of love for your Glyndebourne debut season, and always,

Madison xx

I left it propped up against the mirror in the boys' dressing room before I went to my own to start my make-up and stayed ensconced there till the beginners' call. I imagined Andy and Megan arriving, hoping that they had managed to stay on friendly terms during their journey from London. I imagined Gerry, twitching with excited impatience, conducting the air, and talking non-stop. Annie and Clarissa were introspective too. The seriousness of the occasion and the enormity of the privilege it bestowed upon us hung in the air, and suddenly there were no words to express how we felt. Even the murmur from the auditorium sounded different to the refined hubbub that had surrounded us as we sat in the audience. It was insistent, cajoling and wooing us onto the stage.

And so we responded. As the curtain rose and we followed Tamino, emerging out of the swirling dry ice to declaim *Triumph!* it was indeed a triumph. Time passed more swiftly than seemed possible. We moved from each scene, to the interval, into the second act and to the finale without conscious thought, led on by Mozart's sublime music, and playing into the hands of the happy and appreciative audience. It was an audience free of critics, of course. Our friends and family cheered us on, but also many knowledgeable and discerning opera lovers, who were analysing our performances as closely as any journalist would do on Saturday. As the applause rose and swelled, Ben and I turned simultaneously to meet each other's glance. His smile filled my already bursting heart to overflowing. 'We've done this together, and isn't it cool?' it said, and I knew mine conveyed something of my deep love for him, as well as for the wonderful job we were doing. Finally, backstage, I held out my arms and we hugged excitedly.

'Oh, Mads, wasn't it wicked?'

'Darling, it was awesome,' I laughed, through tears of happiness. Annie and Clarissa were jumping around clutching each other and I let go of Ben briefly to join in a three-way embrace. Even Annie was excited enough to hold out her hand to Ben and include him in our triumvirate.

At the door to our dressing room I told Ben, 'I'll see you in the lobby. Tell your dad not to go till I've had a chance to say hello.'

Ben punched me on the arm and loped off down the corridor.

'If we're this crazy today, it'll be bedlam on Saturday,' Clarissa drawled as we changed.

'Absolutely,' Annie agreed. 'But goodness, isn't it the most thrilling thing you've ever done? How can we beat this?'

'With a principal role that has an aria,' Clarissa quipped, and we laughed in wry agreement.

I met Ben in the corridor, heading for my dressing room.

'Dad's back here, are you coming?' he asked.

'I'd better look for Andy and my mum, and I'll bring them back, too,' I told him, and he scuttled back from whence he had come.

Andy and Megan were waiting at the doorkeeper's desk, Andy already engaged in a conversation with him. Megan looked anxious and cross as she so often did when off her own territory and waiting for me to do something, but her face wreathed in smiles when I approached.

'Darling,' she cried, holding out her arms.

We hugged and she heaped proud endearments on my ears.

'You were wonderful, Madison. We could hear you so well, even in the middle of those other two big voices.'

I chuckled to myself. This was a classic Megan backhanded compliment.

Andy beamed in the background.

'Well done, *Oh Bella Suprema*. Very impressive. I like the set.'

I smiled, kissing him chastely.

'Thanks. Come and see the dressing rooms,' I urged, knowing I was leading them in to a danger zone, but unable to resist it. And sure enough, passing the door of the boys' room, Ben called to us imperiously.

'Mads, come here.'

I felt Andy stiffen with irritation, as I gestured to them to follow me. Gerry was leaning against the mirror, hands in his pockets, looking beautiful and rakish, beaming with pride. An elderly, grey-haired woman sat silently on a stool at the make up counter, smiling softly at Ben – I guessed her to be his maternal grandmother. I met Gerry's happy grin with one of my own, feeling a thrill of joy to see him again. The restaurant and Emily's outrage seemed a very long time ago.

'Hi,' I said, catching my breath. 'Wasn't he wonderful?'

'Wonderful,' Gerry agreed. 'And you were pretty impressive yourself, Dr Brylmer. I wouldn't like to be on the receiving end of that sword.'

Andy looked frosty and Megan was breathing down my neck, waiting to be included in the conversation. I pulled her forward.

'You remember my mum, Gerry, who came to the Solent Music Club concert back in April.'

'I certainly do,' he said, sauntering forward leisurely to shake her hand.

'Mum, you haven't met Ben, though, Gerry's son, who was the First Genie tonight.'

'Hello Ben,' Megan greeted him. 'You did very well this afternoon. It must have been exciting.'

'Yeah,' said Ben casually, headbutting his dad's arm.

'We've had enormous fun,' I said, feeling Andy's simmering resentment as he avoided looking at either Ben or Gerry.

'You must be very proud,' Megan said.

'Oh, yes,' Gerry laughed. 'I'm very good at playing the role of proud father, as you are of being proud mum.'

As Gerry said this, he shifted his glance from Megan to catch mine, and raised his eyebrows, eyes dancing with amusement. It was an intimate glance, his smile softening as I let my gaze meet his squarely, and we held the look for a beat longer than necessary. He broke it first, turning to Ben in a businesslike manner.

'Come on then, young man. Have you got everything?'

'Yes, hurry up dad, you're keeping me waiting.' Ben grinned at me, slinging his bag onto his shoulder. 'Come on, Madison, we don't need to wait for him.' He grabbed my arm and propelled me out of the room.

We trotted up the corridor, the others following in our wake, Gerry, never at a loss in company, regaling Andy and Megan about some aspect of the opera, so I didn't have to worry that their silence might make things awkward. As we crossed into the car park, I urged Ben to hang back and we let the adults catch us up.

'Are you coming again?' Gerry was asking Megan.

'Of course. The end of the month, isn't it, Madison?' she said, turning to me.

'Oh, yes. I got my cast tickets fixed at the first rehearsal.' I smiled.

'I think I'll be seeing it five, perhaps six, times,' said Gerry happily, as we reached Megan's car.

'Wow!' Ben exclaimed in awe. 'A Morgan!'

'Goodness, that's an impressive piece of machinery,' Gerry concurred mildly.

Ben was running his hand over the smooth paintwork.

'That is so cool. Are you going home in it, Mads?'

I nodded.

'Can I come, too? Please, Dad, can I go with Madison?'

The panic that surged up inside me must have been visible on my face, for casting a swift glance at me, Gerry cut in smoothly.

'Of course not. It may be a four seater, but it's a pretty tight fit, and there's already three of them, plus their baggage. I'm afraid you'll have to travel home the boring way, young man.'

I sagged with relief. As much as I would have loved Ben's cheerful company on the way home, Andy's anger would have definitely cast a shadow over the occasion. I rolled my eyes at Gerry who winked.

'See you soon,' he said with a wry grin.

'Definitely,'

I saw Megan and Andy move to get into the car so, greatly daring, I added quietly, 'Ring me.'

'Yes, I will.' Gerry's voice was low too, and I brushed his hand with my fingers as I turned to open the rear door.

'Bye,' he murmured softly behind me, fading away in the direction of his own car.

As we drove out in the car park, I caught Ben's faint farewell and waved my arm randomly in his direction.

'That boy is definitely too much,' Megan declared as she drove onto the main road. 'He's far too confident for his age. It must drive everyone mad.'

I wasn't sure that it was possible to be too confident, surely it was a valuable life skill, but then I was biased.

'He's a bloody pain in the neck,' Andy growled, 'but Madison doesn't agree, do you, Mads?'

The edge to Andy's voice alarmed me, but I kept my reply light, hoping that by the time we were home he would be less inclined to create a scene.

'We get on fine. Mum, what did you think of Sarastro? Isn't that voice incredible?'

Megan, it seemed, had surprisingly not picked up on the tension emanating from Andy, or surely she would have not been easily deflected, but she was. We conversed happily enough between the bucket seats, as Andy retreated further into glowering silence. Eventually, as the miles stretched out behind us, I dozed and the summer night breeze blew through the car and the moon went before us all the way home.

CHAPTER 23

I had spoken too soon. Megan phoned the next day, and after five minutes or so of casual conversation she went for the jugular.

'You seem to have become very friendly with the pianist,' she said.

'Which pianist?' I asked, deliberately vague.

'The man who played for you in Portsmouth,' she clarified needlessly. 'I suppose that's because his son is in the opera with you.'

'Yes,' I agreed smoothly, 'and I do the odd job for him now and then. Don't forget he's conducted me before, and he's MD on *Tito* in the autumn.'

'Hmm,' Megan murmured cryptically. 'You all seem to have a rather more than professional relationship, I must say.'

I adopted an increasingly upbeat note.

'Yes, we have. It's lovely how well Ben and I get on together.'

Megan left the subject there, but the conversation had not been as casual as it may appear to an observer unfamiliar with her ways. In typical form she had registered that she had seen and heard something which caused her to wonder, and her conjectures had lead her down a path she did not find congenial. That she had conveyed all this in what may appear to be the mildest terms would indeed be misleading to someone who had not experienced thirty-eight years of the Megan method. If her curiosity and imagination were not fed, the issue would die, but if fostered, the subject would run. I left it closed for the time being. I had enough trouble dealing with my feelings for Gerry without seeking it elsewhere, but there was an awful fascination in waiting to see what Megan might guess, and how she would react if ever, finally, wonderfully, I had reason to believe that Gerry returned those feelings.

So we moved towards the official opening on Saturday, tidying up one or two corners and consolidating our midweek efforts. Gerry and Josh had tickets for the first night, but I had little reason to expect to see them. Lizzie Swallow and her sister were coming as my guests and I would need to spend time with them even if Gerry made himself available. It was, at least, an excuse to phone him on Saturday morning, since he had conspicuously failed to do so. I caught him on his mobile while I was on the train.

'Gerry McFall.'

'Hi. It's Madison.'

'Hello. Hold on, let me put the phone on handsfree. I'm in the car.'

There was a rustle and clatter of static.

'That's it. How are you? I was supposed to ring you, wasn't I? Sorry.'

'I'm fine.' I ignored the opportunity to upbraid him on his failure to call. 'Might I see you tonight?' I asked.

'I expect so,' Gerry said cheerfully. 'We'll be collecting his nibs from the stage door, so perhaps you'll be around then.'

I couldn't think of any reason to keep him on the line longer so I hung up, discouraged. I had a clear sense that Gerry had gone as far as he was going to do – or perhaps as he felt able to do. He'd involved me in his family life where our professional associations had made it reasonable for him to do so. I had taken extraordinary advantage of those occasions and I knew I had caught his attention and interest, but now I was stuck. I was also impatient. I had to think of something soon, some reason for Gerry and I to be alone, away even from Ben and Josh, and then maybe I could work out where we could go from here. I gazed out of the window at the passing fields, letting my thoughts wander. As I flipped through my diary for inspiration, I remembered that Graham Fellowes was singing Renato in *A Masked Ball* at the Coli and I had promised to see it, and now it occurred to me that I could ask Gerry to join me. That was the answer; I could work out the details later. Pleased with my decision, I put it to the back of my mind to concentrate on the huge responsibility ahead of us. *Die Zauberflöte* was finally up and running and tonight's high paying audience would expect the very best.

I think they got it, too, if the applause was anything to go by. It went on for nearly twenty minutes, and we were weak with excitement and exhaustion as we changed. Lizzie and her sister, Karen, were waiting in the lobby as I emerged, and so was Gerry.

'Hi,' I said cheerily, especially concerned not to appear overly eager now I had a plan. I gestured towards Lizzie.

'Do you know Lizzie Swallow, one of my long-suffering accompanists and a very good friend?'

They shook hands amicably and I winked at Lizzie, signalling to her to bear with me as I engaged Gerry for a moment.

'What did you think? Better than the dress?' I asked.

'Oh, yes, tighter, more fluid; it's looking great. Did Ben behave himself?'

'Of course not,' I laughed. 'He was wonderful. Where's Josh?' I asked, looking over Gerry's shoulder.

'Gone back to the car. He's had about as much as he can take of opera and opera fans for one day. He knows Ben's done well, though, and that this is important.'

'I'd like to meet him again sometime.'

'I'm sure you will,' Gerry said non-committally.

Determined to be the one to break off the conversation, I turned to Lizzie and Karen.

'Let's be gone then, shall we? I want a blow by blow critique in the car.'

As we moved towards the door I looked casually over my shoulder.

'Bye,' I called, only catching Gerry's eye briefly. I hated not to linger in his presence but it was all in the interests of a new long-term strategy, I told myself. At least, that was the theory.

'Was Gerry there tonight?' Andy asked, as I climbed into bed.

'Yes, with his older son,' I said lightly. 'I only saw him to say hello as I was leaving with Lizzie. I don't know what he made of it.'

'You mean to say you didn't come home with them all, Madison? Or invite them back here to stay the night?'

'Don't be ridiculous.'

'I'm not the one being ridiculous,' Andy retorted coldly. 'I'm not the one who looks like a lovesick cow when Gerry McFall's in the vicinity. I hope for your sake that he feels the same. It would be pretty humiliating if he didn't, don't you think?'

Andy's cruel words cut like a knife into my heart.

'Ah, yes, that hurts doesn't it?' he laughed.

'What are you talking about?' I snapped, irritated that I had been so transparent.

'You know', he sneered. 'When are you seeing him next?'

'I've no idea,' I replied honestly.

'What a shame. Perhaps you'll have to make do with Ben now. I'm going to sleep now, Madison. If I can.'

In the darkness, I lay still, knowing that Andy was awake. Tears ran from beneath my eyelids, which I knew would look swollen and heavy in the morning. It was true that Gerry didn't feel the way that I did. If he did, he would have said so by now, I was sure. In silent anguish I thought of the women he had loved, those who had returned his love and those who had turned from it. In the painful darkness of the night I hated every one of them and I wept for the love of a man who had unwittingly taken my heart and every fibre of my being, and made them his own.

CHAPTER 24

The good news was that Andy started work full time at The Restless Dragon on the Monday after *Flute* opened, and having vented his spleen over Gerry at the weekend, he was inclined to be cheerful. Now we were into the run, rehearsal calls for revision purposes were lighter, and I was at home when Andy left for the theatre.

'Have a wonderful day,' I urged. 'It'll be marvellous, I know.'

'I hope so,' he said, feigning terror, and I laughed easily with him as he departed.

I missed going to rehearsal. We had a call on Tuesday, and another performance on Wednesday, but suddenly the days had lost their rhythm: the anticlimax after the thrill of the final night. I made coffee and sat at the computer, toying with the prospect of starting work on an article I had promised a colleague I would write for a classical musical magazine. Procrastinating, I checked my email first and the thrill of seeing Gerry's name in my inbox was so wonderful that I gazed entranced for several seconds before clicking open the document. I tried to remember to breathe.

Hi Madison, I read,

I feel very conscious that I haven't thanked you properly for looking after Ben so beautifully during the Flute *rehearsals. It has been very reassuring for me to know that he has been in your care and I hope he has not been too much for you! Thank you for all the kindness you have shown to him and to me. See you soon.*

Love from Gerry

I had to read it several times before I'd absorbed every word, as the air seemed to close around me and I didn't just forget to breathe, I couldn't if I'd tried. The sheer unexpectedness of it magnified its wonder a hundred times. I buried my face in my hands and hyperventilated with joy. Eventually, I recovered sufficiently to consider my response.

Hi Gerry, I wrote,

Thank you for your sweet message. It has been the most wonderful pleasure to look after Ben, not that he has needed much looking after. I rather think that he has been chaperoning me, actually! There are not many ways I can show you both that I love you, so it's good to be able to do so when I can.

Love from Madison

My heart beat heavily as I clicked on 'send' and then I put my head on the desk and cried quietly for a while. It was over to Gerry again and I would just have to wait to see if my brave and foolish words brought a response.

Nevertheless, as the day progressed, my natural inclination to exert control reasserted itself. I rang Gemma, pleased to hear her answer in person.

'Hi, Gem. It's Madison.'

'Hello!' she cried, 'How nice to hear from you. Are you okay after the weekend?'

'Just about,' I laughed. 'It was great, wasn't it?'

We burbled for a bit about the show and then I asked, 'Gemma, are you taking the boys on the train on Wednesday?'

'Yes. Do you want to come with us?'

'Oh, yes, please,' I sighed. 'Oh, Gemma?'

'Madison?'

'Has Gerry told you yet if he's bringing Ben to Victoria?'

'I haven't heard anything to the contrary,' she replied. 'Why? Are you plotting?' she asked.

'Of course, but you can't really tell, can you?'

'Absolutely not,' she reassured me. 'So, two o'clock at the departure boards, then?'

'I'll be there at one thirty,' I told her. 'Just in case.'

'In case of what?'

'In case I miss something.'

I was there at 1 pm, drinking coffee in the café opposite the departure board, my eyes glued to the concourse. At one thirty I took position to wait for Gemma and the boys, and at one forty-five, my tenacity was rewarded. Typically, I was looking in the other direction as Ben landed on me from behind and then walked ahead a few paces before swinging round again.

'Hiya.'

'Hi, Ben,' I grinned, mussing his hair.

I didn't dare look around for Gerry, but waited for him to come into my line of vision. 'Hello,' I said casually, but I couldn't stop my smile broadening.

'Travelling with the *hoi polloi*, Dr Brylmer?' he quipped. 'I can't believe I'm actually not going to see the show tonight.'

'It's been a real anticlimax since Saturday,' I told him. 'I'm longing to get back there tonight.'

'His nibs has been even more hyperactive than usual,' he said. 'I hope this will channel his energy more productively.'

As Gerry was speaking, Gemma wandered up, already in possession of young Oli, so we only had to wait for Dusan, and once he had arrived, I would have no further opportunity to talk to Gerry. I took swift advantage of Gemma's arrival, barely greeting her as she and Oli were accosted by Ben.

'Gerry, you know that Graham Fellowes is singing Renato at ENO?'

'Yes,' he nodded.

'He promised me two tickets for next week's opening if I wanted them. Would you be interested in seeing it with me?'

I held my breath.

'When is it?'

'Tuesday.'

Gerry was silent, making some mental calculation, though I couldn't be sure what was being calculated.

'I think that would be fine,' he said eventually. 'But can I email you to confirm?'

'Of course,' I said, trying hard to sound offhand. 'I've got a rehearsal at St John Smith Square in the afternoon, but I'd be free by five or five thirty. I could meet you at the theatre, or wherever, so just let me know.'

Dusan was being delivered by his mum by now, and we had to move.

'Okay,' Gerry nodded, 'I'll be in touch.'

There was a flurry as he said goodbye to Ben and Gemma moved us all off at high speed towards the train. I deliberately didn't look round as we walked down the platform, but hurried to catch up with Gemma, apparently engaging her in a fascinating conversation about precisely nothing.

Gerry emailed me the next day.

Hello

Tuesday is fine. Shall I meet you from St John's and we'll have something to eat first? Tell Graham we'll be rooting for him.

Love from Gerry

I had five days to survive, relieved a little by the chance of seeing Gerry at our Sunday performance of *Flute*. But I resolved to keep things light if I did, anxious not to give him any reason to have second thoughts about our outing. I made no special travelling arrangements on Sunday. Quietly going to Lewes alone, enjoying the peace of the gardens whilst I ate smoked salmon sandwiches I had made as treat, I was sitting in the sun with my eyes closed, when Annie slipped on to the bench next to me.

'Hello,' she whispered. 'Am I disturbing you?'

I smiled, keeping my eyes shut.

'Hi, there. How are you doing?'

'Cool. You looked as if you were thinking especially nice thoughts.'

'I was.'

'Might I be so bold as to suggest their subject?' she asked.

I chuckled.

'Is it really obvious?'

'Crashingly.'

I opened my eyes and looked at her. She was smiling mischievously.

'Oh dear.'

'Don't worry, it's only me and Gemma who ever get to see it.'

'Apart from Megan and Andy,' I said wryly.

'That could be a problem.'

'We've got a proper date on Tuesday,' I told her. 'I'm so excited.'

'That's nice.' Annie looked at me kindly.

I sighed, passing my hand through my hair as I lifted my face to the sun again.

'I love him, Annie.'

'I thought so.'

'And Ben too, It's wonderful being with them both. It makes me very, very happy.' I looked at her and grinned. 'And I very much want to go to bed with him.'

We giggled foolishly.

'Oh, Madison.' Annie took my hand. 'Do take care. Don't get hurt.'

'I hurt already. I actually feel sick with love for him. But it's okay. I've never felt like this before, and it's amazing, even when it makes me cry.'

'That sounds heavy stuff,' Annie murmured, 'I'm not sure I could live with it.'

'I didn't know I could till it happened,' I told her. 'It took me totally by surprise.'

'What are you going to do?' she asked quietly.

'I don't know. It depends on Gerry. I'll just have to wait and see.'

'Take it easy, Madsy,' she said, patting my knee. 'Remember you've got a willing ear here if you need one,' she added, pulling at her earlobe.

'Thanks, Annie.'

'Shall we?' she asked, rising from the bench.

'Let's,' I agreed, standing to join her, and we wandered through the beautiful gardens back to the house, each lost in our own thoughts.

CHAPTER 25

Gerry was waiting outside St John's as I emerged from the cool darkness of the church in to startlingly bright early evening sunlight. Incredibly, he was beautifully coordinated: blue blazer, blue and white striped shirt, grey slacks, blue and silver tie. He looked positively smart and my heart warmed at this evidence of his clearly having made an effort. He looked sweet and self-conscious, but smiled as soon as he saw me, kissing me a brief hello.

'I thought we'd have something to eat first, if you'd like that,' he said.

After the long day of waiting, I felt less nervous now, and was excited and happy at the prospect of a whole evening in Gerry's company. I enjoyed being propelled briskly down the street. Everything Gerry did was at top speed, but it was lovely to feel he was in control. Even the very act of walking down the road was so different with Andy. Where Andy meandered, Gerry sped forward with purpose, and where Andy would have studied the menus in the windows of four or five different restaurants before we ended up going into none of them, Gerry stopped at the first place we saw, and we were seated at a table without a second's hesitation. I knew it was mean spirited to make trivial and invidious comparisons, but such simple things made me feel safe and protected. I enjoyed Gerry's ability take charge easily, tired of playing the lead, of things never being straightforward, and forever wondering whether Andy would be prepared to fit into a situation without special allowances always having to be made for him.

I took pleasure in so many things that evening. Sharing a table with Gerry, and hoping that people noticed us and assumed that we were a couple; Gerry's easy conversation, smattered as ever with tales of this and that; settling into our theatre seats as I read extracts from the programme to him. And above all, as I tentatively slipped my arm through his, hoping I could rest my hand there, he took it and held it in his all evening. As his fingers traced patterns over my hand and wrist, up the length of my arm, and as I pressed closer against him, I thought I might faint with joy and pleasure. I tingled from head to foot, sighing deeply as I moved my free hand to rest on his warm thigh. Even after we returned from the brief interval, Gerry continued to run his fingers tenderly along my palm, stroking my cheek as I rested my head on his shoulder.

Incredulous, incandescent with happiness, I didn't want the opera to end. Once we moved from the dark auditorium, I had to face going home alone, leaving Gerry to go his own way. But real hope at last welled in my heart, mingling joyfully with my love for him. I had so longed for this sweet moment, for his loving touch, and at last, Gerry had reached out to give me that for which I had so hungered. I hardly dared imagine what lay ahead for us, but I knew my expectations were already running too far ahead.

Of course, the opera had to end, and we walked quickly back to Gerry's car, hand in hand, talking over what we'd seen. Even as we chatted, my brain beavered away in another compartment, marvelling at how natural it was to walk with my hand in his, and how I loved the sense of belonging it bestowed, albeit transitory. It was crazy; after the longest four months of my life, from the day that I had woken to the knowledge that I loved this impossible, wonderful man, to now, time had seemed an eternity in which I had blundered from day to day in ignorance of how Gerry felt. But now, suddenly we were together, as I had longed us to be, his touch real, no longer a fantasy, his presence close and overwhelmingly powerful.

In the car, he took my hand again as he drove, and each time he had to change gear, I feared he would not take it again, but he did, rubbing his thumb across my knuckles, and drumming his fingers on mine as if my hand were some soft percussion instrument. And all the time, he kept talking to me of this and that, as if there were nothing incredibly, wonderfully strange about this evening. But his easy manner made me relax and the tension of waiting and longing that had paralysed me so often faded away, and I felt open and expansive.

I resented the quickly passing streets and, as we pulled up off the heath, I turned to Gerry in ill-concealed anguish.

'I don't want to go.'

'Don't you?' he smiled, reaching out for me.

I snuggled into his chest, then raised my head to kiss his neck, and buried my face into the hollow of his neck.

'You are so lovely,' I murmured. I wanted to say more, but held my tongue.

'So are you,' he whispered.

We sat like that for a while as I enjoyed the feel of Gerry's arms around me at long last.

'I want to stay with you.' I couldn't keep silent any longer.

'I know,' he answered softly.

I wasn't sure what that meant: that Gerry wanted me to stay; that he was glad I wanted to be with him; was it an acknowledgement that it would be nice, but was impossible? I slid my hands underneath his jacket and hugged him closer to me.

'I think it's time you kissed me properly, Gerry McFall,' I coaxed.

'Do you now?' he laughed.

'Way over time, in fact.'

So he did. Several times. The effect, of course, was to make me even more anguished at the prospect of leaving him. Gerry patiently let me cling to him, stroking my bare shoulders tantalisingly.

'Come on, beautiful,' he said eventually. 'You'd better go. I'm worried about that husband of yours.'

'Don't be,' I urged. 'Let me be concerned about him.'

He pushed me gently away from him, laughing softly.

'Go home. We'll get some time together soon.'

'All right,' I said reluctantly, but let my fingers linger a little longer over his sweet features.

'You are completely gorgeous.'

'No, I'm not. I'm a beaten up old man, and if you don't go now, I'm not going to be responsible for my actions.'

'That sounds promising.'

'Madison! Go! See you tomorrow.'

I knew when I was defeated. I stood on the pavement as Gerry sped off into the distance, and gazed into the darkness of the trees. Despite the lateness of the hour, and the much-vaunted danger of walking alone on the heath, I couldn't go home yet. Joy drove away fear, and I pushed my way into the dark woodland, finding a path which led to an area of grassland. I sat in the silvery moonlight, listening to the mysterious crackle and sigh of the trees as my heartbeat slowed and my breathing steadied. Four months of waiting and longing, of hope and despair had culminated in this beautiful night. Nothing could be the same again after this, although Gerry still had the power. I had to wait for him to make the next move, and the one after that. I tried to convince myself that even if he never again touched me as he had tonight, I could savour forever the sweet memory, but I knew I was fooling myself. I wanted Gerry more than ever, and I was prepared to risk everything for him.

Andy was working at the computer when I reluctantly turned the key in the front door.

'Sorry I'm so late,' I quickly apologised, anticipating a short response, but Andy looked at his watch absently.

'Goodness, I had no idea it was that time already. I've been making some major changes for tomorrow's call. It's a definitive rehearsal on the final scene.'

'Oh, good.'

'Did you enjoy yourself?' Andy asked cheerfully enough.

'Yes. It was lovely. Well worth seeing. Graham was excellent as ever.'

Andy closed down the computer. 'I think you'll like the work I've been doing.'

I sighed softly, as Andy elaborated on the changes he'd made, listening with half an ear. In little more than twelve hours I would see Gerry again. I could survive – just.

CHAPTER 26

I was standing out on the heath ridiculously early, waiting for Gerry and Ben, enjoying the warmth of yet another beautiful day, and the delicious anticipation of several hours in the company of the two dearest creatures in my life. Ben was already in full cry as I got into the car.

'Madison, sit in the back with me. You've got to play me at this all the way there.' He waved his Nintendo at me.

'Oh, Ben, can we wait a bit?' I pleaded. I wanted to be close to Gerry. 'Your dad will feel like a taxi driver if we're both in the back. Perhaps later.'

'If you insist,' Ben said disparagingly. 'But you've got to talk to me, Dad's in a bad mood.'

I glanced at Gerry, expecting to see him smile and make some joke in response, but none was forthcoming. He raised his eyebrows in irritation.

'I'm not in a bad mood, Ben, I'm just tired. Madison doesn't need a lot of hassle from you all the way to Lewes. You've both got a performance tonight.'

I looked at Gerry in surprise. I had rarely heard him speak sharply to Ben.

'It's all right, Gerry, I think I've got enough stamina to make it through the day.'

'Good for you,' he replied without humour. 'I can't say the same goes for me.'

I was lost for words, as my heart sank heavily. My instinct was to ask if I'd done something to upset him, but I just managed to stop myself. I'd only seen Gerry twelve hours ago and couldn't possibly have offended him in my brief absence. I felt sick with disappointment, despite the strict lecture I'd given myself earlier that morning: *'Don't expect anything, Madison. Don't assume, don't push, don't build up your hopes.'* Nevertheless, I had hoped and expected and assumed, and so far Gerry hadn't even managed a smile. I wished I had sat in the back with Ben, but now the car was speeding down the A3, and I didn't think it wise to ask Gerry to stop to let me change over. Given the two available options of bursting into tears or twisting uncomfortably in my seat to half face Ben, I took the second, trying to persuade my emotions back into some semblance of order. Ben, undeterred, leant forward between the seats to show me how to play his electronic game and we ignored Gerry's brooding silence. It took us by surprise when he pulled into a service station.

'I need to get petrol,' he said shortly. 'Ben, go into the shop and buy us some chocolate,' he added rummaging around for change in the dashboard.

'What's the magic word?' Ben demanded.

'Please,' Gerry added, thrusting several coins into his outstretched hand.

Ben scrambled out of the car and we were alone.

'Sorry,' Gerry rubbed my knee, looking contrite. 'I'm appalling company today.'

I put my hand over his, but he didn't move to take it.

'Are you all right?' I ventured.

'Not really.' Gerry looked straight ahead of him. 'I'm exhausted, I guess. Sorry,' he added again. This time he turned to face me. 'Are *you* all right?'

'Yes, of course.'

The air was laden with all the things we weren't saying. Gerry took my hand at last, briefly kissing it.

'I'd better get this petrol,' he said apologetically.

I pulled my hand away in irritation. I shouldn't let him get away with this thoughtless inconsistency, but I knew I was going to do so.

'I'll go in the back with Ben,' I said abruptly. 'I'm getting a crick in my neck sitting like this.'

'If you want,' Gerry said quietly, climbing out of the car.

Ben hurled himself at me on his return. We shared out the chocolate he'd purchased, and against my better judgement I poured Gerry coffee from his flask, and passed the cup to and fro over the back of the seat until he'd finished it. My eyes were heavy with unshed tears as Ben leaned into me to finish his current game. When he was done, he grinned triumphantly.

'Try to beat that,' he said, handing the gadget to me.

'Not much chance,' I laughed as I took it from him.

'Are you all right, Madsy?' he asked, looking at me closely. 'You look as if you're going to cry; your eyes are all glittery.'

I blinked rapidly.

'It's the sun,' I said as an errant tear made its escape. I brushed it away quickly, but Ben had noticed.

'Madison!' he exclaimed.

'Ben, I'm fine. Now, just watch and be awe-struck.'

To my relief, he was sufficiently distracted by my incompetence and the subject was abandoned. I saw Gerry glance up at the rear view mirror several times as we continued on our way, but I kept my eyes averted.

Gerry kissed me briefly as Ben and I prepared to disappear through the stage door. I tried to catch his hand in mine as he did so, but he let my fingers trail his palm without response.

'Are you going to join us in the break?' he asked.

Ben's grandparents were going to be in the house tonight, having made their own way from further down the south coast.

'I'll see later,' I said. 'I might stay with the girls tonight.'

'Whatever,' he shrugged.

Annie was reading in our dressing room when I arrived, having despatched Ben into Gemma's care.

'How was your hot date?' she asked with a grin.

My reserve deserted me entirely.

'Oh, Annie, it was wonderful. Totally, completely, beautifully wonderful.'

'Ah, I can sense a 'but' coming,' she countered.

'Last night he treated me as if he wanted me almost as much as I want him, and then today he picked me up from home in a foul mood, hardly spoke, could barely bring himself to touch me, and it's as if yesterday never happened.'

The tears I'd been holding back in the car finally fell, as Annie's sympathetic arms came around my shoulders.

'The bastard,' she said fiercely. 'After all you've done, all the hassle you take for him.'

'I don't mind that. It's what I want to do. But it hurts so much today. He led me on, Annie. He made me think he likes me too, and now he regrets it.'

'Now, come on, honey,' she chided. 'You sound like an infatuated teenager here, not the cool, intelligent, professional woman that you are. If Gerry McFall isn't man enough to follow through on whatever he said or did last night, it's his loss, do you hear me?'

I nodded, unconvinced.

'If you still want him, that's your business, but if you let him get you into this state every time he messes you about, is it really worth it?'

'But, Annie, I love him.'

'I know you do, and he doesn't deserve it, but since when has love been fairly distributed?'

I sat back, wiping my eyes.

'Now, Madison Brylmer, just remember one thing tonight. Who is that going up on the Glyndebourne stage? Is it you or him?' She gave my shoulders a gentle shake. 'It's you. *He's* not going into the pit, but *you're* going to sing in an international house to a capacity audience.'

'I'm not in competition with him, Annie,' I protested.

'I know you're not. If you were a conductor, you'd give him all your gigs, I know. But listen, sweetie, what I'm trying to say is that you are talented, clever and gorgeous, and you don't need Gerry McFall for anything. You certainly don't need him making you miserable.' Annie paused and looked at me questioningly. 'And this may be way out of line, but I'll say it anyway. You've also got a marriage you might not want to lose, and certainly not over some guy who's not going to play fair with you. Don't burn your bridges, Madison, that's all I'm saying.'

I nodded again, glad of Annie's frank words, even whilst I was aware that I was not able to apply her wisdom just yet, if at all.

'I know you're right, Annie, but I'm beyond rational argument at the moment.'

'I know. I have been there too, you know,' she laughed, and we hugged and I wiped my eyes again.

'The show's the thing, eh?' I joked.

'It certainly is,' she agreed. 'Are you seeing him in the interval?'

'I don't know. His parents are here to see Ben. To be fair, he did ask me to join them, but I left it open.'

'Well, for what it's worth, I think you should leave him to stew,' said Annie firmly. 'And what's more, I've got the car with me today, and you're more than welcome to come home with me.'

'Thanks. I'll see how I feel. I do appreciate it,' I squeezed her hand, 'but I do have to think of Ben, too. It's not fair if I go off in a huff and he wonders why.'

'Just let me know, kiddo.'

The prospect of curtain up worked its usual magic, and by the time the three of us stood in the wings, ready to slay the serpent, I was focussed and alert. 'Thank God for this,' I thought, realising that although singing and Gerry were now inevitably and inextricably linked, I could still sing and enjoy it without him. 'It's got to stay bigger than him,' I reminded myself. 'If I can remain complete and satisfied as a singer, then whatever Gerry does, I'll survive.'

Ben came looking for me in the long interval. I'd stayed with Annie and Clarissa, but half an hour in, he found me drinking tea with them on the grass outside the stage door.

'Madsy, Dad's sent me to find you,' he puffed, having run all the way.

'Why?' I asked with deliberate vagueness.

Ben looked puzzled.

'Aren't you coming to join us?'

I felt Annie breathe heavily down my neck, but stood up anyway.

'Oh, well, for a few minutes, I guess,' I said, avoiding her eye. 'See you guys later.'

Ben didn't bounce ahead as he usually did, but hung back at my side, looking up at me curiously.

'You're odd today,' he announced.

I laughed. 'What? More than usual?'

'I think you're upset about something,' he observed astutely.

I just looked at him and winked.

'I'm cool, darling. And you sound fabulous tonight.'

'Thank you,' Ben said meekly.

'Don't be humble, it doesn't suit you,' I laughed and reassured, Ben then did run ahead, and I was glad he'd dropped the interrogation.

CHAPTER 27

Gerry scrambled to his feet as soon as I reached the McFall party.

'Madison, where did you get to? These are my parents, Pauline and Richard. Mum, Dad, this is our good friend, Madison Brylmer.'

We all shook hands and I politely refused food and wine, but accepted a coffee.

'Ben's talked about you so much, Madison,' Pauline told me. 'I understand you all knew each other before this season.'

I nodded, sipping my coffee.

'Yes, we all met last year doing *Butterfly*. It's been a lovely coincidence that Ben and I were both booked to do *Flute*.'

I noticed Gerry watching me carefully and eventually I allowed my glance to intercept his. I widened my eyes in acknowledgement and he smiled tentatively. Perhaps I would go home with him.

Which, of course, I did. Annie made a half-hearted attempt to persuade me otherwise, but didn't pursue it.

'Don't blame me if you feel miserable tomorrow,' she chided.

'Annie, I'll feel even more miserable if I don't go with him.'

She shook her head in despair.

'Ring me if you want to,' she said, and was gone.

Gemma took her lively charges, Ben included, on the cast bus to Lewes to spend the night in their hotel, and I waited at a polite distance whilst Gerry and his parents said their farewells. His mum waggled her fingers at me, and I returned the gesture. I felt sick as I leaned heavily against the car, wishing now that I'd gone with Annie. But it was too late; Gerry was striding over quickly and, in his usual flurry, we were driving out of the grounds before I had a chance to seriously wonder if Annie may still be somewhere around.

'I think there's some coffee still in the flask,' Gerry said, and I took this as an indication that he wanted some and I was supposed to do the honours. Which I did, and rummaged in the picnic boxes for bits of fruit and cake. Gerry ate and drank as I passed food and coffee to him and he pronounced at length on the details of the evening's performance. I was glad to let his chatter wash over me. It suddenly all felt very familiar and normal. Indeed, if it were not for the previous night's events, I would have been happy just to be ministering to him whilst he kept me entertained.

I decided to take a risk. What was there to lose now? As Gerry turned to me asking my opinion about Pamina's performance, I rested my hand on his leg as I replied. Deliberately keeping my answers light, I responded as I would have done on any other night, hoping Gerry couldn't feel the tension in my body as I longed for him to take my hand. But he didn't and, as the miles passed, even as we chatted easily again, my hand felt lonely and foolish as it rested unattended on his thigh, and eventually I took it away, covering the movement by fishing in my bag for chocolate we'd saved earlier.

Gerry grew quiet as we drew nearer to London, fidgeting nervously with his hands on the wheel and on his knees. He looked at me mournfully as we drew up outside Exeter House.

'I'm sorry I've been useless today,' he apologised, but offered no further explanation. I was tongue-tied, lacking the courage to press him. I said the first thing that came to mind.

'It was nice to meet your mum and dad.'

Gerry smiled. 'My mum thought you were sweet.'

'Goodness, I barely said anything to her.'

'She could just tell.'

We looked at each other.

'Madison?'

'Gerry?'

'I feel awful asking you this.'

'Asking me what?'

'It's a cheek, I know, but Ben's got to be at the cover run on Friday and Gemma can bring him back to Victoria, but can't take him all the way home. Is there any chance you can meet them and get him back to Dulwich?'

I looked at Gerry mutely.

'I'm sorry. I shouldn't have asked. Forget it.' He spoke hurriedly.

'It's okay,' I said quietly. 'What time does the train get in?'

'Are you sure?' Gerry looked at me sheepishly.

'It's fine. I can be free if I manoeuvre things a bit.'

Gerry stroked the back of my hand absently.

'You are wonderful,' he said, looking even more hangdog.

'I know,' I said briskly. 'Ring me and let me know what time I need to be there.' I opened the car door and began to clamber out.

'Thank you.'

'It's okay,' I said reassuringly, knowing that I was effectively letting him off the hook for the whole disappointing day, and whatever had precipitated it.

'Bye.'

Without a backward glance, he sped away.

'Bastard,' I whispered half-heatedly as tears began to trickle down my cheeks. I sat on the wall and let them flow unrestrainedly, sobbing noisily into my hands. I jumped when I felt a hand on my shoulder.

'Miss Brylmer? Are you all right?'

It was the night watchman, who had seen, and doubtless heard, me from his station.

'Oh, goodness!' I sat up quickly. 'Yes, I'm fine. I'm so sorry.'

'You don't look it, love.'

'No, no, it's really okay.' I scrambled to my feet. 'Just a bad day. I'm sorry to have disturbed you, Mark.'

'No problem, as long as you're all right.'

In deep embarrassment, I scuttled through the front door, hoping that Mark would not consider it his duty to tell Andy that I'd been in obvious distress after getting out of a black VW.

I pretended to be asleep when Andy let himself in an hour later.

'Mads?' he whispered as he climbed into bed. 'Are you awake?'

I lay still and breathed slowly and deeply.

'Goodnight,' he said softly.

I waited until there was no movement except the steady rise and fall of Andy's chest before I buried my head in the pillow and let silent tears flow once more.

I moved through the next day in a haze of tears, pausing occasionally to wonder at the notion that in all my thirty-eight years, no one and nothing had reduced me to such a pathetic mess. My feelings for Gerry and my reactions to his behaviour – good or bad – were utterly beyond reason, though perhaps sometime in the future I would be able to analyse them. Andy was concerned by my demeanour.

'Madsy, did something happen yesterday? Was it an awful show?'

'Of course not.'

'You're crying.'

'No, I'm not,' I denied as I brushed away a treacherous tear which had conspired to fall as I made some toast.

Andy pursed his lips in annoyance, and any guilt I felt at causing him concern fled.

'How did you get down there yesterday?' he asked.

'You know I went with Gerry and Ben.'

'Ah.'

I didn't have the spirit to challenge him and the morning passed in a heavy silence as we went about our own concerns. By early afternoon I could stand it no more and took my music, CD, and phone onto the heath to do some learning and to await Gerry's call. I didn't have to wait long.

'It's Gerry.'

'Hello.'

'Are you still all right for tomorrow?'

'Of course. What time shall I be there?'

'Four o'clock, if you can.'

'That's fine, and I'll take him straight home?'

'Please. I really appreciate this, Madison.'

'No problem.' I paused. 'Shall I ring you in the evening, or Saturday morning?'

'Yes. We'll speak soon.'

He gave me no opportunity to prolong the conversation and I hung up sorrowfully. I had a good cry again, and tidied myself up as best I could before wandering home. Andy and I looked cautiously at each other as I entered, but he had clearly elected a truce. Buoyed up by the prospect of doing something for Gerry the next day, I made a fair stab at acting as if everything was all right, until exhaustion claimed me in sleep.

CHAPTER 28

I trembled with love as I watched Ben come through the barrier at Victoria. His easy gait and cheerful smile were so like his dad, and I knew that part of my love for Ben was a projection of how I felt for Gerry. But not all of it. Ben would have won my heart under any circumstances, I thought, as I hugged him, and we tussled playfully for a moment.

'He's all yours, Madsy,' Gemma said, 'and you're very welcome to him.'

She still had Dusan and Oli in tow, and she looked around the station searchingly.

'If Dusan's mum is here, I can get this one back home.' She indicated the dark, serious little fellow who sang the Third Genie. 'Thanks for relieving me of Ben today. I can't take them all home individually, and Oli lives on my route so it's the obvious way round to do it.'

'Gemma, you don't know what a privilege and pleasure it is,' I said, gazing fondly at Ben, who was jumping up and down impatiently.

'Oh, Madsy,' Gemma smiled, and touched my arm lightly. 'He is very special, isn't he?'

I nodded, not trusting myself to speak as I furtively brushed away a tear. Gemma remained tactfully silent as I composed myself.

'See you on Saturday, Gem,' I said. 'My mum's coming to the show again, so I'll have to be on my best behaviour.'

We laughed, said our farewells, and Ben and I disappeared in search of the Dulwich trains. I was sorry that it was only a short train journey, a brisk walk (no chance of dawdling in the company of Ben), and too soon he was unlocking the door, and we entered the chaos of the McFall residence.

We'd arranged that if Josh wasn't at home, I would stay until he arrived to relieve me, and I was pleased to find the house still and quiet. Ben threw his bag into a corner already crammed with clutter, and banged into the kitchen.

'You make the tea, Madison, and I'll turn the computer on.'

Having received my orders, there was nothing else to do but carry them out and when I went in search of Ben, bearing two mugs and some biscuits I'd found lying abandoned on the kitchen table, he was already engrossed in his email.

'For goodness, sake, Ben, would it be patronising of me to ask why you need email?'

'Yes it would, so don't,' he declared.

He showed me his messages which essentially consisted of ridiculous animated attachments that were being mailed amongst the high-minded young scholars of St George's.

'Shall I forward this one to you?' he asked, laughing uproariously at some penguins doing bizarre things on the screen.

'If you insist.'

'What's your address?'

'madison.brylmer@virgin.net'

He forwarded the attachment.

We continued with these mind expanding activities for a while, venturing into some obscure sites of peculiar interest to eleven-year-old boys, until we heard the front door slam.

'That'll be Josh in a bad mood,' Ben pronounced.

'Can you tell by how he closes the door?' I joked.

'He's just always in a bad mood,' Ben said. 'He's driving Dad bananas,' he added as Josh stuck his head around the door.

'Hi,' he grunted, then, catching sight of me, allowed a faintly surprised expression to cross his beautiful, sullen features. 'Oh, hello,' he added.

'This is Madison,' said Ben, without taking his eyes off the screen.

'Yeah. We've met.'

I noticed that since I'd seen Josh at the beginning of June he'd been busy refining his personal style. He was dressed in unremitting black with matching nail varnish, contrasting with sparkling silver gel in his jet hair.

'You look fabulous, Josh,' I exclaimed, meaning it sincerely. His striking good looks were quite remarkable, and could surely earn him healthy modelling fees.

'Yeah, thanks,' he mumbled, deeply embarrassed.

'Don't let Dad hear you say that,' Ben laughed.

'Your dad should be proud to have two such fantastically handsome sons,' I said.

Josh inched further into the room.

'What are you doing?' he asked.

'Just messing about,' Ben replied. 'I'm hungry,' he added, turning to me. 'When's Dad coming back?'

'I don't know, darling. I ought to go now Josh is here, or shall I make you something to eat first?'

'Yes, please.' Ben fluttered his eyelashes winningly. 'And I'll carry on here.'

'Just this once, perhaps,' I laughed, 'but Josh, I'll need you to show me where things are.'

I expected him to balk at this, but he got up quite willingly from the chair he was flopping in.

'Cool. I could do with something now,' he said and led me downstairs with surprising speed. Once there, he was awkward again, casually showing me the fridge and cupboards, hanging back, unsure of his role.

'Would you help me a bit, Josh?' I asked. 'It's a slow process getting used to someone else's kitchen. Do you know what you were supposed to be eating tonight?'

Together we found some frozen chicken Kievs, broccoli, sweetcorn and new potatoes, and I chatted to Josh whilst I put it together. He didn't respond much, but he was evidently listening, and once, when I turned around from the hob, I caught him staring at me intently. I smiled.

'You okay?' I asked.

'You said you used to be a teacher?' he said.

'Yes. Philosophy mostly.'

'I've got ADD,' Josh said suddenly.

'I remember your dad telling me.' I smiled at him. 'Does it make school work tough?'

'Yeah. I get so bored, then I just produce crap.'

'Are you on Ritalin?'

'I'm supposed to be, but I don't take it.'

Josh moved irritably across the kitchen to poke at the potatoes and I sensed the conversation was over.

'These are done,' he said. 'I'll get the infant.'

It was after eight when Gerry arrived home to find us idly chatting at the kitchen table and drinking tea. The remains of the boys' dinner – empty plates and crumbs – had been pushed aside as Ben and I actually succeeded in raising a laugh out of the taciturn Josh with our tales of the rest of the *Flute* cast. I fell silent when Gerry walked in, looking over the little scene in surprise.

'Hello. You still here?'

'Madison got dinner for us,' Ben piped up.

'So I see,' Gerry replied, eyebrows raised enquiringly.

'I'm sorry.' I scrambled up. 'I guess I've overstayed my welcome, but the boys were hungry, and I was here, so it seemed…' I trailed off.

'Very kind of you to step in, that's what,' Gerry interjected.

'I'll be on my way now your dad's back,' I continued, addressing Ben and Josh. 'I've had great fun. Thank you for entertaining me.' I kissed Ben on the top of his head. 'See you on Saturday. Bye Josh. I'm glad to have met you again today.'

He offered me a brief smile and I longed to hug him. I smiled instead.

Gerry followed me into the hall.

'Madison, you didn't need to do that.'

'I'm sorry. It won't happen again,' I apologised.

'No, no,' he said hurriedly. 'I'm not cross. Quite the contrary. It was lovely of you to stay with them. I don't know how to thank you.'

I looked at Gerry ironically and he averted his gaze sheepishly.

'Oh, Madison, what can I say?'

'Whatever you want to say, Gerry.'

He stared at me again, touching the tendrils of hair that had fallen across my face, and gently moving them back into position.

'You are wonderful,' he said quietly.

'So you keep telling me.'

Gerry breathed in deeply as if to say something important but evidently thought better of it.

'I won't see you on Saturday. I'm not going to *Flute* again for a couple of weeks.'

I nodded curtly. 'See you around then.'

'Madison, don't be…' He trailed off helplessly.

'Don't be what?'

'Nothing.' Gerry kissed me briskly on the mouth. 'I'll ring you. Okay?'

'Okay,' I sighed, unable to bear the agony any longer.

'Bye.'

I heard Gerry's faint farewell as I walked briskly on to the street. I held the tears back until I was on the train. The commuter line was quiet at 8.30 at night, but a small, sad-looking man watched me from the end of the carriage. We exchanged sympathetic smiles as we exited the train at Victoria, and I felt his enquiring eyes still on my back as I disappeared in the direction of the tube.

CHAPTER 29

Megan descended in full glory on Saturday and ferried Andy and I down to Lewes in the Morgan. It was a glorious day yet again. There had barely been a cloud in the sky since the beginning of May. What a magical summer it was: enough rain, miraculously falling at night, to keep the grass green, with bright sun and fresh breezes during the day. I sat in the back of the car, and let Andy and Megan chat over the rushing wind and revving engine. I had heard nothing from Gerry the previous day, and had been glad of a rehearsal call that kept me in Sussex the whole day, driving back with Annie in the early evening. Inevitably, she had been deeply disapproving of my activities the day before.

'Madison, I'm really beginning to doubt your sanity. He moves in on you, then behaves like it was some aberration, and you still do his dirty work for him.'

'I'd hardly call spending several hours in the company of Ben and Josh dirty work!' I laughed. 'It's wonderful.'

'Maybe, but it leaves you feeling awful when he kicks you in the teeth again. Cut yourself loose from him Madsy.'

'What about *Tito*?' I asked.

'You're a professional, that's another matter. Just compartmentalise your feelings. Tell him to be straight with you, or he can find someone else to walk over.'

'I can't do that, Annie.'

'Don't want to, you mean.'

I smiled at her cross little face.

'Yes, I suppose I do mean that.'

I could certainly have done without Megan's sharp glances and probing questions at the weekend, but I galvanised myself to be cheerful when I joined them briefly in the long interval.

'Lovely, darling!' Megan cried as she rose to hug me.

'Fabulous, Madsy,' Andy grinned.

'She's the best of three, isn't she?' Megan went on. 'The others don't have her stage presence.'

'Oh, I don't know about that,' I laughed. 'What's different to last time you saw it?'

So we chatted about the show and for a while I was able to forget my sadness and curb my longing to be in the dressing room with Gemma and the boys. As I rose to return backstage, Megan suddenly asked.

'Is that boy's father here today?'

'You mean Gerry? No, not today,' I replied shortly.

'Umm.'

Megan and Andy should take out copyright on meaningful monosyllables.

'Come backstage afterwards,' I said, refusing to be drawn, and gave them a cheery little wave as I trotted away.

I was called over the tannoy as we were changing after curtain down.

'Visitors for Dr Brylmer.'

I covered my face with embarrassment.

'Oh, God, that's my mother all over, just making sure everyone thinks I'm a snob.'

I scuttled off to whisk Megan and Andy out of sight as quickly as possible.

'You mustn't ask for me as Dr Brylmer,' I said crossly, 'it's not the done thing.'

Megan pursed her lips and said nothing, but Andy put on the charm offensive with Annie and Clarissa, and Megan relaxed as we showed her our costumes close up and she responded to Annie's direct manner. But I wouldn't leave without saying goodbye to Ben and there was no way I could be furtive about it.

'I'm just popping into another dressing room for a minute,' I said casually as we made our exit.

'Shall we wait outside?' Andy asked.

'Yes, fine. I'll see you out there,' I agreed, but Megan had pricked up her ears.

'Where are you going? We don't want to be waiting around.'

'I'll be two minutes,' I promised.

As I spoke the door to the boys' dressing room opened, and Gemma emerged looking hassled.

'Oh, Madison, thank goodness,' she gasped. 'Just who I need.'

I felt a faint prickle of alarm. What was coming next would not please Megan, I was sure.

'What's up, Gem?' I asked, trying to signal with my eyes that she should be circumspect. Either I was too subtle, or she was too stressed to notice.

'Ben's in floods of tears. I don't know what the matter is, and he won't take any notice of me. Please will you see what you can do?'

My concern to avoid annoying Megan and Andy gone in a trice, I sped into the dressing room. Ben sat at the dressing table with his head on his arms, shoulders heaving. My heart turned over as I put my arms around him and smothered his soft hair with kisses.

'Darling heart, it's Madison. What's the matter, my angel?'

Ben sobbed harder and I drew him closer to me. I realised that not only Gemma, but Megan and Andy were staring at us, transfixed. I wanted to motion to them to leave, but I concentrated on encouraging Ben to speak to me.

'Precious one, please tell me what it is. I'd like to help if I can.'

'You can't.'

144

'Try me.'

Ben's tears quietened momentarily whilst he thought this out.

'I want my mum,' he said finally, before sobbing afresh.

'Oh, lovey,' I murmured as Ben moved to let me cuddle him properly. 'She would be so very, very proud of you, darling,' I said softly, stroking his hair. 'Her love for you means that she'll always be with you, even though it's not in body anymore. You can keep it close to your heart forever, and feel her presence with you. And all the lovely things that you are and that you do, are a testimony to her, so you and Josh keep her alive in a special way, too. I know that won't be much comfort to you right now, but if you think about it tomorrow, it might make a bit of sense.'

Ben sighed deeply against my shoulder and his arms held on to me tightly.

'I really missed her today, Mads,' he said sadly.

'I'm sure you'll often miss her, darling, however much time passes. But that's part of remembering her, rather than forgetting her, and that's good. Just think that she'd always want you to remember her happily, though, and to be happy as you grow up and develop your talents and relationships. But some days you'll want to cry, and that's okay, too. Today's one of them.'

Ben lifted his head and looked at me blearily.

'I shouted at Gemma.'

'Sweetheart, don't worry, she'll understand.'

'Did she fetch you?'

'Yes.'

'Good.'

Ben rested his head on my shoulder again.

'I love you,' I said quietly.

'I love you, too,' he murmured.

I felt three pairs of eyes boring into my back, but I didn't flinch.

'Madison?'

'Yes, darling?'

'If I had another mum one day, I'd like it to be you.'

Ben was the only one oblivious to the sudden tension in the air at this, but I had no intention of rejecting this sweet boy's affection. 'I wish we could take you home in the Morgan,' I said, 'but I think you're firmly under chaperone rules today. I'll see you on Friday.'

'Bye, Mads,' Ben wiped his eyes for the last time.

Reluctant to leave, I turned to face the firing squad. Gemma was looking relieved and faintly amused; Andy was tight-lipped; Megan was nowhere to be seen.

'Where's Mum?' I asked Andy.

'Gone to the car,' he replied sharply.

As we walked across the car park, he said, 'Megan wasn't very impressed by that little scene. Neither was I, come to that, but you know what she's like.'

I sighed.

'What was I supposed to do? Leave him to cry?'

'No, but you could have been a little less all over him. I've never heard so many endearments in one brief conversation.'

'I'll edit them out next time,' I said sarcastically.

'What next time?' Andy snapped. 'All I ever hear about is the *Magic* bloody *Flute*, Ben, and Gerry – not necessarily in that order. I think you should move in with them, Madison. Ben would clearly enjoy that, and I can't imagine that old Gerry would refuse.'

We were at the car by now and I had to stem the tears that were quick to rise at Andy's words. On current showing, even a cup of tea at Gerry's house was unlikely to be forthcoming.

Megan looked grim and although I tried to generate some amiable conversation, she was having none of it. I fell back on the old ruse of pretending to fall asleep in the back of the car. When we finally drew up on Putney Heath, she let Andy get out of the car before addressing me.

'Madison, wait a moment. Do you mind, Andy? I just want to speak to Madison in private.'

He trundled obediently up the driveway.

'What is your relationship with this boy and his father?' she asked directly.

'We're friends,' I answered in similar tone. 'Thanks for coming today, Mum. I'm sorry you were delayed at the end.'

'I'm not concerned about the delay, rather the cause of it,' she said. 'How have you become so close to that child? I've never seen you like that before.'

'We work together; he's good fun; we get on. Mum, what's the agenda here?'

'Don't use that tone with me,' she snapped. 'The 'agenda' as you put it, is that Andy is clearly unhappy, and you're swanning around with this other man and his children and neglecting your husband.' She emphasised the last two words.

'I don't know how you've reached that conclusion. Andy and I will sort ourselves out if, indeed, anything requires it. Now, thanks again for coming, drive safely and I'll ring you in a couple of days.'

'I never knew I'd raised such a rude daughter,' she said angrily, slamming the car into gear. 'Goodbye, Madison.'

I sighed as she sped off. Gerry was clearly no longer interested in me, Andy was brooding and tense, and Megan was livid. I was rapidly running out of adult relationships. Thank goodness for Ben, I thought. At least one person still loves me.

CHAPTER 30

As the weekend passed into the following week, it was as if Gerry didn't exist. The phone remained silent and his greeting never met me as I opened my email. Whilst the Ladies had a midweek rehearsal call, the genies were not required, so I caught no glimpse of Ben. In a week that felt like a month, never had I checked my mobile for messages or missed calls so often. Gerry was the first thought as I woke and the last as I fell asleep, and I barely made it into the shower each morning before the tears began to fall. I had never known it were possible to cry so much as I reached Thursday with the realisation that I had wept every day since Sunday, and it was getting tediously predictable.

On Thursday I sat on the heath and sobbed long and hard for an hour, mulling over every minute I'd spent with Gerry, virtually every word we'd exchanged, every touch I'd enjoyed. I thought it might be the healing release I needed, and whilst it did feel good to pour out my heart in tears, I woke the next morning to the knowledge that my love was still intact, still churning in my stomach and heavily weighing down my limbs. On Thursday morning, dressing in trousers I hadn't worn since the previous summer, I realised how much weight I had lost. Since April I had been steadily losing a few pounds every week as my appetite waxed and waned, but in the last ten days I had shed nearly half a stone. I examined my reflection from all angles and liked what I saw, wondering whether my costume would need taking in.

The ringing of the telephone took me by surprise as I was examining formerly discarded items from my wardrobe and discovering with pleasure that they could resume active life.

'It's me.'

'Oh. Gerry.'

'How are you?'

'Um, all right, I think. Are you?'

'Now and then.'

I rested my forehead against the cool bedroom wall, desperate to keep him on the line.

'To what do I owe this pleasure?' I said, trying not to sound too interested.

'I've got a cover run of *Boheme* on Monday and my assistant's let me down. Will you take notes for me?'

I recognised the leafy fronds of an olive branch. There were several other people who would have been a more obvious choice for this task. The only reason for Gerry to ask me had to be for the pleasure of my company! It was time to play hard to get – just a little.

'Hold on, I'll get my diary,' I said, then covered the mouthpiece and counted to twenty.

'That looks as if it'll be all right,' I said as if I was giving it considerable thought. 'I assume you're going to make it worth my while?'

'Standard MU rates, Madison. What can be fairer than that?'

I allowed a chuckle to pass my lips.

'You're on. When and where?'

Before we hung up he said, 'Madsy, Ben tells me you were very kind to him at the weekend. He didn't let me press him on details, but whatever it was, thank you.'

'That's no problem, Gerry,' I said, warmer now. 'You know he's the love of my life.'

After we'd hung up, I examined the contents of my wardrobe with renewed interest. Assuming that Monday's weather stayed as glorious as the summer had thus far proved, I had exactly the thing, I thought, extracting a low cut white top, just this side of appropriate for day wear. Suddenly I didn't feel like crying anymore. I phoned Lizzie. She and little Gaby came over for the afternoon and we ate like pigs.

The *Boheme* rehearsals were at the Maida Vale studios Gerry used as his base. I felt shy as I found the room and watched as Gerry worked with a handsome young Marcello. By the time they had finished, the cast had assembled and the rehearsal pianist was poised to take over the keyboard. Gerry caught sight of me and smiled warmly.

'Excellent. Thank you very much for this,' he said, depositing a score, notebook, and pencils into my hands. 'I'm going to have to shout things at you as they happen. Sorry about that. We don't want to stop.'

I took my appointed seat, and poured coffee for us both from my flask, deeply contented to be part of the morning's activities.

I had decided not to prevaricate when, the previous evening, Andy had asked me about my plans for the following day.

'I'm doing a dep. job on *Boheme* for Gerry,' I said bravely.

'Why?' Andy asked in surprise. 'You told me there's no mezzo part in it.'

'I'm just assisting him at a cover run. I'll be paid,' I added hastily.

'I should think so,' Andy said firmly, and with remarkable restraint, left it at that.

He looked at me narrowly as I left that morning, however.

'What time will you finish?'

'Early afternoon I should think,' I calculated, giving myself a safe margin.

'Come down to The Dragon afterwards, then,' he suggested. 'See how rehearsals are going.'

It was wise to fall in with his plans, I thought, and, in truth, I was interested to see how *Lethal Desires* was coming along. But for the present moment, I sat back, pencil poised, to luxuriate in Puccini's romantic score. I had long adopted the approach that if an opera didn't have a mezzo role it wasn't worth the effort, but now I itched to sing along with so many of Mimi's wonderful lines, and did so mentally, as she and Rudolpho played about with the candle and key. I loved her subtle commentary which underlay the second verse of *Quando men vo*, and her glorious aria, *Donde liete*, sang as she parted from Rudolpho in the third act. But most of all, I loved the sweet deathbed farewell: '*I had so longed to be alone with you, there is so much I want to tell you. Most of all this, you are my love and all my life.*' I was emotionally shattered! Tears rolled unchecked as I sang the words in my heart to Gerry. How perfectly, in both libretto and score, did they capture the deepest feelings I had for him.

Apart from the times when Gerry half turned to call out notes, he was unable to see my face, and I was glad that my raw emotions were concealed from him. Despite my intense involvement in the musical drama, I managed to concentrate on Gerry's brisk instructions: 'Musetta came in two beats early'; 'I must speak to Colline about that bit,' and so on. At times I was ahead of him, having noticed a discrepancy between the score and what the singers were doing, and it was very satisfying to already be writing when Gerry turned briefly to call out a note.

I sighed with pleasure as the final chords sounded, and considered it a morning well spent, even without building into the equation the alluring presence of Gerry. I chatted amiably for a while to one of the chorus mezzos as he finished up his work. She recognised me from *Rigoletto* at the Coli.

'Hello, you were Maddalena last year, weren't you? What are you doing here?' she asked curiously.

'Gerry McFall is a friend,' I said casually. 'I'm doing him a favour.'

We engaged in a pleasant conversation about why it was technically possible for a mezzo to sing Mimi, acknowledging, however, that it wouldn't be very enjoyable for the audience, until Gerry bounced up to relieve me of my score and notes.

'Thanks, Madsy,' he said easily. 'Can I offer you a quick sandwich or something, before we reconvene?'

Does a duck swim?

We bought sandwiches from a corner deli and found a garden square around the block from the studio. The sun shone sweetly on soft perennial beds in pink, lilac and blue, the grass as smooth as a bowling green.

'I'm sure this is a private square,' I said as we sat on the velvety grass.

'If the gate's open, it's an invitation to us,' Gerry replied firmly, passing me my sandwich.

I gazed at him lovingly as he ate and told me exactly what he'd thought of the run, glad not to be the object of his more barbed criticisms. He was looking the most gorgeous shambles in a washed out shirt and baggy blue shorts that afforded a tantalising view of his beautiful legs as he stretched them out before him. They were long and smooth, lightly tanned and perfectly proportioned. Indeed, it was an outrage that a man should have such good legs. To compensate, I breathed deeply, pulling back my shoulders to facilitate a better perspective of my rather more satisfactory physical features. I tried to look relaxed and casual about everything, even as I longed to lay my head in his lap and sob my heart out. But of course I didn't, and we were amiably gathering up our rubbish when Gerry said, 'We've got a few people coming to see *Flute* next Wednesday. I thought we could have a really exclusive picnic, if you'd like to join us. I hope you will.'

Gerry was studying me seriously as if he really cared about my reply and I was so overjoyed at this unexpected glimmer of hope I didn't have it in me to mess about.

'I'd love to. I'll bring a contribution, shall I?'

'If you like,' Gerry smiled.

Throwing caution to the wind, I held my hand out to him. He took it in his and we looked each other squarely in the eye. I felt sick with longing.

'Hello,' I said quietly.

'Hello.'

'You are lovely.'

'Not as much as you think I am,' he said, but as I leaned towards him he kissed me briefly and looked at me with that wry, half mocking expression that told me precisely nothing.

'Come on, Dr Brylmer.' He took his hand away decisively. 'I've got to get back.'

As we parted he said, 'I'll ring you before next week, then.'

It seemed an age.

'Sure,' I nodded. 'I enjoyed this morning.'

'Good.' He raised his eyebrows in amusement. 'Glad to hear it.'

'Madison Brylmer, repeat one hundred times, 'You are a tediously foolish girl',' I told myself as I descended into the depths of Maida Vale tube station. I may have got up to twenty before I dismissed it as a pointless exercise.

On Friday, Gerry called me in the evening as Andy was helping me to make supper. I'd had quite a good week by current standards. Encouraged by the prospect of some time with Gerry, albeit in the bosom of his family, I had managed the odd tear-free day, and after Monday's visit to The Restless Dragon, I'd found myself taking a genuine interest in the progress of *Lethal Desires*. I was feeling quite mellow as I lifted the phone without first checking the caller display.

'It's me.'

My heart lurched in surprise.

'Oh, hello.'

'Is it a good moment?'

'Not particularly.'

Inevitably this caught Andy's attention and he cocked his eyebrows enquiringly. I didn't flinch.

'Can you talk?'

'Yes, fire away.'

I tried to sound businesslike and Gerry responded in kind.

'The chaperoning arrangements for next Wednesday have gone awry. Can you take Ben on the train with you? I can't drive down till nearly show time.'

'Of course. What time train?'

'Whatever suits you.'

'Is 2.20 okay?'

'Wonderful.'

Andy was still watching as I hung up.

'Who was that?'

'Annie. She's not taking the car next week. She wants to meet at the station.'

'You sounded a bit off with her,' he said, puzzled.

'Did I? Well, she doesn't mince words, does she?'

Andy shrugged and continued to stir the sauce.

Later, I caught my reflection in the kitchen mirror. My face was flushed and my eyes sparkled. I was suffused with joy, I thought poetically. So *that's* what it looked like! I had always wondered.

CHAPTER 31

I was desperately excited as I waited for Ben at Victoria
Station. Although technically we didn't need to head for
Lewes so early, Gerry had been agreeable to Josh escorting
Ben to Victoria, from whence we would both board the Lewes
train, leaving Josh to disappear to do whatever fifteen-year-
olds do on a Saturday afternoon in London. Gerry and his
party would come down in their respective cars later and we
would meet in the long interval. I clutched my snazzy new
wicker carrier containing my contribution to the party:
smoked salmon, a particularly fine Australian Shiraz,
strawberries marinated in amaretto, and a tub of especially
crusty clotted cream.

Ben played his usual trick of pretending not to see me
when he and Josh emerged through the ticket barriers,
spinning around after walking past me for about ten paces,
then sauntering back, smirking.

'Hi, sweetheart.'

'Hiya, Mads.'

'You okay, Josh?'

'Yup.'

Josh looked particularly dark today. It couldn't do his street
cred any good at all to be escorting a hyperactive younger
brother up to town, and he was clearly keen to disappear. I
liked Josh, though, despite his brooding appearance, and I
longed to get to know him better. There was something about

the sensitive intelligence in his wary gaze that I understood and recognised from my years of teaching. I had taught lads like Josh, and knew how rewarding they could be when they laid aside the public myth they so carefully created.

Today was not the moment, however, and after a brief farewell to Ben, Josh slunk off into the crowd, his funereal black ensemble soon blending into the throng.

'Ready?'

'Ready!'

We drifted over to our platform, looking out for fellow Glyndebourne bound travellers. I felt nostalgic already for this journey – only two more performances to go, and after the long summer, with its emotional and musical challenges, it was virtually impossible to imagine feeling so passionately involved in anything ever again. Logic told me that I would be; every performance comes to an end, together with the enforced camaraderie that goes with it, and it is soon replaced by the next one and that by the one that follows it. But I knew, too, that I would never be the same after this summer, whatever lay ahead. I only had to look in the mirror and see the light in my eyes and the radiant glow in my usually pale complexion. I had been transformed from within, and nothing could ever take me back to where I'd been.

As we settled on the train, I looked at Ben with love, marvelling afresh at the joy he had so unwittingly brought to my life. Today, two more performances, and then, I knew not. Only that I had to keep seeing Gerry and Ben; I had to still be part of their lives, however superficial it may be to them. How much I hoped that today would seal the promise that hovered in the air. Three weeks had passed since Gerry had touched me for the first time with what I had thought was love and desire. Two weeks and six days since he'd drawn back again into enigmatic silence. No word of explanation, and yet no outright rejection either. He had tolerated the touch of my hand, the obvious longing in my gaze, neither reaching out nor turning away.

Familiar tears burned my eyes and lonely hunger tightened my throat. I brushed them away before they could fall, not wanting Ben to see me cry. I needn't have worried; he was already immersed in his latest diversion: *One Hundred and Fifty Card Tricks to Amaze Your Friends*.

'Madison, pick a trick, and I'll do it for you.' Ben handed me the book.

'Any one?'

'As long as it doesn't involve a glass or Sellotape.'

I suggested several tricks, which, not surprisingly, were apparently not appropriate under the restrictions of train travel, but eventually hit upon one that could be accomplished with ease. As we pulled into Lewes station an hour and ten minutes later, I enjoyed seeing a middle-aged woman, her dress identifying her as one of tonight's audience, smile at us indulgently. I gathered my wicker basket and Ben's sports bag from the luggage racks above us as she leant over the aisle to speak.

'Your son is lovely. I'm sure you're very proud of him.'

If Ben had heard I would have corrected her, but since he didn't I allowed the error to stand.

'He's wonderful', I agreed.

'Is he in the cast tonight?' she asked. 'One of the boys?'

'Yes, how clever of you to guess', I responded with pleasure. 'In fact, we're both in it. I'm the Second Lady.'

I began to panic a bit then, realising that the remarkable coincidence of mother and son appearing in the same opera in the same season at Glyndebourne might not bear too much scrutiny. I pretended to have dropped something on the floor, and bent down low, averting my face from the woman's fascinated stare.

'Hope you enjoy it!' I called out cheerily.

'What are you looking for? Ben asked loudly.

I peered over my shoulder to make sure the kindly woman had moved out of earshot.

'My sanity.'

'Oh, you'll never find that', Ben responded with a laugh.

From the mouths of babes and all that…

The cast bus was waiting, and I was pleased to see Annie already ensconced, reading the paper. Ben dived for the back seat, digging out *One Hundred and Fifty…* et cetera again. I sat down next to Annie with a sigh of pleasure.

'Uh, oh. She's with wonder boy again,' Annie murmured.

'And my cup is full.'

'Give me an update then, kiddo,' she demanded, folding her paper away.

So I did.

We were all in high spirits during the performance. It was a beautiful day, one of the finest that the Sussex countryside could produce for us: skies blue and clear, the sun brightly glittering on the waters of the lake, the flowers in the gardens and the courtyard an array of multicoloured splendour. Everyone responded enthusiastically to the best weather we had enjoyed so far, and we sang on fine form. I loved the unity and precision of the ensembles, relishing the tight harmonies as we Ladies sang with Tamino and Papageno in the first act quintet. The audience seemed to relish it, too, and we changed for the long interval with applause ringing in our ears. It continued to surprise and please me that the sophisticated Glyndebourne audiences enjoyed *Flute* so much. There was a sense almost of relief in the air on *Flute* days, as if the audience could lay aside their perceived preferences for the tense drama of *Simon Boccanegra*, or the pain of *Peter Grimes*. *Flute* was pure pantomime and the audience gave themselves to it completely. There are deeper messages in *The Magic Flute*, of course, which may not be immediately obvious. The symbolism of Masonic rituals and pagan worship hover over the action, but it is possible to be absorbed by the music and pageantry of the opera without being influenced by these dark overtones. The characters are deeply ambiguous, but exist on two levels and the audience make a choice whether to be troubled by the Svengali-like Sarastro and the angry possessiveness of the Queen of Night, or to simply enjoy the larger than life characters as one would enjoy a pantomime dame or villain.

I retrieved the contents of my wicker basket from the fridge and moseyed over to Ben's dressing room. The boys were, as ever, inordinately excitable, and Gemma looked ready to flag. 'I've come for mine,' I told her, as she fought a losing battle trying to get the boys to hang up their costumes.

'You've no sense of loyalty, Madison,' she complained. 'Taking Ben off and leaving me alone with these two for an hour and a half. Great!'

'Gemma, you know better than that,' I chided. 'Nothing would separate me from you, except this little treasure!'

'If you say so, Mads,' Gemma laughed. 'Have a good time.'

I bundled Ben out of the dressing room and he chatted gaily as we moved through the throng of picnickers towards our designated spot, far from the house, by the edge of the lake.

'Dusan's getting a new computer on Saturday.'

'That sounds good,' I offered. 'With his earnings, I assume?'

'Yes. I'm going to get one, too, now. With a scanner, DVD, and telephone camera thingy. That would be awesome. I can ring Grandpa and he can see me on the screen. Cool, or what?'

'Cool,' I acquiesced.

'He's given me his magazine.' Ben waved a glossy brochure in my face. 'You can look at it while we eat.'

'I can barely wait.'

My sarcasm was lost on Ben as he spotted Gerry's gangly figure in the distance. He ran ahead as I slowed my footsteps, approaching the party with sudden caution. I don't know what triggered off a warning bell as I paused to observe Gerry and his friends in the near distance, but ring it did. I held back as

Ben bowled head first into his dad, and watched as they greeted one another with their usual casual but obvious affection. There were three other adults with Gerry. A man, plumpish and square, must be Ben's second cousin, a relative of his mum, whom, obviously, I'd had no previous reason to meet. One of the two women would be his wife; my guess was the dark haired female, reaching now into the hamper to remove glasses and plates. A second woman was greeting Ben, hands reaching out expansively to ruffle his hair and to pull him to her, planting a kiss on his cheek. From my vantage point she looked ten years my senior, straight bobbed hair fell just short of her shoulders, a honeyed dark blonde. She was wearing a good deal of heavy jewellery – a thick bronze choker, with earrings and bracelet to match. Her gold tunic matched them well, and her wide legged silk trousers completed a sophisticated ensemble. I stood frozen, staring at the scene ahead.

Ten paces and I would be with them. I could turn around now, taking my hamper, and binge on Shiraz and strawberries alone. What an appealing prospect that suddenly seemed, but the sense of dread which hung over me was paralysing. Something was horribly wrong. As I hovered uncertainly Gerry looked up and saw me poised for flight. He beamed, gesturing to me to hurry, and with leaden feet I moved across the grass.

'Hello. We've already started the champagne. Have a glass.'

Gerry thrust a champagne flute into my hand as soon as I had laid down the basket. I sipped at it tentatively, my eyes fixed on the unknown woman who was speaking.

'Pâté, olives, cheese, and home-made brownies,' she declared, opening plastic containers for approval.

Her voice was loud and forthright, making a simple announcement with what seemed unnecessary authority. Her outfit was lovely though, the fabrics soft and shimmering in the late summer sun. I looked down at my simple dress: a silky turquoise shift with delicate embroidery on the bodice. I had chosen it with such care; now I hated its lack of sophistication, and my pretty turquoise and silver earrings looked cheap.

'Hi.'

I greeted Gerry, hoping to put off the moment when I had to acknowledge mystery woman.

'Are you okay? You seem a bit disassociated. Was it a tough first half?' Gerry was smiling his usual grin, full of easy charm and good humour. If there was something wrong here, Gerry clearly didn't know it yet.

'No, it was fine. I'm just hungry,' I replied. 'I've brought some stuff here. Let me unpack it and we can all dig in.'

I thought I managed to sound pretty normal, and I must have pulled it off, since Gerry turned his attention, as I'd intended, to the hamper.

'Excellent! What have you got? Oh, smoked salmon, strawberries, and clotted cream. Marvellous!'

Food was always guaranteed to focus Gerry's interest, so I left it to him to unpack my goodies, whilst I looked again at the interloper.

He set everything out on the remarkably smart picnic blanket which provided a backdrop to the enormous quantities of food already displayed. I'd bet my season's pay cheque that it belonged to Ms Bronze Jewellery. I'd never seen anything in Gerry's possession that so obviously reeked of class as that blanket.

'Madison, meet George and Mavis, Susan's cousins.'

I congratulated myself on a flawless identification as the plumb man genially held out his hand.

'Hello, Madison. Good to meet you. We're really enjoying the opera. Very impressive.'

George's wife nodded in enthusiastic agreement.

'Yes, it's wonderful. This is our first Glyndebourne visit, and its so exciting to watch Ben, and to meet you, too, now. We're very privileged.'

I did the gracious opera singer bit, nodding and smiling, and murmuring thanks.

'And this is Vanessa Hargreaves. Vanessa, Madison Brylmer, who you've just been watching doing ghastly things with a spear.'

I met Vanessa's gaze boldly.

'Nice to meet you.' She held out a large, masculine hand.

'Hello,' I responded shortly.

I knew we were in big trouble here and I had no desire to offer insincere formalities. I dropped her hand like a hot brick, deciding that my best option was to get Ben over to my side of the picnic blanket. If I could focus on him for the next forty minutes, then I might just make it.

'Ben, were you going to show me that computer magazine?' I ventured. 'You'll have to explain it to me personally if I've any hope of understanding it.'

Bless his heart, my little saviour scrambled around to me, magazine in one hand, chicken leg in the other. I studiously ignored everyone else, feeling mildly guilty for giving the innocent George and Mavis the cold shoulder, but I needed time to gather my resources and analyse exactly what was wrong here. I didn't have to wait long.

'Don't *do* that!' Vanessa's strident tones rang out. 'Wait, and I'll do you a plate.'

I looked up from Ben's magazine. Gerry had been caught with his fingers in the salad bowl. Vanessa's had grasped his wrist and was chiding him fiercely. Releasing his hand she slapped his leg with ease born of long established familiarity.

'I hope you're going to behave yourself,' she continued.

'Don't I always?' responded Gerry, and I knew I was lost.

Vanessa piled a plate full of salad, chicken, and salmon (*my* salmon), handing it to Gerry with a spotless napkin and sparkling cutlery.

'That'll be a start,' Gerry laughed.

'There'll be plenty to eat on the way home. We've far too much here,' Vanessa opined, 'and you'll be ready for more by then.'

162

I clenched my fists so tightly that my extra long, red varnished, Second Lady's nails virtually punctured my palms. If she thought there was too much food, I was more than happy to take away my salmon and eat it all by myself, as far from her as possible.

'Madeleine?'

It took me a few seconds to realise Vanessa was addressing me. I looked up slowly from the computer magazine.

'It's Madison. As in Madison Square Gardens,' I corrected her coolly.

'Oh, sorry. It's such an unusual name, I expect you get it all the time,' she smiled.

'Quite the contrary,' I replied, with all the dignity I could muster. 'People tend to remember it because it is unusual.'

There was nothing she could say to that, and in the awkward pause that followed, I saw George and Mavis exchange a puzzled glance, obviously wondering what soap opera they had stumbled into. Gerry was oblivious to it all.

'Madison, are you going to eat?' he asked. 'This is good stuff.'

He handed me a plate and I cautiously helped myself. My throat had closed up as tight as a drum, and I had no idea how I was going to eat anything. I longed to be back on stage; there I was in control. I had proved that all this season, and even now, I would sing like an angel, although my heart was breaking. I wished I was going back in the second half to sing a huge aria, full of love and pain and passion.

Conversation had resumed around me, and I picked at my plate, exchanging banter with Ben as we continued to weigh up the relative merits of rival computer systems. Eventually, Gerry began to realise something was awry.

'Madsy, you're not eating much,' he remarked. 'I thought you were hungry.'

Vanessa was looking at me hawk eyed.

'Have some salad, Madison.'

She passed the bowl over, and I tried to be gracious, failing dismally.

'Tell everyone about the spears in the last show,' Gerry asked me.

I gathered my thoughts sluggishly. The last thing I felt like was being a raconteur, but I stumbled through the tale of the missing spears which had mysteriously turned up in the orchestra pit. It lost something in the retelling, but everyone laughed in the right place.

'You should write a book of all your funny conducting stories, darling,' Vanessa piped up, placing her hand possessively over Gerry's. 'And you can start keeping a diary of your experiences now, Ben,' she continued.

To Gerry's credit, he didn't move to take her hand in his, but I knew it meant very little. Gerry and Vanessa were an item, and had been so for a long time. My eyes burned, and my breathing tightened. I grappled for my handkerchief, blowing my nose vigorously. It had the desired effect of stemming the tears, but I knew it wouldn't last long. I needed to escape, to put some space between me and Gerry and Vanessa, to weep unrestrainedly before I could begin to rationally process this new information. Utter misery washed over me. In the part of my brain that continued to function in cool, intellectual lines, irrespective of what happened around me, I was able to wonder at the fact that never before had I felt such desperate unhappiness. Gerry's ambivalent behaviour, too, over the last three weeks began to make sense. The spineless rotter had made a move on me, knowing that he was already in a relationship which, presumably, he had no intention of ending for me. Rather than come clean, he'd left me hanging on a thread, waiting to make his next move. And this, it appeared, was it.

Around me, conversation buzzed on the still summer air. Late evening sun was gently fading over the lake, and soon Ben and I would have to return to our dressing rooms to prepare for the second half. What could be more perfect than this magical place, doing the job I was born to do? But in a stroke its perfection had been demolished. I didn't move quickly enough to stem a fresh fall of tears, and salty drops splashed on to Ben's brochure. He didn't notice me wipe them away, engrossed in a hunk of bread smothered in taramasalata. Vanessa did, though. I hastily looked away as our eyes met, feeling small and foolish.

'Ben, I'm going back, sweetheart. Are you coming with me now, or shall your dad walk you back in ten minutes or so?'

His mouth full, Ben spluttered messily, 'I haven't had any strawberries yet. Dad'll take me back.'

'Madison, you're going already?' Gerry queried.

'I don't want to be in a panic for the second half,' I said. 'Don't worry about my stuff. Finish it up, and Ben can bring the basket back.'

I couldn't bear to be in Vanessa's predatory presence any longer and I would happily have given up my basket forever just to get away.

I scrambled to my feet, letting my eyes briefly flicker across George and Mavis.

'Nice to meet you. Enjoy the second half. See you, Gerry.'

It hurt to say his name, and new tears of betrayal and pain brimmed again. I turned quickly, but didn't brush them away. I let them fall as I walked with consummate dignity through the picnickers, out of the garden, across the courtyard, and through the stage door. Blindly, I made my way to the dressing room I shared with Annie and Clarissa, hoping it would be empty. To my enormous relief, it was. Annie must be elsewhere drinking tea from her ever-present flask, and Clarissa still with her parents, who were in house for the show. Trembling, I closed the door behind me, leaning heavily against it, burying my face in the fluffy robe Annie hung there on performance nights. Finally my tears could flow unchecked, my body heaving with anguished sobs. As I wept, glad of the emotional relief my tears allowed, I thought of a telling aphorism I had read earlier that day, in a book aptly entitled *If It Hurts, It Isn't Love*. 'Every broken heart is a broken expectation,' I'd read, as I idly flipped through it whilst I waited at Victoria station for Ben. It had rung true even then. Gerry had already broken my heart, shattering the expectations he had, I thought, given me reason to have. If I had tentatively begun to piece it back together, today's events had left it in fragments again. I could easily admit to my expectations: a life with Gerry and Ben, sharing our music, fun and friendship, enjoying the mutual engagement of wit and intellect, laughing at the same things, caring for them both, and – let's face it – long days and nights of passion with Gerry.

Even in my pain, I felt angry. Gerry had already hurt me deeply, but today's callous display had gone too far. I had to deal with the pain and the anger, but now was not the time. Sitting down at the dressing table, I began to repair my damaged face, moving creams and brushes quickly over my face, hoping to anticipate Annie's and Clarissa's return. I had made good headway by the time they trundled in, and I was able to give the impression that I was so deeply engrossed in the task of re-costuming, conversation was not on my mind. As I fixed my wig, a cursory knock on the door was immediately followed by a whirlwind entrance.

'Here, Mads, your basket.' Ben hurled it through the door. 'Dad says he'll meet us at the car.'

He was gone in a flash, and I realised that my trials were not over. When Gerry and I had arranged that I would bring Ben down on the train today, we had also agreed that I would return with them by car. That the three of us were unlikely to be returning alone had not been mentioned, and after Gerry's thoughtless behaviour I knew that it had not been an accidental oversight. I groaned, pressing my forehead against the dressing table top.

'What's up, Mads?' Clarissa asked.

Annie looked up sharply.

'Oh no, that man hasn't upset you, surely? Not in the middle of a performance? I just don't believe it!'

'It's okay, Annie. Just chill. I'm just hoping Ben will sleep on the way home. I'm too weary to play card tricks all the way back as well as all the way down.'

I could see Annie wasn't convinced, but we had a show to do, and she busied herself with her own preparations.

Later, she hugged me as we waited for our entrance. I briefly laid my head on her shoulder as we watched Ben, Dusan and Oli sing their fabulous quartet with Pamina. Pamina was ready to die for love and, for all my intellectualising, that day I knew how she felt.

CHAPTER 32

I saw Gerry pacing as Ben and I approached the car park at the end of the evening. Cars were still streaming out from the grounds and along the country road that would take them to Lewes and thence home, but we had missed the worst of the queues whilst we changed. It had been tempting to take the company bus to the station and to soothe my battered psyche in the comforting presence of Annie, but ultimately I didn't feel up to the explanations it would have involved. I could give no good reason for suddenly rejecting a lift home and felt incapable of coming up with one. Now the curtain was down I felt numb and utterly exhausted. I would sleep in the car, blocking out the reality of Gerry and Vanessa in the front seats (I had no doubt who would be sharing the back with Ben), make a hasty exit on Putney Heath, regroup, and tomorrow would be a new day.

I walked towards the car on leaden feet, awash with sadness as I studied Gerry from a safe distance. How dear to me he was, every feature and characteristic precious and infinitely sweet. I loved his ever-moving hands, always playing an unseen piano, or conducting an orchestra visible only to him. How I longed for those beautiful hands to touch and hold me. My misery grew as I joined Gerry at the car and with a sinking heart saw that it was not his companionable black VW, but a smooth metallic blue BMW, Vanessa at the wheel.

'You didn't come down in your car?' I asked unnecessarily.

'No, Vanessa's car is faster, not to mention tidier', Gerry laughed. 'We'll have you home in no time.'

I shrugged, not wanting to meet Gerry's eyes. If I did, he would smile, and I couldn't condone his thoughtlessness by smiling back as if everything was all right, yet I knew I couldn't be tough enough to coldly stare him down. He opened the boot to stow my bags as I climbed into the back with Ben. Ah well, at least there was a chance of a cuddle on the way home, even if it wasn't the type I'd had in mind.

I let Ben chat as we left Glynde and pulled onto the A4, murmuring appropriate responses to Ben, whilst keeping one ear open to Gerry's and Vanessa's conversation in the front. It was innocuous enough, but run through with the casual ease of a well established couple. Vanessa rested her hand proprietarily on Gerry's knee as she drove, bracelets jangling. I made no attempt to join the conversation. Ben soon flagged and I gently shifted my position to let him rest his head on my knee, his long legs curled up along the seat as he slept.

'Are you asleep, Madison?' Gerry turned around to look at us.

'No.'

'Do you want to sleep? Do you mind Ben lying across you like that?'

'It's fine. I like it,' I answered shortly.

'Why don't you doze, darling?' Vanessa asked Gerry.

'With you two in the car? I wouldn't be so rude,' he replied.

Vanessa laughed throatily and I considered throwing up all over her plush upholstery. Instead, I stroked Ben's soft hair away from his face and leant my head back, gazing out of the window at the beautiful full moon that followed us as we travelled. Tears of loss trickled down my cheeks and intermittently I brushed them away. Even as he slept on my lap, I felt that I had lost Ben. Another broken expectation. All that we had shared during the summer had joined us so close, but though he had not changed, Vanessa's appearance had brutally severed the link. Without the hope of a future with

169

Gerry and Ben, what was the point of all that had gone before? It was nothing but a meaningless fantasy.

I took comfort from Ben's warm head resting on my lap, closing my eyes to feel the tears still creeping from beneath their lids. Conversation continued in the front seats, Gerry occasionally throwing a question or comment to me. I answered briefly, initiating nothing myself. Food was inevitably produced as we passed the halfway mark of our journey, Gerry reaching his hand back to pass me grapes and cherries. I took them carefully, thinking sadly how I would usually have taken the opportunity to teasingly squeeze his fingers as I took the fruit. Now I was as stiff and cold as a fish straight from the freezer, avoiding even an accidental touch.

Gerry had obviously already told Vanessa where I lived, for eventually we joined the A3 and the familiar landmarks began to appear, signalling that home was near.

'Sweetheart, sorry, I have to disturb you.' I spoke gently to Ben, softly nudging his shoulder.

'Are we home?' he murmured sleepily.

'We're at my home. I've got to get out here.'

He raised is head and gazed blearily around him.

''S'okay. See you Mads.'

'Yes, next Tuesday. Same time, same place. I'll ring your dad to confirm details.'

'Umm.'

He was already starting to drift off again as I climbed out of the car. I wanted to reach back in and hug him fiercely to my poor, tear-weary breast, but even had I not wanted to overwhelm him with too much misdirected adult emotion, the moment passed as he settled back down to sleep again. On the pavement I called out a perfunctory 'Bye. Thanks for the lift,' closed the door far more gently than I would have liked, and stomped fiercely up the driveway of Exeter House. I didn't look around even as I heard the car rev and pull away, but set my face like stone towards the front door.

CHAPTER 33

Andy was in Birmingham with the rest of The Restless Dragon production team, and I was deeply grateful for his absence that night. Although I could perhaps have coped with seeing him briefly before I staggered into bed, the prospect of waking to a new morning, unable to deal privately with my grief would have been overwhelmingly ghastly. Although it was past midnight, I was fired with energy; emotion-charged adrenaline spurred me into activity. I took in the washing drying on the balcony, sorted the mail I had left lying on the kitchen table, unpacked my picnic basket, and washed up the containers. Finally, I surrendered, made a large mug of lemon, ginger, and honey tea which I hoped would help me to sleep, and climbed into bed. At last I was dry eyed, and as I sank back against the pillows, I gave in to healing slumber.

Despite everything, I woke early the next morning, as was my habit those days, I thought dispassionately. My biorhythms, or whatever, were so completely out of synch that I could survive on half the food and half the sleep than was my usual quota. I felt like an invalid, nevertheless. My movements were sluggish as I made tea and cautiously wandered around the flat, making a kind of reality check. Here were all the familiar things I loved: my plants and books, my piano and music. I ran my hand over the spine of my doctoral thesis, marvelling that it belonged to a life in which I hadn't even known of Gerry's existence. On the piano sat my *Flute* score and my throat tightened with emotion as I leafed through its pages. Next to it lounged my copy of *Tito*, its bright blue cover looking so optimistic. But I couldn't bear to think about *Tito* today; only yesterday afternoon had Annie and I been singing our sweet little duet as we changed. No wonder I felt like an invalid, I thought. I had been beaten up yesterday, my heart and my psyche was bruised and battered, and now I needed careful handling. Oddly enough, though, I didn't want to be alone, and I was glad that with no singing commitment today I'd agreed to go to The Tuition Box to do some summer revision with a sixth form student.

At 10 o'clock Andy rang, sounding cheerful and friendly. He'd enjoyed the play they'd been to see and the huge curry and plenty of beer afterwards; he had just got up and expected to be home in the early evening. How had *Flute* gone? I uttered a platitude or two, before claiming that weariness and pressure of time to get to South Kensington precluded further conversation. Dressed and ready to leave I just had time to check my email. I sipped a coffee as the computer screen twinkled into life: Inbox (1). Without much interest I clicked it open.

From: Gerry McFall.

Re: Tonight.

Hello

I've just got in and wanted you to read this in the morning. You've been totally miserable all night, and I think it's my fault. If it is, I'm sorry. I don't want you to be unhappy. Talk to me today if you can.

Love from Gerry.

I looked at the time that the message had been sent: 1.15 am. Trembling and weak, I laid my head on the desk as I allowed this new development to sink in. My analytical mind began to process the salient facts: Gerry had discerned my distress, knowing that he had blundered, though not necessarily how. I had been sufficiently on his mind for him to email me before he went to bed and he wanted to talk. This was all immensely gratifying, but I was still too hurt and angry to let him entirely off the hook. He had a lot of explaining to do yet. Quickly I clicked the reply icon, and without pondering my choice of words for long, mailed him back.

> *Of course it's your fault. It would hardly be Ben's, would it? At least he's consistent with me and doesn't make me feel a complete fool. Ring me on my mobile.*
>
> *Madison*

I checked that my phone was fully charged, aware that my poor student would not be getting my full attention today whilst I waited for Gerry's call. As I locked the door behind me I felt a glimmer of hope.

'You stupid girl, you're supposed to be angry with him,' I muttered. And I was. I wanted to beat my fists against his spare chest and sob with fury. And then I wanted him to take me into his arms and tell me I was the most important person in his life, and he would love me forever. I wasn't going to hold my breath. But I was smiling as I boarded the train at Putney Bridge, and the August sun shone warmly on me, glad that my spirits were cautiously recovering.

My phone rang while I was drinking coffee with Maeve, the efficient administrator who ran The Tuition Box. She was immensely loyal to me, knowing that despite my recent successes, I needed to keep a toe in the academic waters. She would find me a student every month or so, a sixth former or undergraduate who needed a Madison Brylmer Special as she called it. It never interfered with my singing; indeed, now that I was appearing in international houses, I couldn't even let it be known that I still tutored a bit on the side. It would have immediately been interpreted as demonstrating a seriously questionable lack of professional commitment. So there we sat, dunking digestives, as I told her about *Flute*, and the terrific feeling it was to be on the Glyndebourne stage. I grabbed my phone on the first ring. I knew it was Gerry, of course, since his name, long since programmed into the memory, flashed insistently against the luminous display. I feigned ignorance.

'Hello?'

'Madison?'

'Yes.'

'It's me.'

'Oh, hi, Gerry. You okay?'

'Yes, I'm not happy about last night, though.'

'Um, well. I sent you an email this morning.'

'I got it. Can you talk now?'

'Not really. Are you around later?'

'I'm rehearsing *Boheme* all day, and I've a meeting tonight. What about tomorrow?'

'Hold on a minute.'

I held the phone away for a moment, while I rubbed my hand across my face and collected my thoughts again. I saw Maeve watching with interest.

'I'm here again. I've got coaching in the morning, but otherwise I'm free.'

'You going to Robert in Crystal Palace?'

'Yes.'

'Then come over afterwards. I'm working at home tomorrow.'

'What time?'

'Midday suit you?'

'Call it 12.30.'

'Okay. See you then.'

Gerry hung up abruptly, but that was his usual practice, and I thought nothing of it.

'Everything all right?' Maeve asked, trying to sound casual.

'I guess so.' I put the phone away slowly. 'Men!' I smiled back at her.

'Andy?' she queried sympathetically.

In answer I shook my head, raising my eyebrows ironically.

'Oh, Madison, you getting your fingers burned?'

In the pleasure of a little girlie bonding, the awfulness of my situation was briefly diffused.

I gathered up my bag.

'Let me know how it goes,' Maeve called after my departing figure.

'If I can work that out myself, I will,' I called back.

CHAPTER 34

'Yes, that's going to be good,' said Robert as we packed up. We'd enjoyed an invigorating hour or so on Rossini's *Stabat Mater* and I felt confident about my forthcoming weekend gig in Winchester cathedral.

'Thank you, Robert. As ever, I couldn't do it without you.'

'It's all in the score, but if you could find it there yourself, I'd be out of a job,' he beamed.

We parted in our usual good humour, and I wandered slowly back to Crystal Palace station. My stomach began to lurch and dip again, now that I could no longer distract myself with music. A few slick manoeuvres between trains and I was disembarking at West Dulwich, shaky with nervous tension. As I rang Gerry's doorbell, I thought of the previous occasions I'd been here over the last months. Today felt different. My earlier visits had been exhilarating as I'd discovered more about the fascinating object of my sudden and wonderful love, thrilled by every little gesture that even faintly held out some hope that my feelings might be reciprocated. But today's visit marked a watershed. Its outcome would be decisive, and I could fantasise no more. We were dealing with reality now.

Gerry looked distinctly sheepish as he opened the door and I decided to take things gently. If I was to benefit from his own awkwardness and concern for me, then it wouldn't do to set up a confrontation. We went through to the kitchen, circumnavigating discarded coats, hockey sticks, bags and instrument cases.

'Tea?'

'Lovely.' I smiled at him and to my relief he smiled back.

'I'm sorry I upset you,' he began as he took out the tea caddy.

'Hang on a bit, Gerry, get some tea. I think we need to have a real talk today, so let's be comfortable first.'

I marvelled at my own boldness as he turned back to the kettle and I prattled on about Rossini and *Flute*, and asked him about *Boheme*.

'I wish I could sing Mimi,' I complained, 'but that would mean I'd have to be a soprano, and that's just unthinkable.'

Gerry laughed, as I'd intended, and brought tea to the kitchen table.

'Madison,' he began.

'Please, Gerry, let me speak first. I don't know if you realise why I was such a misery on Wednesday – and I'm sorry about that – but unless I tell you properly, whatever else we try to say just won't be helpful.'

'Okay.'

I took a deep breath, then another, opened my mouth, closed it, and tried again. This time sound came out. I'd been practising this speech the previous evening, and rehearsed it *ad infinitum* since.

'Gerry…'

'Yes?' He looked at me intently with his wide, enquiring eyes.

'I *was* cross and upset and I'm sorry if I made things difficult for you. I wouldn't knowingly upset you, and I'm sure you appreciate that. But I do think we need to establish where we both stand now. I obviously made a gross misjudgement three weeks ago when you gave, what seemed to me, a clear indication that you liked me too, and wanted to take our relationship further. Although you didn't immediately pursue things – and I guess I do need to know why you didn't – I thought that, in principle, you were still interested, and I was prepared to wait for your next move. But this week, you put me in an impossible position, making unambiguously clear that you are already involved with someone else. I admit I was desperately hurt. You had had so many opportunities to say, 'Look, Madison, I like you, but despite what happened the other day, I'm already in a relationship, and I can't be involved with you.' But you didn't. You took the coward's way out, and said nothing, leaving me to draw my own conclusions. And then you humiliated me, Gerry, in front of that woman, and potentially in front of Ben, though, thank goodness, he was blissfully unaware of the sub-plot on Wednesday.'

Gerry opened his mouth to speak. I quickly took another breath.

'No, please wait, Gerry. I've nearly finished.'

He sat back further in his chair as I continued.

'I guess I have to take the blame for some of this. I've assumed an awful lot which perhaps I had no reason to assume, but I thought we'd been building a relationship, not just because of what happened a few weeks back, but over the last five months. But we've just been feeling our way, and not actually saying anything. If we'd both been more open about things, then we wouldn't have got into this mess now. I was very cross with you on Wednesday and yesterday, and now I've calmed down, but we can't carry on as we have been. We've got to be honest with each other now about what we both want.'

I stopped abruptly. I was suddenly afraid to look Gerry in the eye, but I knew that if we were going to establish the openness I wanted, I had to be tough with myself.

'Oh, Madison,' Gerry sighed, 'I'm so sorry. You've been so good to us, and I would never hurt you.'

I waited.

'I'm in the wrong here, I know. I also know I haven't been honest with you, and I've made you the victim of my own feebleness. That was deeply unfair of me, and my only excuse is that you are always so easy going and cheerful, so adaptable and positive, I didn't stop to consider how you might be really feeling about things. You've given me and Ben so much love and I know you've given us time that can't always have been easy to give. Although you haven't said as much, I guess that Andy hasn't always known when you've been with us, and I get the impression he wouldn't be pleased.'

I nodded silently, not wanting to break Gerry's train of thought.

'When you sent me that email saying you loved me and Ben, it was so sweet and nice. And I wanted to show you how it pleased me, that I enjoy you being with us and caring for us. You're lovely, but now I've hurt you, and I don't know how to put it right.'

Gerry's beautiful hands were drumming the table nervously, but with their characteristic grace. I wanted so much to take his hands in mine, but even more, I wanted the gesture to come from him. Now he looked at me appealingly and I realised that the next cue was mine.

'You can start by telling me if you feel anything for me, or if I should walk away now, and let us try to get back to our old relationship, before any of this happened. I just need to know, Gerry, and then I can fit in with it, readjust my hopes and expectations, get my life back into some kind of order, although I don't know what that would involve at this stage.'

I decided I had nothing to lose, so I may as well go for it now.

'Gerry, I love you, and I want to be with you. I want to share your life, and you to share mine, to look after you and Ben, to get to know Josh. I want to be the best friend and lover you could ever have, and to be there for you whenever you need me. Let's start from there and negotiate downwards.'

I tried to inject some humour into what had become an increasingly impassioned speech, knowing that I had taken a serious risk in so ruthlessly exposing the deepest desires of my heart, but now that we had got this far, what point in prevarication?

Gerry rubbed his hand wearily over his face, and looked at me with tired eyes. I waited for my fate to be decided.

'Okay,' he began. 'Let me say that if all things were equal, I wouldn't want to negotiate downwards.'

At last, Gerry took my hand, and I enjoyed the feel of his long fingers tracing my palm. I breathed a deep sigh of pleasure, but I knew we were a long way from closure yet.

'But all things are not equal?' I offered, more willing now to help him out.

I mentally patted myself on the back for thus far holding back the inevitable tears, but feared too much self-congratulation would be premature.

'I've known Vanessa for a long time,' Gerry continued. 'Since before Susan died. She was a friend of the family long before Sue got ill and she's known Ben and Josh since they were small.'

The realisation that Vanessa had enjoyed years of input into the boys' young lives was profoundly hurtful, and I winced painfully, but Gerry didn't seem to notice, and continued speaking, still absently stroking my palm.

'In the last year of Sue's life, when she was so ill, in and out of hospital, and finally in the hospice, Vanessa was very good to me. She was still with her husband then – she's divorced now – but, I'm not proud of it, we began a relationship then. She was having a tough time; so was I. We knew each other and our circumstances, and could empathise, sympathise, whatever. But I felt so guilty after Susan died, that for about a year, I hardly saw Vanessa alone, but two years ago we began to see each other again, and by that time she was in the throes of leaving her husband. She gave me what I needed: support, encouragement, a sense of worth after so much misery and helplessness, and, I admit, a sexual relationship, when I was beginning to contemplate that possibility again. I'll always feel guilty about our affair whilst Sue was still alive, but two years later, the guilt had faded enough to start again.'

Gerry paused, dropping my hand, and leaning back heavily in his chair. He looked at me keenly.

'Do you want me to say all this, Madison?'

I nodded mutely, my heart pounding, but sure that we needed to speak frankly now, whatever the outcome.

'Vanessa had done me a lot of good and our relationship has a great deal going for it. We know many of the same people, we're a similar age, she's got children who are contemporaries of the boys, she enjoys the world I move in without being directly part of it, and she gives me space away from it. She loves me, and I can't tell you that I don't love her.'

Despite my brave intentions, I wasn't sure if *this* was what I wanted to hear and I shifted unhappily, aware of my brimming eyes.

'And then I met you.' Gerry paused, waiting for me to settle again. 'Or rather, I became aware of you gradually infiltrating my life.'

I laughed through my tears.

'You make me sound like a spy.'

'Bit by bit, you were increasingly, well, just *there*, I suppose. Wanting to do things with me, and for me, singing in my operas, talking with me and Ben, loving him to death, and I began to sense that you might be feeling something of the same for me. And all the time, so friendly, and caring, and clever, and funny.'

I sobbed afresh at this lovely testimony. Gerry took my hand again and kissed my knuckles softly.

'I could see that you were taking time to be with me, and the way you behaved with us was always the same – so consistent and loving – I began to wonder if there might be something for you and me. When you told me you loved us, and I knew it wasn't my imagination anymore, I was so touched, Madison. But then I couldn't see how it could all fit

181

in – my life, your life, Vanessa, Andy, everyone who knows me and you, Susan's parents, the boys. Madsy, it just felt too much to cope with, and I backed off. I was foul to you, too much of a coward to say all of this three weeks ago when I should have done, and spared hurting you now.'

Gerry stopped speaking, kissing my hand again.

'I'm sorry, Madison. Can you forgive me?'

'I've already forgiven you. I did that yesterday,' I smiled tearily. 'I can't go on being angry with you for long. And I am grateful that you've told me all this. But it still leaves me in love with you, and that feels pretty tough at the moment. Isn't there any place for me?'

I was weeping openly now, ashamed that I was virtually begging Gerry to let me have whatever crumbs he could offer. What price the feminist revolution, for goodness sake? And me – a Doctor of Philosophy!

'Would you leave Andy?'

That took me by surprise, but I didn't hesitate, not even for a second.

'Yes.'

'I'm not asking you to do so.'

'I know.'

My answer had been quite involuntary. I hadn't given the reality of leaving Andy conscious thought, especially not after Wednesday's debacle, but I knew, without the slightest doubt, that I would if Gerry gave me reason.

'Madison, I want you in my life. Of course, there's a place for you; you occupy it already. But can you put up with my feebleness? I can't offer you much, but what I do offer, I offer for me as well as for you. I'm selfish enough not to turn down the love of a wonderful woman who says she wants me, but I can only give you part of me in return. Is that really enough for you?'

I tried to lighten the mood again.

'Depends what part?' I snuffled.

Gerry smiled.

'We won't be able to be together very often, you'll be sharing me, not only with Vanessa, but with a whole world of people who make endless demands on my time and energies, with the boys…'

'I'd like that,' I whispered. 'They're part of you and I want to share in your relationship with them.'

'Whatever,' Gerry continued. 'I'm usually exhausted, often moody and self-obsessed – as if you didn't know that already – and I carry so much baggage you could book me into left luggage at Victoria station. But you are a sweet and lovely ray of light in my chaotic life, and if you can put up with that, I'd count myself very lucky.'

I was crying so hard that a coherent answer was impossible. Gerry let go of my hand and got up to come round to my side of the table. Kneeling by my chair, he took my arms firmly, turning me around to look at him,

'Madison, do you want to tell me to get lost?'

I shook my head blindly.

'I'm sorry I look so ghastly,' I sobbed, 'I can't cry tidily.'

Gerry laughed and took my crumpled handkerchief from my fist to wipe my face gently.

'You look lovely. Like a crushed flower,' he chuckled.

'I love you.' I passed my hand over my face miserably.

'I know you do.'

'Try not to break my heart too many times. At least let it mend properly between breakings.'

'Madison, I promise I will do my utmost not to hurt you at all.'

I knew it was a vain promise, given the conditions Gerry had just laid on our relationship, but I stroked his cheek, rapt with love.

'I know you're a miserable old thing already, so that's nothing new, and even without Vanessa, I reckon we'd be in for a pretty bumpy ride. But if you're not sending me away, I've no intention of leaving.'

We stared at each other, wide eyed, and I managed to stop crying long enough to drink in the pleasure of his sweet face.

'Please kiss me, Gerry.'

For a painful moment, I thought he was going to pull away again, but as I trembled with love and desire, he pulled me firmly towards him and kissed me. My mouth and hands and body responded like a firecracker to a flame, and Gerry felt the urgency of my response. He pushed me back gently.

'Madison, are you sure this is what you want? You deserve better than this.'

'Gerry, shut up.'

And this time, I kissed him, pulling him hard against me, and this time, it was he who responded.

'You are lovely.'

'Are you sure about that?'

'Of course.'

'Don't you think you ought to investigate more closely, just to be certain?'

It would be romantic to say that I swooned with pleasure that afternoon, as Gerry took me to his bed, and made love to me for the first time, but I remained very conscious indeed, and so did he.

CHAPTER 35

F ive days later, I watched daylight trickling through the curtains and sighed with happiness as I turned on my side to bury my face in Gerry's shoulder. He lay on his front, face crushed against the pillow, one arm casually thrown over me. I manoeuvred so I could feel the length of his body against me, but he slept on despite my fidgeting, so I resisted the temptation to waken him, satisfied instead to enjoy the sight and feel of him.

I marvelled at how my life had changed in five brief days. Outwardly, everything had remained the same. I hadn't left Andy. I went home after that momentous afternoon, weak with love, and desperate at having to leave Gerry. Andy was already there, happy with another successful day at the theatre, watching the rehearsals that were bringing his script to life, and enjoying the collaboration with the director as the play took shape. How ironic, I thought wearily, that his angry suspicions of June and July seemed to have abated at the very time when Andy finally had something concrete to be angry about. It was incredible that I had been forced to defend myself, to deny that anything had happened between Gerry and me that justified his anger, and yet now, when I was fresh from Gerry's bed, still trembling from his touch, he was oblivious to the radiant glow that shone from my face. I sat in the kitchen, drinking red wine, and nibbling at olives, whilst Andy shared his day, happier and more enthusiastic than I'd seen him for along time. He ran his hand through his curly hair, his broad shoulders swelling with pride as he described how he'd been permitted to direct a key scene. I nodded and murmured at what seemed to be the appropriate places, and must have got it right, since Andy never queried my responses.

'So how was your day, Mads?'

I pulled up sharp, trying to remember what I was supposed to have been doing.

'Oh, fine. I had a good session with Robert on the Rossini for tomorrow.' That, at least, was true.

'So you're all set for Winchester then?'

'Yes. Are you coming?'

I dreaded the prospect of a whole day with Andy. If I couldn't be with Gerry, I wanted to be alone to savour the thought of him, but I knew I had to maintain some semblance of normality.

'Of course. I said I would. Don't you want me to come now?'

'Yes, yes,' I assured him hastily. 'We have to leave by eleven.'

'Marvellous.' Andy stretched luxuriously. 'You'll be fab!'

So I sang my *Stabat Mater* in Winchester cathedral, every note a pure liquid offering to my lovely Gerry. Andy had done his own thing round the city during the rehearsal and thankfully we'd had little time alone. I closed my eyes in the car on the way home, feigning sleep. Already, my voice had a new vibrancy and depth; I'd heard it as I'd sung, full of joy and confidence. If this was the result of being so much in love, it was worth money in the bank. Keep it up and I'd soon be at the Met.

But I missed Gerry painfully, longing for him to call me. As I'd left his house, we'd arranged that I would wangle him another ticket for *Flute* on Tuesday, and this time he and I would have the special evening I'd hoped for last week. With the diversion of *Stabat Mater* over, Sunday dragged, and it was a relief when Andy departed for the theatre on Monday. I spent the morning working gently through *Tito*, getting Sesto into my voice and brain. Gerry finally rang at lunchtime, sounding as rushed as ever.

'Hello. It's me.'

'Hello, me.'

'Are you all right?'

'Umm. Very much so. I miss you though.'

'Good,' Gerry laughed smugly. 'I've got tomorrow afternoon entirely free. I can drive you and Ben down to Sussex if you'd like that.'

'Yes, please. Where shall I meet you?'

'We'll pick you up at home if that's helpful. Get lots of food ready for us. We'll be there at, what, 2 o'clock?'

'It's a deal.'

'Madison?'

'Yes?'

'Can you come back with us, and stay over?'

'You bet.'

My mind began to process a range of excuses I could offer to Andy. A cast party should do it.

'See you tomorrow, then.'

The brevity of Gerry's phone calls hadn't changed, but I liked the content much better.

Andy accepted the fiction of a last minute cast party without blinking an eyelid. I sprinkled the crucial conversation liberally with Annie's name, and it paid off. He liked the fact that she and I had established such a good friendship so quickly, and he seemed keen to encourage it.

'So I'll see you sometime on Wednesday, then?' he asked as he left on Tuesday morning. 'Time of arrival depending on level of hangover?'

'Andy!' I feigned shock. Never was there a more sober article than me, as Andy well knew, but I wasn't averse to the suggestion that on this occasion, my level of consumption might necessitate an extremely slow return from Sussex on Wednesday morning.

And so we finally had our special day. Gerry was utterly, beautifully, attentive and Ben in high spirits. I was so happy you could have used me to light the Olympic flame. Annie knew something was up, of course, as soon as I bounced into the dressing room.

'Do I detect a certain *joie de vivre* today? she asked.

I giggled foolishly.

'I take it this means that our esteemed Mr McFall has deigned to look kindly upon you?'

'That's one way of putting it.'

'Oh, Madison, you haven't?'

'Haven't what?'

'Bloody well gone to bed with him, as a refined creature such as you would put it?'

All I could do was grin.

'Oh, well, lovey, if it's what you want.' Annie conceded, giving me a hug, 'Don't let him get his own way all the time, eh? Promise me. Don't give him all the power.'

'I'll try.'

'Try very hard,' she admonished.

Gerry decided he had already broken enough rules with Ben's chaperoning regime and we travelled back to London alone after the show. Ben was holed up, as per the regulations, in a hotel in Lewes, and would return the next day with Gemma. I saw her eyeing Gerry and me curiously as we said our farewells to Ben and the other boys. I caught her eye and winked, and she grinned back. Let her work that one out!

Our journey home couldn't have been more different than the sad affair the previous week. My breath caught high in my chest, leaving me almost hyperventilating with joy as we sallied forth through the dark Sussex night. At last I was free to hold Gerry's hand, to rest mine on his warm thigh, to enjoy his proximity without already anticipating the moment when I would leave the car and he would drive rapidly away without even a backward glance. He chatted happily as we travelled, in his most vociferous form as he pronounced on this and that. How I loved him! I didn't think of Andy for a moment, I'm ashamed to say. It was only as I hesitated, uncertain what to do with my mobile when we arrived back in Dulwich, that he even crossed my mind. If he were going to ring, he would have called by now, I calculated, switching it off, and that was that.

Next to me, Gerry stirred softly as I stroked his back, letting my hand move over his shoulder blades, his rib cage, and down his thighs, savouring the warm smoothness of his skin. I pressed closer to him, holding him fast with my leg, burying my face in his chest. He groaned, and opened his eyes.

'Madison.'

'Gerry.'

'Are you trying to seduce me at some unearthly hour of the morning?'

'Of course.'

'I'm not sure if this old man can cope with a young thing like you, after all.'

'You coped pretty well last night.'

'Umm, I suppose I did.' Gerry's eyes twinkled as he roused himself fully from sleep. 'Perhaps we'd better check it wasn't a fluke.'

I giggled, loving the intimacy and humour of the moment. Already, our lovemaking had softened and deepened. On Friday, I had been so tearful and stressed that I had been on a knife-edge of emotion. We had made love with urgent passion, as if quickly sealing an agreement before it could be revoked. Last night, united by the pleasure of the day, talking and sharing, enjoying Ben's lively company, and the friendly warmth of the drive home, we came together with a sweetness that was overwhelmingly beautiful. Now, as Gerry pulled me close to him, and we kissed deeply, I knew without doubt, that I had never before known such love as this. I felt him hardening against me, and his sensuous fingers stroked me in my own dark places.

'You are so gorgeous,' I murmured softly against his mouth.

'I try.'

'My lovely Gerry.'

'My beautiful Madison.'

'Don't make me cry now.'

'Why? What did I say?'

I silenced him with a kiss, and it was a good while before either of us said anything coherent again.

An hour or so later we were idly drinking tea and nibbling toast, talking about the day ahead. Gerry was playing for a special service at Windsor chapel, and later I had a rehearsal for a short Bach cantata at St Martin's in the Fields – not usually my kind of thing, but such was my mood I was prepared to enjoy anything! Josh wandered downstairs at about 9 o'clock giving no indication that he shared my current positive outlook on life. Gerry greeted him cheerfully though, and Josh didn't seem to find my presence odd enough to question.

'Ben did brilliantly again last night,' he told Josh.

Gerry worked firmly on the principle that his sons were to be encouraged to appreciate each other's achievements.

'That's good,' Josh conceded, helping himself to toast.

'What are you up to today?' Gerry asked him.

'Sleeping.'

'Haven't you got work to get ready for school?'

As Gerry said this I realised how quickly the summer was flying and our final performance of *Flute* next week would be rapidly followed by the beginning of a new academic year.

'Yes.' Josh managed a monosyllable.

'Isn't it a good idea to do it this week, rather than leave it till just before term starts?' Gerry suggested.

I could see the way this conversation was going and tried to calculate how welcome my intervention might be. Not very, I guessed, but I'd give it a go anyway.

'This is your GCSE year coming up isn't it?' I asked.

'Yeah.'

'What do you think you'll do best in?'

'Not much,' Josh grunted 'but I suppose English, History, Art, Drama, if I'm allowed to do it my way.'

'Aren't they very flexible at St George's?' I asked. 'Is it very traditional?' I knew, of course, that it was.

'Umm, I guess so.'

'Are you involved in lots of things there?'

'Not really.'

I tried to find the key to unlock this little problem.

'Have you good friends there?'

'Not really.'

I clearly wasn't asking the right questions to encourage Josh to open up, but I was getting a picture. He hated his school, dreaded going back, and was unlikely to do the required holiday work before he did so.

'Does Ben enjoy it there?'

'Oh, yes, but he's the conventional type,' Josh drawled disparagingly.

I smiled inwardly, thinking that 'conventional' was hardly the epithet that I would apply to the sparky and forthright Ben, but it was interesting that this was the way his brother viewed Ben's ability to fit in where Josh clearly didn't.

I decided to throw in a wild card.

'I used to teach at Doddington Carter and Paine before I started singing full time. Do you know anyone who goes there?'

Josh looked slightly more interested.

'Yes, some guy in my class, his sister goes there.'

Gerry cleared his throat forcibly, bringing the conversation to a halt. He looked at me narrowly, and I knew he'd sensed the direction in which I'd been heading. Good. I'd leave him to ponder it!

'I've got to be going,' he told us. 'Do you want a lift anywhere, Mads?'

191

'Yes, sure, I'll get out when we get to a convenient tube station.'

I looked at Josh, sorry not to be able to spend longer talking to him. We were still new to each other, and I hoped that in time, something would spark between us.

'Nice to see you, Josh,' I said. 'See you around again soon.'

'Uh, yes, sure.' He was toying disconsolately with his toast. 'Dad, when will you be back?'

'For supper. I'll ring you.'

My heart went out to Josh, who looked lonely and fed up, but I knew it wasn't appropriate to suggest he spent the day with me.

In the car, however, I dared to tentatively broach the subject of Josh's school.

'Gerry?'

'No. Absolutely not!'

'What? I haven't said anything!'

'Josh is not going to give up a place at St George's to go to a drop outs' college.'

'Ah.'

'Is that all you've got to say?'

'Just let me get a prospectus for you. I can pop in there today.'

We drove in silence for a bit whilst Gerry looked mutinous. At last he spoke.

'Just to look at, all right? Out of interest.'

I grinned, averting my head to hide my smile, but I couldn't keep it up for long and turned back to catch Gerry's eye. As we pulled up at traffic lights he opened them wide, his impatience gone. He leaned over to kiss me.

'I think you might be a genius,' he chuckled, taking my hand, which, to my satisfaction, he held all the way into town.

CHAPTER 36

Over the next few days I began to appreciate the course our relationship was going to take, and exactly what Gerry had meant when he said I would have to share him with all and sundry. I thought, too, of what Annie had said to me: don't let him have all the power. But I didn't see what the alternative was. Gerry held the cards – the whole pack. Despite our wonderful day and night together the phone remained silent and my inbox empty. I tortured myself, imagining him with Vanessa, missing him and Ben desperately. I felt disconnected and empty, and by Saturday night I was climbing the walls. The final *Flute* performance was less than a week away, but before then we had our first music call for *Tito*. I would feel terribly wrong-footed if the next time I saw Gerry was when I walked into the rehearsal room, but I feared this was going to happen. The Doddington prospectus burned a hole in my bag, but I was reluctant to post it, thinking that would effectively be an acknowledgement that I wasn't expecting to see Gerry soon enough to give it to him.

'Let him wait,' I muttered bitterly to myself, but immediately felt guilty, because it was Josh I was letting down if Gerry didn't get to look at it soon.

By Saturday, too, I couldn't avoid Andy any longer. Although he was at the theatre during the day, we had arranged to go out with friends in the evening, and I was glad that I didn't have to be with him alone. The only hope I had of getting through the evening was if I'd heard from Gerry, and the chances of that were getting slimmer by the moment. Just before I left the flat, I gave in and turned on the computer. Reluctantly, I emailed him, knowing I should be holding out, waiting for him to contact me, but quite unable to do so.

Hello, I wrote.

Have the DCP prospectus. Do you still want it? What's going on re Flute *on Wednesday? Shall I take Ben on the train? Ring me before* Tito *on Tuesday.*

Love from Madison

The tone of my message was no different to that I'd used in previous emails – concise and businesslike, with just a touch of friendly affection. I didn't think it gave away my desperation. I hoped not. Sighing, I logged off, feeling very sorry for myself.

To my surprise, I managed to keep my end up pretty well with Jim and Sophie, two old friends Andy and I had known since my teaching days. I'd met Sophie when I'd been regularly singing solos for a local choral society to which she belonged. Her husband, Jim, was a lawyer, acerbic and witty. He and Andy got on exceptionally well, and I'd always enjoyed our evenings with the couple. They had been to one of the early performances of *Flute* and wanted an update. I enjoyed the opportunity to talk about the show; it made me feel close to my boys for a while.

'So how's the little lad you're friends with, Mads?' Sophie asked.

'Oh, Ben?' I clarified casually. 'He's doing fine. A real star.'

I knew I should stop at that, but the need to talk about him was too great.

'We have such a laugh together. He's working through *A Hundred and Fifty Card Tricks to Amaze Your Friends* at the moment, and I'm supposed to be catching on, but I can't say that I am!'

Sophie and Jim laughed, although Andy remained ominously quiet.

'You work with his father, too, don't you?' asked Jim.

The quality of Andy's silence darkened, but still I couldn't keep my mouth shut.

'Yes. We're doing *La clemenza di Tito* in the autumn and he comes down to see *Flute* quite often.'

'How cosy for you all.' Andy broke his silence at last.

Attack is sometimes the best form of defence, I thought, and launched my rocket.

'There's no call for a remark like that,' I snapped. 'His son is singing a principal role at Glyndebourne before he's twelve-years-old. What else is he going to do but take the chance to see him as much as possible?'

'Did he go to the cast party last week?' Andy asked edgily.

'Of course not!'

'Umm.'

Andy looked sceptical and I kicked myself for my self-indulgence. I should have kept quiet. Sophie saved me from further blunders with a smooth interjection.

'Shall we order, then?'

And we did, the dangerous moment passing. Later, when she and I were alone, she looked at me approvingly.

'Mads, you're looking really great. You've lost a lot of weight.'

'Yes, over a stone since May,' I nodded.

'And you look really happy. Glyndebourne must be doing you good.'

I smiled.

'It's great fun. I shall be sad when our last performance is over on Wednesday.'

'Well, honestly, Madison, I've never seen you looking better.'

I'd have looked even better if I'd heard from Gerry before I'd come out tonight, I thought miserably, but I patted her arm gratefully.

'Thanks, Sophie. If I discover the recipe, I'll pass it on.'

Gerry finally rang me on Monday morning. Yes, he wanted the DCP prospectus; would I bring it to *Tito* the following day? I managed to gather my wits quickly.

'Are you free after the call? I can talk you through some of it then.'

'Yes, I think so. As long as I get my orchestra parts finished today.'

'What about *Flute* on Wednesday? Do you want me to do anything?'

'Ben's going down on the train in the morning with Gemma and the others, and staying overnight, so I think we're okay,' he replied, crushing me with disappointment. Too many expectations again.

'All right.' I tried to sound as if I couldn't care less. 'I might go down with them anyway. I'd like to travel with Gemma. See you tomorrow then.'

I burst into tears as soon as I had hung up. It was as if our wonderful time in bed and the closeness of our day together had never happened. I buried my head in my arms.

'Here we go again,' I thought. But this time it was worse, and I only had myself to blame for accepting Gerry's terms and conditions.

I cried for a long time that morning, and then brushed myself down and trotted off to practice. I hadn't completely lost the plot, I thought with relief. Some things did remain constant at least, and music was one of them. Thank God.

My stomach felt ready to hit the floor when I walked into the rehearsal room the following morning. Gerry's withdrawal had thrown me utterly, and it seemed as if we were starting all over again. He was already at work with Francesca, who was singing Vitellia, when I arrived. I tried to look nonchalant as I took out my music and made a show of making some random notes. I hoped I looked suitably devil-may-care. I had no intention of meeting Gerry's eye, far less smiling.

Despite my anxiety, it was lovely to hear Frances singing *Non piu di firori* and I felt fresh excitement at the prospect of doing this wonderful opera, and singing a role tailor-made for me. I gave in to the music and by the time Annie arrived I had relaxed, and greeted her warmly.

'I can't bear it that *Flute* is over tomorrow,' I whispered.

'I know,' she replied sorrowfully. 'I want to cry just thinking about it.'

'I've been so ridiculously happy,' I added. 'But at least we still get to sing together.'

We squirmed with pleasure.

'*Tito* and *Carmen*. Aren't we lucky girls?' she grinned. 'How's it going?' she continued, inclining her head in the direction of the piano.

I shrugged.

'So-so,' I admitted. 'He's playing hard to get again, but I intend to do likewise today.'

'Good girl.'

John, who was singing Publio, had arrived and Gerry wrapped up what he and Francesca were doing, to start work on the two trios that involved John and the girls. I was deeply glad of my ability to become totally absorbed in a rehearsal, relishing the music and the profound pleasure of hearing us all blending and interweaving, my voice responding with delight to music which came especially naturally to me. Gerry was businesslike, singling me out only when the musical requirements of the rehearsal demanded it, but always doing so with ease and humour. Incredibly, I found myself smiling and laughing, and by the end of the session, I had to admit that I'd almost forgiven him. It was so lovely to watch him at work, and I felt an involuntary rush of love and desire as I remembered the feel of those beautiful, capable hands dealing with me as skilfully as they now dealt with the piano! I wanted that again, but I knew that if I made a fuss I would only diminish any inclination on Gerry's part to pursue our affair, and I was determined to follow his lead.

'Do you want a lift anywhere?' Annie asked as we packed up.

I shook my head.

'I'm okay, thanks.'

She squeezed my arm.

'Take care, kiddo.'

By the time everyone else had drifted off, I'd run out of things to do to look busy, and Gerry, never one to tarry, was ready to leave.

'Hello,' I ventured. 'Are you all right?'

'Yes, of course. Are you?' Gerry scrutinised me closely, and I wondered if this was his acknowledgement that his silence may have been unwelcome.

'Umm. Sure.'

We looked at each other for a moment.

'I'm so glad to see you,' I finally admitted.

'Oh, yes, why?' Gerry rolled his eyes at me teasingly. 'Shall we get a coffee, then?'

I nodded, sagging with relief.

We settled in a little Italian café by Warwick Avenue, and Gerry chatted on about what he'd been doing since last Wednesday, though I was sure it was a heavily edited version. I found his lack of self-consciousness incredible. If I were in his position, I would be anxiously justifying my failure to have been in touch, feeling desperately awkward until I was sure that I'd re-established my ground. But then I wasn't Gerry, and I was actually pleased that he found it easy to simply pick up again as if nothing could possibly be amiss. It gave me time to calm my nerves, and his infectious good humour was, as ever, impossible to resist. At last, Gerry paused in his narrative, and looked me over appraisingly. He took my hand, lying empty and idle on the tabletop.

'It's nice to see you. You sounded lovely this morning.'

I entwined my fingers with his, trembly and grateful.

'Darling, I've missed you so much.'

'I'm sorry I was so busy this weekend,' he said.

I snuffled up this crumb with pathetic gratitude.

'That's all right.'

Five days of misery faded away as if in smoke. Spot the victim.

'You're not going to *Flute* tomorrow, are you?' I continued.

'No, we've a *Bohème* Sitzprobe. Whatever time it ends, it'll be too late to get down to Sussex. Are you going down with Gemma and the boys?'

'Yes. I've arranged to meet Gemma at Victoria. Do you want me to collect Ben from you first?' I held my breath in hope.

'Yes.' Gerry spoke slowly as he thought it out. 'It'll save Ben coming all the way to Maida Vale with me first thing, only to go over to Victoria two hours later. Josh can be at home in the morning with him if you're okay to pick him up from there.'

I nodded coolly, absolutely delighted.

'Are you sure, Madsy? It means you have to come right across London, then back into town, before going on to Lewes.'

'It's no problem, Gerry. You know I enjoy it.'

'I'm very grateful.' He tried to look humble and failed.

'I've brought the DCP prospectus. Do you want to look?'

I handed it to Gerry, who leafed through it carefully.

'Did you say anything to Josh?' I asked.

'No, I thought I'd talk to you more first.'

I glowed and, buoyed up with the confidence that I could talk to Gerry about something that I definitely knew more about than him, I began to explain the DCP ethos further, and why I thought it may be the answer to Josh's problems.

'Everyone who goes there does so either because they don't fit in with the traditional system, or because they feel their school is not where they'll flourish best. It may have already let them down, or they have become disillusioned with it. But they're not dropouts. Quite the contrary; they're trying to drop in to a set up that suits them well enough to enable them to fulfil their potential. Small groups, personal supervision, a more adult environment, and no extra curricular activities if the kids don't want them.'

Gerry nodded slowly, still flicking the pages.

'And no dress code,' he laughed.

I nodded, keeping quiet as he absorbed what I said.

'When does term start? St George's are back next week.'

'Not till 16th September. Plenty of time, though I guess you'd lose a term's fees at St George's.'

He shrugged fatalistically, so I continued.

'I can organise you both an interview for Friday.'

Gerry sighed and looked pensive for a moment.

'Okay! Let's do it. Can you ring them now?'

I fished out my mobile and the deed was done in less than five minutes.

'I'll talk to Josh about it tonight. If you get a chance tomorrow morning, say something helpful, won't you?'

I grinned. I'd done something useful for Gerry that no one else he knew could do, and I was puffed up with joy.

'What are you doing on Friday yourself?' he asked.

'Shall I meet you after you've been to DCP?'

'Good idea. In fact, meet us there, if you can?'

This was getting even better.

As we left the café, Gerry took my hand in his, chatting easily again as we strolled up the street. At the tube we paused as I retrieved my travel card and he kissed me briskly but warmly.

'See you on Friday, then.'

I held fast to his hands, not wanting to leave him.

'Gerry.'

'Yes?' he smiled.

'I love you.'

I hated myself for saying it so easily.

'And I'm very lucky that you do.' He kissed me again. 'Have a nice day tomorrow. Don't let Ben give you any trouble.'

I sobbed from Warwick Avenue to Baker Street, and from there to Waterloo. On the overground train I recovered enough to get out my music, but it blurred before my eyes and I was still shaky with tears when I emerged at Putney. No one said anything, but if I were them, I'd ignore me, too.

CHAPTER 37

I was distinctly nervous about how things were going to
work out as I woke the next day, but Andy, remarkably
open-minded about my movements, raised no query about my
need to take an earlier train, and I left the flat in good time to
collect Ben from home. He was definitely not ready, but I
admit to thoroughly enjoying the excuse to be maternal and
organising. Josh hovered in the background, saying nothing,
and looking lost. I took pity on him.

'You're going to see DCP on Friday, aren't you? My friend,
Sara, is meeting you. She's pretty cool.'

Josh nodded.

'Have you looked at the prospectus?' I asked.

'Yes.'

I waited, and Josh pushed himself to continue.

'It might be okay.'

'It's worth going to see,' I offered casually. 'What are you
doing today?'

'Not much.'

The kitchen table was covered in art materials but Josh
toyed with them disconsolately.

'Darling?' I turned to Ben, 'where's your dad at the
moment? Can we get him on his mobile do you think?'

'Dunno. Why?'

'I was wondering if Josh fancied coming down with us
today. I'm sure we could sneak him in backstage. We might

even be able to find him a cast ticket if we were really lucky. But we need to ask your dad. What do you think?'

I looked at both boys.

'Would you like to come, Josh?'

Josh's sweet, sullen, face had transformed.

'Yes, please.'

'Then we'd better get hold of Gerry.'

We dialled his mobile number and, incredibly, he replied immediately.

'Oh, hello. Everything all right? Is the little one ready for you?'

'Yes, everything's fine. Actually, we were wondering if Josh could come with us for the day. Gemma and I can squirrel him in backstage if I can't get him a slips seat.'

'Oh? Does he want to go?' Gerry sounded surprised.

'Do you want to talk to him?'

Josh and Gerry exchanged a few brief words before I took the phone back.

'What about getting him home?' Gerry asked me. 'I don't think Gemma can sneak him into Ben's hotel as well.'

'It'll be a bit late for you to pick him up at Victoria, won't it?' I turned to Josh. 'Would you be happy to stay with me tonight and come home in the morning?'

Josh nodded.

'Does that sound all right?' I asked Gerry.

'It sounds wonderful. Call me later.'

So we rang off, everybody looking terribly pleased with themselves.

'You'd better get your things quickly, then,' I told Josh, and he leapt into action.

Time was still on our side as we left Dulwich, bound for Victoria. Josh and Ben jostled together on the suburban train and I was glad for a moment's grace to think through the complicated scenario that I'd created rather too easily. Andy's current mellow mood notwithstanding, it was going to be a tough job explaining how I'd ended up with Josh in tow when

I got home later. A pre-emptive strike would be necessary, I decided. I'd leave a suitably garbled message on Andy's voicemail and avoid his calls for the rest of the day. He could hardly throw the child out on the street once we were home.

Gemma took the arrival of my additional charge in her stride. We occupied two adjacent table seats – she, Dusan, and Oli at one; me and my boys at the other. It was beautiful to watch them together. Their undemonstrative devotion to each other was clear, and Josh, despite his customary aloofness, was infinitely tolerant of Ben's boisterousness. The six of us travelled happily, sharing drinks and chocolate, Gemma and I gossiping quietly when beyond Haywards Heath we shunted Josh and Ben over to join the other boys, and she sat with me at my table.

'What's going on, Mads?' she asked. 'You're up to something with Ben's dad.'

'Oh, Gemma, it's early days, sort of, although it feels as if it's been going on forever.' I looked over at Ben and Josh. 'It's wonderful having them both with me today. I've so wanted to get to know Josh. I already love Ben so much, as you well know.'

'And his dad?' Gemma looked mischievous. 'That sounds like a lot of trouble brewing.'

'It's worth it.'

As I said the words, I appreciated afresh that I was prepared to go a long way for a relationship with Gerry. I didn't know where it was leading, if anywhere, but I knew I wanted to give it my best shot.

'You're wonderful with Ben, Madison,' she said seriously. 'They're lucky to have you around, I'd say,' she added.

'I couldn't agree more,' I agreed, and we raised our coffee cups to one another.

'To whatever love and life bring,' she said.

'If I'm brave enough for it,' I joked.

But I could already feel the cold fingers of guilt and fear running up my spine. I wanted Gerry passionately, but the prospect of domestic upheaval terrified me.

'Madison,' Gemma cut across my ruminations, 'the love that's written all over your face when you look at that boy and his dad, it's to die for.'

I blinked, and spoke more vehemently than I'd intended.

'Well, let's hope it doesn't come to that.'

Suffice it to say, we had the most glorious day. We descended *en masse* on the company office, and after a good bit of wheedling, extracted a slips ticket for Josh. Copious amounts of food were consumed before the show and in the long interval, and we all chatted away non-stop, except when we were singing. Annie and Clarissa joined us in the interval, and we sipped a minuscule amount of champagne to bid the lovely season farewell.

'Here's to the coolest three Ladies ever!' Clarissa toasted, and we drank to that with verve.

Dusan and Oli had family with them, so once the girls had returned backstage I was left with Ben and Josh, lazing on the grass and contemplating the punters from a distance.

'That's for bringing me.' Josh spoke quietly. 'I came with dad earlier in the summer, and it was okay, but I like it better today.'

'You need to see an opera more than once to really appreciate it,' I said. 'You have to get familiar with what's going on musically and dramatically. It still takes me a while to really get into something.'

Josh nodded slowly.

'And this whole set-up.' He gestured around him expansively. 'I thought it was just pretentious when we came before, but today, it feels sort of natural.'

'It is,' I agreed. 'I don't think most people come here just to pose around. They're here because they love it. The whole opera scene is utterly compelling, and speaking from my side of the footlights, it becomes a way of life you couldn't envisage abandoning.'

'Yes,' murmured Josh thoughtfully. 'It's good for Ben to have done it, isn't it? I mean, who knows whether he'll be able to sing as an adult? But at least he's done it now.'

I was delighted by the maturity of Josh's thoughts but, not surprisingly, Ben had other ideas.

'What do you mean, I might not be able to sing when I'm an adult? I'm going to be *the* international tenor of the twenty-first century; bigger than Pavarotti, Domingo, David Rendell.'

'Not physically, I assume,' I laughed, critically surveying Ben's slim frame.

He pantomimed around for a bit, pretending to be a twenty-stone tenor. I wondered what his life would hold if indeed his youthful promise didn't make the transition to adulthood, but I felt confident that whatever it did, he would be a success, publicly and privately. Ben fell over next to me, as if bouncing on several layers of blubber.

'I think it's time to calm down and consider the second half intelligently,' I suggested.

'Intelligently! What's that?' Ben laughed, and Josh grinned companionably.

'What you're not, obviously,' he joked.

Ben made to launch himself physically at his brother, but I caught his arms and hugged him to me instead.

'Come on, gorgeous, time to get back.'

He allowed himself to be hugged for a second longer before breaking away to whirl excitedly again. I stood up, ready to go, Josh still sitting on the grass. I held my hand out and, to my gratification, he took it to lever himself to his feet. We stood still, our hands lightly clasped for a moment.

'Thanks for a cool day, Madison.'

It was the first time he'd spoken my name, and I liked it very much. I squeezed his fingers briefly.

'It's a pleasure, Josh.'

My heart was bursting with love as we wandered back, Ben and I to change again, and Josh to saunter mysteriously to the slips. My love keeps expanding, I thought with delight. First to embrace Gerry, then to encompass Ben, and now Josh, and each time my heart reached out to take in someone new, my love for the others increased as it did. It felt just lovely.

CHAPTER 38

It was hard to leave the dressing room that night. I was leaving behind so much: my debut in an international house, and with it the feeling of having come to maturity as a singer – for the time being at least. But forever in my mind, Glyndebourne would be associated with my relationship with Gerry. They were inextricable now, and to leave Glyndebourne for the last time marked more than just the end of my season there. I would return to the Sussex house; already I had been booked to sing Fenena in two years' time. I was happy and proud about that, but my mind was occupied with thoughts of what might have happened by then between me and Gerry.

Annie, Clarissa and I hugged a tearful farewell, and then Gemma and I took the boys to the cast bus waiting outside the old house.

'Keep in touch, Madison,' she instructed me. 'Let me know what Ben does next, and I'll try to muscle in on it.'

We separated outside Lewes station, the genies, despite their protests, flagging and ready for bed. Ben and Josh pushed one another in a suitably casual 'See you tomorrow' gesture, and Josh and I were left to sink gratefully onto the train. We were silent; each lost in our own thoughts for a while. As I began to drift off, Josh's soft voice stirred me.

'Ben's lucky to have such an important thing in his life.'

I nodded, sensing there was more to come.

'I know what I enjoy now, and what I think I want to do in the future, but none of it feels really important, not like Ben's singing.

'What do you think you want to do later?' I asked quietly.

'Write,' he replied very firmly. 'I want to write plays especially, and poetry.'

He studied me, gauging the level of my interest.

'I write quite a bit now. Would you like to see something?'

'Of course.'

Josh drew out a dog-eared notepad from his jacket. It was full of small, intelligent script.

'Here.' He handed it to me, turning over pages. 'I wrote that yesterday.'

I read.

Grey clouds and bright sun
Blue skies and black night
Folly and wisdom
Love and hate
Evil and good
All in me and around me
Life in death and death in life
Duality in unity
Unity in duality

Goodness me.

I read it again. It did make sense, though it was pretty heavy for a fifteen-year-old.

'Josh, that's good. What else is there?'

He took the book from me and picked out some other pieces. They were witty, observant, and hauntingly sad.

'I'm impressed, darling,' I told him. 'You have a real facility with language. Writing is wonderful, isn't it? It doesn't just entertain, or inform, but it helps you to express things you wouldn't otherwise say.'

Josh nodded enthusiastically.

'That's just it. Do you ever write, Madison?'

'A little, articles mostly, and I write a bit of poetry occasionally. Just for me. Not your sort of stuff; very girlie,' I laughed.

'I'd like to see some,' said Josh seriously.

I rummaged in my bag for my Filofax. Leafing through the pages I handed it to him. He took it and read.

In your sweetness and your beauty
You tear my life apart
I know not if you want me
But I know you'll break my heart

I struggle in confusion
Your kindness has me lost
Why do you let me close to you
Yet not your love entrust?

I wait to be rejected
To be spurned, my love denied
And though you do not do so
So many tears I've cried

All this can bring is heartache
No happy end for me
But every time I close my eyes
'Twill be your face I see

'Madison, that's really sad.'

'It's just life, Josh. Sometimes the painful things, like our relationships with others, are the sweetest, too. Although I wouldn't choose to have the hurt that inspired that poem, I wouldn't choose not to have the relationship that caused the pain.'

I wondered if I'd gone too far, but Josh opened his dark eyes wider.

'That's awesome, Madison. It's like you have to see everything as part of one huge pattern and if you try to remove one element of it, the whole pattern disintegrates. So to keep the pattern, you need to accept all of it, even the hurting parts.'

'Quite,' I said. 'It's only when there are more parts of the pattern that cause pain than bring joy that you need to make an adjustment. And that's really a very individual thing. Some people can integrate more pain than others without the pattern disintegrating. It's important to learn about your own pain threshold and when and how you have to act to protect yourself.'

This was the most bizarre conversation to be having with a fifteen-year-old boy, but Josh continued undaunted.

'Being at St George's is spoiling the pattern,' he said firmly.

'And that's why you and your dad are looking at alternatives.'

Josh nodded.

'And having ADD is part of the pattern,' he continued. 'But I write my best stuff when I can't focus on other things, so I guess that's part of the pattern too, and the pain is worth the good bit.'

I smiled in agreement.

'I find it helpful to think of it in that way. It puts things into perspective, if that's not too much of a cliché.'

'No, it's not,' Josh said. 'You're not a cliché kind of person.'

I took that as a compliment, and it made me smile all the way back to Clapham Junction, as Josh closed his eyes and drifted off peacefully.

CHAPTER 39

I wasn't surprised to find Andy up and about when we let ourselves into the flat soon after midnight. He was stony faced and I knew my voicemail hadn't gone down well. I'd kept it brief, attempting to convey the impression that arriving home with Josh was utterly normal. To do him justice, he was courteous to Josh, asking after his day, and showing him his room, the bed turned down neatly, and the side lamp switched on. It wasn't until Josh had closeted himself behind the bedroom door that Andy confronted me coldly.

'What the hell is this all about?'

'Josh came down to the show with Ben today, but the hotel couldn't accommodate him with Gemma and the other boys, so we worked out that the best option was for him to come back with me.'

I was pleased that this not implausible and entirely true version of events tripped off my tongue so easily. Its main advantage was that Gerry's name wasn't included, but Andy soon filled that particular gap.

'And I take it that Gerry knows about this arrangement?'

'Of course. He had to know where his son would be.'

Andy was silent, so I forged ahead.

'We had a wonderful last night. It was a shame you couldn't come.' I hoped I sounded convincing.

'Oh, yes?' Andy sounded disbelieving, with reason. 'Quite convenient, I would have thought. You could spend all your time with Gerry's kids rather than have to keep me company. The rest of the cast probably think Gerry's your husband.'

'Don't be ridiculous,' I snapped, using my anger to cover the wave of sadness that washed over me. Despite my own longings, Andy's pain hurt me, and I was frightened of where all this was leading. We were both silent now.

'Did you have a good rehearsal today?' I asked.

Andy's own opening night was a mere five days hence.

'Yes,' he said grudgingly. 'We think we've got a hit. Do you plan to be in attendance on Monday, or will your new family be needing you for anything?'

I gripped the edge of the kitchen counter.

'Of course I'll be there. I wouldn't miss it for the world.'

'Well, I wouldn't want to inconvenience you, would I?' he replied sarcastically, stalking out of the kitchen.

I moved to follow him, but thought better of it. I didn't want to disturb Josh, so I stayed in the kitchen for a little longer before venturing into the bedroom. Andy was already in bed; the covers pulled firmly over his shoulders and his back to me. I spent as long as I could getting ready, hoping that Andy would fall asleep and no further conversation would be possible. It didn't work.

'How's he getting home tomorrow?' he asked as I climbed into bed.

'He'll get the train himself. He is fifteen.'

Andy grunted and said no more.

I switched off the light, and nestled down, every nerve and muscle taut as wire fencing. I waited for his next move, but it didn't come, and eventually I heard the heavy breathing that indicated he was finally asleep. I began to relax and let my mind wander over the day's events. How satisfying and deeply happy they had been. I sighed with pleasure, but with sadness too. At thirty-eight years old I had found the family I had never known I wanted, and the man with whom I longed to share them. What awful, hopeless timing. But when I tried to think of a better time to have met Gerry, I couldn't. If I'd met him before he was married, I'd have been too young for him to have been interested in me, and once I'd reached a realistic age, he already had a family. How cruel fate was, that I should meet him now, when the age gap was no longer important but still we could not be together. I thought of my conversation with Josh earlier on the train. What would I prefer? Not to have met him at all? I knew the answer to that without giving it another thought. Gerry was part of the rich pattern of my life, and I would no more unpluck its threads, despite their painful colouring, than I would those that had brought me nothing but joy. And for now, it was enough to know that Josh slept in the bedroom next door, secure, I hoped, in the knowledge that he'd spent the day receiving unconditional love and friendship, and had given back so richly.

All my tomorrows would just have to look after themselves.

I left Josh to sleep late in the morning and didn't stir him with tea until after Andy had left. To my relief, our parting had not been acrimonious. Andy seemed to have recovered overnight, and it wasn't until he was going out of the door that he looked at me intently.

'You're not out today, are you?'

I shook my head.

'Do you want to come down to the theatre later, see a bit of the rehearsal, go for a drink afterwards with some of the crew, perhaps?'

I suspected that this was a test, and I didn't feel up to scoring a failing grade today.

'Sure,' I smiled. 'How about I drop down about 4 o'clock?'

A shadow seemed to lift from Andy's eyes, and I felt awful.

'Great, see you then.'

Josh was clearly not a morning person. He rose slowly, not inclined to chat. I left him to leaf quietly through my bookshelves as he drank tea and ate a pastry. I made the beds, sorted some laundry, and passed a duster not too assiduously around the place. At 10 o'clock I suggested we ring Gerry to let him know Josh was in one piece. He sounded gratifyingly pleased to hear from me and joy welled in my heart as we spoke happily.

'Shall I despatch him to you directly?' I asked.

'When he's ready, there's no hurry. Just check he's got his front door key.'

'Okay. I'm not going out till this afternoon, so he can stay as long as he likes. Where shall I meet you tomorrow?' I asked. 'At DCP or elsewhere? South Kensington tube?' I suggested.

'Oh, God, yes, we've got that tomorrow haven't we?' Gerry sounded suddenly tired.

'It'll be fine. There's no obligation to buy the product,' I joked.

'No, except that Josh has set his heart on it now. Ah, well, see you at 11 o'clock at the station.'

Josh sauntered off at about 11.30.

'I like staying here,' he commented as he left. 'Thanks.'

'You're welcome anytime, Josh.'

'I don't think your husband was too impressed.'

Josh was clearly even more perceptive than I'd given him credit for.

'Don't worry about him,' I laughed. I felt a pang of disloyalty, but squashed it quickly. 'You and Ben and your dad are my friends,' I said quietly. 'There's never any problem if I can help you out.'

Josh nodded shortly.

'See you tomorrow then.'

I would have liked to hug him, but contented myself with a pat on the shoulder.

'See you.'

And he was gone.

CHAPTER 40

I watched Gerry and Josh approach the tube station for a good while before they saw me waiting. They walked together down the Old Brompton Road, moving easily in long strides, Gerry talking animatedly to a silent Josh. Josh was in his usual garb: black jeans, black tee shirt, and black jacket. He'd slicked his jet black hair with gel and it gleamed wetly. Inevitably, Gerry was less coordinated: saggy dark blue blazer, pale olive trousers, crumpled and worn, white shirt, red tie. It didn't bear close examination, but I braced myself, and gazed at him with love. How does he do it? I wondered. What's his secret? On a scale of one to ten in the glamour, sophistication, and drop-dead gorgeous stakes, Gerry would score about three on a good day, but nevertheless, he exuded charisma and sexual magnetism from every pore. The sad fact was, of course, that I wasn't the only one who was susceptible to it. I shivered involuntarily. I longed to be in his bed again – or indeed anywhere that gave me exclusive possession of Gerry's body and attention for several hours.

Josh smiled shyly as they drew level with me, and I beamed at them both. Gerry bounced up and down on the balls of his feet and waved his hands around meaninglessly.

'Let's go and get this over with,' he said. 'If I'm to pay two sets of school fees this term, I might as well start getting used to it.'

I winked conspiratorially at Josh, who grinned back sweetly. There were just too many cute guys in my life at the moment.

I wasn't entirely sure what I was doing there with Gerry and Josh, except perhaps to lend moral support, I guessed. But it was fun to introduce them to my former colleague, Leanne, and to wait with her whilst they trooped off to chat with Sara Grayson.

'What's your connection with these chaps?' she asked.

I tried to look mysterious and fascinating and Leanne raised her eyebrows.

'He's a bit scrawny, isn't he?' she asked incredulously. 'And he hasn't got much hair. Now, the lad, that's another matter altogether! Is he a model?'

'Good heavens, no!' I laughed. 'Josh would despise anything so commercial.'

'I bet he wouldn't mind the money,' she retorted. 'But honestly, Madison, is his dad, your, whatever…' she finished lamely.

'"Whatever" describes our relationship very well,' I concurred. 'Whatever he feels like today, and I just go along with it.'

'That doesn't sound too satisfactory,' Leanne replied, 'but I guess I'm not the one to judge.'

We moved on to college gossip and I enjoyed being part of another, familiar, world for a while. When Sara Grayson reappeared with Josh and Gerry in tow, the smile on Josh's face said it all, and even Gerry had lost his nervous rabbit look. I hung back as they said their farewells and waited till we'd settled in the café next door for them to tell me what they thought.

'Dad, I want to go there.' Josh spoke quietly, but firmly. 'I won't go back to St George's. I just can't.'

'Okay,' said Gerry simply. 'I think I've got the message.'

'But you did like it, too, didn't you?' Josh was anxious for his father's approval.

'Yes, I did,' he nodded. 'It looks right for you, and that's the important thing.'

We talked about subject choices and travelling, the daily routine, and so on, until Josh got restless.

'Dad, can I go to the Victoria and Albert Museum?' he asked Gerry.

'Let's get this registration form filled in first,' Gerry answered, 'drop it back to the college, and then you go off wherever you want. Madison and I have got things to do ourselves, so we'll probably go back home for a while before I have to go out again.'

That sounded promising, I thought, managing not to look too keen. So I watched Gerry fill in the form, and waited outside DCP whilst they took it in. Gerry gave Josh some money, and he meandered off towards Exhibition Road, and finally we were alone. Gerry took my shoulders and turned me to face him.

'You are completely wonderful to us,' he said quietly. 'Thank you. I do know how lucky we are.'

My eyes filled with tears and I buried my face in his chest. He stroked my hair and kissed the top of my head.

'I don't know what I've done to deserve you,' he said.

'Being gorgeous and lovely.' My voice was muffled in his jacket.

'If you say so. Actually, I think I'd like to take all your clothes off, and make love to you several times,' he added matter of factly.

'Hmm, yes, please.'

He grinned and kissed me in a businesslike fashion.

'Come on, then, beautiful. Let's not waste precious time.'

I cried in Gerry's arms as we lay in bed that afternoon. He stroked my hair and shoulders, kissing me and wiping away my tears with gentle hands.

'Darling Madison, please don't cry. Am I so awful to you?'

I shook my head.

'No, you're lovely,' I sobbed. 'That's why I'm crying. I love you so much; I can't bear to leave you. I don't want to go home.'

I sounded pathetic even to my own ears. Gerry said nothing, but sighed deeply and held me closer to him, kissing my neck softly. I entwined my legs tighter around him, pressing as close to his slender body as I could. We stayed like that for a while. I knew there was nothing Gerry could say to make it any easier for me. He'd made his position clear enough: if I was prepared to accept a part-time relationship, he could offer me that; if I didn't like it, I knew what I could do. I also knew that I couldn't bore him with tears every time we met. I lifted my head and smiled at him. He looked sad and concerned.

'I don't want you to be unhappy,' he said.

'I'm not,' I reassured him.

I kissed him slowly, hoping he would respond, and be diverted from my tears. He was. I willed myself not to cry as I pulled him on top of me and felt the sweet heaviness of his body. I lost myself in the pleasure of loving him, and for a man who couldn't say he loved me, he nevertheless put up very little resistance.

On the day of Andy's opening I received a card from Josh with the morning mail.

Dear Madison, I read

Thanks for your help with Doddington, et cetera. I'm looking forward to going there.

I hope you are happy. See you soon.

Josh

What's that? Andy asked.

If I'd guessed what was in the small white envelope I'd have hidden it away and opened it later, but now it was too late.

'Just a note from Josh McFall,' I told him casually.

Andy picked it up and read it over. He looked up in surprise.

'He's going to DCP?'

I nodded briefly.

'Yes. He wasn't happy at his school.'

'So you just happened to get it all fixed for him.'

'Please, Andy, don't make a big deal out of nothing. I was able to help, so I did, simple as that.' I looked at the clock. 'Shouldn't you be getting underway?'

I hoped that Andy would be prepared to let the matter drop in favour of his own concerns.

'You'll be at the theatre tonight, won't you?' he asked.

'Of course.'

Andy turned away reluctantly, and began getting his things together.

'At least you won't be flogging down to Sussex with them any longer. You might have to see that bloody Gerry for *Tito*, but I can't see any reason for you to spend time with the boys.'

I shrugged silently.

'Well?' he persisted. 'Is there?'

'I don't know, Andy.' I tried to sound matter of fact.

He slammed his hand down hard on the kitchen table.

'Madison, what's with you and these people? Ben isn't in *Tito,* is he?'

'Of course not. Don't be ridiculous.'

'So there's no reason for me to expect to find him here, is there? Or his brother? Or for you to take them anywhere?'

'Andy, they're my friends.'

'Friends! You're obsessed with them, and it's been going on for months. I've had enough, Madison.'

'Of what? What possible harm can it do? They're great kids.'

'They're Gerry's kids, that's the harm it does. If you never see him again it'll be too soon for me.'

'Well, that's simply not going to happen. We work together.'

'That's just the tip of the iceberg, Madison, and you know it. Don't tell me it's normal for a singer to be so heavily involved

220

with a conductor and his family. You can't kid me that all you have is a professional relationship. I didn't see you getting that much involved with Colin Davis at Glyndebourne.'

Andy was furious now.

'Don't be silly,' I responded. 'It's an entirely different set-up altogether.'

'And isn't that the truth.'

'You know what I mean, Andy. Please can we just drop this pointless conversation? Today is far too important to spend quarrelling.'

I tried to sound calm, though my heart was racing, and Andy looked distinctly unprepared to let it go. Reaching over to take Josh's card from my hand he tore it briskly in half, dropping the pieces curtly into the bin.

'If they're nothing special to you, then you won't be keeping this, will you?'

I tried not to wince, and just stared at Andy's back as he stalked down the hall. I said no more until he was leaving.

'See you later, then.'

'Fine,' he said brusquely.

'Andy, please don't be like this.'

The fight seemed to drain from him. He needed this even less than I did today. He nodded in acknowledgement of a truce, reaching out a hand, then drawing it back immediately.

'Bye.'

I buried my face in my hands as he closed the door, feeling drained and sick. What was happening to me? Just two years ago I would never have envisaged allowing this emotional drama to unfold. But two years ago I hadn't met Gerry. Now I dreaded the coming evening but, gathering my strength, I began to review my wardrobe. One way or other, a special effort was needed. But first, I rescued the fragments of Josh's card from the bin, and hid them away with my precious photos and letters.

CHAPTER 41

The atmosphere was electric at The Restless Dragon, and Joe Budzynski was happy as a clam, delighted to see such a large audience, and anticipating healthy box office receipts for the forthcoming run. Andy was excited and glowing, this morning's scene forgotten as he basked in Joe's approval.

'The lovely Madison,' beamed Joe in his heavily accented English. 'Such a radiant beauty as you only serves to enhance an already perfect night. This boy, he has done very, very, good, don't you think?' He patted Andy paternally on the arm; although he was barely fifty-five, his manner was always that of the patriarch. 'He has done very good indeed, with the writing, the directing, yes, all good. He may have a future with us, indeed.'

I smiled encouragingly. Any success for Andy could only be a good thing. Joe nodded enthusiastically.

'He is, of course, you would know, a little stubborn, pig-headed, you may say, but he has talent, and Joe Budzynski knows how to stretch it.'

He beamed again, flourishing his arms extravagantly as he turned to introduce Andy to one of the theatre's sponsors.

I looked around at the gathered throng. They were hardly the sophisticated Glyndebourne crowd I had observed over the summer, but they were just as enthusiastic. In this small south London venue, an evening was about to unfold that was as important to them as any opera performance in the lovely Sussex house.

Danielle sidled up to me as Joe led Andy away to meet more human chequebooks.

'Exciting, isn't it, Mads?' She clearly found it so, her eyes sparkling with pleasure. This was a big night for her and Steve, too. I couldn't muster up quite her enthusiasm but I gave it my best shot.

'It's great. All these people here to see Steve in Andy's play! What a double act!'

'What if it transfers, Mads?' she burbled. 'If it goes to the West End!'

'They'll be too good to speak to us then,' I laughed.

'To me, possibly, but you're grander than any of us,' she said.

'Oh, Dani, don't say that, it makes me sound awful.'

Danielle linked her arm into mine as we trundled off to find our seats and I pondered over what she'd said. I had always thought I wouldn't be changed by whatever success came by me and, essentially, I was sure this was true. But I did feel remote from those who I'd loved so long before I'd even met Gerry. My thoughts were so often far away, occupying a sweet, but painful, world which revolved around Gerry and his boys. I could see my remoteness appearing as an arrogant, I'm-beyond-all-this separateness. But perhaps I was reading too much into Dani's casual remark, for she was as friendly as ever, and her enjoyment was infectious. By the time Andy had settled himself into the adjacent seat, I was feeling more connected, and Danielle and Andy generated so much nervous tension it was impossible not to become part of it.

The play *was* good, excellent even, although for Andy, Joe, and Ron, the director, it would be the reaction of the critics and the box office response which would ultimately declare *Lethal Desires* a success or failure. We didn't dare celebrate during the interval, though we kept our ears open for audience comments. While Joe, Andy and Ron worked the sponsors again, Danielle and I could fade into the background and eavesdrop.

So far, so good. Steve's powerful acting as the menacing Mort Williams was capturing people's imagination, and we heard encouraging remarks about strong dialogue, atmospheric direction and gripping plot. By curtain down, it looked as if The Restless Dragon had another success on its hands. At the after show party Andy clung to my side, introducing me to crew and cast I hadn't yet met, repeatedly asking me what I had thought of this and that, actors, set, lighting, refinements to the script which had taken place during the last stages of production.

'Andy, it's marvellous,' I urged him sincerely. 'It's a wonderful play, wonderfully produced, and wonderfully acted. Well done.'

He looked at me, the pain in his eyes showing through the excitement.

'Your opinion matters more than anyone else's, Madsy,' he said seriously. 'I'm glad you're here today. It wouldn't be the same without you.'

'Of course I'm here. I wouldn't miss it for the world,' I responded cheerfully, hoping Andy wouldn't get maudlin. I was glad when Ron accosted Andy with yet another congratulatory handshake.

'We've got a hit, Madison. Tom Woodward is talking to Joe even now.'

Tom Woodward was in charge of scheduling for a chain of important regional theatres. It was a good sign.

'Well done, Ron,' I said. 'This is a marvellous night.'

I found Danielle again before we were due to leave.

'Ron says there's a possibility of regionals already,' I whispered.

'Oh, Madsy, how cool!' she gushed. 'But are you okay? You've been a bit subdued tonight.'

I nodded, sad that I couldn't share fully in the joy of the evening with everyone.

'I'm fine, Dani, just a bit tired at the end of the *Flute* run, I think. It's all rather an anticlimax now.' I realised how very self-centred that sounded; Andy's success tonight should outweigh any malaise I felt now that *Flute* was over. I tried to salvage things. 'But this is more than worth it.'

Danielle didn't look too convinced, but I changed the subject, hoping to dispel her doubts. I was feeling increasingly fraudulent and wondered if I really liked the person I was becoming. I didn't think I did, but I was powerless to change it. Gerry had me in his power now, and there was not a single thing I could do about it.

CHAPTER 42

I sat in Gerry's music room several days later, describing the opening of *Lethal Desires* and the rapturous reviews that had been in several important dailies, as well as the trade press.

He listened carefully, looking serious and interested.

'I expect Andy's chuffed to bits then,' he said.

'Oh, yes. He's like a kid with a new toy, only now the play's opened there's nothing much for him to do. Joe Budzynski wants him to do some more work at the Dragon but I don't know when that will be. If *Lethal Desires* gets a regional tour, then Andy will go with them, but that won't be till next year anyway.'

'Hmm.'

I wasn't sure what that meant, but I was getting used to Gerry's inscrutable comments and wry observations and tried not to analyse them too closely.

'Darling?'

'Madison?'

I plucked at the ancient braid around the piano stool whilst Gerry tapped at the computer keyboard.

'I can come to *Boheme* this week, can't I?'

'Yes, of course.' Gerry looked surprised that I asked.

'When's Ben going?'

'Saturday, I think.'

'I'll go then in that case,' I said, pleased.

Gerry murmured inarticulately and shifted awkwardly.

'Is that not convenient?' I asked warily.

'Hmm, not really. Come on Tuesday. I'll get you a seat with some of the VIPs.'

'No disrespect to them, Gerry, but I'd rather be with Ben,' I objected mildly, sensing that I was about to venture in to rather deeper waters than I cared for, but unable to stop.

'It's better if you come on Tuesday,' Gerry said more firmly.

I sighed. I knew what the inconvenience was. Bloody Vanessa would be going on Saturday, Ben in tow, openly with Gerry, acknowledged as his publicly acceptable companion. And I doubted he would be going home alone after the excitement of a Saturday night show.

'Fine,' I said abruptly. 'Leave me a ticket at the box office, then. You won't have to speak to me afterwards. I'll leave quietly. No one will even know I'm there.'

'Madison, please.' Gerry hunched his shoulders over the keyboard as if in pain. 'I don't know what to say when you're like this.'

'Like what? I'm not like anything. I just said, leave me a ticket, okay?' I was close to tears now, cross with myself for precipitating this conversation. 'Actually, leave me two. I'll ask Annie to come with me.'

I thought how Annie would lecture me for my continuing involvement in this fiasco and I choked back my tears. I got up from the piano stool and Gerry turned round to look at me, his face contorted with confusion.

'I'm really trying, Madison.'

'You certainly are, Gerry,' I agreed. 'Don't bother to see me out.'

He was probably still rooted in his computer chair as I banged the front door behind me and began trudging tearfully down the drive. I was just about to turn into the main road, heading for West Dulwich, when I heard feet hurrying behind me. Gerry grabbed my arm bringing me to a halt. I let him turn my shoulders to face me.

'Please don't walk out on me,' he said.

'Why not, Gerry? You've made it quite clear that my presence is acceptable only when convenient to you. It's not actually very convenient for me to be here at the moment, so I'm going home.'

'But we were going to do some singing.'

'I don't really feel like it today. Sorry.'

To my horror, my resolve failed me and I burst into tears. Gerry's arms were round me straight away.

'Madison, I'm sorry,' he murmured against my hair. 'I'm such a clumsy oaf. I can't change things now. It's all arranged for Saturday.'

'Then unarrange it,' I wept.

'I can't.'

'Why not?'

'I just can't. It's just... Well, I just can't. Please try to understand.'

'All I understand is that I love you so much and you don't love me,' I cried into the front of his shirt.

'It's not as simple as that.'

'Oh, Gerry, for goodness sake, of course it's as simple as that. You either love me, or you don't; you either want me to be with you, or not.'

'I do want you to be with me.'

We stared at one another. It was clearly the best he could offer me and I had to choose – again – whether to take it or leave it. I took it, resolving to at least try not to stage another prima donna scene like this again. I put my arms around Gerry's neck, kissing him softly.

'Good,' I said, and we laughed, at ease again. 'I'm sorry to pull a diva fit on you.'

'I'm sorry to upset you. I really don't want to do that, but I seem to be very good at it,' he said meekly.

I held him close.

'You're wonderful to me.'

'I know I'm not, but I'd really rather you didn't go away.'

'I'm not going to,' I whispered. 'I was only calling your bluff. And it worked.'

Gerry slapped my rump in mock rebuke. 'Come on, you she-devil, shall we go inside and sing?'

He kept his arm round me as we walked slowly back to his house. I leaned against Gerry's shoulder and thought about what he'd said. He wanted me to be with him, on his terms and when he chose, maybe, but it would do for now.

I rang Annie and told her about *Bohème*, though not about Vanessa. I couldn't admit that even to Annie; it was too humiliating.

'Please come with me, Annie. I'll feel horribly vulnerable on my own.'

'Of course I'll come, but he shouldn't make you feel that way, Madsy. If you're good enough for him to sleep with, you're good enough for him to make a bit of fuss of at his poxy opera.'

'Oh, Annie, it's not that simple,' I said sadly, smiling wryly at the irony as I echoed Gerry's own words.

'It seems pretty simple to me,' she retorted sharply, 'except for the fact that you're married. But somehow, I don't think that's what holds Gerry back.'

'Annie, just come with me, there's a dear, and give me the lecture afterwards.'

After all the fuss, the Tuesday was the best night for me to see *Bohème*. Two performances the previous week – including the infamous Saturday – had bedded the production down, and both orchestra and singers were at ease with stage and score. Even better, Andy was at The Restless Dragon, serving one of his shifts as assistant director on duty. Whilst he didn't look exactly thrilled when I told him where I was going, he was mollified by Annie's appearance.

'I see I'm serving as an alibi, too,' she complained in the car.

'I'm sorry,' I said humbly.

'Darling, I'm only joking,' she laughed. 'I may not approve of your liaison with the conductor from hell, but I'm starting to learn that somehow, amidst all that pain, he nevertheless makes you happy. Have you thought of joining Masochists R Us?'

'Thanks Annie. I'm really glad you're here!'

'Just make sure I know what the signal's going to be for me to scram and let you and himself do whatever you do.'

'I'm not going home with him, Annie, I've got no reason to stay out, and it's too late to invent one. Anyway, I wouldn't dump you like an unwanted wallflower.'

'That's my role in life,' she cracked, as we parked close to the theatre.

Poor Annie was patience itself as I sobbed through *Boheme*. Gerry looked beautiful in his tails, and I drank in the sight of him as the music washed over me. I ran out of handkerchiefs before the final curtain, and Annie rummaged in her bag for tissues.

'Don't get any ideas now,' she whispered. 'Dying of TB is not the best way to get a guy to commit. Rudolpho's just a wimp who's only prepared to go the distance when he's sure that Mimi won't be around much longer.'

I bit my lip to stop laugher escaping in an undignified gulp, and I was glad when the first ripples of applause offered a hiding place for our mirth.

'Annie, you are good for me,' I chuckled. 'God, I must look a mess.'

'Fetchingly dishevelled,' Annie declared. 'Now, what do you want me to do, honey? I honestly don't mind making myself scarce.'

'Come backstage and let's take it from there. Sorry to involve you in these machinations.'

'I'm fascinated,' she said as we moved through the crowds, 'I could write a book after observing you.'

I punched her lightly, grateful for her humorous take on what was otherwise unremittingly traumatic.

Gerry was holding court backstage and I hung back, waiting for him to notice us. Annie, with nothing to lose, headed straight for him.

'Hi, Gerry.'

'Annie-Annio, hello there.'

Gerry looked over her head, his eyes searching me out.

'Madison,' he said with a twinkle.

'It was lovely,' I greeted him quietly, happy to see his smile widen just for me.

I stood by whilst Annie engaged him in banter for a while, before turning to me and saying remarkably naturally, 'I'd better be going, Madsy. Are you okay for getting home?'

I was afraid that Gerry might miss his cue but, bless him, he didn't. He was working hard to make up for his previous gaffes.

'I'll take you home,' he said quickly. 'We can get a coffee first, if you like.'

Annie patted my arm.

'See you at rehearsal.'

She winked as she left, and I thought again what a good friend she was. Even whilst she believed I was treading a disastrous path, she was still unswervingly loyal.

We toyed over coffee and dessert in an Italian restaurant near the theatre. Gerry was on a high, even more infinitely pleased with himself than usual. I thought of what Megan would say seeing him now, so thrilled with what he'd done: 'That man is far too flamboyant for my liking. No woman should be taken in by him.'

Well, maybe she was right, but I loved him fit to burst as I sat back and let him talk. Eventually, he paused and smiled at me.

'Are you all right?' He took my hand in his long fingers.

I nodded. 'I wish we could go to bed now.'

'Can you come home with me?'

'Not really. I didn't set up any reason to stay out.'

'Can you say you've gone to Annie's?'

'I don't think it would sound very convincing.'

Gerry shrugged his shoulders. I couldn't bear it.

'Gerry, Andy is away next week. He and Joe are going to Southampton about transferring the play. Can I stay then? Or you come to me?'

'That sounds worth waiting for,' he grinned, and I breathed again. 'Perhaps we could do something with the boys too,' he continued, 'if you're going to be free.'

'I'd love that.' I stroked his palm gently. 'You know I want to be with you guys,' I added, feeling fresh tears closing my throat.

'Good.'

I looked at Gerry under my lashes. He was smiling with such tenderness it caught my breath.

'I love you.' I wished I could stop myself from saying it so often.

'I know,' he whispered, but he spoke the words more gently than usual, kissing my hand, and holding on to it as we left the table.

We hugged each other and kissed for a long time in the car before I reluctantly dragged myself away.

'Madison, it's time to go home,' Gerry said with his more customary firmness. 'I'll see you at rehearsal on Thursday, and we can talk about next week.'

I nodded against his shoulder.

'Umm. Okay.'

I left very slowly and as Gerry drove away I thought that perhaps something almost imperceptible might have changed, but I didn't dare think about it too hard.

CHAPTER 43

Rehearsing *Tito* was bliss. Whilst the venues we would be playing may not have the prestige of Glyndebourne or even the Coli, it was of no account when I had the finest mezzo role Mozart wrote. Not everyone would agree with that. It is arguable that Sesto is a soprano role, and that indeed Mozart wrote none of his female roles for what we now call a mezzo, but either for *musicos* (male sopranos) or tenors, or that indeed he made little distinction between sopranos and mezzos at all. Thus, Cherubino, Dorabella, or Sesto could be sung by either a soprano or a mezzo, but certainly by a singer who can bring warmth and depth to the musical line. It was an interesting debate. When I sang Zerlina in the *Don*, we had considered at some length whether it should be sung by a mezzo, as so many interpretations of the role used a light lyric soprano. Now I was keen to sing Elvira and therein lay another debate!

But what I knew beyond doubt was that Sesto was a role I was born to sing! Vocally and dramatically, I was in heaven. Annie was a fine tomboyish Annio and every one of our colleagues were beautiful singers and happy folk to work with. It was the first opera that I had sung with Gerry since six months earlier I had come to the life changing realisation that I loved him, and I wondered briefly whether our radically altered personal relationship would affect our musical one. I was delighted to find it had altered not a jot. As soon as we were in the rehearsal room, I was focussed and alert, able to separate my turbulent emotions from the hard work we were engaged in. I could still look at Gerry with pleasure, feeling a thrill of desire as I thought how later that day his beautiful hands, now working at the piano, or raised to conduct a tricky passage, would be touching me, but as soon as I sang I could lay it aside and concentrate on the music. Production rehearsals were just beginning and we all enjoyed analysing our roles, exploring the tensions between the characters who felt so passionately about love, honour, and betrayal.

And Gerry was wonderful to me. Something subtle had happened the night I had seen *Boheme*, so subtle I couldn't identify how it had occurred, but Gerry was softer with me. He reached for my hand more easily, not simply in response to my own touch. When he took me home, he lingered longer in the car, talking companionably, relaxed and gentle. My heart was light in those first weeks of September. There were still days when I didn't see Gerry, or even hear his voice on the phone, and I knew that on some of these days at least he must be seeing Vanessa, but his obvious affection made it easier to bear.

When Andy and Joe went to Southampton for an overnight recognisance trip, Gerry decided that Josh – actually admitting to having enjoyed his first few days at DCP – was responsible enough to keep an eye on Ben overnight, and he stayed with me, in my home and in my bed. We dined leisurely, and drank a bottle of rich dark Shiraz, curled up on the settee with the lights low. With no clock to watch or teenagers to listen out for, we kissed luxuriously, holding and touching one another until Gerry took my hand and led me to the bed I had made up for us in my music room. We made love till late into the night, sleeping only to wake as early light filtered through the curtains and to make love again. I was so weak with bliss I could barely stand.

'Umm. You're gorgeous,' he murmured, kissing me. 'Every time I finish making love to you, I want to start all over again.'

He stroked my full breasts tantalisingly. I groaned softly, and caught his lower lip gently between my teeth, exploring his tongue with mine.

'Dr Brylmer, you are far too sexy for your own good. One day I might just have to take all your clothes off in rehearsal, right in front of everyone else.'

I giggled and we were silent as Gerry buried his face in my hair and we held each other for a while.

'You make me so very happy,' I murmured eventually. 'The happiest times of my life are those I share with you.'

'I'm glad,' he said kindly.

'Are you?' I asked him tentatively.

'Of course. I don't want you to be sad when you're with me, do I? Or any other time for that matter.'

'As long as you're happy, too,' I dared, venturing onto dangerous territory.

'Haven't I just proved that?'

'I don't just mean…' I petered out feebly.

'I know what you mean,' he said, 'and, yes, you do make me happy. You are wonderful in every way.'

I smiled to myself, knowing that even though he could not tell me he loved me, Gerry had revealed more than was usually the case.

'Mr McFall, I am so in love with you,' I said as his gentle hands explored the contours of my stomach and thighs.

'I know,' he drawled, 'and I intend to take full advantage of it.'

'Gerry!'

'Are you complaining?' he asked, manoeuvring me on top of him.

'Well…'

'I thought not,' he chuckled, and it was some considerable time before we contemplated getting out of bed again.

As Gerry had suggested, I joined with him and the boys and we went indoor bowling in Streatham the night Andy was due home. I hasten to add it was not my choice of venues, but I was keen to learn! Gerry's family were clearly going to introduce me to a whole new way of life. Josh considered it beneath him to participate in such an uncool activity, but he chatted to me quite animatedly about DCP as we drank tea.

'I've got a brilliant English teacher,' he said with pleasure. 'He says I can do poetry for coursework. And the drama's great too, and art. We can do ceramics as well as painting. Some things are a bit pointless though. I don't know why I have to do physics and geography. I want to give that up. It's such a stupid subject.'

'Which?' I laughed.

'Both of them,' he said with disgust.

'Are you getting there on time in the mornings?' I asked.

'Nearly.' Josh fluttered his dark eyelashes plaintively.

'Oh, Josh, they'll get really cross if you're late all the time.'

'They haven't done yet.'

'I'm glad you like most of it anyway. Is it better than St George's?'

'Oh, yes, definitely,' he said, nodding vigorously. 'I'll never really like school, but this is better than it was.'

Gerry caught Josh's words as he came into the kitchen.

'We owe you many thanks, Madison,' he said. 'If it wasn't for you, well, I certainly wouldn't have thought about an alternative to St George's. I know I wasn't very positive about it to begin with, but you were absolutely right.'

I glowed with pleasure.

'It's all about knowing the right people, Gerry,' I laughed.

He smiled broadly.

'I expect there'll be another potential disaster you can rescue us from soon. Josh, are you sure you don't want to come with us?'

Josh brooded darkly.

'Do you really want to be on your own again tonight?' Gerry continued.

'Come and keep me company, Josh,' I urged him. 'You know how hyperactive these two are. I need someone sane around me to redress the balance.'

Josh grinned.

'Okay,' he agreed, 'but I'm not doing any stupid bowling, I'll just watch and criticise.'

'Great,' Ben complained. 'When do you ever do anything else?'

They scuffled briefly as we left the house, and I caught Gerry's eye and smiled happily.

'I hope you know what you're letting yourself in for,' he sighed.

Much against his better judgement, Josh clearly enjoyed himself that night. When he saw how inept I was at tenpin bowling, he took pity on me and we formed a team against Gerry and Ben. We still lost hopelessly, but we managed to maintain an air of intellectual superiority which had us giggling as we sat down to burgers and cokes.

'I have to admit that a PhD isn't very helpful when it comes to sporting activities,' I laughed.

'You can be clever and be good at sports, too,' Ben declared.

'Well, we're not,' said Josh companionably, 'and it doesn't worry us, does it, Madison?'

'Absolutely not,' I agreed. 'We're just happy to be here with you, Ben.'

It warmed my heart to see Gerry smiling at us with a look of tender pleasure.

'Did Dad tell you I'm singing the Fauré *Requiem* in Chichester next month?' Ben asked me, not to be outdone.

'No, he didn't, darling.' I looked at Gerry accusingly. 'Why didn't you say before? That's great.'

'I probably thought I'd bored you with it already,' he said. 'It's going to be a bit awkward actually, which is a nuisance.

It's a *Bohème* night, so I can't be there. I haven't even thought about who's going to go with him. My parents will go to the concert, but they can't flog up to London first and take him to Chichester in the morning. I expect it'll get sorted out though.'

'When is it?' I asked.

'October 10th,' Ben piped up.

I made a rapid mental calculation.

'I might be able to go,' I said casually. 'As long as the trains back from Chichester run late enough.'

'Madison,' said Josh with disgust, 'surely you don't want to spend a whole day with the infant? Didn't you have enough of him during the summer?'

I ignored him whilst I looked questioningly at Gerry.

'That might be the solution,' he smiled. 'We'll talk about it later.'

Later was the next day, after rehearsal.

'Madison, I know we're taking advantage of you again, but if you are free on the 10th it would be such a relief if you could chaperone Ben.'

'I'd love to, Gerry,' I said with pleasure.

'It's always nice to know that he's with you,' he said.

'Good. I like being with him, you know that.'

'I'll cover your fares and things, obviously,' he added.

'Don't be silly.'

He stroked my cheek thoughtfully.

'I'm starting to wonder what we did before we met you.'

I leaned into his chest as he put his arms round me.

'Well, you don't have to do without me now, do you?' I said, trying not to sound too pleased about it.

I was worried about how happy I was. Things were going too well. But I needn't have done so because, of course, it didn't last.

CHAPTER 44

By the end of September, The Restless Dragon team knew that *Lethal Desires* had secured a regional tour for the forthcoming year. Theatres were being booked all over the south of England, not only in Southampton, but Oxford, Plymouth, Bournemouth, Canterbury, Brighton, and Hastings. The play would then work its way back up towards London, stopping at Guildford, Dartford, and Richmond. The possibility of a West End transfer was remote now, but Andy, Ron, and Joe were nevertheless delighted with the success of their first joint venture.

It wouldn't be an exaggeration to say it had transformed Andy's professional life. He was utterly wrapped up in The Restless Dragon and was already planning a new play with Budzynski, a true story based on the adventures of a Polish émigré, who was allegedly some distant relation of Joe's. *Lethal Desires* would run until the second week in October at The Dragon, and I hoped that Andy would not find its close too much of an anticlimax. He would be involved in the regional tour in the new year, but I knew how hard he would find the intervening months after such excitement. Every third night Andy did a tour of duty at the theatre as AD, and he would come home thrilled to bits, his pleasure almost entirely eliminating his suspicion of me. I knew that once *Lethal Desires* finished he would be more aware of my movements again, and would have time to think over the possible implications of my continuing professional involvement with Gerry, but for the time being I enjoyed my freedom.

On one of Andy's AD nights we had a late call on *Tito*. We didn't wrap until nearly eight, and unusually Gerry was persuaded by Tom, the director, to join some of the cast for a drink afterwards.

'What do you think?' Gerry asked me quietly. 'Do you want to go straight home?'

'I really don't mind; whatever you fancy.'

'Well, perhaps tonight, then, just for a quick one,' he said to Tom. 'But I mustn't be long. I've left Ben alone with Josh a bit too often lately. I think they're getting on each other's nerves.'

I was quiet whilst everyone else chatted and joked, sitting across the table from Gerry, trying not to watch him too closely. I loved studying him when he was holding court, always managing to make himself the centre of attention. I would have liked to sit close to him, to lean against his shoulder and stroke his hand, but since – thankfully – no one but Annie knew of our relationship, it was better to sit where such temptation could not overcome me.

At nine o'clock Gerry looked at his watch.

'I'd better make a move. Do you want to come now Madison, or stay here?'

I saw Annie smirk at Gerry's attempt to be subtle.

I rose from the table.

'See you guys tomorrow.'

'Darling, if you need me to stay with Ben some evenings when you're out, you only have to ask,' I said when we were settled in the car. 'If Josh needs a bit of space, or whatever.'

Gerry took my hand.

'It's very kind of you, but you do enough for us already.'

'I'm not keeping score, Gerry.'

'Ben is very much looking forward to your Chichester trip,' he continued. 'He seems to think you will let him get away with anything.'

'I can't see that there'll be much scope for anything more exciting than doing the job,' I laughed.

Gerry's reply was cut short by the ringing of his phone. He released my hand to make the connection, driving erratically with one hand on the wheel as he did so. The phone often rang while we were in the car, his voicemail service delivering the many messages which were left for him as he worked, or fellow musicians ringing him late at night, knowing that it was often the only time they could be sure of catching him. Often he would put the call on to the hands-free mode, and I would hear both sides of the conversation as we drove. This time I sensed something was untoward as soon as Gerry answered the call. Although I could only hear his responses – significantly, he didn't put the call on to the speaker – the tone of his voice sent my hackles rising.

'Gerry McFall... Hello.' Gerry's voice dropped and he sounded hushed and confidential.

'We've just finished... Just hitting the Edgware Road... Yes, it was fine....'

He looked as his watch.

'About an hour, I should think.... Yes, of course... *Of course*... Well, about ten o'clock... Is that all right?'

I wondered briefly if he was speaking to Josh or Ben, anxious to know when he would be home, but I knew that if he was he would have put the call on to the speaker.

'Umm... Yes... Madison's here... *Madison*...'

Gerry kept his eyes facing squarely ahead, sounding increasingly furtive.

'Yes... I would, yes...'

I knew as well as I knew my own name that he was speaking to Vanessa and I felt despair sweep over me. I began to shiver involuntarily as unbidden tears trickled down my cheeks. I was furious with myself, but incapable of stopping them. I turned my face towards the passenger side window, wiping my cheeks as the tears fell, but fresh ones immediately replaced them. I couldn't believe his brazen nerve! Gerry had told me he had to get home to see the boys, but he was clearly planning to drop in on Vanessa on the way there. And not for a quick coffee, I was sure. How many times had he done this after we'd been together? Did he go round to see her after we'd spent the afternoon in bed? I winced painfully at the prospect, too agonised now even to wipe away my tears. I just let them fall.

'I'll be there… *Yes*… No, not now…'

Gerry sounded tense.

'Umm… I love you… Okay… Bye for now.'

My heart felt as if it was being ripped out.

Gerry hung up in silence and I kept my tear-streaked face averted.

He drove for a while without saying anything, negotiating Park Lane with unnecessarily intense concentration. Eventually he sighed heavily.

'Madison.'

His voice was like a lead weight and it pulled me sharply out of my catatonia.

'Stop the car, please. Just stop right here. I want to get out.'

'Don't be silly, we're in the middle of a dual carriageway.'

'I really don't care. Just stop. *Stop!*' I was raging with fury and pain.

'I'm not abandoning you in the middle of London at night,' he objected wearily.

'I have lived here all my life. I can find my way home, and it's only twenty past nine, as you are well aware, since you have an *appointment* at ten o'clock,' I spoke with heavy sarcasm.

With another sigh, Gerry pulled turned into a side street and turned off the engine.

'Madison, I would really rather you didn't get out of the car. Please let me take you home.'

I put my face in my hands and sobbed.

'How could you do that?' I wailed.

'I'm sorry.' Gerry wrung his hands helplessly. 'What can I say?'

'You can tell me that I'm wrong in thinking that you've gone straight from being in bed with me to her.'

'Of course not!' Gerry sounded genuinely horrified, but I didn't trust him.

'Why the hell should I believe you? You've been caught out now, Gerry. All those times you've taken me home, kissed me, told me – in your favourite phrase – that I'm 'wonderful', and let me think that you were going back to the boys, and now I know where you were going. To bloody Vanessa.'

'Madison, please, this is not like you.'

'Of course it's not like me, is it? Sweet little Madison, who's a bit of a laugh and a real sucker when it comes to the kids, who's so goddamned in love with you that you can get away with anything as long as you're kind to her now and then.'

'That's not how I think of you, you must know that,' Gerry said pleadingly.

'Why should I know that? I thought we'd been having a really lovely time over the last month. I don't expect you to be there for me all the time, I certainly don't expect you to say you love me, but forgive me if it was all my imagination, you seemed to be enjoying it, too. Well, now it counts for precisely nothing, because I'm clearly not important enough for you to protect my feelings.'

'We have been having a nice time,' said Gerry sadly. 'I don't want it to stop, do you?'

'Of course I don't want it to stop. You're missing the point completely. You have just treated me and my very fragile feelings with the utmost disrespect. It's one thing not to be in love with me, but it's quite another to tell that cow that you love her in my hearing.'

'What could I do, she was pressing me to say it?' Gerry looked utterly helpless.

'You could have given her one of the amusing little brush off lines you give to me when I tell you that I love you. But the difference is, of course, that since you don't love me, it's rather easier to do so.'

'I obviously can't say anything right,' Gerry said crossly. 'I'm not going to talk to you when you're in this state.' He went to start the engine.

'So it's all my fault,' I complained childishly. 'Of course, why didn't I realise that?'

'Madsy,' he said more gently, 'when we talked in August, and we, well, started to see each other, you knew my limitations. You accepted it, and I know you want more, but I can't deceive you and pretend I can give you any more.'

'I did accept it, Gerry,' I sighed, wiping my eyes, 'but that was weeks ago now, and I'm starting to have real trouble working out why you can't give me more. I can't actually see anything physically or morally preventing you from doing so.'

'But even if I could, what about you?' he asked. 'You're married.'

'What's that got to do with it? It doesn't change how I feel about you.'

'But it has to be a consideration.'

I knew Gerry was right, but it didn't let him off the hook.

'It's my consideration, not yours, Gerry. You can't use it as an excuse for hurting me in the way you've done tonight. I may be the one who's married, but I never give you the slightest reason for you to doubt my commitment to you. If, of course, that's important to you anyway. Perhaps it's not.'

We were silent for a while. Then Gerry reached out for my hand; I let him take it.

'Can I take you home now?' he asked quietly.

I nodded, saddened beyond words.

'I'm really sorry, Madison.'

'At least I've made you late for her.'

'Look, I won't go, I'll ring her and tell her I have to get back to the boys.'

'Do whatever you like, Gerry.'

He held my hand all the way home, rubbing the ball of his thumb across my knuckles in the way he knew I liked. Even as I yearned to turn to him I held back, staring out of the side window as my thoughts raced. I had to confess to being surprised that Gerry took my outburst so stoically. If he wanted an excuse to be rid of me from his complicated personal life, I had given him a good one tonight. But evidently, for reasons best known to himself he wanted our relationship to continue and was prepared to make a concerted effort to smooth my fiercely ruffled feathers. And whilst I believed that he had acted hurtfully and thoughtlessly, he was right to remind me that I was, after all, married. He was not asking me to leave Andy, and somehow that made it unreasonable of me to ask him to jettison his relationship with Vanessa. I knew this was an over simplification but there was more than a grain of truth to it. I was as sure as I could be that if Gerry did ask me to leave Andy that I would do so, but he hadn't; until he did, I couldn't be truly certain of what I would do. Ultimately, the arrangement I had entered into with Gerry was the one that suited him, and if I didn't want to lose it, I had to accept it.

With a heavy heart, I moved my fingers to entwine them with Gerry's and I felt him relax. Whatever else he thought and felt, Gerry wanted to make peace. We smiled tentatively at each other.

'Are you all right?' he asked.

'I'll survive.'

'I'm sorry. I always get it wrong.'

'No, you don't. You get it right an awful lot of the time.' I paused. 'I'm sorry for shouting at you.'

'It's all right,' he smiled wanly. 'It was just a bit of a shock. I've never heard you so angry.'

245

'Madison, I really don't see you how you described. I think you're beautiful and kind and clever, and... well, as Ben would put it, totally awesome.'

Tears began to well up again as Gerry said this. It was lovely, but evidently still not enough for him, otherwise why would we be in this situation now? I made a weak joke of it.

'I should think so.' I squeezed his hand and moved closer towards him.

On the heath, Gerry pulled into a side road and turned in his seat to face me. I wiped my eyes again, feeling a wreck. We stared at each other in silence.

'Oh, Gerry,' I sighed eventually, 'what a mess.' He looked sad and I stroked his cheek gently. 'But I do love you.'

'I don't deserve it.'

I shifted in my seat again and he held out his arms to me. With enormous relief I let him hold me, stroking my back as he buried his face in my neck. As I raised my head I noticed with grim pleasure that it was already past ten o'clock. Let Vanessa sweat.

'See you tomorrow,' he said quietly.

'Yes.' I couldn't face leaving him just yet. 'Don't you want to kiss me?' I asked sadly.

'Oh, Madsy, of course I do.'

He kissed me very tenderly for a long time and inevitably I began to cry again. I knew I had to let Gerry go, wherever he was headed.

'Bye,' I said reluctantly, pulling away.

'Bye.' His voice was very low as I closed the door and walked towards Exeter House without looking back.

Sometime after two o'clock I must have slept, for I woke with a start when Andy stirred me,

'Mads, it's eight thirty. Hadn't you better get up? I thought you had a call.'

I felt ghastly, heavy lidded and sluggish.

'Yes, I have.' I buried my face in the pillow.

'I've made you some tea.' Andy indicated the mug beside the bed.

'Thank you.' The sight of it made me feel terribly sad.

'Are you okay?' he asked.

I nodded, keeping my eyes closed.

'I didn't sleep too well.'

'You were fast off when I got in,' he said.

I had, of course, been feigning.

'I woke up later and couldn't get off again,' I improvised. I opened my eyes again. 'But I'm awake now. Thank you.'

Andy studied me closely.

'See you in a minute then,' he said.

I nodded again and, once he'd closed the door, I let my tears fall. The prospect of the day ahead was horrendous, but I knew that once I'd struggled through it, I would start to feel better. There was a great deal to be said for having a strong constitution, and I was glad that mine was proving to be made of the toughest fibres.

CHAPTER 45

As only Gerry could, he managed to behave as if absolutely nothing had happened, and in my characteristic way, too, I let him do that. I didn't know whether he'd gone on to see Vanessa after we'd parted, how he'd explained his delay to her, or how he'd felt in the dark hours of the night about what had happened. I decided I didn't want to know. But he was gentle with me the next day, inviting me to go home with him after our rehearsal, chatting easily about his other projects as he drove. Once ensconced on his settee, eating toast and peanut butter, he kissed my hand, holding it tightly in his.

'How are you today?'

I gave him a wry smile. 'I'm okay. All the better for being here with you.'

'Good. Are you in a rush to get away?'

Andy was expecting me home for supper, but I didn't intend to lose a minute with Gerry that day.

'Everything's negotiable,' I teased.

'Darling Madison.' He stroked my hair and we exchanged peanut butter flavoured kisses. 'I want very much to take you to bed. Is that all right?'

'Gerry, you haven't needed to ask before, and you certainly don't have to start now.'

He looked humble.

I put down my plate and, standing up, held out my hand to him.

'Come and be seduced, Mr McFall.'

'Oh, Dr Brylmer, I love being dominated by a PhD with the voice of an angel.'

'Just as long as I'm the only one.'

We were convincingly reconciled that afternoon. Although I knew that at some point we had to make some serious decisions about the future, they could wait for now.

Two weeks before *Lethal Desires* closed at The Restless Dragon, Joe Budzynski called Andy in for a serious meeting. He hadn't told Andy what it was all about and I anticipated the worst. I expected that, as usual, Andy had managed to fall foul of the system and would be given his marching orders. I couldn't have been more wrong. Andy rang me on my mobile as I got off the train at Waterloo one lunchtime on my way to an afternoon rehearsal.

'Madsy,' he said with excitement, 'you'll never guess what's happened.'

The tone of his voice was reassuring. It could only be good news.

'What's up?'

'Joe Budzynski has offered me a permanent contract as assistant director at The Dragon. Not just for the *Lethal Desires* tour, but for all productions coming into the theatre.'

'No!' I laughed, 'You're having me on! How can they afford it?'

'They've got a new grant, and I'm the one he wants for the job.'

'Andy, that is just fantastic! What a result!'

Indeed, it changed things dramatically. A year ago, Andy was effectively financially dependent on what I earned, as he had been all through our marriage. Now he would be earning a regular salary, on top of the money he had already been paid for his work on *Lethal Desires*. It was a liberating prospect. Even before I'd met Gerry this was a development I had long hoped for, but now it took on a new dimension. If ever, remote though the possibility might be, I was to leave him for a life with Gerry, at least now he could support himself. Perhaps not in the style to which he was accustomed, but it was no longer all down to me, and I felt enormous relief.

Joe Budzynski would make Andy's appointment public at the last night party for *Lethal Desires*, but I told Gerry and Megan.

'That's good, isn't it?' said Gerry. 'Are you happy about it?'

'Overjoyed. It feels like an enormous burden has been lifted from my shoulders. Not just financially, but psychologically too. All he has to do now is keep the job.'

'He wouldn't blow a chance like this, surely?' Gerry asked.

'With Andy, anything's possible,' I said darkly.

'It's not your responsibility, Madsy. If it works, or if it doesn't, is down to Andy, not you.'

'I know,' I agreed, 'but it's hard to lay aside ten years of taking responsibility.'

Megan claimed to be pleased but characteristically managed to make it sound as if something deeply troubling had come about.

'Are you sure he'll be up to it, Madison?' she asked. 'That sounds like an enormous amount of responsibility. He'll have to work very hard.'

'Of course, Mum, he knows that.' I hated feeling defensive and wrong-footed yet again.

'You'll have to be there for him quite a lot, you know,' she warned. 'He needs you to support him in this.'

I took my courage in my hands.

'Mum, it's a professional job and if Andy's a professional he'll be able to do it. If not, he won't. I don't look for him to hold my hand while I pursue my career. I just get on with it.'

'And you're very different to Andy, Madison, as you know. I think it's very good for him; tell him I'm delighted, but I do worry about you both.'

'Then don't.'

I felt the burden of Megan's anxiety deeply. I would never be the perfect daughter she wanted, open and confiding, successful and yet putting family first, always offering a soft answer to even the most brutal criticism. And yet I knew I had never done anything concrete to warrant her censure. I had never been on drugs, been in prison, lost my job, failed an important exam, had a nervous breakdown – all things which to Megan were the sign of a life ruined and shamed, but neither had I had an illicit relationship and considered leaving my husband. Until now.

Despite everything, I looked forward to the party which would bring the curtain down on *Lethal Desires* in London. We could invite a number of our own guests, and I enjoyed drawing up a list: Sophie and Jim, Annie, Megan, Lizzie; Danielle would be there already as Steve's partner. I wondered if I could get away with asking Gerry, but I thought that might be pushing it.

Although the job didn't become official until the party night, Joe had Andy back working at The Dragon almost every day before the play closed. It meant again that I could see Gerry as often as he found time for me and I happily anticipated our *Tito* tour. Although Gerry usually liked to get home after a show, however late it was, when we were in Plymouth and Exeter, York and Birmingham, we had to stay overnight. The company manager had booked us all into hotels, putting Annie and I together. As MD, Gerry got a room to himself.

'Annie, will you mind if...?' I was deeply embarrassed by her knowing grin.

'Say no more, Madsy. I won't expect any midnight feasts with you, let's put it that way.'

And in the New Year, Andy would be away with *Lethal Desires*. Perhaps even without leaving my home and disrupting the lives of so many people, I could begin to carve out a more permanent role in Gerry's life – if that was what he wanted. I began to feel happier again as the memory of the Phone Call (definitely an upper case event) didn't go away, but at least faded. I loved Gerry, and ultimately I knew I that nothing he did would change that.

CHAPTER 46

Andy was not happy that I was chaperoning Ben to Chichester. I had tried to think up all kinds of alternative scenarios for my disappearance that day, but in the end I bit the bullet.

'I'm chaperoning next Friday for a concert in Chichester,' I said vaguely, 'so I'll be out early and back late. I'll be bright-eyed and bushy-tailed for the party on Saturday though.'

Foolishly, I hoped that Andy would not press me for details.

'Chaperoning? What do you mean? Who needs you to chaperone them?' I could see the suspicion in Andy's eyes. I wished I could substitute another name, Oli or Dusan from *Flute* perhaps, but I had to allow for the possibility that Andy might want to see the concert programme, or, in the way it does, that the truth would be revealed anyway. Better take the flack sooner rather than later.

'Ben McFall.'

'Oh, great! I thought it was a long time since I'd heard his name. I have noticed that Gerry doesn't get mentioned much these days, although you must be seeing him often enough at rehearsals. Gone off you, has he? Not such good friends these days?'

This was worse than I had anticipated.

'There's no one else to do it,' I said feebly.

'But why does that mean you have to go with him?' Andy stormed. 'It's nothing to do with you, surely? Or perhaps it is. How *is* your relationship with the First Family of music progressing, Madison?'

'Andy, it's not very helpful if you get angry. I've agreed to go and I can't let them down now. It's a done deal. I shall take my publicity to give to the conductor of the choral society down there, and there might be some useful work out of it in the future.'

This hadn't even occurred to me before, but I thought it sounded good. Not surprisingly, Andy wasn't convinced.

'Don't treat me as if I'm stupid, although I know you think I am. Just have fun, okay. I may expect to see you back home afterwards, or not, whatever you and Gerry decide.'

One day I knew that I would push Andy beyond the point of no return, but this wasn't it. As I rose early in the morning to collect Ben from home and take him to Chichester, Andy was quiet, but no longer angry.

'Have a nice day, then,' he said neutrally. 'See you later, I expect.'

'Yes. I have to go to Dulwich once we get back into town, remember.'

'How will you get back from there?'

'If Gerry's home, he may give me a lift, otherwise I'll call a cab from their house.'

Andy nodded non-committally and I left without further issue.

The house was in its usual uproar when I arrived to collect Ben. Gerry took me through a list of things I had to do and needed to know, before noticing my amused and tolerant expression.

'Oh, you know what to do, Madsy. I don't need to explain it all in triplicate, do I?'

'I think we might manage. Don't worry about us. Just have a wonderful *Boheme*, and enjoy your day. He's in the safest hands.'

I held them out and Gerry took them, smiling.

'I know.' He kissed my palms. 'I would trust you with his life.'

That was so sweet. I put my arms around his neck and hugged him tightly.

'For God's sake, Mads, put him down, you don't know where he's been.'

I sprang away from Gerry as if scalded. Josh was grinning in the doorway. We had never even held hands in front of the boys. I had contented myself with touching his arm or shoulder, or kissing him a cheerful farewell when they were around and saved my hugs for Ben; that had always seemed the safest option. I was flustered now and searched around anxiously for something that would deflect Josh's intelligent gaze. Gerry came to the rescue.

'You're just jealous. You and Ben think that Madison is your personal property.'

Josh just laughed and winked at me most uncharacteristically.

'Good luck today,' he smiled. 'Rather you than me.'

'Oh, Gerry, I'm so sorry,' I said contritely as Josh sauntered away.

'Don't be silly.' Gerry busied himself with packing an inordinately large amount of food for us. 'It's not as if he walked in on us in bed. If he takes offence at you giving me a hug in my own kitchen that's too bad.'

'He didn't take offence. He was amused!'

'Then what are you worrying about?' Gerry retorted.

I thought he was being incredibly dense, but I left it.

'Shouldn't he be in school, anyway?' I asked.

'He says he's only got library periods till noon and it's not worth going in for that.'

'Gerry!' I admonished. 'You'll really get their backs up if you condone unauthorised absences.'

'Madison, what is this? The KGB? Unauthorised absences, for goodness sake! He'll be in for his class at twelve.'

I looked at my watch. It was nine fifteen.

'I bet you a Mars bar that someone from DCP will ring in the next five minutes and ask where he is.'

I won my bet, and had to stuff my handkerchief into my mouth to stop laughing out loud as Gerry tried to justify himself to Josh's tutor at DCP.

'He can work just as well at home... No, he's still under sixteen... Punctuality? Well, have you tried to get out of Victoria station in the rush hour? It's like a war zone... If I can get him out of bed, yes, if not, no... No, I'm not free to come to see you today, I've got a living to earn... Josh is enjoying it with you much more than his old school, so I don't see there's a problem... Oh, I see... He'll be there shortly... Goodbye.'

Josh and Ben had come back into the kitchen during this exchange and by the time Gerry hung up we were all laughing at his discomfiture.

'It's not funny. I don't have time for this,' Gerry complained. 'Josh, I think you better make a slightly earlier appearance than originally planned, okay.'

Josh opened his mouth to object, but caught my eye before he spoke. I gave him a wry grin and he shrugged his shoulders.

'Okay, I'm out of here.'

Gerry leaned his forehead against the kitchen units.

'Who would put up with this every day?' he joked wearily.

'Me,' I ventured.

'Oh, heaven help you woman, you must be crazy. Take my younger son away please and leave me in peace.'

Ben and I approached Victoria station with the familiarity of seasoned travellers. The Chichester train was satisfactorily swish and we treated ourselves to frothy rich hot chocolates from Costa Coffee, deciding to keep the flask till later, when no more tempting options presented themselves. We examined the contents of the food bag that Gerry had provided: chocolate, yoghurts, grapes and biscuits.

'That'll do nicely for this morning,' Ben announced, 'but I hope we're going to Macdonald's later. Or Pizza Hut? KFC?' he looked at me enquiringly.

'I'm sure we can find somewhere that suits you,' I laughed.

It was like travelling to Glyndebourne again. Ben told me in considerable detail about his new computer, and the advantages of not having to share computer time with Gerry and Josh any longer.

'You'll have to send me an email again,' I told him. 'More of those ridiculous animated things you were showing me in the summer.'

It seemed so long ago, and so much had changed.

'Madison?' Ben asked, looking at me seriously.

'Yes, my darling?'

'Can you be my chaperone all time, you know, when I get a job, and Dad can't come?'

He sounded like an international artiste with a full diary, bless his heart.

'If I'm not working myself, of course, and if it's okay with your dad.'

'Oh, it'll be all right with him,' Ben said with a grin.

'You sound very sure about that.'

'Yeah. Josh told me that you were cuddling him in the kitchen when you got to our house this morning.'

'So? Is that a big deal? I have been known to cuddle you on occasions.'

'That's different.'

'What kind of different? You're both my friends, and Josh too.'

'It's just different. But it's cool, okay?'

It sounded as if Ben was giving me permission for something although I wasn't quite sure what, and I certainly didn't intend to question him.

'Anyway, do you want a biscuit?'

Ben was diverted, as I knew Josh would not have been, and I was glad not to be under his dark-eyed scrutiny. We dug into the biscuits as Ben asked me rather randomly what *Carmen* was about, and I managed to stretch the answer out long enough until we pulled into Chichester station.

It looked as if Ben was going to have to forego Pizza Hut. A member of the choral society's hospitality team swept us up at Chichester station, and I could see that it would be difficult to escape her clutches.

'Hello, dear,' she greeted Ben. 'How nice to meet you.'

She looked at me without much interest. I held out my hand.

'Hello, I'm Madison Brylmer. I'm chaperoning Ben today.'

'Oh, good,' she said briskly. 'I hope you won't be bored.'

We were frogmarched to the car as she kept up a stream of chatter. Our first port of call was to meet the conductor, Ralph Burgess. He was an old friend and colleague of Gerry's so we were sure of a warm welcome there. Hazel (Ms Hospitality) spoke to Ben as if he were five years old and to me as if I were a rather dense drug pusher. Ben rolled his eyes at me when we managed to exchange surreptitious glances.

'So is that all clear, Ms…' Hazel turned to me bossily.

'Please call me Madison.'

'She's Dr Brylmer.'

Ben and I spoke simultaneously, stopped, and laughed out loud before seeing that Hazel clearly was not amused. I waited a beat.

'It's Madison, and yes, that's all clear. I'm very familiar with this kind of routine.'

'Do you chaperone for a living, then?' she asked.

'Madison's an opera singer,' Ben said loyally.

That stopped Hazel in her tracks.

'How nice,' she murmured.

Ben blew down the back of my neck and I giggled again. Hazel looked bewildered and I took pity on her.

'Ben and I are friends and colleagues,' I said cheerfully. 'I'm here today in lieu of his dad.'

She must have been very glad to leave us in the rather more genial hands of Ralph Burgess, who hugged Ben warmly.

'Hello, old chap. How are you doing? Missing Glyndebourne?' He beamed at me. 'You must be Madison. Gerry told me you were coming along today. And you were in *Flute* too? I went to see this young man, but I must admit that I don't recognise you with your normal clothes on!'

We laughed and Hazel looked even more confused. I sensed she would spend all day trying to work out our relationship. Not that it mattered a jot. I wouldn't have minded if she thought I was the dustman, I just loved being there with Ben. He and Ralph worked on Ben's solo – *Pie Jesu* – at the piano before lunch, which Hazel was to serve in Ralph's kitchen. I wandered off to see if she wanted any help.

'It's very nice of you to come down with Ben today,' she said, 'especially if you're more used to being a soloist yourself.'

'It's great fun,' I told her, mixing a bowl of salad. 'I love him very much.' It was quite unnecessary to tell her that, of course, but I did enjoy saying it and Hazel was a safe audience.

'Yes, I can see that,' she said with surprising perspicacity. 'And he obviously loves you.' Perhaps my first impressions of Hazel had been a misjudgement too.

To my delight, Graham Fellows was the baritone soloist, and he rolled up for lunch in high spirits.

'Hello, gorgeous,' he greeted me, taking me in his extravagant embrace. 'What a treat! My favourite mezzo thrown in for nothing! But what are you doing here? There's no solo for you today, darling.'

'I'm chaperoning Ben.'

'Are you indeed?' Graham looked hugely amused, and I knew this titbit would go back to London with him.

He kept us entertained throughout lunch and the afternoon rehearsal. When Graham and Ben didn't have to sing we sat and listened to the choir, wandered around the cathedral and gossiped quietly. He played cards with Ben on a back pew and spent a lot of time watching Ben and I closely. As Ben rehearsed his solo with the orchestra, he whispered in my ear.

'What's going on then, Madsy? I can smell a scandal.'

I moved away from him stiffly.

'What do you mean? A scandal?'

Graham chuckled, raking his hand through his jet black hair. He was an attractive man who knew how to use his charm.

'You and the young man seem to have become very friendly. I presume this relationship extends to his dear father, too.'

'Yes, Gerry and I *are* good friends.'

'*Just* good friends?' he laughed.

'Graham, I don't see that it's any of your business.'

'And there, my dear, is the answer to my question.'

Graham kissed me, his eyes sparkling with mischief as he drew back.

'Don't worry, darling, your secret's safe with me,' he said, bounding to his feet. 'And now I think I've got to sing.'

Ben leaned against me as we listened to Graham rehearse, his rich voice filling the cathedral and sending shivers down my spine.

'He's fabulous, isn't he?' Ben murmured.

'He certainly is,' I agreed.

Ben cuddled up closer and I put my arms round him, kissing the top of his head.

'I love you,' I whispered.

'I love you,' he muttered in response.

If only it was that simple with Gerry.

Hazel came bustling up after the rehearsal.

'Come with me now, dears, tea at my house.'

'Pizza, pizza, pizza,' Ben whispered behind my back.

'What was that, dear?' she asked.

'Nothing.' Ben looked innocent.

Graham came to our rescue.

'Hazel, I wonder if you would permit me to entertain my two dear friends here? It is such a special blessing to see them both today. I would very much like to treat them to a repast at that much vaunted centre of culinary delight, the Pizza Hut. Perhaps afterwards I might bring them to your house so we can change and prepare ourselves for the evening.'

Hazel melted under Graham's oozing charm, and we made a run for it.

'Graham, only you could pull that off!' I laughed as we walked into the town centre.

'Lots of practice.' He winked at us. 'And a highly developed sense of when a boy needs some junk food.'

'Pizza's not junk food,' Ben objected. 'It's mostly tomato.'

We all tucked in to a huge pizza which was definitely not mostly tomato, and I sipped a glass of wine, whilst Graham kept Ben company with a coke. A wave of something akin to homesickness washed over me as we ate, and I wished that Gerry was here with us, but I was grateful to Graham for entertaining Ben, and I enjoyed his ridiculous posturing.

Walking to the cathedral later, I realised with pleasure that Ben was starting to treat me with some of the causal affection he bestowed on Gerry. He pulled at my arm, pushed and mock punched me, and prodded me imperiously when he wanted my attention. The happiness he brought to me blossomed to a new dimension as for the first time in my life I felt the love of a child. I rested my hand on my stomach and wondered what it would be like to carry a child for nine months, to give birth, and eleven years later to look at a beautiful boy like Ben and know that he was truly mine. It made me want to cry with longing, but I swallowed my tears till I sat in the cathedral listening to Ben's sweet voice ringing around the ancient building. He was not mine, and never would be, but I was grateful for the precious day we had spent together.

CHAPTER 47

T he memory of it kept me going the next day as we prepared for the last night at The Restless Dragon. I'd got home shortly after Andy the previous night, having taken a cab from Dulwich. Gerry was not back when Ben and I returned, and after our tiring day I hadn't lingered long with the boys. Josh was flat out in front of the television and greeted us with a distinct lack of interest. As I kissed Ben goodnight, I stroked his smooth cheek and hugged him close.

'Goodnight, my darling. Thank you for a lovely day. You were totally wonderful.'

'Thanks for taking me, Mads. It was fun.'

'It certainly was. See you soon.'

'Hmm.' Ben had already started to drift off.

Josh waved a hand vaguely from the settee as I left, his attention quickly turned back to the TV.

Andy had made little comment about my day beyond asking if Ben had sung well, where we'd eaten, and what time we'd got back to town. I answered briefly, but honestly, and encouraged him to focus on events at The Dragon.

'You will be there in good time, won't you?' he asked as he left long before I needed to set out.

'Before good time, Andy, I promise.' Megan was collecting me and we would meet everyone else at the theatre.

After he'd gone I felt sad, thinking about Gerry, Ben and Josh, wishing I were with them. The good days, like yesterday, were invariably followed by this melancholy: my limbs dragged and I felt ominously tearful as I tried to set about my overdue paperwork. It lifted as soon as Gerry phoned.

'I hear yesterday was a resounding success,' he said.

'It was lovely. You would have been very proud.'

'I am,' Gerry said warmly. 'Ben tells me that a good time was had by all, including Graham Fellows. I bet he was pleased to see you.'

'Yes, I think he was,' I replied coolly, glad to hear what I dared to think might be an undercurrent of jealousy. 'Darling,' I continued more plaintively. 'It's the Dragon party tonight, I don't think I can bear it.'

'Oh, Madsy, I'd offer to come with you, but I don't think that's a good idea, do you?'

We laughed.

'No, I don't think the surprise factor would work to our advantage.'

'I'll see you next week, and send lots of positive thoughts in your direction in the meantime,' he consoled.

As we hung up, Gerry said, 'Thanks again for yesterday. It was reassuring to know he was with you.'

My heart swelled with love for them all, and I went about my business in better shape.

I really tried to lose myself in the spirit of things at The Restless Dragon that night. It was a genuinely happy occasion: *Lethal Desires* had played to good houses throughout its run, justified the sponsors' faith in the venue and Joe's faith in Andy; the tour was arranged, with every reason to expect the play to be as successful in the provinces, and Andy's pleasure in his new role was matched by The Dragon team's pleasure in having him on board. Even Megan seemed to find no fault with anything as she flirted openly with Joe.

'How does this all fit into the great scheme of things?' Annie asked me as we sat quietly sipping champagne.

'I don't know, Annie,' I replied. 'When Andy's not suspicious and cross, I feel as if I could carry on like this indefinitely, especially now he's doing so well. When he's angry, even about the little he knows of my relationship with Gerry, I wonder how I can go on with it at all; I get so frightened of how it will all work out. But when I'm with Gerry and I'm so happy, or when I'm away from him and missing him desperately, I feel as if I'd do anything to make a life with him, and deal with the trouble later.'

'In other words, you're confused.'

'Sometimes. I wish I could just fix it, Annie. Put Andy with someone who loves him unconditionally, happy and successful, and me with Gerry and the boys, all our emotional dysfunctions smoothed out, happy ever after. Then it would be so easy.'

Megan came over to join us, and we changed the subject, but as I watched and listened that night, I thought that possibly, conceivably, if one day Gerry left me with no option, I could slip back into my old, pre-Gerry, life. I would not be unchanged, but I could hang in there if he told me to go my way, and I would survive. With that thought I let myself go a little more, responding more cheerfully to old friends and Andy's new colleagues. I could see that Andy was pleased, and it made me feel better to show some enthusiasm about a night that represented everything that Andy had been hoping for as long as I'd known him.

As we fell into bed at 3 am, Andy said quietly, 'That was a great night, Madsy, and you were marvellous. Everyone at The Dragon thinks you're amazing. They can't wait to hear you sing.'

'I would have sung tonight, if you'd asked,' I said, 'Annie too.'

'I didn't think you'd want to.'

'Why on earth not? You know I'll sing anywhere at anytime.'

'You're not much inclined to do much with me or for me these days.'

I groaned inwardly. Not an argument at this time of the night, please. I stayed silent.

'I even think your mother enjoyed it tonight,' Andy said, thankfully not pursuing his bitter observation.

'Then you must have done something right,' I smiled. 'It won't last, of course.'

We laughed softly together, united for a moment in our shared knowledge of exactly how Megan's mind worked.

'Well done, Andy.'

'*Are* you pleased, Mads? Really?'

'Of course. What a silly question.'

'Not so silly these days, is it? We're driving in different lanes, and your car is full of a lot of passengers.'

Bemused by the bizarre analogy, I murmured non-committally.

'You've always accepted my career, Andy; it's inevitable that I work apart from you.'

'I don't mean your singing, you know that.'

'Then what do you mean, Andy?' I said, sitting up in bed.

'If I have to tell you, then you must be especially dense, and I know you're not,' he replied heatedly.

I said nothing.

'Just leave it, Madison. Go to sleep.'

I did eventually, after lying awake, my mind whirling. As much as I just wanted everything to go away except for me and Gerry and the boys, it simply wasn't going to do so. My relationship with Andy was clearly reaching crisis point, and soon enough he was again going to ask me directly if I was having an affair with Gerry. I didn't know what my answer would be. As I fell asleep my last thought was that if Gerry could say he loved me things would fall into place. Possibly.

CHAPTER 48

On Monday morning as I was walking away from The Tuition Box, having spent a couple of happy hours working with a pretty teenage girl on *Language, Truth and Logic*, I checked my mobile for messages. *1 message received* the display read. I fiddled about to reveal its contents:

Hello, it read. *I love you. G.*

After I'd received Gerry's astonishing message – the first, incidentally, that he'd ever sent to me – I found a café and sat for a long time over a hot chocolate. After staring into space for half an hour or more, I picked up my phone and sent my own message back.

Hello. I'll believe it when you tell me in person. M.

It took ten minutes for him to call me. I was still gazing into my hot chocolate when the phone tinkled and I watched his name flash on the display several times before making the connection.

'Hello.'
'Hello. It's me.'
'I didn't think you knew how to send text messages.'
'I worked it out.'
'So I see.'
'Are you free this afternoon?' he asked.
'Conceivably.'

'Come on, Madsy, give me a break here.'
'I think I can be free for you, Gerry.'
'Meet me at home at three o'clock, then?'
'I'll be there.'

I tried to be cool and unbothered, but it lasted precisely ten minutes after walking through the front door. I said nothing about our messages, but made us tea whilst I encouraged Gerry to tell me about his new music writing software which was lying on the table top, until he was the one who could bear it no longer. He took the mugs from my hands, and pulled me firmly into his arms.

'Madison, I love you. Josh and Ben love you. You are the most wonderful and adorable woman and I am deeply happy and grateful that you love me too.'

I burst into tears and we went to bed.

I'd thought that things would be easier once Gerry could tell me that he loved me and in some ways, of course, they were. The last remnants of reserve fell away and I had never before felt as at ease with anyone, man or woman. I told him how I felt about everything; I encouraged him to open up to me about his life, present and past, and we would lie in bed, sit over the kitchen table with tea, or in the front of his car in purply darkness, and talk contentedly. I felt radiant and fulsome, my coffers rich with so much love that was at last returned with gentle tenderness by the man I adored. But after that day in his kitchen, although Gerry showed me in many little ways that he loved me, the words that had come so slowly from him didn't come again. It was bewildering. I had no doubt that he had meant it, but evidently he felt that once said, repetition was unnecessary. I told him that I loved as often as I had ever done, biting back the temptation to seek reassurance; I had to trust him. When, about ten days after he had so wonderfully texted me, he said, 'By the way, I've told Vanessa that I can't see her any more,' I knew that I couldn't expect any more of him. He had done all that I had asked of him, and the only thing left was for him to decide if one day we had a real, permanent future together, and I would wait for as long as that took.

We were rehearsing *Tito* every day as we fast approached the first performance at the beginning of November. It occupied all our time and energies and with the whole of the forthcoming month devoted to it, I couldn't think of a happier way to spend six weeks. I grew into my role more each day until I felt as if I could understand the motivation behind every breath poor, weak, besotted Sesto uttered. The music had come to fit my voice as a hand in a fine leather glove, not a wrinkle or blemish marring its smooth line and rich texture.

I threw my arms around Gerry every evening when we'd wrapped our rehearsal.

'Thank you, thank you, darling, for giving me this! I never want to sing another role again, it's so perfect.'

Gerry laughed indulgently.

'I wouldn't have asked you if I didn't think you'd do it wonderfully, would I?'

I thought of how dramatically our relationship had changed since he'd originally approached me to sing the part. Over a year had passed and never would I have imagined the passion we would be sharing twelve months hence. I knew it filled my voice and body as I sang.

'Despite my deep reservations, I can see that man does wonderful things for you,' observed Annie laconically.

Tom, the director, was pleased too.

'Madison, you should be singing this role all over the world,' he told me as Gerry lounged against the piano, smiling proudly.

'Put a good word in for me then, Tom,' I said. 'All offers considered.'

Throughout all this, Andy seemed to be making a good fist of his first official weeks as AD at The Restless Dragon. He was working with Joe on a Christmas production of *Puff the Magic*

Dragon, which they thought very droll, and it did promise to be enormous fun, with an original libretto written by Andy, and music by a thin, intense young man, who burned with creative energy. Andy did some work in the office too, but I was reluctant to examine him closely about this, given his appalling track record with anything that involved attention to detail. I hoped that Joe wouldn't give him too much responsibility too soon, but it was nothing to do with me, and I kept my counsel.

It was a strange time. Twelve months earlier I would have felt an integral part of all that Andy was doing, despite my involvement with *Tito*, but now I felt more like an observer, watching with detached interest, waiting to see how the picture was going to form. We were both out all day in the last weeks of October, seeing one another only briefly late at night or early in the morning, or on Sunday when The Dragon was closed. We maintained a well crafted façade of geniality, built, I knew, on many years of avoiding confrontation, but we nevertheless circled each other with the underlying unease of wild animals defending their territory.

Ironically, we were so busy working that Gerry and I shared less time alone than we had during September, and there was no opportunity to stay with him overnight, but the quality of the time we shared had changed, and it transmitted itself to our hours in rehearsal, too. The fragile threads that had bought us together over the summer had become soft chords, strong and firm.

'I've got tickets for you and Megan for the opening night, and there'll be cast tickets available if you want to come to one of the more accessible touring venues too,' I told Andy a week before we went up.

'Good,' he said neutrally. 'All the time you're spending on it, it should be brilliant.'

I bristled nervously. 'It's always like this before we go up, you should know that.'

269

'I do,' he nodded. 'I'm sure you're enjoying all this time with Gerry, all up front and official.'

'What's that supposed to mean?' I responded irritably.

'Absolutely nothing,' he snapped, walking out of the room.

After that, I think Andy and I made something of an unspoken pact not to mention Gerry unless it was absolutely unavoidable. I wondered if Andy was sure that I was having an affair with him, or just guessing, or if he simply thought that we were attracted to each other but had done nothing about it. Some days I wished he would challenge me directly, but I knew that I was still too uncertain of a future with Gerry to precipitate such a confrontation. Even though it was I who was married, I would be the one to make the compromises, to fit in to Gerry's life, rather than he into mine, and I knew it meant that it would have to be he who determined where the next stage of our relationship would take us. I could take no chances and assume nothing. In the meantime, I felt rich with music and love, and if I could have held back time in those last weeks of October, you couldn't have stopped me.

CHAPTER 49

Annie and I stood side by side, staring into the long mirror that filled an entire wall of our dressing room in the theatre.

'I don't think Sesto is supposed to have a bosom,' she observed critically.

'It's not my fault,' I objected, 'it's the costume.' We were dressed in battle fatigues, olive green T-shirts and combat boots for this modern dress production of *Tito*. 'I think we look cool.'

'You look ridiculous,' a voice piped up behind us.

'Ben, nobody asked your opinion, and we certainly don't need it,' Annie retorted. 'At least, I don't, although I know that your friend Madison is more accommodating.'

Ben and I grinned at each other. Annie never gave him an inch and we enjoyed baiting her.

'Darling, I think you'd better give us a bit of space before curtain up.' I looked at my watch. 'I'll meet you in the wings just before the overture starts.'

He skulked off, but not before he had to be physically restrained from taking with him the replica machine guns Annie and I carried during Tito's entrance.

I felt a natural adrenaline rush and nervous excitement as I stood waiting in the wings, but today there was an added frisson to my nerves. Megan and Andy were sitting in the auditorium, and they would be backstage at the end of the show, doubtless coming face to face with Gerry for the first time since our affair had begun. I wasn't sure that even Gerry could carry it off with absolute composure now that there was so much between us. My stomach churned anxiously but the sound of the overture reaching its climax focussed my mind. Sesto and Vitellia opened the opera with a long and difficult passage of recitative, and our concentration had to be total. As soon as the last vestiges of applause died away, the harpsichord signalled our cue and we were off.

There were some special moments that night: two wonderful arias for my character, one accompanied by the most fabulous virtuoso clarinet solo; the tense first act finale, and the rousing power of the ensemble which closed the opera. Vocal fireworks were set off at every available moment in an opera full of classic pieces, but they were conveyed with an intense feeling for the drama and the complex web of emotions that united the unhappy, proud and passionate characters. I didn't want it to end, but was comforted by the prospect of ten more performances that lay ahead. I revelled in the curtain calls. Deeply gratified by the cheers that rang out as I took my bow, I squeezed Gerry's hand tightly when we joined for the final line-up. He squeezed it back and I felt the joy of our special partnership. This beautiful man who had conducted me with assurance and intelligence was the one who held me in his arms and filled my heart and mind and body with unimaginable love and longing. If I could only be his forever, my cup would be full.

We were all excited as we changed, high on the energy and buzz of a successful first night. Dressed and ready to face the fray, I looked myself over critically in the mirror. My cheeks were flushed, and my eyes bright with happiness. I looked about twenty-five years old, and I knew that the radiance that welled up in me would be obvious to Megan. But I couldn't quench it even if I wanted to do so; so much love for Gerry,

Ben and Josh coursed through my veins that it could not be hidden.

Andy and Megan were talking to Annie in the passageway.

'You look so different from in *Flute,*' Megan was saying, 'Your combats are really glamorous; because you and Madison are both so beautiful you carry them off brilliantly!'

Annie laughed heartily.

'Madsy, did you hear your mum? She says we're sexy in our combats.'

'I didn't quite say that,' Megan objected, but she laughed along with Annie, and I could see she'd thoroughly enjoyed the evening.

Andy looked wary and on edge, but relaxed as I smiled at him.

'Were we cool?' I asked.

'Extremely cool,' he nodded. 'Your best role to date.'

'I hope the critics agree. There was supposed to be someone from the Garden out there tonight.' I raised my eyebrows at Annie. 'Our time has come, don't you think?'

The four of us talked easily enough about the production until Annie hoisted her bag.

'Okay then, *amica mia fedel,*' she said, 'I'm off to get my beauty sleep.'

'Yes, I suppose we are, too,' I agreed, reluctant to go before I had said goodnight to Ben and Gerry.

As I shuffled in indecision, Ben appeared at the end of the passage. He headed straight for me, bearing Gerry's suit carrier, which he promptly deposited at my feet.

'I'm not carrying that any further,' he declared mutinously.

I managed to catch Annie's eye and she set her own bag down again, recognising my mute plea for help. Andy said nothing.

'This is my mum, Ben. She came to see us in *Flute* if you recall.'

'Yeah, hi.' Ben smiled sweetly as he repeatedly bounced off the wall, using his hands as springs.

'You look as if you've got far too much energy at this time of night,' Megan remarked dryly.

'I'm always energetic, aren't I, Madison?' he said cheerfully.

'I think I have known the odd quiet moment in your company,' I replied, feeling Annie closing ranks as Andy's muttered curse caused even Ben to look up in surprise. Megan's lips pursed as if she'd bitten into a lemon, and the moment was crowned as Gerry strode into view. He didn't hesitate, but walked straight up to us.

'Hello,' he greeted Megan. 'You do get around don't you? Did you enjoy it?'

Even as he addressed my mother, his gaze shifted to meet mine, and my smile widened and my heart swelled with love. He looked dishevelled and exhausted, but his eyes were characteristically full of humour. His white tie and tails packed away he had returned to his more usual retinue: a mismatch of trainers, tie and jacket. He looked vulnerable and eccentric and utterly beautiful and I longed to hold him in my arms, but for the moment we just grinned at one another.

'Yes, it was marvellous,' Megan was saying, her eyes bright and alert. I knew she was registering something and that she would not hold back later if she wanted me to know it.

'Come on, Dad,' Ben complained impatiently, and Gerry heeded his son's tired tones.

'Nice to see you,' he told Megan, 'I hope you're going to come again. We've got shows all over the place this month.'

'I'm sure I'll get to at least one,' she agreed, as, anxious for the potentially awkward scene to conclude, I began to turn away.

'See you on Friday,' I said to Gerry, knowing that we nevertheless planned to meet before the performance at the end of the week.

'Yes, have a good week.' His voice was teasing and I marvelled that he could not realise how he was setting me up for a blistering scene with Andy, or Megan, or indeed both, so obvious was the intimacy in his voice. His eyes rapidly passed over us all: me, Annie, Megan and finally Andy. The two men held each other's gaze for a brief moment, Andy's black with anger and resentment, Gerry wide eyed and ingenuous. I made a final move to walk away, forcing the others to follow me. Annie turned to me deliberately, talking loudly and casually about the show, until we hit the safety of the street. Kissing me on the cheek as we separated she whispered, 'Good luck. Ring me if you need to.'

I squeezed her hand warmly.

'Thanks. I'm braced for the worst.'

Andy was quiet, but Megan kept up a stream of chatter as we drove home.

'How about meeting for lunch tomorrow?' she said as we left the car on Putney Heath. '1 pm at my office.'

It was a royal command; I could do nothing but agree.

CHAPTER 50

How many nights will you have to spend away for *Tito*?' Andy asked when we got in.

'About four, perhaps five,' I said, deliberately casual. 'Most times we'll be close enough home to drive back.'

'*We* meaning you and Gerry, of course,' he said sharply.

'Any of us.'

'But you'll be travelling with Gerry,' he insisted.

'Sometimes, I should think. But other times with Annie.'

I thought that the best policy was to act as if none of it was especially important.

'Crap,' he retorted aggressively.

'Andy, please. What's that supposed to mean?'

'That if you think I'll believe you won't be travelling in cosy companionship with Gerry and doing whatever else you do with him, you must reckon I'm a total idiot.'

'You're making an issue out of nothing,' I tried feebly to bring the conversation to a close.

'I don't think so, Madison,' he replied coldly. 'Well done tonight. I'm going to bed.'

I could say no more as he stalked away, but I knew Megan wouldn't let me off so lightly.

We toyed with chicken Caesar salads and glasses of cold white Oxford Landing in Megan's office, sitting by the huge plate glass window that offered a panoramic view over the city. Megan had enjoyed a successful morning in court, dealing with an acquisition and merger case, and she contented herself with filling me in on it as we ate. It was not until we drank frothy cappuccinos and each ate a single Belgian truffle that she launched her missile.

'So, you'll be touring with *Tito* after this week's performances are over?'

'Hmm,' I murmured. 'We should have a review in tomorrow's papers,' I added with rather more enthusiasm.

'Can you get back home after many of the shows?' she asked, refusing to be deflected.

'Most of them.'

'What do you plan to do for the others?'

'We'll all be booked hotel accommodation – good quality too, I hope!' I laughed.

'How does Andy feel about that?'

'Mum, I've stayed away before. It's not exactly my first out of London gig is it?'

I heard my defensive tone and braced myself for Megan's inevitable reaction.

'I suspect that he views this rather differently, Madison,' she said crisply, 'especially given the atmosphere last night.'

'What atmosphere?' I asked foolishly.

'Come on, Madison, we're both intelligent women, let's try to be honest with each other. You've clearly got an enormous crush on the conductor. It's obvious to Andy and it's obvious to me. Get it sorted out now, or you're going to make a fool of yourself and make Andy very unhappy while you're doing so.'

Red-hot anger raged through me.

'A crush?' I said furiously. 'A *crush*? What exactly do you mean by that?'

'You're impressed and flattered by him, and you encourage his son in an entirely overly familiar relationship with you,' she replied succinctly.

I pushed aside my coffee cup and stood up furiously.

'That sums up exactly what you think of me, doesn't it?' I spoke quietly, too angry to shout. 'In your eyes I'm nothing more than a foolish teenager with a crush on their teacher; some fourteen year old who doesn't know how to control inappropriate emotions. Well, even if I was, you're being unfair. If I was fourteen and infatuated with my music teacher, it would simply be a normal part of growing up. But you never saw it like that, did you? You thought it was shameful and embarrassing if I admired someone in authority with charm and charisma. It was a weakness to be stamped out by your disapproval and anger. And nothing's changed now. You can't imagine that I might feel anything deeper than a crush, and you can't imagine that anyone like Gerry could feel anything for me. You assume that I'm infatuated by him and that he's tolerant of my affections and amused by them, but probably also embarrassed, and he will eventually tell me to direct them elsewhere. That's what really hurts, Mum; not so much your accusations, but the assumption that if I feel anything for Gerry it couldn't be a proper grown-up, loving devotion, and still less would you expect him to feel that for me.'

Megan had sat silently through my tirade. Finally she spoke.

'How interesting that you should direct it all back at me,' she mused. 'So one of my doubtless numerous failings as a mother was not to encourage you to express unwise and foolish fancies over unattainable idols. I'm sorry it caused you so much trauma, Madison. Now I have work to do, and I think this lunch is at an end, don't you? Think about what I've said, if I were you, if both your career and your marriage mean anything to you.'

She walked away from her office with stiff-backed dignity. I had no idea where she went, and I stood still, staring at the scene from the window until it was clear that she was not going to return. I collected my bag and coat and left the building, utterly at a loss to know how I could rebuild the bridges I smelt burning behind me.

Megan made no effort to contact me later that day, or the next. Andy was quiet, and I slipped away to see Gerry with a heavy heart. As we lay in bed the evening before our second performance, I told him about my scene with Megan

'Can you believe it, Gerry, she thinks I've got a crush on you, as she so flatteringly put it, as if I'm not capable of having a mutually consenting and reciprocated relationship with someone of your rarefied stature!'

'Well, I am, of course, far superior to you in every way,' Gerry laughed. 'You'll sit at my feet and learn from me, if you're wise.'

We laughed and I cuddled close to him.

'I've emailed her, but she won't respond. I don't know what to do now. I was pretty spiky with her, I know; I was defensive and angry, but I don't want us to be on bad terms.'

'I can't imagine that she wants to be either, Madsy,' he reassured me.

'You don't know my mother,' I said darkly. 'She's capable of sending out the UN troops over a missed phone call, never mind the suspicion of an unsuitable relationship. I'm walking on eggshells at the moment.'

'You can walk all over me instead if you like,' Gerry teased.

'That sounds far too energetic,' I sighed, acknowledging that I couldn't expect Gerry to understand the tense and fragile relationship I shared with Megan.

But I couldn't bear the tension and the next day I turned up at Megan's office at lunchtime, our glowing *Daily Telegraph* review in hand. She was with a client, so I waited in the outer office, chewing my fingers. She ignored me as they were ushered out, speaking only after the door was firmly closed behind them.

'What do you want, Madison?'

'I've come to say sorry for flying off the handle on Tuesday.'

Megan turned away, tight-lipped.

'Please Mum, can we be friends again? I am sorry.'

'Madison, you're going to be away a lot over the next month. If there is anything you need to resolve, then resolve it now.'

I resisted asking her to clarify what she meant. I knew, and I knew too that nothing was going to be resolved in the way that she envisaged. I needed this time with Gerry to see if we had any future together, if the love that I held in my heart was worth all the pain and distress, but I kept these thoughts to myself.

'There's nothing to worry about,' I told Megan, hoping I sounded more convincing than I felt. 'He's my friend and colleague. He's good to me and I'm good to him.' This was nothing other than the truth, if not the whole of it.

Megan looked at me silently, but I felt the atmosphere thaw fractionally. I held out my precious newspaper cutting.

'Look what we got in the *Telegraph*.'

She took it and walked over to the window to read the glowing praise our lovely production had earned.

'Oh, how nice, Madsy.' At last Megan smiled and I felt the tension in my shoulders dissipate. *'Madison Brylmer, as the troubled Sesto, sang with an enormous range of dramatic colour, and her fluid and flexible stage movement contrasted brilliantly with the statuesque poses of Peter Radin's magnificent Tito,'* she read with pleasure.

I glowed.

'Well done, darling,' she said warmly. 'Can I keep this?'

'Of course, it's your copy. Can you come again tonight?' I asked, anxious to consolidate our reconciliation.

'I've got late meetings, or I'd love to,' she said regretfully, 'but I'll see it again in Cambridge, won't I?'

I looked at her with relief, deeply glad that the awkward moments had passed, but acutely aware that many more would lie ahead if she discovered the true nature of my relationship with Gerry. It panicked me even more than the prospect of further confrontations with Andy, such was the power of Megan's approval or disapproval, but for now, it was postponed.

'I'll ring you tomorrow, and tell you how it went,' I told her, preparing to leave.

'Yes, please do. I'll be thinking of you.'

On the train I looked at the review again, rereading the paragraph about which Megan had not commented:

One of the highlights of the evening was Brylmer's inspirational singing of Parto, Parto. Conductor Gerard McFall united singer and clarinet soloist, Sven Raingold, in a perfect balance of melody and sheer virtuosity. McFall and Brylmer are becoming an operatic partnership to watch, although at this stage Brylmer's career seems to be the one in the ascendant.

I chuckled aloud, oblivious to my fellow travellers. Gerry had laughed appreciatively over that.

'This time next year, you'll be too good to speak to me,' he teased, 'and then I'll be the one with the crush on you.' He stroked my hair, quieter now. 'I do love you, Madison, and I'm extremely proud of you.'

I put my arms around him, hugging his slender body tightly to me. At last, Gerry had told me again that he loved me, and I wanted the moment to last forever. I raised my head to look into his eyes, suddenly clear and bright, his characteristically enigmatic gaze gone for a moment.

'And I love you,' I told him softly.

'Hmm,' Gerry grinned, 'I know.'

'Oh yes? How?' I teased.

'I'm just clever like that,' he said. 'But you do give me the odd clue now and then.'

Andy and I ate out with Sophie, Jim, Steve, and Danielle, before the *Tito* tour began. Loyal friends that they were, they had seen the opera in town and were suitably impressed.

'You get better every time we hear you,' said Steve seriously. 'And your sense of drama, how you use the stage and work with the other characters, is maturing all the time.'

'Good.' I valued Steve's knowledgeable opinion.

Conversation turned to other things and it was a happy evening. Andy and Steve talked excitedly about the latest events at The Dragon until eventually, in a predictably sexist way, the women huddled together to talk, leaving the men to do their own thing. Everyone came back to Exeter House for coffee and liqueurs after we'd eaten, and I found myself leaning against the lintel of the lounge door, watching and listening with a new intensity. These were my friends, loyal sharers and supporters over many years. They had helped Andy and I in too many practical ways to remember, as we had them, and together we had been part of happy and engaging musical activities long before my career had begun its exciting progression. Andy and Steve went back even before I'd met him, and Dani had been my friend before she'd met and married Steve. How often she had laughingly accused me of matchmaking.

I watched Andy in the midst of them all, happy and laughing, at ease with people he loved and trusted, who loved him, who rejoiced with him in his success at The Dragon, and who would be dismayed by my treachery. All this I was risking, wittingly and with careless folly: these friendships honed over the years; my marriage, which may not have been passionate, but which had been friendly; and, of course, Megan, whose rigid code I was betraying, and whose confidence in me as a loving, responsible wife and daughter would be cruelly shattered. I watched it all as through a glass, separate from the action, and yet all I had to do was walk through it and be part of it again. Dani looked up to see me hovering at the doorway, half lost in reverie, half urging myself to be drawn into the safety of their circle again.

'Are you all right, Mads?' she asked, smiling easily.

I nodded, matching her comfortable smile with my own.

'Fine. Can I get you a refill?' I held my hand out for her coffee cup.

'Oh, thank you.'

She made as if to follow me into the kitchen, but I was glad when Sophie distracted her with a question, and I slipped away alone. As the kettle boiled I felt pain and longing for Gerry catch inside me like a knife in my solar plexus. It made me gasp as quick tears came to my eyes. Where was he now as I cried for him? Who was he with? What was he doing? Where were my sweet boys? All I knew was that they weren't with me, and if, at that moment, he called me to say he was waiting downstairs in the car to take me away to be his forever, I would have walked out of the front door without a backward glance.

CHAPTER 51

We completed three London performances of *Tito*, then took it to Southampton and Oxford before it was necessary to stay overnight. The York date took us away for two nights since Gerry and Tom had decided that we needed a full technical rehearsal with the orchestra on the morning of the show. Loud groans resonated at the prospect.

'Oh please, Gerry, Tom, it means three days' childminder's fees rather than two,' sighed Christina, our pretty Servillia.

'Sorry, Chrissie,' said Tom firmly. 'We haven't refreshed the show yet and we're half way through. We can't risk it getting stale or being thrown by a new venue because we haven't walked it properly on the stage.'

Gerry just pulled a face. I guessed he'd had to find ways around child care far too often to have much sympathy for those who were less resourceful. You either did the job, or you didn't.

As we packed up the dressing room after our brief sojourn in Oxford, Chrissie sighed again.

'They don't realise how expensive it is to have a childminder for an extra day. I was banking on being able to drop Simone at ten o'clock on Tuesday and pick her up before noon the next day. Now I'm paying for two overnighters.'

Annie patted her shoulder.

'There's nothing you can do about it, sweetie. Just accept it, and get yourself a nice *Messiah* to cover the extra cost,' she soothed.

Christina was not that easily placated.

'Madison,' she said entreatingly, 'will you try to persuade Gerry that we don't need it?'

I blinked and looked at her quizzically.

'I don't think it's in my power to do that, Chris. It's a production team decision. Pulling a diva fit about it won't be very helpful.'

Realising that I sounded rather po-faced, I grinned to soften my words.

'Oh, come on, Madsy,' she persisted. 'He'll listen to you, even if he doesn't listen to anyone else.'

'Why do you say that?' I asked, suddenly wary.

Christina laughed, and turned to Annie and Francesca. Annie looked helpless, but Francesca chuckled knowingly.

'Don't play innocent with us, Mads. We're not blind, you know.'

'I'm sorry, Francesca, I'm lost here. What are you talking about?'

My heart was thumping hard as I realised with horror that my precious secret, known only, I thought, to Annie, appeared to be company knowledge, or at least, speculation.

'You and Gerry. It's obvious.'

'What's obvious?' I was going to make them work for this.

'Well, that you and he are, well...' Francesca petered out, suddenly intimidated by my fierce stare.

'In a relationship,' Christina finished off with a smile.

I fell silent, staring into the middle distance, wondering what I had done to betray us. Annie's troubled face told me that it had not been she who had amused our colleagues with gossip, it was my open, obvious, and total devotion to Gerry that had done the damage. The moments we had shared a giggle or whisper in rehearsals; the proximity to which I always stood or sat to Gerry; our smooth departures in his car, always together, always quick to be gone once the job was done; the look in my eyes as I watched him at work. I could blame no one but me.

Smoothly I resumed folding my costume ready for Wardrobe to pack away with the others for transportation to York. Annie reached out her hand to me, gently pulling at my shoulder.

'Madsy, don't worry. Nobody thinks badly of it.'

I whirled around in anger.

'I should think not. It's no one's business but ours. I trusted you Annie, I thought you knew how much it meant to me, but now I discover that you've all been laughing about me behind my back.'

'We haven't, Madsy, I promise,' Annie said anxiously.

'Madison, I'm sorry.' Christina was contrite. 'I was really stupid. Please don't blame Annie. She hasn't said anything. It's just that you and Gerry are obviously close. You're really sweet together.'

She held out her hand to me, genuinely distressed, and I softened.

'It's okay, Chrissie, I'm overreacting. Sorry, Annie, I do know better than to accuse you of tittle-tattling.'

I squeezed Chris's hand, then held my arms out Annie. She hugged me hard, and tears closed my throat.

In the funny ways these things do, the episode united us that night, and the girls seemed reluctant to leave for their respective vehicles as we lingered at the stage door. We were talking still as Gerry sauntered towards me ready to depart.

'Are you coming with me, Dr Brylmer?' he asked in the casual way he invariably adopted before an audience.

'Yes, please,' I smiled, suddenly shy as Annie, Francesca and Chris studied him appraisingly.

Gerry raised his eyes mockingly. 'Why are you all looking at me like that? What have I done?'

'Nothing, Gerry,' said Annie innocently, and we broke up in laughter.

Gerry shrugged his shoulders dismissively.

'Have you all been drinking in the dressing room?' he enquired.

'Oh, no, we can find entertainment in anything, without the aid of alcoholic beverages,' Annie quipped and we giggled again.

'I'm lost. Are you ready?' Gerry turned to me.

The girls all reached out to hug me as if I was going away to sea, and suddenly I was glad that they knew. I realised now why Christina had always seemed slightly wary of me, and why Francesca had apologised to me after she'd flown off the handle at Gerry during one tense rehearsal. I'd thought she was just being courteous to me as her stage partner, but now I recalled her words with new understanding.

'I'm sorry I blew up at Gerry like that, Madsy. Are you angry with me?' she'd asked contritely.

I'd laughed and said that of course I wasn't angry and that I didn't think that anyone was, but now I appreciated her concern better.

I disentangled myself from my colleagues and padded down the street after Gerry, who, tired of waiting, was already unlocking the car. As we climbed in we saw them all still standing outside the stage door, gazing after us.

'What are they up to?' Gerry asked me. 'You were all behaving very oddly in there.'

'They seem to have decided I'm in need of special care and attention.'

Gerry turned to me with wide eyes as I settled in the passenger seat.

'Don't I give you that?' he grinned.

'You certainly do,' I replied. Resting my hand on the warmth of his thigh I buried my face in his shoulder, sighing deeply.

'What's this all about?' Gerry murmured against my hair.

'I just love you.'

'That's all right, then. Come on, I've got to get back to young Joshua and Benjamin.'

Gerry manoeuvred me gently away so he could start the car, but gradually I let my head rest on his shoulder again and I slumbered fitfully as he drove through the night.

CHAPTER 52

Andy saw me off with a long face as I left for York. 'Do you have to travel with Gerry?' he asked. 'Why can't you go with Annie?'

'Because I've arranged to go with Gerry, and Annie's not travelling from London anyway. She's been in Manchester for the last two days.'

'I don't like it, Mads.'

'Andy, he's the conductor,' I sighed.

'That's not all he is to you,' Andy retorted angrily, 'and I don't like you going away with him. But I'm obviously going to have to accept it.'

I was silent.

'No answer came the stern reply,' Andy muttered darkly. 'Have it your own way, Madison, you usually do.'

It wasn't the most propitious departure, but I was comforted by the fact that Andy was happily engrossed at The Restless Dragon. *Puff* was due to open in the first week of December, running into early January, so the team were busy from early in the morning till late at night, determined to build on the success of *Lethal Desires*. Nevertheless, I left with injunctions from Andy to phone him at every conceivable moment, to keep my mobile permanently switched on to receive his calls any time of the day or night.

I despised myself for the excitement I felt as I headed over to Dulwich to meet Gerry. My behaviour was utterly unjustifiable, driven by a love and passion I should have quashed as soon as it had made its first appearance. But with deliberate determination I had fanned its flames, battling against the odds as I sought Gerry's love, pushing my way through pain as sharp as thorns, and staring Andy's anxious fears in the face with a callousness of which I would never once have believed myself capable. The love that had made me more open and giving, reaching out in compassion and tenderness to Ben, Josh and Gerry, came at a cost and I hated what I had let it do to me even as I welcomed it.

But that night I rejoiced in our time together. Eight of us shared dinner in a seafood restaurant in the city centre before retiring to our charmingly rustic hotel. Sitting in the warm diner, my leg pressed tight against Gerry's, I basked in the rosy glow that bound us all together. I caught Francesca watching me stealing fries from Gerry's plate and she grinned warmly, but I knew that neither she nor Christina would pursue that subject again unless I volunteered it. Nevertheless, if they had put together the small, but plentiful clues, and reached the same conclusion, so must have the rest of the cast and the production team, and if our relationship was now an open secret, so be it. If it were up to me, I would pronounce it from the rooftops. But it wasn't, so I contented myself with entwining our fingers under the cover of the table, safe in the knowledge that soon we would be sharing the velvety darkness of our hotel room, lost in the heartaching pleasure of the love for which, it appeared, I was prepared to pay the price.

By ringing Andy from the hotel lobby at 11.30 I hoped he would consider it late enough to wait till morning had truly broken before tracking me down again. I knew I was in danger of precipitating a crisis with no confidence in how Gerry would respond, but at least I was taking the risk with my eyes open. And despite the danger (certainly not because of it) as I lay in Gerry's arms I felt nothing but peace and joy. The pleasure was less in the freedom to make love all night should we so desire, but in sharing the warm, tender companionship of our bed, not for a few snatched daytime hours, but through the long night watch. As I stirred in the early hours of the morning, the faintest glow from a streetlight filtered through the thick curtains, softly illuminating Gerry's gentle features. I kissed his shoulder, curling close to him again as I felt him move against me.

'I love you,' I whispered as he opened his eyes, already smiling.

We kissed drowsily.

'Can I sleep with you forever?' I asked softly as I settled again in his arms.

'I'll think about it,' he murmured.

I was so astonished that by the time I found my voice Gerry was asleep and I lay awake for some time wondering exactly what *that* meant.

When I reached home two days later, flushed with the pleasure of another wonderful performance and such precious time with Gerry, Andy was anxious and restive.

'How many performances have you got left?' he asked dourly.

'Just four,' I told him sadly. 'I can't bear the prospect of it being over. I'll never sing a role like that again.'

'Don't be silly,' he chided. 'Another year or so and you'll be able to write your own ticket.' He didn't sound too happy about it.

'I wish I had your confidence,' I laughed.

'How many more nights are you staying away?'

'Plymouth and Birmingham. Don't forget that you and Megan are coming to Cambridge.'

'And after that, you're not doing anything with Gerry are you?' he asked, staring at me hard.

'Not immediately, Andy. You know I'm mostly on an ENO contract next year, apart from *Figaro*.'

'*Figaro*?'

'You also know that I'm signed with Gerry to do it in Cornwall next summer, but that's a long way ahead.'

'Not long enough.' Andy closed his book with a slam. 'And doubtless before that there'll be chaperoning duties and God knows what else.'

'I've no idea,' I said calmly.

'Well, I have,' he said, 'and I know that if there's a chance to be with that man and his children, you'll take it, whatever it is.'

This was, of course, the truth, and my denial had no conviction.

'Oh, just go and live with him, Madison. Ring him up now and ask him to come to collect you. I'll be gone by the time he arrives.'

Andy banged his way out of the flat, returning long after I'd retired to bed. I guessed he'd gone back to The Dragon, so I hadn't been unduly worried, but I was, nevertheless, relieved to see him return safely.

'You're still here,' he observed.

'Of course.'

'Didn't he want you?' Andy laughed unpleasantly.

'I didn't call him and neither am I planning to do so.'

Andy was silent as he prepared for bed, and I feigned sleep as soon as it seemed realistic to do so. Lying still and quiet, I hardly dared to breathe as tears filled my eyes, trickling silently into the pillow, and whether or not he was convinced by my charade of slumber, Andy settled back against the pillows and said no more.

CHAPTER 53

The last weeks of *Tito* sped by on winged heels, and I savoured each special performance, finding new depths to Sesto's anguished confusion. We were well rested between performances and came to each as if it were the first, whilst benefiting richly from what we had learned. Megan and Andy came to Cambridge, and though she was a little reserved, my mother refrained from her trademark barbed words and looks.

'I don't understand it,' I told Gerry later. 'She didn't say a word about you, nor offer any unsolicited advice as to how I should be treating Andy. It's very strange.'

'Perhaps she's just decided things will happen as they happen and there's nothing even she can do about it,' Gerry suggested.

'Maybe, but she's getting very hard to read. It must be where I get my inscrutability from,' I laughed.

'Madsy, you're an open book.'

'Oh yes, and what do my pages read, then?' I challenged him.

'That you love me,' he grinned.

'Then I shall have to do something about that. I can't have you getting complacent and sure of yourself,' I teased. But I was glad that Gerry was sure of my love. I enjoyed showing him – and doubtless others – that he was the greatest love of my life, and I wanted him to know it. Nevertheless, as far as I could see Gerry was happy to carry on exactly as we were and was making no moves to precipitate anything further. But I was acutely aware that it need take no further action from Gerry for Andy to call in his cards. On the basis of supposition alone he had correctly deduced that more lay between Gerry and I than a professional relationship, that somehow I had bonded with him and his boys in a way that lay far beyond the opera stage.

At our final performance in Birmingham we were emotional and sad to see the opera put to bed. It had been special for us all, and the weeks that lay ahead would leave us bereaved in some way. We would all move on to the artistic challenges that lay ahead, but there is always a period of mourning when an especially satisfying project finally comes to an end. I was mourning too the loss of special time with Gerry. Once *Tito* was over, it was inevitable that we would see each other less and our meetings would again have to be carefully arranged, and organised to fit into family life, even without Andy's increasing vigilance and the separate demands of two busy careers.

The shadow of impending loss hung over our day and night in Birmingham. I cried on Annie's tolerant shoulder before we changed for our final show, weeping that my sorrow as our beautiful month ended had been painfully exacerbated by Gerry's strange mood.

'I don't know what I've done wrong,' I cried helplessly. 'He barely spoke all the way here. It was as if we'd turned the clock back to those funny old days in the summer when he was messing me about. Like he suddenly didn't know whether he wanted to be with me after all. It was such hard work, Annie. I eventually gave up and tried to learn *The Music Makers* off my CD!'

'That's my girl,' she chuckled. Then, more seriously, 'Didn't you ask him what was wrong?'

'I asked him if he was all right about twenty times, and all I got was 'Hmm' and 'I don't know', classic Gerryisms designed to keep me at arm's length. And Annie, you know he hasn't told me he loves me since we opened *Tito* in London. I tell him every day, and I send him emails and text him when we can't see each other, but he hardly ever emails me now. It doesn't usually matter because we have such a wonderful time when we are together, but after today, I'm frightened he doesn't love me at all. That he's just waiting to get rid of me after the show's over.'

Annie studied me thoughtfully before she answered. It gave me time to stem my tears and to think how often in our brief acquaintance she had been strong and comforting for me. I hoped that if the day came I would be as loyal and patient in her time of need as she had been in mine.

'I think that's unlikely, darling, given the little you've told me, and what I see of the two of you. Gerry may not be the world's greatest romantic, but I see he cares for you, even as you both try madly to play it cool in public. It's so funny sometimes, Madsy, because you make it more obvious by ignoring each other.'

I smiled. 'It's hard to get out of the habit of trying to hide what I feel, even though I guess everyone knows by now.'

Annie took my hand.

'Look, sweetie, if Gerry's giving you grief, ask him about it. Don't you think you've gone through enough together now to do that? You seem to think that he controls every aspect of your relationship and you have to take whatever he throws at you. Take charge now and again. After all, you're the one with something to lose in all this. He's not married and you are.'

'I'd just die without him, Annie.'

'That's rubbish and you know it,' she rebuked me sharply. 'Don't be so melodramatic. There was life before Gerry and there can be life after him if that's how the cookie crumbles. Don't demean yourself by suggesting otherwise. But, for what it's worth, if you want this relationship to continue and you think there's a problem, for goodness sake, talk to him about it.'

Annie sat back, her piece said. I squeezed her hand gratefully.

'Annie, I do love you. I'm sorry you always bear the brunt of this.'

'I love you, too, Madsy, and I'm glad to be here when that idiot upsets you, but I'd rather see you happy. You don't need to submit yourself to this all the time.'

I knew that Annie was right. It took so little for Gerry to reduce me to a crumbling heap, just as it took so little for him to send me onto clouds of rapture. He could break my heart with one ill chosen word, and then mend it again with a kiss, leaving it more tender and vulnerable each time. I nearly broke down as I sang *Parto, Parto* to Vitellia's unyielding back that night, but I used my pain, letting it fill my voice and my body until the final anguished bars. The applause as I left the stage told me that I had never sung it better, so perhaps it was all worthwhile after all.

We marked our final performance with a celebration in the theatre bar after the curtain fell. Gerry was expansive and overexcited as he received praise and thanks from everyone. I left him to his own devices, as I mingled with the cast and crew, laughed uproariously with Annie and Francesca, and talked seriously with John, our kind bass who'd sung Publio. But eventually we all drifted back to the hotel and I had to face Gerry alone.

I was tense with anxiety and pain, suddenly sure that I was facing my last night with him, and he was quiet as we got ready for bed, though put his arms around me readily enough as I cuddled up to him. He sighed deeply, saying nothing as we lay in the darkness.

'Gerry?' I ventured when I could bear it no longer.

'Hmm.'

'What have I done to make you angry with me?'

'Nothing. I'm not angry with you,' he said quietly. 'Why should I be?'

'Because you're fed up with me?' I sounded five years old, but I'd left my pride on the stage two hours earlier.

'Of course not.' Gerry kissed my hair, and stroked my back gently as I buried my face in his neck.

'But you've hardly spoken to me today. I know there's something wrong. Please tell me so I can put it right.'

Gerry was silent, but he held me closer, so I waited.

'I've been thinking about where we go from here,' he said eventually.

'Where do you want to go?' I asked, hoping he would keep talking.

'I don't know,' he replied slowly. 'I just don't know.'

I lay very still, willing myself not to cry, knowing that I must not confuse this important moment with indulgent tears.

'Have you considered what the options are?'

'Hmm... yes... I think so.'

'And?' I laboured on.

'We carry on like this, or we could consider something rather more, well, more permanent, I suppose.'

I raised my head to look at him, daring to meet his eye. He fixed me with his sweet, quizzical stare.

'Or we could call it a day, of course,' he concluded.

'That doesn't sound like a good option to me,' I said tremulously.

'Possibly not,' he responded calmly.

I felt anything but calm as I concentrated on the tender warmth of Gerry's hands on my back.

'Are you considering it nonetheless?' I asked with trepidation.

'Not really. I don't know.'

'What do you know?' I said more strongly, my heart beating so fast I fancied that Gerry could feel it against him.

'That you are very beautiful to me.'

'If that's so, it's because I love you.'

'I know that too.'

'Good.'

He smiled at me at last.

'And I know we have a very nice time together,' he added, kissing me softly.

'So what's the difficulty?'

'I don't know if there is one,' he answered thoughtfully.

'Oh, Gerry,' I sighed, having serious trouble holding back my tears. 'I belong to you so completely. I am yours in every way, whatever you want, wherever we go from here.'

'But you are married. We can't escape that fact.'

I looked at him, wide-eyed.

'But I want you. I love you. I want to be with you and look after you and Ben and Josh, and, well, everything that goes with that.'

Gerry wiped away the tear that had finally escaped.

'I know you do, but how is that going to be possible, Madison?'

'I could come to live with you.'

'That's a pretty drastic step.'

'And it's not what you want,' I interpreted sadly.

'I don't know.'

I wanted to press him further, but just shifted position so he could entwine his long legs around mine and I feathered his soft mouth with kisses until he laughed again.

'Lovely Madison.'

'My beautiful Gerry.'

'If you say so.'

'I do.'

'That's all right, then.'

CHAPTER 54

As I went about my business the following week I felt sad and weepy again, and it was as if the clock had been turned back. I remembered the tearful days of the summer, crying for Gerry on the heath and in the shower, hoping against all the evidence that one day he, too, would love me. Although he was cheerful and easy-going again the day after the Birmingham show, affectionate and sweet as we drove home, I couldn't forget our inconclusive conversation. It had left me no surer of his feelings or his hopes for the future, and as we settled back into the busyness of our individual lives, I feared I never would. Andy was deep into work at The Dragon, but when he was around there was an awkwardness between us. There was no confrontation, but things had changed. He watched me closely, as if looking for something that would prove his suspicions, and almost every day he found a reason to make a barbed comment about Gerry.

'Why don't you ask Gerry?' he said infuriatingly when I asked him genially enough to explain some facet of the American presidential election.

'Because I don't want to ask him, thank you, I'm asking you.'

'That makes a change,' he sneered.

'Andy, stop this, please.'

'Stop what?'

'Making these ridiculous comments about Gerry all the time,' I snapped.

'Oh, you seem upset. Isn't the course of true love running smoothly?'

'What's that supposed to mean?'

'So you and Gerry aren't having the love affair of the century then?' Andy smiled unpleasantly. 'Oh, forgive me Madison, I thought he was the axis around which you revolved, the sun to your moon, the…'

'For goodness sake, Andy,' I interrupted him, 'don't be sarcastic.'

'I wasn't being sarcastic. Just making an observation,' he replied coolly, and I took the line of least resistance and left the room.

Puff opened at The Dragon and Andy seemed to lay aside his grievances for the evening as Megan and I joined the production team and the cast for the first night celebration. But I was in poor shape, desperately missing Gerry, who I'd not seen for a week, and unjustifiably resentful of the things that kept us apart.

'Are you all right, darling?' Megan asked more gently than usual as we ate pizza slices and drank red wine in the foyer of The Dragon. Her kind tone brought tears to my eyes and I had to turn away, pretending to seek out a refill.

'Madsy?' Megan, sharp-eyed as ever, saw my distress.

'I'm fine, Mum,' I assured her, burying my face in pizza.

'Are you missing *Tito*?' she probed.

'Yes, I am,' I replied honestly. 'It was so good. Funnily enough, although it was a far less prestigious production, I miss it even more than *Flute*.'

'It was very special to you, wasn't it?'

'Yes, it was.'

I looked her in the eye, suddenly wanting to pour my heart out to her. My mouth trembled as I fiercely held back my tears. We held each other's gaze for a long moment.

'Oh, Madison, be happy for Andy tonight,' she said heavily.

'I am. It's a lovely show.'

She shook her head and I knew that the moment of understanding, had it ever existed, had disappeared.

My pent-up emotions poured out all over Gerry when I finally saw him two days later. In his kitchen I sobbed against his chest as he held me close, murmuring in anxious tenderness.

'Please, Madsy, I don't want you to be upset. Don't cry. What is it? Please tell me.'

'I've missed you so much,' I wept. 'I can't bear it without you.'

'I know, I know,' he whispered helplessly.

'I can't go so long without seeing you, Gerry.'

'I couldn't help it,' he said, stroking my hair. 'You know how much I've had on since we got back.' As he began to remind me of what he'd been doing over the last week, I cut him off gently.

'Darling, I know, I do. I'm not getting on to you. I'm just telling you why I'm crying. I'm so glad to see you.'

'And I you, little one.'

My tears had dried when Ben and Josh returned from school, and I hugged them both with joy.

'Hey, take a chill pill, Mads,' said Ben, looking me over in amusement. 'We haven't just got back from Australia.'

Josh rolled his eyes, but smiled with infinite sweetness.

'Perhaps it just seems like that,' I laughed, as grateful to see them as I was their dad.

So we ate supper together, and Josh showed me his latest English coursework, and when the boys eventually drifted off Gerry studied me across the table as he idly entwined his long fingers in mine. I smiled. It was lovely to be happy again.

'Hello.'

'Hello.'

I loved Gerry's faintly ironic emphasis on the last syllable.

'It's so wonderful to be with you all again.'

'Good.'

'I've missed the boys, too.'

'So I see.'

If I didn't already know that this was a typical Gerry-Madison dialogue I would be screaming with frustration, but I was finally learning that when he was at his most monosyllabic and non-committal, Gerry was thinking carefully and deeply. I stroked his cheek and waited.

'I've been thinking a lot about us this week,' he said quietly.

'Really?' I smiled encouragingly. 'Is that good or bad?'

'Oh, good, I think,' he went on. 'Were you all right at home? Since we got back, I mean?'

'I missed you very badly. Andy was cross. I thought Megan was going to be supportive when she saw I was unhappy at the *Puff* party, but it didn't last.' I shrugged. 'I had one small job, saw a couple of students, caught up on everything I'd neglected during *Tito*, looked at *Carmen*. I survived. I'm here now, as you see.'

'How are things with you and Andy?' he asked.

I was irritated.

'How do you think they are? I'm not his favourite person because he's angry at how much time I spend with you. He regularly hints and implies that he knows the full extent of our relationship, but is never specific, so he just simmers angrily most of the time. I can't put anything right with him because I'm missing you and just waiting for the next time I can be with you, and he can see that. He's proved far more perceptive than I ever thought he was. I say very little; he concludes much, usually correctly.'

Gerry nodded slowly.

'What do you want to do about it?' he asked.

'I want to live with you and the boys.'

'You make it sound very simple,' Gerry mused.

'I didn't say it was simple; the implications are horrendous. But you asked me what I wanted and that *is* what I want – what I would like.'

'Hmm.'

Gerry got up from the table, returning with wine and glasses. As he poured he said, 'Do you think you'd enjoy it if you did?'

'I'm sure I would. And would you?'

'What do you think?'

'Gerry, I've no idea. Help me out here. You're not exactly forthcoming about how you feel about me, and what you'd like to happen. As far as I can tell, you carry on exactly the same when we're apart, and I'm the one who's grieving. We have a nice time when we're together, and you're lovely to me, but otherwise it makes no difference to your life.'

'Madison, that's not true.' He paused, looking at me seriously. 'I love you, you know that.'

'No, I don't. I don't know that at all.'

We both fell silent and I studied Gerry's beautiful hands, fiddling now with the stem of his wineglass.

'That's not fair,' he said eventually. 'We might show it rather differently, but you should be as sure of my love for you as I am of yours.'

'Then let me come to live with you.'

'Isn't it a bit soon?' he asked reasonably.

'Not for me,' I told him. 'You are the dearest love of my life, and I was made to be yours.'

'Maybe so.'

I looked up at Gerry's sweet face, checking to see if he was laughing at me. He winked and laced his fingers in mine again.

'I promise I'll think about it. I *am* thinking about it,' he said.

'I don't know what there is to think about,' I said sadly.

'Madison, I've said I'll think about it, and I mean that.'

'I love you.' I didn't know what else to say.

'I know you do. Now come here and give me a hug.'

So I moved round to his side of the table, and sat on his lap and we cuddled and kissed a bit until Ben came looking for his flute. I wondered if Gerry would move me off his knee, but he didn't, which I took as a good sign, and neither did Ben look surprised or disapproving. In fact, he didn't even seem to notice, as he searched under the table.

'Where's my flute, Dad?' he asked, a disembodied voice as he disappeared from sight.

'Where you left it, I expect,' Gerry said matter of factly, prompting Ben to relocate his search to the hallway.

'Found it!' he called out in triumph.

'Now there's a surprise,' Gerry laughed.

As I left, with great reluctance, to return home later that night, Ben let me hug him without demur and I made the most of it.

'Bye, darling. See you soon.'

'Bye, Madsy,' he said winningly. 'I hope I will.'

'Charmer!' I accused him. 'I don't know where you get it from.'

'From Dad I expect,' he replied innocently.

'That must be why I love you both,' I laughed, and his soft smile warmed me all the way home.

CHAPTER 55

The critics enjoyed *Puff* enormously and it was clear that Andy's arrival at The Restless Dragon and the success of both *Lethal Desires* and now *Puff* were seen by Joe Budzynski to be inextricably linked. I marvelled afresh: a year ago Andy was picking up the odd job here and there, pessimistic about his future prospects, and, I sometimes wondered, on the verge of resenting the success that had come my way. Now his future as The Dragon's assistant director seemed secure and he would soon be in a position to cast his net wider on the back of two critically acclaimed productions. He and Joe were still working on Joe's Polish émigré story and the first pages of script that I saw boded well.

'We're going to need a singer for *Elushka*,' Andy told me. 'Someone really classy to sing Polish folk songs.' He scrutinised me closely. 'You will do it, won't you, Mads?'

'Oh, Andy, I don't know at this stage. It depends when it goes up and what my other commitments are at the time.'

He looked crestfallen.

'But Joe wants you.'

'That's terribly nice of him, but what if it coincides with an ENO job? You'll have to fit around me Andy, not the other way round.'

Andy's disappointment quickly turned to anger.

'What else should I expect? Why should you slum it with us when you could be with Gerry?'

'It's nothing to do with Gerry. He's not at the Coli, is he?'

'Maybe not, but even if you said you'd sing for us, and then Gerry called you up and asked you do something with him, you'd drop us like a hot brick.'

'Of course I wouldn't. If I was contracted to The Restless Dragon that would be the end of it.'

Andy looked sceptical. Shrugging, he indicated the subject at a close.

'Well, anyway, you probably won't be around. You'll have moved in with Gerry by then.'

'I don't think so,' I said quietly.

'Do you have to sound so sad about it?' Andy asked bitterly.

'I can't win at the moment, can I?'

'Not for as long as you go on seeing Mr Wonderful,' he agreed.

Despite this, I was comforted by the knowledge that Andy was enjoying himself at The Dragon and I was quite unprepared when he returned from his stint as duty AD in a towering fury a week after we'd had the conversation about *Elushka*. I'd managed to spend almost a whole day with Gerry and I was dozing contentedly, my only regret that I'd not stayed longer in the warmth of his arms and his bed. The slam of the front door jerked me fully awake and I lay still as I heard Andy's footsteps making heavy progress into the kitchen. I sighed resignedly. I couldn't pretend that his loud arrival hadn't wakened me, and better to face him voluntarily than be commanded out of bed.

In the kitchen Andy was pouring a whisky, his face like thunder.

'What's the matter?' I asked nervously.

'Nothing,' he spat fiercely. 'Absolutely nothing.'

'Please, Andy.'

He tossed down the Scotch, his rigid back communicating nothing. I waited.

'Joe's pulled me off the *Lethal Desires* tour. He's sending Ron with a new AD and wants me to stay in London with him for the spring season at The Dragon.'

'Oh, is that all?'

'Is that all?' Andy was incandescent. 'It's my play, remember.'

'You had so much input when it was on in the autumn, surely you can feel it's in safe hands now,' I tried to placate him.

'That's not the point. Joe said I wasn't experienced enough to tour and that he still needs to watch my work. After all I've done!' Andy slammed his glass on the counter, and poured another drink, shimmering with self-righteous anger.

'I think you're grossly overreacting,' I chided him. 'You should take advantage of working closely with Joe on new projects.'

'Like I'm overreacting about you and Gerry McFall, I suppose?'

'Oh, no, please let's not go down that route again,' I begged.

'At least it'll put paid to whatever plans you and he had for my absence,' he laughed unpleasantly. 'I'm afraid I'll be home now.'

'You didn't get cross with Joe, did you?' I asked without much hope. This was all horribly familiar.

'Of course not, Madison,' Andy sneered. 'I didn't do anything to jeopardise my job. I know exactly what you'd think of that. Don't worry, Joe didn't sack me. I just might decide not to go back. And I can withdraw author's permission for *Lethal Desires* to tour if I want.'

'Oh, no, Andy, I don't believe this. It's quite out of proportion.'

'Just as your relationship with Gerry is out of proportion,' he stormed back. 'But that's all right, Madison. There's the phone. Ring him now, why don't you?'

'No thank you.'

'Then go to bed and leave me alone.'

I retreated, my heart heavy. Lying against the pillows, sleep a remote possibility, I wondered why I hadn't foreseen this. So caught up with Gerry and my own career, I had blithely assumed that Andy's relationship with The Dragon a match made in heaven, safe from the usual disasters. I'd thought he valued his life there enough not to jettison it with a fit of pique. It was a long time before Andy came to bed, and I lay awake until the early hours, wondering what was to become of both of us.

I recognised the pattern that subsequently emerged and I knew where it would lead if Andy followed his familiar course. Moody and secretive, he stopped talking about The Dragon and I strongly suspected that he was absenting himself from work. I didn't know how he'd left things with Joe, and didn't dare to ask. At the weekend, I had a concert in Salisbury, Andy was supposed to be on duty at the theatre, and I'd persuaded Megan to drive me down there. Gerry was away, conducting in Amsterdam, and I felt bleak. Before I left, I broached Andy with trepidation.

'Have you sorted things out with Joe regarding the spring?' I asked.

'Thank you for checking up on me, Madison,' he snapped. 'And who's going to Salisbury with you tomorrow?'

'You know it's Megan.' I refused to let him deflect me. 'Andy, please tell me what's going on.'

'What's going on,' he mocked nastily. 'What's going on is that you're only interested in what happens to me in so far as it might affect you and your lover.'

'I want things to be all right for you at The Dragon,' I sighed. 'It's so nice there and everyone loves you. Please resolve things with Joe.'

'How do you know they're not resolved?' he asked.

'Does that mean that they are?'

'Just leave me alone,' he growled.

'I'd like to see *Puff* again next week. Is there any reason why I can't?' I wondered if the prospect of my making an unscheduled visit to The Dragon might spur Andy into something – action or explanation.

'I expect you'll do whatever you want, Madison.'

'I think Andy might have walked out on The Dragon,' I told Gerry as he took me through Bach's *Christmas Oratorio*.

'Why so?' he asked, eyebrows raised questioningly.

I filled him in.

'But you don't know for sure?' he queried.

'No. I'm just surmising.'

'Can't you ask him directly?'

'It doesn't work like that with Andy,' I told him. 'If things go well, he's positively loquacious; when they go badly, he'd insist Tuesday was Wednesday rather than tell the truth. If I ask him he won't tell me, and he'll just get angry.'

'That's ridiculous.'

'I know, but that's the way it goes.'

Later, as we drank tea in the kitchen, Gerry asked me, 'If Andy has finished with The Restless Dragon, what will he do?'

'Go back to his old regime, I expect. Doing as little as humanly possible,' I said wryly.

'That doesn't sound very fair on you.' Gerry looked at me with concern.

'He doesn't think I'm fair to him, so that argument won't work either,' I told him.

'Because of me, you mean?' he asked.

I nodded.

'Have you talked to him about us?'

'No. What is there to talk about?' I looked at him questioningly. 'If and when there's something to tell him, I'll do so.'

'Do you want to stay tonight?'

'I think my absence would be noticed,' I said, surprised that Gerry had asked.

'Ring him and say you're not coming back till tomorrow.'

'I don't think I can do that,' I told him reluctantly. 'I can't precipitate another crisis before I've established what's going on at The Dragon.

'Okay,' he said easily, 'but don't say I didn't ask.'

In bed later that night I cried into my pillow, thinking what a fool I had been not to stay with Gerry. Andy stayed out till after midnight, and when he returned I doubted he would have noticed if my side of the bed were empty or not.

I trundled through the *Christmas Oratorio* in Salisbury, unusually glad of Megan's company, and I ended up enjoying myself so much as I sang Bach's cheerful music that I knew I couldn't let the unsatisfactory situation at home continue. I phoned Annie on the Monday.

'Listen, mate, I need your help. Can you bear to sit through a performance of *Puff the Magic Dragon*, and lurk protectively if I have to do some detective work?'

Trooper that she was, Annie agreed readily enough and two days later we turned up at The Restless Dragon, slipping into our seats just as the lights went down. We bided our time until the final curtain before trooping backstage in search of Andy. He wasn't there.

'Madison?'

Joe Budzynski bustled up to us in surprise.

'Hello, Joe. Sorry to bother you. We were just looking for Andy.'

Joe was clearly deeply embarrassed, flapping his hands helplessly as he looked around for someone to rescue him.

'Joe, it's okay. Don't feel awkward. I take it he's not been around for a few days, since you told him he wasn't doing the *Lethal Desires* tour?'

Joe nodded anxiously.

'Is there still a place for him here if he wants it?'

'Of course. He's being a very stupid boy, but I like him. Tell him that Joe wants him at The Dragon. He's got to do as I say, but if he does that, he can't go wrong.'

'Fine, Joe. Thank you. It might take a few days, but I'll get it sorted.'

'Ye gods, Madsy,' Annie marvelled as we left. 'I'd bloody kill him if he was my husband.'

'Don't think I haven't been tempted,' I answered her grimly, 'but I'm not exactly on the moral high ground these days, am I?'

'I suppose not.' She paused a beat. 'What are you and Gerry going to do?' she asked curiously.

'I don't know, Annie. It's up to Gerry, but first I've got to get Andy safely back to The Dragon. I owe him that.'

'Why? He's the fool if he walks out because his pride has been wounded,' she opined.

'It's not as simple as that,' I sighed. 'He's done this before, and I suppose he should have to learn the hard way, but he doesn't learn. He'll do this until there are no more opportunities left. Annie, if I'm even thinking of leaving him to live with Gerry, I can't let things stay like this. He's got to be able to support himself and have a life without me so, you see, I'm not being entirely altruistic.'

'But you're still waiting on Gerry to determine your future?' she said with an ironic lift of the eyebrow.

'I'm not proud,' I smiled sadly at her. 'He knows what I want, so what else can I do?'

'Dump him?'

I shook my head.

'I can't do that. My life is utterly bound up in his now. I can't begin to imagine it without him. It makes me feel ill,' I confessed frankly.

'Oh, Madsy, what a situation,' Annie said with feeling.

'Hmm. I wouldn't exactly recommend it, but it exists, so I have to deal with it. Now, let's get a drink and you can help me work out how I'm going to persuade Andy to go back to The Dragon.'

CHAPTER 56

Ultimately, I knew that there was no way round it but to tell Andy that I'd been to see Joe. I risked his wrath, his accusations of interfering, of humiliating him in the eyes of Budzynski, but set against the ongoing drama that was my life, it seemed a small price to pay. What was one more argument if there was a chance that from it Andy might be inclined to set things right with Joe? With nothing to be lost, and something to be gained, the next day I metaphorically and physically took a deep breath and tackled him.

'Annie and I went to see *Puff* last night,' I said, without rancour.

'Oh, I see,' Andy growled. 'I expected this sooner or later.'

'Expected what?'

'That you'd go checking up on me. So what did you discover? Apart from the fact that I wasn't there, of course?'

'That Joe wants you back at The Dragon. He was quite unequivocal about that.'

'And he'd let me tour with *Lethal Desires*?' Andy asked.

'No, I don't think so. He says that you must do what he tells you. But that's reasonable, surely? He is the manager. Look, Andy, he wouldn't want you back if he didn't think you're good news for the theatre. That place is a venue to be reckoned with and if you can stick it out there (which should surely be a pleasure) then you'll have enough credit and kudos to be considered by the bigger provincials and eventually, perhaps, the West End.'

'Says she who knows exactly how to play the system,' Andy sneered, 'with a little help from Mr McFall.'

'Stop it, Andy. This is nothing to do with my career, or Gerry, or anything other than getting you to see reason. You are throwing away the best opportunity you have ever had. Joe won't wait indefinitely, but if you act now, everything will be as it was, I'm sure of it.'

There was little else I could say, short of repeating it all over again, so I stayed silent whilst Andy brooded.

'Stop seeing Gerry and I'll go back to The Dragon,' he said eventually.

Irritation snapped like a taut wire inside me.

'For goodness sake, Andy. This is just ridiculous. I'm not working with Gerry till the summer again in any case.'

'That doesn't mean you won't see him,' he observed.

'Maybe, maybe not. I don't know.' I was getting onto dangerous territory here, and was keen to steer us back to the issue at hand. 'Andy, go back to The Dragon and you'll have a serious career. Ditch it now and I'm even more convinced that you'll regret it. Separate it from anything else; it's not just me nagging you to go back for my own reasons, or even because I think it's wrong in principle to have walked out. I'm begging you to go back for *you*. If you can't accept anything else, please try to accept that.'

'I don't have to accept anything you say, Madison,' Andy replied coolly. 'You don't have the answer to everything, you know.'

'I'm not advocating that I do,' I ploughed on in desperation. 'I just don't understand why you're prepared to let something as good as The Restless Dragon go so easily.'

'And I don't understand why you've allowed Gerry McFall and his family to take over your life. How's the older one doing at DCP by the way? Bringing honour on your good name, I hope.'

I said nothing.

'That's fine, Madison. Don't answer me, but don't expect me to give you an answer either. It's up to me if I go back to The Dragon, not you. So I suggest we leave this conversation right here.'

I was too exhausted to pursue it, but I knew I couldn't leave it indefinitely. I recalled Andy's cold ultimatum: stop seeing Gerry and I'll go back to the Dragon. He knew that even without an opera in rehearsal I was spending time with Gerry, and for all I could tell, knew too that I loved him. Pressing my face into my pillow I sighed with regret for so much, yet utterly unable to do what Andy demanded. He needed to find a reason to go back to The Dragon that was not contingent upon me, a reason for him to be happy and satisfied in his own achievements there. But whilst he was blinded by his bitterness and disappointment with both Joe and me, he was unlikely to find it.

In the midst of all this, I had something of a respite, an oasis of pleasure and happiness, when I took Ben to Cambridge to sing *Rejoice in the Lamb*. Gerry was working and couldn't chaperone him, and my heart warmed with joy to have Ben entrusted to my loving care for a whole happy Friday. Andy watched me go with looks of dark fury. He had made no move to resolve The Dragon situation and I feared that Joe's patience would wear thin, but it was, without a doubt, an enormous relief to escape the tense atmosphere of the flat for a day. I cared desperately about the outcome of Andy's situation, but to surrender to Ben's uncomplicated company was like sunshine after a storm.

I hugged him tightly when we met at King's Cross station, as Gerry gazed benevolently upon us.

'Darling Ben, you have made me a very happy girl today,' I told him.

'Why? I haven't done anything yet,' he asked, grinning broadly.

'Just the pleasure of being in your company, my angel,' I said, mussing his hair. 'I love you very much.'

'I know,' he said smugly. 'I'm enormously loveable.'

My emotions were on a roller coaster, and I was close to tears before ten o'clock in the morning. Gerry saw that I was fragile, and took my hand as he issued instructions in which Ben clearly had no interest whatsoever. I leaned against Gerry and he kissed the top of my head, still trying vainly to engage Ben's attention. Eventually, he gave up.

'Oh well, over to you Madsy. I surrender any attempt at control. Look after Madison today, young man,' he instructed his son.

We all grinned at each other and my poor heart nearly burst with love. Gerry held his arms out to us both, and for a beautiful moment the three of us hugged each other tightly.

'Have a nice day,' he said. 'I love you.'

Whether he was addressing Ben or me wasn't clear, but we both answered him.

'Love you, Dad,' Ben muttered.

'I love you, too, sweetheart,' I murmured into Gerry's jacket, and we all laughed.

I basked in the glow of Ben's undemanding presence all day, and thought with pleasure how close we'd grown since the summer, even since I'd chaperoned him to Chichester in October. He chatted to me without restraint, pulled onto my hands, arms, or shoulders, as he demanded my attention or, more endearingly still, when he was engaged in something else entirely. On the train he leaned heavily against me and the warmth of his thin young arms silently comforted me. In Cambridge he grilled me closely on the rehearsal and to my amazement even asked me to run through his solo with him alone as we prepared for the evening, a privilege I thought he bestowed only on Gerry. It was a healing, wholesome day, and as Ben dozed against my shoulder on the train home I allowed my imagination to wander, dreaming idly of a time when I might wake each day free to pour out my love on this beautiful boy, his brother and his dad. As I kissed his soft hair and laid my cheek against his head, he stirred, sitting up quickly to see what he might be missing.

'Where are we?' he asked.

'About twenty minutes out of King's Cross, I think.' I smiled at him, drinking in his intelligent and precocious countenance.

'Madison?'

'Yes, darling?'

'Josh says he thinks you might come to live with us.' Ben looked casual, but I sensed my answer mattered.

'Is that a question, a statement, or an opinion?' I asked.

'Dunno.'

'I'm sure it would be fun,' I said slowly, 'but I'm not sure it's very practical.'

This seemed to satisfy him, and he turned his attention to the ubiquitous food supplies that Gerry had provided for the journey.

'Better eat these up quickly,' he said. 'We can't go home with anything left over.'

CHAPTER 57

I was glad of my lovely day as we inched towards Christmas. I sang here and there, skirted around Andy, who was still considering his options as far as The Dragon was concerned, and I tried to work out what I could live with and what I couldn't. Everything hung heavily in limbo and I longed for the new year when I vainly imagined something would change: Andy would go back to the theatre, Gerry would ask me to move in with him and the boys, and we'd all be fearfully amicable about the whole thing, Megan included. It was a fairy tale, I knew, but an attractive one nevertheless. But the new year seemed achingly far off, with Christmas under Megan's close scrutiny yet to endure.

'Please, Andy,' I shamelessly wheedled, '*Puff* is half way through its run. You're missing all the fun, and you'll have no chance of being involved in the *Lethal Desires* tour if you're simply not there.'

'Any other reasons you want to offer me, Madison?' he sneered. 'Like you want me out of the house so you can entertain your lover here? It doesn't matter anyway. If you don't see him here, you'll see him somewhere else, not to forget your cosy little chaperoning trips.'

The script never changed much: I pleaded with Andy to go back to The Dragon, he made snide remarks about Gerry and the boys, and I held off from saying 'All right, I'll go and live with them now if that's what you think I'm going to do eventually' because I simply feared that whilst the door of 22 Thurlow Park Road might not exactly be slammed in my face, it wouldn't be opened too widely either. And in any case, I wanted the initiative to come from Gerry. I wanted him to say that he loved me so much he couldn't bear the prospect of life without me. But for all his gentle tenderness, his soft look of amused pleasure in my company, the warm touch of his hands and mouth, and his arms around me, he couldn't, or wouldn't, say the words I longed to hear.

A week before Christmas I wept in the passenger seat of Gerry's car as he stroked my hair and murmured nothing in particular.

'Oh, Madsy, I can't leave you like this,' he sighed.

'Then don't leave me at all,' I sobbed.

Gerry shrugged helplessly. 'What do you want me to do?'

'I want to be with you permanently. You must know that by now. You now how much I love you all.'

'Yes, I do,' he said softly, without his customary irony, and I smiled through my tears.

'How do you know?' I teased.

'Because it's written all over you, in everything you say and do, in every look and every touch.'

My face flushed with love and shyness and I buried it in Gerry's jacket.

'How embarrassing. Everyone notices, don't they?'

'Yes,' he laughed softly.

'Oh, no, Gerry, do you get asked awkward questions?' I was mortified.

'No, just knowing smiles when your name is mentioned.'

He put his arms round me and we held each other in silence for a while.

'It would be very difficult for you if you left Andy, wouldn't it?' Gerry said eventually.

'Enormously. It wouldn't be easy for you either.'

We looked at each other frankly.

'No.' Gerry shook his head. 'It would be an incredible adjustment for us all to make.'

'I am very worried about Andy and The Dragon,' I told him. 'I want nothing more than to be with you, but the biggest practical obstacle is Andy's security. If he were still happily ensconced at the theatre at least I'd know he'd have a decent income, whatever he chose to do with it. I wouldn't even worry about him having Exeter House. All I'd take would be my own things.' I stopped abruptly. 'It feels peculiar even talking like this.'

'I know,' Gerry soothed. 'But all that side of it is your concern Madison. I can't help you with any of that.'

I was surprised to find that I didn't mind Gerry's evident reluctance to be involved in the workings out of my own personal circumstances. He was right that only I could make such hard choices, and I knew that it was enough that I ask him to consider making such sweeping changes to his own life, and the boys' lives. And I liked his independence, his freedom to stand aside from my own concerns, refusing to be burdened by matters that I had to resolve in my own heart. All I needed from Gerry was that he be sure of his love for me, and he had to work that through without my help, just as I had done in the long, painful months before he ever returned my love for him.

'And you can't help me with how I feel, with the issues I have to consider about Ben and Josh, about what I want to happen in their lives as well as mine,' Gerry went on frankly. 'I'm sorry, Madsy, I'm so hopeless. Perhaps we'll arrive at the same point together and it will all be clear what we should do.'

Although my skin was perceptibly tougher than it had been in the spring, still I felt desperately bleak at his words, as the prospect of a future with him seemed unutterably remote. I pulled back.

'When you've decided what you want, let me know, Gerry. You know where to find me.'

'Madison, that's not fair. I could say the same to you. If I asked you to come home with me tonight and stay for good, could you do that without hesitation?'

'In my heart, yes,' I told him. 'It's everything else that would be a problem. But since you're not asking me to do that, isn't it totally hypothetical anyway?'

'If you really love me, you'll wait for me, and hold out for what you want,' said Gerry seriously.

'Oh, Gerry, only you could say something so complacent and arrogant and manage to make it sound like an offer I can't refuse,' I laughed.

He looked affronted.

'What do you mean?'

'You're so sure of me, aren't you?' I said.

'Am I wrong to be so?'

'No.' I shook my head.

'You are lovely.' Gerry stroked my cheek softly.

'So are you.'

'I don't think so,' he smiled, 'but I'm glad you do.'

CHAPTER 58

Of course, we were no further forwards after that. But finally, Andy went to see Joe. It was too late for him to go back to The Dragon for *Puff*, but miracle of miracles, three days before Christmas he told me that he was resigned to staying in London in the spring if Joe would take him back.

'Please, Andy, go to see him today. Don't waste another moment.'

To my surprise, he went without argument or question, and returned smiling. *Lethal Desires* would tour without Andy, but suddenly he had accepted staying with the next in-house production and resuming work on *Elushka* with Joe. With *Puff* in its final two weeks, Andy was due to start back in the second week of January. I sighed with relief, but couldn't help but be cautious. Lips, cups and slips betwixt had coincided before now, and not until Andy was firmly reinstated at the theatre would I believe it. But he seemed to have relaxed a little and whatever had driven him to bury his pride and see Joe again, I was grateful for it.

It certainly made things easier with Megan. I had wondered how we would get through the Christmas holiday on the pretence that all was well at The Dragon. Her rampant inquisitiveness would have doubtless found our responses to her endless questions wanting had we not been buoyed up with the assurance that Andy was once again in harness, and without her having even known that there had been a hitch.

Only Annie had known, by virtue of her visit with me to The Dragon, and not for the first time I wondered at how, in so short a time, she had become such a trusted friend.

On Christmas Eve afternoon, neither of us gainfully employed, we giggled in my kitchen as we made canapés for the evening. In a rush of enthusiasm and a desire to blank out the empty seasonal days without Gerry, I had invited Annie, Graham Fellows and his wife, Sophie and Jim, Danielle and Steve, Ron Stryker, Megan, Lizzie, and various acquaintances of ours to drop in for drinks and nibbles, and incredibly I had found many people not only able, but apparently keen, to spend an hour or two with us before moving on to other festivities or engagements. Annie and I played the CD of *Carmen* as we worked and sang along to our roles, eagerly anticipating the start of music calls at the end of January. We didn't talk about Gerry, gossiping instead about work, colleagues and family, and when Andy appeared at four o'clock with liquid refreshment, apparently in better spirits than he'd been for several weeks, the atmosphere was positively light. Annie joked easily with him, and I wondered what she really felt about me and Gerry and the situation that I had so comprehensively cultivated. Perhaps she despised me for it, awaiting the opportunity to tell me how wrong she believed that I was, though I never saw it in her eyes or heard it in veiled censure.

As I retrieved tiny, hot mushroom tarts from the oven, I was suddenly overwhelmed with sadness, separated from Gerry not by ten miles across town, but by a universe. Tears filled my eyes as I placed the tarts onto a large serving plate, brushing my hand quickly across my cheeks.

'Madsy, don't cry, darling.' Annie's warm arm was around my waist in a trice. 'You're doing brilliantly, and you'll see him again very soon, won't you?'

I nodded miserably.

'I'm such a mess, Annie.'

'Come on, don't think of it like that,' she chided. 'All the lovely singing you've done this year, *Carmen* to come, *Figaro*, and *Cosi*, and if you really love him, isn't it all worthwhile in the end?'

'Oh, Annie, I thought you might be angry with me about it all.'

'Mads, these things happen. I've been there, kiddo.'

I was brushing tears away as Megan breezed in.

'Are those mushroom things ready?' she asked, holding out her hand.

Just too late, Annie and I looked up and Megan saw my flushed face, recovering from my moment of disarray, but still definitely pink.

'What's the matter?' Megan's eyes were wide with alarm.

'Nothing, Mum. Just the blast of air from the oven,' I quickly improvised.

She wasn't fooled.

'I don't think so, Madison. What's happened?'

'Please, Mum, nothing, I promise. Will you take these in?' I proffered the plate of canapés.

'Hmm,' Megan grunted. 'Well talk later.'

I groaned as she retreated.

'I'd better think quickly,' I sighed to Annie.

'Good luck.' She rolled her eyes and we laughed.

'Let's hit those tarts before they all go,' she urged, taking my hand, and I let her drag me into the lounge.

I caught Megan watching me closely several times during the evening, but I was saved further interrogation. Her sister, Finty – my aunt – was staying with her for the holiday and they were due to see friends of my mother's after leaving our little party. Although they left before she had a chance to speak to me alone, I knew it couldn't be put off indefinitely, but never did I envisage the sheer ghastliness of the moment when it did arrive.

Andy had risen on Christmas Day in an apparently good frame of mind. The previous night we'd attended Midnight Mass with Dani and Steve after our visitors had left, shared a little champagne with them on our return home, and gone to bed without incident. Driving to Megan's house for lunch, he was amenable and good-natured, and I realised selfishly that I was able to handle Gerry's absence so much more easily when Andy wasn't being angry. So I relaxed and began to enjoy the convivial day in Megan's lovely home. I chatted happily with her friends, ate heartily, and saw and heard myself as if from a distance, growing jollier and more gregarious as the day wore on. In the late afternoon Megan and I sat in the capacious overstuffed settee, drinking burgundy and eating ripe brie and red grapes as Andy leaned against a book case, listening to us talking to Megan's closest male friend, a loyal escort named Doug.

'So, Madison, tell me what's happening next for you,' he enquired genially.

I told him about *Carmen*, then backtracked a little and filled him in on *Tito*. Andy took it all without comment, expressionless.

'And how was Glyndebourne?' Doug enthused. 'Megan was thrilled by her trips there.'

'It was lovely, darling, wasn't it?' Megan trilled. 'We had a marvellous time and we were so proud of her.' She looked up at Andy, urging him to confirm the wonderfulness of it all. 'Don't you agree, Andy?'

She looked faintly put out by his blank stare and my heart began to beat perceptibly faster.

'Oh, yes, Megan, I'm sure that Madison had a lovely time. Glyndebourne holds some very special memories for her, doesn't it, Mads?'

He sounded casual, genial even, but neither Megan nor I could miss the edge to his tone. Doug, quite reasonably, did.

'I'm sure they'll stay with you forever, Madison,' he smiled. 'And you'll have lots more to add to them. What stood out especially for you in your first time there?'

Andy gave a bark of sarcastic laughter and this time Doug did blink in surprise, and looked at Andy enquiringly.

'That's easy, isn't it?' Andy asked me, his smile shark-like. 'The beautiful new relationships that you developed there.'

I could feel Megan tensing beside me and I babbled hopelessly to cover the ghastly moment.

'Yes, Doug. I met some lovely people, especially Annie Winkworth, another mezzo. We did *Tito* together afterwards, and we're both in *Carmen*. But the best thing is that we became very good friends.'

'Don't forget Gerry and Ben though, Mads,' Andy cut across me sharply. 'They're the ones you really bonded with, aren't they? Your little surrogate son, and his brother, of course, not to mention his father. What's his role? Your mentor? Your muse? Or are you his?'

By now Doug must have realised something was distinctly odd, but I kept bowling on.

'Ben was one of the genies, Doug,' I explained. 'A boy treble, of course. I knew him and his father a little before the summer season, and we've worked together since.'

'Among other things,' Andy sneered, as Megan looked increasingly tight-lipped.

'Yes,' I interjected smoothly. 'They've been good friends to me and I've chaperoned Ben to a couple of choral gigs.'

'Megan, did you know that Gerry's older son has been at DCP this term?' Andy asked, deceptively mild.

'No.' Megan was short. 'You can tell me about that later, Madison.'

I smiled as if nothing could possibly be untoward about it, which, of course, it wasn't really. Gerry could send his sons wherever he wished, and I didn't even teach there anymore. That wouldn't be the point, of course, as I was fully aware.

'But the great thing now, Doug, is that I'm on an ENO contract for the next three years. I'll get to sing some excellent roles and barely have to leave London.'

'Well done, Madsy,' he praised me, 'I remember when you were just starting out at all this, nearly ten years ago, and you've done yourself proud. I know it's a great source of pleasure to Megan.'

My mother managed a stiff smile, taking Doug's glass as she rose.

'I think it's time for a refill,' she said shortly.

I covered her exit, turning the conversation to Doug's latest business ventures. He knew her well enough to realise that she was aggrieved, but he was too kind and well mannered to pursue the matter with me, for which I was grateful. The damage done, Andy stalked away and Doug patted my hand reassuringly.

'What a clever girl you are, Madsy,' he said kindly. It was the most he was able to say, but it spoke more than enough in support and affection, in a mutual awareness that Megan was a tough prospect when crossed and that he sympathised without really knowing what had precipitated her anger.

'And you're a very kind man,' I told him.

CHAPTER 59

The blow finally fell after the other guests had left. Finty still remained, but this was no deterrent to my mother.

'Finty, why don't you relax for a bit. Madison will help me to clear up.'

Megan swept out, leaving no option but to follow. She was running the hot tap as I moved on leaden feet into the kitchen. Her back rigidly turned away, she said, 'Get a tea towel, Madison.'

We worked in silence for a few moments, as I searched vainly for a neutral topic. I gave up quickly, aware that Megan was not in the mood for idle banter. I waited.

'So what was all that about?' she asked at length.

'What?' I tried innocence.

'Don't be ridiculous, Madison. You know what. What's going on between you and Andy or, perhaps more to the point, between you and the conductor? I suppose whatever it is explains your tears in the kitchen last night. Which suggests to me also that Annie knows about it.'

Her lawyer's mind had quickly analysed what she'd observed, and I suspected that she'd already drawn alarmingly accurate conclusions.

'Mum, really, there's nothing.'

'No, I'm sorry, Madison, but this has been simmering since the summer and it's time we came out with it all. I still stand by what I said to you at the beginning of November:

that you've an unhealthy and inappropriate interest in and involvement with that man, and conceivably with his family, too. I was prepared to think that it was essentially a crush, a passing phase, that would blow over if you applied a little of your customary sense and decency. Now I'm not so sure. Reluctantly, I'm rather more inclined to think it's considerably more than that.'

'He's my friend,' I said truthfully.

'I don't doubt he's your friend,' Megan replied.

I looked helplessly at her, her stare pinning me to the spot.

'Are you in love with him, Madison? Is he in love with you? Tell me what's happened to make Andy so angry. What's happened to change you so much? Look at yourself.' She grabbed me and turned me to face the mirror. 'You're so thin you'll start looking anorexic soon. But there's something different inside you, too. I saw it happening during *The Magic Flute* and it was there for everyone to see when you were singing Sesto. I'm not questioning for a moment that you're singing wonderfully well, you've blossomed and flourished like a hothouse flower, but I'm not sure I'm comfortable with the cause of it, and Andy certainly isn't.'

Megan paused for breath as we looked at each other in the mirror. Her face was set, and I knew I would find no compassion there. Never would I be able to pour out my heart to my mother, hoping to receive understanding and sympathy. If I told her the agonies of my love for Gerry, the bittersweet pain and joy of the last nine months, my longing to be with the man who, whatever the future might hold, was my soulmate, I would meet nothing but cold anger and disappointment. But perhaps that's all I deserved and I was fortunate enough to have received unconditional support from Annie.

'Well?' Megan wanted an answer, and I knew not what to say. 'Do you love him?'

I stared blankly at my reflection in the mirror, utterly dumb.

'Yes, she does.'

Andy stood in the doorway, set like granite and his voice as flinty.

'Your daughter loves another man and, oddly, his children, too. She spends every moment with them that she can. She cries into her pillow at night, and I think she's going to leave me to be with them.'

I stared at Andy in shock, horrified to hear the simple truth suddenly on his lips.

'Whether Madison sleeps with him, I don't know, but whatever she does, it's him she wants now, not me. You've seen the way she looks at him, and at Ben. She belongs to them, heart and soul, and I don't think there's anything I can do about it.'

Too stunned for tears, I awaited Megan's reply in silence. Andy held my gaze unflinchingly, challenging me to deny all that he'd said.

'I thought so.'

We looked at Megan as she spoke, nodding softly, as if mulling over some legal precedent.

'There you are, Madison, it's all been made easy for you now. The truth is out and you haven't had to breathe a word of it yourself,' Andy sneered.

I swayed, feeling nauseous and weak, knowing that I would not be allowed to remain silent much longer.

'It's not as simple as that,' I finally whispered.

'Pardon?' Megan looked at me sharply. 'You'll have to speak up, Madison.'

'I said it's not that simple.' I cleared my throat and looked at them, turning from one to the other in desperation.

'Well, tell us how it is then?' Megan asked sharply.

'Yes, go on, Madison. Exactly what has been going on between you all?' Andy persisted.

'Nothing,' I shrugged vaguely, quite unable to share anything with this hostile audience.

'Okay, that's it.' Andy slammed his hand down on the counter. 'I've had enough of your prevarication. I don't care what you and Gerry have been up to, whatever it's all about, but I'll tell you this, Madison. If you want me to go back to The Dragon, you'd better promise me you'll not be seeing him again.'

'Andy!' Fresh alarm swept over me. 'That's got nothing to do with it.'

'Oh, yes, it does. You can have your association with Gerry or you can have the satisfaction of me going back to The Dragon, but you can't have them both.'

'But The Dragon's for you, not me,' I wailed.

Andy shrugged.

'I can take it or leave it, you're the one who's obsessed with it.'

'Andy, what's the matter with you? Why do you refuse to see why it's so important to you? Surely it's what you want to do? I thought you loved it there.'

At last I was crying, hot childish tears coursing down my cheeks. Megan watched, silenced for a time, as Andy and I fought out this intensely private battle.

'I suppose so,' Andy agreed. 'But I'm making you an ultimatum. I don't care whether it's the wise thing to do or not, but unless you give me some assurance – real, tangible assurance – that you've finished with the McFalls, you can ring Joe Budzynski yourself and tell him not to expect me back. Is that clear?'

Andy stood upright, tall and unyielding.

'And now, I'm going home, if you don't mind, Megan. I'm sorry this has spoiled the lovely day you prepared for us. Madison, I'll see you later, or not, as the case may be.'

Stunned, I watched Andy leave with more dignity than I'd previously seen him muster. As the front door closed behind him, Megan asked, 'What was all that about going back to The Restless Dragon? I didn't know he'd been away.'

Two hours previously, I would have protected Andy, fudging some vague answer, but I could no longer see the point. Megan couldn't be angrier than she was, and at least Andy could share some of the flak.

'He walked out at the beginning of December, but he's arranged to start there again in the new year.'

'Why did he walk out?'

'Artistic differences,' I told her briefly.

'Umm.'

I could see that Megan was deciding which issue to pursue – my relationship with Gerry, or Andy's comings and goings at The Dragon. I knew better than to attempt to deflect her from the hornet's nest I had stirred, and said nothing.

'I don't need to ask you if all that Andy said is true,' she told me coldly. 'I can see that it is, and to be honest, it's nothing I couldn't have worked out for myself. I did what I despise in others – went into denial, believed your ingenuous reassurances that you and the conductor were just friendly colleagues, despite the glaring evidence to the contrary.'

'What evidence?' I asked, genuinely interested.

'The looks, the smiles, the familiar manner the boy has with you. The way Annie looks protective and fierce when there's a danger you and he are going to give it all away. I knew he was trouble from the first day I saw him with you.'

I looked up in surprise.

'When?' I asked stupidly.

'In Portsmouth, when he had his eye on eating the food I had brought for you to take home.'

'We had the chocolate and the peaches,' I said softly, nostalgic at the memory, even in the awfulness of the present moment.

'Yes, I knew you would,' she said, oddly smug.

I leaned against the kitchen cabinets, weeping softly as I thought of that lovely day, and all the lovely days since, of the happy times I'd shared with Gerry, and of the painful ones too. I wanted him there and then, to hold me and take away the fear that now ran through my veins.

'So, what are your plans, Madison?' Megan asked, looking grim.

'I don't have any plans,' I protested tearfully.

'Well, you'd better start thinking fast, my girl,' she retorted. 'What I think about Andy's position at The Dragon notwithstanding, if you want him to do what's right for him, you know what you've got to do. I don't condone his emotional blackmail, but if there was ever a time when it may be excusable, if not actually justifiable, this is it. Sort yourself out sharpish, Madison. You make me ashamed to call you my daughter.'

'But Mum, you know nothing about it. Nothing about Gerry, or me, or about Andy, for that matter. You don't know what's happened between me and Gerry, how much I've cried, how hurt I've been. You know nothing of what it's been like all these years being married to Andy.'

'I don't want to know. I know enough, thank you. Get out of that relationship now, or face bitter consequences, Madison. And don't think you'll escape all of them by doing that alone. What you've done, whatever the extent of it, has changed things beyond measure.'

'What things?'

'Your relationship with Andy, with me and, I suspect, with yourself. You may think you have gained much through your relationship with this man, but I question deeply whether it will be worth what you have lost.'

I could do nothing but weep, wishing with all my heart that the clock could be turned back, and Doug, in his innocence, had not set us on this path. Perhaps it was a path we would have inevitably taken, but today it could surely have been avoided.

A movement behind Megan finally distracted us. Finty stood in the doorway, her expression as concerned as Andy's had been angry.

'Megan, Madsy, I can't bear it any longer. I know it's nothing to do with me, but please will you both stop this.'

Ten years Megan's junior, Finty felt closer in age to me than to her sister. Megan patronised and bossed her sibling, a delicate and gentle woman, but she loved her, and a spasm of anxiety crossed Megan's face as she saw Finty's distress. She tightened her lips and turned to me angrily.

'A great Christmas Day you've given Finty now,' she snapped.

'Mum, that's not fair,' I gasped. 'You could have ignored Andy's comments. You didn't need to pick them up; Doug didn't.'

'Of course he didn't. It doesn't directly involve him and in any case, he thinks you can do no wrong. It seems he doesn't know you well enough. None of us do.'

'What is all this about?' Finty asked in bewilderment.

'Madison is clearly intent on proving that she's not the girl I brought her up to be,' Megan said sharply.

'I'm sorry for all the row, Finty,' I told my aunt quietly.

'Marvellous,' Megan crowed sarcastically. 'You apologise to Finty, but not to me.'

'I've got nothing to apologise to you about,' I wept, 'I didn't start this.'

'And you didn't start a relationship with that insufferably self-satisfied man?'

'Gerry's not like that. He's just very confident and enjoys what he does.'

'I don't care,' Megan cut across me, lest she be subjected to a litany of Gerry's virtues.

'Who are you talking about?' Finty asked looked from one to another in puzzlement.

'Never mind, Finty. I don't think Madison and I have anything more to say to each other at the moment.'

Pushing me aside, Megan stalked from the kitchen, and as Finty and I gazed helplessly after her, we heard footsteps going up the stairs, across the landing, and the study door closing us out. I sagged with exhaustion.

'I am really sorry, Finty. That shouldn't have happened.'

'Where's Andy?' she asked.

'Gone home.'

'How are you going to get back yourself?'

I shook my head.

'I don't know. Oh, ring for a cab I expect.' The prospect of going home was so unattractive, it didn't matter how I got there.

'Let me take you, Madsy,' Finty suggested kindly.

'Fints, you can't do that,' I said, touched by her offer. 'Megan will go ballistic.'

'I can make the odd decision for myself,' Finty laughed wryly, 'although I know rumour would have it otherwise.'

'Thank you,' I accepted gratefully. I had to face it at some point.

CHAPTER 60

Finty scribbled a quick note to Megan – *Taken Madsy home. See you later* – and we fled. As we pulled out on the Finchley Road, I took a deep breath.

'Fints, can I ask you something really cheeky?'

'Yes, darling,' she smiled at me with far more kindness than I deserved.

'Would you be prepared to take me somewhere other than home?'

'Ah.'

I remained silent whilst Finty pondered.

'Where do you want to go?' she asked finally.

'Dulwich.'

'Am I allowed to ask why?'

'I need to talk to someone who lives there.'

'About what's just happened?'

'Yes.'

Finty kept driving. We were nearing Swiss Cottage and I calculated that she would need to make a decision by the time we got to Baker Street where the road divided.

'If I'm about to get involved in this I think it's fair enough for me to ask who it is,' she said, glancing at me sideways.

'Gerry McFall.'

'Do I know him?'

'You've seen his back a few times, most recently conducting *Tito*.'

Finty nodded slowly.

'I see. Are you in love with him?' she asked directly.

'Very much.'

'And does he love you?'

'I think so. Sometimes I'm sure he does. Sometimes, well, I don't really know.'

'That doesn't sound very satisfactory.'

'It's okay,' I told her, shrugging fatalistically.

'And if you go to see him tonight, will it help you find out for certain?' she asked.

'It might do. I hope so.'

Finty drove on in silence, staring out at the dark Christmas night, lit by twinkling beams from shop windows and high apartment buildings. We passed Lord's cricket ground, and around the roundabout at the bottom of Wellington Road, as we headed towards Baker Street. Finally, Finty nodded again.

'Okay, Madsy, I'll probably regret this, but my instinct is telling me to take you there, if that's what you want. Don't ask me why. Perhaps it's because if I was in the same position I'd like to think someone would do it for me.'

I waited for Finty to elaborate, but she didn't and I squeezed her hand.

'Thank you so much. I know I shouldn't ask you to do it.'

'No, you shouldn't, but you have, and I am, so you'd better just show me how to get there.'

It seemed a remarkably short time before Finty turned the car into Thurlow Park Road. She had asked me no more about Gerry or what was going on, and I marvelled at her restraint as she turned off the engine outside Gerry's home.

'Thank you, Finty.'

Now we were there I felt sick with apprehension, glancing anxiously over towards the lighted house.

'Are you going to be all right?' she asked. 'Do you want me to wait out here? I can still take you home if you'd like that.'

'It's okay, Fints, I'll manage from here.'

The prospect of being turned away from the front door had occurred to me, and if that did happen, I wanted to deal with it alone. I reached out to hug Finty.

'How can I repay you?' I asked her tearfully.

She rubbed my shoulder comfortably.

'Get sorted whatever needs sorting, and let me see a smile on that pretty face again.'

'You're amazing, Finty.'

'Yes, I know,' she said cheerfully. 'Go.'

I could see that Finty wasn't going to leave until I was safely in the house, so I had to bite the bullet and ring the front door bell. Closing my eyes, I pressed it heavily, feeling the shape of the button imprinting on my fingertip. I waited for a painful eternity until through the glass I saw a shape moving down the hallway to the door. It was Josh.

'Hi, Mads,' he said in surprise. 'I didn't know you were coming over tonight.'

'Neither did I,' I quipped. 'Is your dad here?'

My heart lurched with fear as I realised I had not yet considered the possibility that Gerry might be out.

'Yes, of course.'

Josh stood back to let me in, and I half turned to wave at Finty as I entered. Josh looked into the street with interest.

'Who's that?'

'My aunt.'

'What's she doing here?'

I didn't feel up to an inquisition from a teenager, and fought to keep an even tone.

'She just drove me over here, darling.'

Josh closed the door behind me as I lurked anxiously in the hall. I wished Gerry had answered the door, hating myself for putting Josh in the position of having to tell him I was here. Voices echoed from beyond the sitting room and I couldn't bring myself to walk in unannounced on Gerry's parents, and, for all I knew, Josh's and Ben's maternal grandparents.

'Sweetheart, would you be very kind and tell your dad I'm here. I only want a quick word with him and I don't want to disturb the party.'

Josh looked quizzically at me.

'Are you going straight away then? Is your aunt staying out there?'

I hadn't heard the sound of Finty's car engine, and I guessed she was waiting to leave until she thought I was safe from eviction into the winter night.

'I think so,' I said briskly, and looked at Josh expectantly, urging him to move.

He didn't have to do so. Doubtless wondering what was keeping his son at the front door at nine o'clock on Christmas night, Gerry swept suddenly from the sitting room.

'Who is it, Josh?'

As his eyes adjusted to the dimmer light of the hall he blinked in surprise.

'Madison?'

'Gerry, I'm sorry.' I twisted my hands helplessly, as I hovered on the brink of tears.

Gerry took over briskly. 'Josh, would you put the kettle on? Your gran wants a coffee and I'm sure Madison would like one, too.'

His kind but firm tone brooked no argument and Josh trooped off obediently to do his bidding.

Alone with Gerry, I was afraid to meet his gaze, desperately regretting my rash journey. Briefly, I contemplated making a rapid exit, fleeing to the safety of Finty's car, which I was sure was still stationed outside the house. As I hovered indecisively, Gerry came to my rescue.

'Madsy, what's happened?' he asked gently.

I risked looking up at him, and the sight of his sweet face, crumpled with concern, set my tears free.

'Oh, Gerry, I'm so sorry. It's just been awful.'

As his arms came about me, I wept into his shoulder, clinging as tightly as a drowning swimmer to a life raft.

'Shh, shh, it's all going to be fine. It's okay. I'm here.' Gerry murmured soft, random words of comfort, as the horrors of the evening overwhelmed me. Eventually, catching a movement over Gerry's shoulder, I fought to get a grip and wiped my eyes unceremoniously on his shirtsleeve. Josh stood at the kitchen door.

'The coffee's made, Dad.'

He looked at me with such tender eyes that I nearly wept again.

'Thank you, darling,' I said with as much strength as I could muster.

'Take your grandma a cup, would you, Josh?' Gerry asked him, steering me gently into the kitchen. 'We'll be in shortly.'

Once Josh had returned to the sitting room, Gerry poured me a coffee and, sitting beside me at the table, drummed his fingers on the back of my hand.

'Is there a short version? I mean, can you tell me the gist of it in about five sentences or shall we wait till later?'

'The short version is that Andy made so many snide comments about you and me in front of Megan that she forced a showdown. Andy made sure that she was left in no doubt about his version of things. She deduced the rest. Andy walked out and Megan effectively told me I was no daughter of hers. Then Finty offered to drive me home, and I persuaded her to bring me here instead. I think that's five sentences.'

'Oh, Madsy,' Gerry breathed, still rubbing his fingers softly across my knuckles. He passed his free hand over his face wearily, and I felt a pang of new sorrow. Gerry would not thank me for my unprecedented arrival on his doorstep.

'I'm sorry, I shouldn't have come here.' I rose from my seat. 'I think Finty might still be outside. If I make my way now she'll take me home. Forget this happened, Gerry.'

He pulled me down again.

'Don't be silly. If Finty's there, tell her it's okay, you're safe and you'll be staying here tonight.'

I shook my head, angry with myself for forcing Gerry's hand. I attempted to get up again.

'No, please, just let me go now, and we can forget it.'

'Madison.' Gerry spoke sharply and I stopped in my tracks. 'Stop it. It's okay that you're here. You did the right thing. Now go and speak to Finty and come back, get a glass of wine and join us in the lounge. Everyone will be going in an hour or so and then we can talk properly.'

I nodded slowly.

'Okay. Will you come with me to speak to Finty?'

'If you really want me to.'

'Yes, please.'

With enormous patience Gerry accompanied me to the front door and, sure enough, Finty was still parked like sentry outside the driveway and as soon as we emerged she was out of the car. Gerry headed straight for her with his usual aplomb, hand outstretched.

'Hello, I'm Gerry. I think I saw you at *Tito* last month.'

'Yes, you probably did.'

Finty smiled genially and shook Gerry's hand without hesitation.

'Look, tell me to mind my own business, but what's the best thing I can do now? Take Madsy home or just leave quietly?'

'Thank you so much for bringing her here,' Gerry told her. 'She's going to stay, if that's all right with you.' His courtesy even when he had been grossly inconvenienced touched me deeply.

Finty nodded, looking us both over with gentle scrutiny.

'Okay, Madsy, as long as you're doing what you want to do.'

I reached out to hug her.

'Finty, don't let Megan blame you.'

'Don't worry about me now,' she said with more assurance than I would have felt. 'Go on, both of you. Get into the warm again.'

She climbed into the car without another word and we did as she bid.

CHAPTER 61

It seemed an eternity until Gerry's parents made their move to depart, but surprisingly I didn't want them to go. It felt safe and snug in Gerry's chaotic lounge, slightly numb from wine and shock, half listening to the conversation that went on around me. Ben seemed to sense nothing untoward and he unselfconsciously showed me his Christmas presents and chatted about the day. Josh glanced over to me now and then with gentle concern, and I tried to smile reassuringly. But finally they were gone and Gerry smartly despatched the boys to bed.

'Guys, it's been a long day, and Madison needs a bit of quiet right now. Can you get yourselves off to bed?'

'Dad.' Ben's whining tone was rapidly silenced by Josh.

'Don't be a pain, kid.' He took his brother firmly by the shoulders and propelled him towards the stairs. 'Bed.'

As Gerry made fresh coffee, he chatted on in his wonderful familiar and easy way about what they'd all done and said during the day, keeping my attention away from my own concerns until we were settled on the sofa. He put his arm round me and I nestled up to him closely, sighing enormous relief.

'Are you all right, little one? You're not, are you?' he said kindly.

'No.'

'Are you frightened? Do you think Andy will hurt you?'

'Not physically, but I am frightened. I don't know what happens from here, Gerry, either with Andy and The Dragon, or with you and me.' I turned to face him. 'He's said again that he won't go back to the theatre unless I stop seeing you, but I don't know if he really means it.'

'That's emotional blackmail,' said Gerry with disgust.

'To you it may seem so, but to him, it's an equaliser. I hurt him; he hurts me. I withdraw myself from him, so he withdraws from something he knows matters to me. What I fail to understand is that he doesn't see that he hurts himself even more by doing so. It's the self-destructive inclination I find so bewildering.'

'So what are you doing to do?' Gerry asked.

I entwined my fingers around his and we sat in silence for a moment.

'I could do with a bit of help, Gerry,' I said finally.

'What kind of help?'

I willed myself not to overreact.

'How can I know what to do if I don't know whether you want me here or not?' Gerry took a breath to speak, but I silenced him. 'I don't mean here now this minute, but permanently. I can't go through all that ghastliness today and walk away still not knowing where my place is, whether you and I have enough of a commitment for me make a life with you.'

My voice caught on tears as I spoke and I stopped abruptly. I didn't want to cry. I needed a serious conversation and there had been enough emotion for one day.

Gerry stared off into the middle distance, still absently linking his fingers in mine.

'I do love you, Madsy,' he said softly. 'And I'm very concerned about what's happened today. I worry about you.'

'I don't need you to worry about me, that's not the point.'

'Maybe not, but I do,' he continued. 'I love being with you, sharing all the things we do. The boys love you. We have a good time together, and you give me such beautifully loving care, it's wonderful. I love going to bed with you, your deliciously sexy body, and the way you make me feel.' Gerry sighed heavily, leaning his head back against the sofa.

'But it's still not enough,' I said sadly.

'It is enough. It's lovely; you're lovely.'

'So why can't I come to live with you?'

'I don't know. It's partly the boys. Not that they don't love you, but I'm not sure if they're ready for another mum or to share me more than they have to already. And I'm not sure if I can give you what you want from me, what you deserve to have – the same unstinting love you give to me.'

Gerry saw my stricken face and pulled me to him gently.

'Darling, I'm just not sure how all this fits into my life at the moment. I take it a day at a time, enjoying you and what we have together, but I still can't see the future clearly yet. I'm sorry this doesn't help you. I know you need me to give you an answer, especially after today, and I'm just being hopeless. I'm sorry.'

Gerry's expression was utterly characteristic, his face crumpled with sweet concern, helpless, loving, and yet still resolute. He was going to do things his way again, just giving me enough reassurance to keep me holding on, loving him so much it hurt, making what he could give me sound like a banquet when we both knew it was little more than a sandwich.

'Shall I go now, then?' I asked miserably.

'No, of course not!' Gerry looked genuinely horrified. 'I want you to stay tonight, and tomorrow, and as long as you need to stay. I'm not making myself very understandable am I, though that's not surprising since I don't even understand myself.'

'Oh, don't worry, I understand quite clearly.'

As much as I wanted to avoid an argument, I couldn't help but be exasperated at Gerry's unhelpfulness. I felt horribly manipulated. Despite his refusal to offer me a life with him and the boys, in a short while he would take me to bed and treat me as if I was infinitely precious to him. But hadn't I accepted this ambiguity and manipulation back in the balmy summer months? I wanted to sleep in Gerry's arms that night, and if the price was to accept, once again, that he would not give me the single-minded devotion that I wanted to give to him, so be it. I met his gaze, my heart contracting with love as I stroked his cheek.

'I love you so much.'

'I know you do. I know.'

Gerry tried to look humble; it was always so funny, and I felt suddenly light-headed as laughter caught me unawares.

'Shall we go to bed?' I asked, hungry for the comfort of his body.

'Hmm. What an excellent idea.'

What other fool would have allowed their life to spiral so spectacularly out of control? I thought ironically, as Gerry slept deeply next to me in the darkest hours of the night. Nothing was resolved, everything lay scattered at my feet, and I still had to face Andy and Megan. I knew not what the morning would bring or for how long Gerry would allow me to take up temporary residence with him. But in the disaster that I had created I knew without the slightest doubt that I would not change a single thing. The incredible, life transforming and stunning passion I felt for Gerry outweighed all else, and guilty, ashamed, and troubled, I could still not regret a single moment of it.

CHAPTER 62

Gerry and the boys were gone in a flurry by ten the next morning. Gerry's older brother lived in Southend, and a Boxing Day gathering of the McFall clan awaited them whatever private dramas might be unfolding elsewhere. The house was heavily silent without them, and I felt unusually lonely. If I had been at home there were a hundred things I would soon have involved myself with, but I was sharply aware that this was not my home, and it felt alien and aloof. I had to occupy myself or depression would soon descend, and I hoped that vigorous activity would help me think more productively about the next step.

I had taken enormous pleasure in making breakfast for them all before their departure into the crisp December morning, so turning on the radio, I loaded the dishwasher, still replete with yesterday's debris, and as it hummed I ran hot soapy water and hunted for scourers. By lunchtime the kitchen gleamed. I gazed proudly at the shiny worktops, polished glass and crumb free surfaces, deeply satisfied with the expenditure of love and energy which had resulted in such a vision of cleanliness. I felt better able to think, too, and sat peacefully over a mug of tomato soup, contemplating my options. I had to speak to Andy. Even if he had assumed I had gone straight from Megan's house to see Gerry, it was not fair to leave him to stew, to wonder whether I was ever returning to Exeter House. But I did not relish the prospect. His anger would doubtless have deepened in my absence, and I was not confident of being a welcome returnee. But return I must; Gerry had made that abundantly clear, even if he had couched it in gentle tones.

I rinsed my soup mug and contemplated where I should next direct my energies: the boys' bedrooms seemed intrusive; Gerry's bedroom too personal. The lounge beckoned. There was nothing I could do with the battered and mismatched furniture, but the abandoned video boxes, newspapers and computer games could be brought to order, and the surfaces polished to a high gloss. And later, as I passed the vacuum cleaner over all the downstairs carpets, I felt pleasantly tired, weary with the comforting sense of muscles exercised in labour that yielded tangible results. It was time to move, but first I rang Annie.

'Madsy!' she exclaimed in surprise. 'How's it going?'

I gave her the potted version, which tripped off my tongue easily on its second airing, but adding, not without a little self-pity, something of Gerry's non-committal response to my plight.

'Oh, lovey,' she soothed, 'he doesn't exactly help you out, does he? He wants all the good things he can get from you without any of the responsibility.'

'I don't think that's true, Annie. He's in a very difficult position. I don't know what the boys think about things so I've got to take his word for it that my moving in wouldn't be good for them, haven't I?'

'Umm, if you say so. I think it would be excellent for them, but who am I to know?' she said acidly. 'So where are they now?'

'Gone to see Gerry's brother.'

'You're on your own?'

'Yes. I've just cleaned the kitchen and tidied the lounge and vacuumed everywhere,' I told her proudly.

'Ye gods, girl. Didn't you have anything better to do? For you personally, I mean?'

346

'Not really. It was odd being here on my own and I wanted to do it. I'm going now, anyway. I've got to face Andy at some point.'

We chatted for a little longer until I let Annie go back to her own choice of Boxing Day revels – a large box of chocolates in front of the television – and sadly gathered my belongings together. Before leaving, I sat at the kitchen table and penned a note.

My dearest Gerry,

I've had all day to think and I guess I'd better go home sooner rather than later. If I cannot stay here permanently, then there is no point hanging about and putting pressure on you. I love you so much, and want nothing more than to be with you, but I cannot force myself on you, and I have to leave it in your hands where we go from here. You are the greatest love of my life, and I belong to you in every way, as I will do forever. Thank you for last night; it was beautiful, as it always is, to be with you. I want so much to sleep in your arms again tonight, but it will only be putting off the inevitable. I'm going home to talk to Andy, if I can. Please ring or email me and let me be with you again very soon.

All my love,

Madison

It was after eleven before I let myself into the flat. It was dark and cold, and as I turned on lights and started the central heating it became evident that Andy had not returned home yesterday either. The mugs were where we had left them in the sink before we set out for Megan's fateful gathering, and the bed still neatly made. A shiver of fear passed down my spine. It had not occurred to me that Andy might not return home and in a spasm of panic I tried to think where he might be. Under a train was all my exhausted brain could offer. As I rested my head against the kitchen cabinets, trying to think clearly, the soft beep of the answering machine filtered through from the study. Hoping to hear Andy's voice, however angry he may be, I hurried to silence its warning note. 'You have two messages in mail box one' the electronic voice intoned. Static hissed in the background and eventually Andy's voice penetrated the crackle.

'If you're at all interested, I've gone to stay with Ron. See you sometime.'

The electronic voice gave the time and date of Andy's message: 2.20 am. Andy had evidently assumed that I was with Megan still since he had not sounded puzzled by my own absence. The second message kicked in.

'Where the hell are you? Silly question. If you ever deign to come home you might ring me on the mobile.'

Andy's second call had been made at midday, since when, silence. I felt sick at the prospect of calling him but knew it had to be done. Despite the hour, he answered on the second ring.

'What?'

'It's me.'

'Oh, yes. Should I care?'

'I'm just letting you know I'm home.'

'Why? Gerry kicked you out?' Andy laughed unpleasantly.

'I left of my own accord. He didn't even know I'd gone. Well, he will do by now, but he wasn't there.'

'Where was he?'

'He and the boys went to see his family.'

'Oh dear, and left you all on your own. What a shame,' Andy mocked. 'What are you doing now?'

'I'm going to bed, Andy. We must talk.'

'That'll be a first.'

'I'm sorry about what happened yesterday. I didn't plan it.'

'It gave you a great excuse to run to Gerry though, didn't it? How did you get there?'

'Finty took me,' I told him, immediately regretting my words.

'The bitch!' he spat. 'Two fucking betrayers together, the pair of you.'

'Please, Andy.'

'Please, Andy,' he sneered. 'Just go to hell, Madison. See you when I see you.'

'Andy. Wait. If you're at Ron's, have you talked about The Dragon, about when you go back next week?'

'You can't trick me into that one so easily, Madison. You keep on seeing that bastard, don't expect to see me at The Dragon again. It's up to you.'

'It's not up to me, Andy,' I pleaded. 'It's your future.'

'Goodbye.'

The line went dead and I hung up wearily. I longed for Gerry's comforting arms and cheery presence, and I realised then with a pang that he had not been in a hurry to call me when he had returned from his brother's house. Oh well, when had Gerry ever done anything straight away? After that terrible day when Vanessa came to Glyndebourne, I remembered. He'd emailed me at two o'clock in the morning then. It felt like another century, not a mere five months ago. How could so much have happened in so short a time? Quite easily, I thought. Quite easily.

CHAPTER 63

Andy came back halfway through the next day as I was making a desultory attempt to practice. Gerry had remained silent and I imagined him with the boys, thinking occasionally of me, doubtless hoping I was okay, but feeling no urgency to make contact. If I could bear it that long, I estimated it would be another couple of days until he called.

'All right, Madison,' Andy declared without ceremony. 'You want to talk, so here's my contribution. If you give up seeing Gerry ever, at all, and his kids, then I'll try to forget about all this and I'll go back to The Dragon. If not, then all bets are off.'

'Andy, what do you think has happened between me and Gerry?' I asked.

'I don't know, and I don't want to know. It's just more than I care for, I do know that much, and I don't want you near him.'

I didn't press him. I certainly did know what had passed between us, that my unfaithfulness to Andy had been total, and all that was left was a fear of the practical consequences of leaving him, and a concern that his self-destructive streak would leave him stranded once my support was gone. But what was there for me if I stayed? An impermanent, fluctuating relationship with Gerry and the boys, whilst Andy raged and stormed, jobless and directionless again?

I felt overwhelmed with emotional exhaustion.

'I can't think now, Andy. I'm going for a walk.'

'Do whatever you wish, Madison. Situation normal, I assume.'

I did manage to wait Gerry out, and I was right. The day before New Year's Eve I had a gala concert at the Barbican, my sole contributions being the Habanera, the Barcarolle, and the Flower Duet from *Lakme* (wretched thing), but it got me out of the house, and in the interval between rehearsal and the concert, my phone rang. I had forced myself to be cheerful with Lois, the soprano soloist, and we were drinking hot chocolate as we looked out over the lake, when I practically leapt in the air at the phone's shrill summons.

'Oh, goodness, sorry,' I apologised to her as I rummaged in my bag. 'I'm waiting for a call and I'm on tenterhooks.' As Gerry's name flashed on the display, perversely I toyed with the option of ignoring it. I didn't.

'Hi.'

'Hi. It's me.'

'I know.'

He laughed. 'Are you all right?'

'I'm at the Barbican.'

'Oh, Madsy, of course. You're singing tonight.'

'It's not much, but it makes a change from Andy's inhibiting presence.'

'Shall I come?' he asked.

I was momentarily stunned.

'Are you free, then?'

'I can be.'

'Oh, please, yes, Gerry. Come to the artists' entrance and I'm sure I can get you a seat. I'd be so glad to see you.'

I started to cry and from the corner of my eye I saw Lois turn away tactfully.

'Then I'll be there,' he said soothingly. 'Don't cry, sweetheart. I'm not there to hug you.'

'I had noticed,' I snapped, immediately regretting my sharp tone. 'Sorry, I just miss you so much.'

'I'll see you later then?'

'Okay,' I snuffled. 'Gerry?'

'Yes?'

'I love you.'

'Jolly good.'

I hung up with a sigh and surreptitiously wiped my eyes with a napkin.

'You okay?' Lois asked.

'Yes,' I smiled. 'Can't live with him, can't live without him. Know the scenario?'

'Intimately.'

We chuckled knowingly.

'I think we've got time for another chocolate, if you can cope with *Sempre Libra* on two double mochas,' I suggested.

'Only wimps can't take chocolate before they sing,' Lois opined, so we indulged again.

Gerry was almost knocked down in the rush when he sauntered up to the artists' entrance at 7 o'clock. I was like a cat on hot bricks, pacing and flapping in my silky green dress, convinced that he wouldn't turn up. It felt like six months, not four days, since I'd seen him, and the sight of his sweet face, gangly frame, and abashed grin were almost more than I could bear. I fell into his arms, kissing him practically into unconsciousness.

'Are you pleased to see me then?' he grinned as I clung to him in anguished joy.

'Desperately.'

'And I'm pleased to see you. Hadn't you better get back there, though? You're on in less than half an hour.'

'Cuddle me first,' I pleaded.

'I am.'

'A bit longer.'

Oblivious to the movement behind us in the lobby, I luxuriated in Gerry's embrace, pulling him close to me in relief.

'That's it,' he said eventually. 'Get to work. I'll see you later.'

Reluctantly I let him go, turning to make my way to the wings to see the security guard grinning in amusement. I flushed, but gave him a wry smile.

'He's a lucky bloke,' he said. 'I hope he appreciates it.'

'So do I,' I mused, 'so do I.'

It was a funny concert with so little to do, but I enjoyed sitting on the platform looking cool and elegant and making the most of the Habanera. I hoped that Gerry was pleased with my efforts and knew I was singing specially for him. He came backstage at the end, looking rakish and bohemian, and beamed triumphantly when he found our dressing room.

'Ah, there you are!' he said, sticking his head round the door.

Lois blinked in surprise as I visibly melted.

'Is this your friend who was coming tonight?' she asked.

'Yes, this is Gerry,' I told her proudly, and I saw her faintly shake her head after she'd greeted him. He clearly didn't fit her mental image of the man who'd apparently reduced me to tears on the telephone several hours earlier.

He did it again not long afterwards as we sat in his car in Whitecross Street. He turned the heater up full blast and I buried my face in his coat as he stroked my hair.

'It's been even more awful than usual not seeing you,' I murmured. 'I'm so happy today.'

'Hmm. I expect you are,' he said wryly, and I punched him softly.

'Cheeky.'

We hugged wordlessly for a moment.

'I wish I was going home to bed with you,' I sighed eventually.

'Are you afraid of going back to Putney?' he asked.

'No. I would just rather be going home with you.'

'And if you do, what then?'

I lifted my head to read the expression in his soft blue eyes.

'Andy will almost definitely not go back to The Dragon, and you'll still send me back tomorrow, won't you?'

Gerry blew out his cheeks and looked helpless.

'Madison, I've been thinking a lot over the last few days. I've thought about every possible permutation of you and me, Josh, Ben, Andy, everyone who has an interest in our futures and our happiness. I want you in my life, I don't want us to quarrel, and I want us to go on talking, and doing all the things we do together, but I can't offer you more than that, as much as I'd like to be able to do so.'

I drew breath to speak, but he silenced me with a kiss.

'And I think you should consider Andy's position very carefully. I agree with you that he would be very silly not to return to The Dragon and he should take responsibility for that decision. But if he does choose not to go back, and there is something you could have done that might possibly have influenced his decision positively rather than negatively, I'm not sure that you'll rest easily about that in the future.'

I stared at Gerry in disbelief.

'So you're telling me you don't want me anymore, and that I should stick by Andy to make sure he goes back to work?'

'No, I'm not. You know that. I'm just saying that I think you should be careful what you decide to do. We can carry on exactly as we are. I'd like that very much, but it's obviously causing you far greater difficulties than it has done previously. I'm sorry that at the moment there's nothing more that I can offer you. There may be in the future, but I just don't know. You may well consider that your best option is to give Andy the support he so desperately needs from you. You could tell him honestly that you're not spending time with me, see him safely installed back at The Dragon, and then just see what happens.'

'See what happens?' I exclaimed bitterly. 'What would happen, Gerry? We'd count to five million and then see each other again?'

'I don't know.'

I stared out of the window as tears ran their course down my cheeks. After a moment, Gerry took my hand, entwining his fingers with mine, tracing patterns on my palm and wrist; the little moves that made my heart turn over with desire.

'Madsy, I have to admit I feel bad about Andy's position.'

'And you think I don't?'

'Of course not.'

'I feel terrible,' I told him. 'Guilty and awful and sick about him.' I turned to look Gerry in the eye again. 'But I simply can't escape the fact that it is you who are everything to me and from whom I don't want to be separated.'

'I know,' he said sadly.

'Please hug me.'

'I suppose I'd better get you home,' he said eventually. 'We'll see each other next week.'

'Okay.'

I thought with some comfort of the lovely day we'd planned for the following week, way before the drama of Christmas Day. Josh and Ben were going to see their grandparents and we were spending the day in Oxford, going to a matinee and to dinner. I longed for proper time with Gerry, free from tears, I hoped.

'Text me everyday till then, you cad,' I teased him.

'And ring me if you need me,' he urged.

'I always need you.'

'Then you'll run up a big phone bill, won't you? You looked very beautiful tonight. Very curvy.'

'It's all for you.'

'Hmm.'

I held back further tears all the way home, and felt ridiculously proud to leave dry eyed as Gerry drove away into the night.

CHAPTER 64

We staggered through the New Year. I made a point of making sure that Megan knew I was home, but the conversation was so painful I ended it as quickly as possible. I called Finty to thank her again for her mercy mission on Christmas Day, and she was kind, but distant, and I knew that she must have suffered Megan's wrath when she had returned that night. Andy was morose and uncommunicative over New Year's Eve dinner with Dani and Steve, and I felt too exhausted to cover up for his mood. The evening was not a resounding success, although they were too polite to ask what was wrong. Andy and I skirted around each other over the following day and the next, and I escaped to see Annie on the afternoon before I was due to see Gerry again.

'You look shattered,' she said succinctly, pouring me a large glass of wine.

'That's probably because I am.'

'Do you need some TLC today?' she asked.

'Please.'

So, true to her word, Annie filled me with good food and wine, and we watched an unashamedly sentimental video during which I wept copiously. She asked no questions, but filled my glass and hugged me.

'This is so cathartic,' I laughed, eating a second helping of Alabama Soft Rock Pie and stretching luxuriously. 'Just what I needed.'

'Good,' Annie smiled. 'Is it all still ghastly?'

'Ghastly at home. Wonderful when I see Gerry. Then I start to cry, he kisses me, I stop for a bit, then I cry again because I've got to leave him, and we start again from the top.'

'Why do you have to leave him?'

'Because he tells me I can't stay.'

'And Andy?'

'He's refusing to go back to The Dragon till I stop seeing Gerry.'

'Stalemate.'

We contemplated the problem. It looked no different after a bottle of wine and a large dish of pasta, but its raw edges were less painful.

'I think I might have to try to live without Gerry for a bit,' I said. Shocked, I looked at Annie in surprise. The words had fallen unbidden from my lips, and I realised that my subconscious had spoken. 'Oh, Annie, how can I?'

'If you have to, you will.'

I shook my head. 'I can't. He's my life.'

Annie squeezed my hand and proffered my glass. I sipped gratefully.

'I'll see after tomorrow. I'm not going to give up my special day with him.'

'Perhaps you won't have to give him up at all. If he tells you tomorrow that he wants you to move in with him what would you do?'

'He won't, but if he did, I'd go like a shot.'

'And what about if Andy just walked out, stopped hassling you about it, but just went?'

'I don't know. If he went back to The Dragon, then I'd feel enormously relieved. I could see Gerry whenever he wanted us to meet and I'd know that Andy was fine – at least professionally. If he just walked out and I didn't know where he was or what was happening to him, then I don't know. It would be much harder.'

'Well, just make sure that you remember what's more important than all of it,' Annie said warningly.

'What's that?'

'Singing.'

'It doesn't feel more important at the moment,' I told her sadly.

'Music's for keeps, Madsy, even when love dies.'

'I'll never stop loving Gerry.'

'Maybe not, but if you're going to try to be without him, then something's going to have to expand to fill the Gerry-sized gap that's left, and I don't think it's going to be Andy, is it?'

I shook my head.

Annie let me cry a little longer then clapped her hands together briskly.

'I've got special cream for liqueur coffees and an as yet unopened bottle of amaretto. How does that sound?'

'Wonderful.'

'Come on then, you mustn't dilute it with tears.'

As I left, I hugged Annie hard.

'Ring me on Thursday; don't brood alone, whatever you decide,' she told me, hugging me in return.

'Thanks, Annie. I love you.'

'You, too. Chin up.'

'How are things home on the range?' Gerry asked the next morning as he pulled off the Hammersmith roundabout in search of the A40 to Oxford.

'The same, but let's not talk about it today. Let me just enjoy every moment of being with you as if none of all that had happened.'

Gerry raised his eyebrows questioningly, then nodded, patting my knee.

'If you say so.'

That done, he held my hand practically all the way to Oxford, and I relaxed pleasurably, as he chatted to me in his lovely way. I knew no one other than Gerry who could make things so easy, investing everything with his natural exuberance and humour. It made the times when he was tired or anxious harder to negotiate, so sharply did they contrast with his usually happy nature, but it softened his emotional reticence, his unwillingness to give of himself completely to me, mellowing it as he did with a ready smile, an intelligent question, a thoughtful response, or willing hug. And I knew that he liked my company, enjoyed my love, my enthusiasm and interest in everything we did. He may not have been prepared to give me the single-minded commitment I craved, but every time he put his arms round me, I forgave the times he had hurt me, and he only had to fix me with his sweet, funny, loving look, and nothing else mattered.

And we had a beautiful day. Though chill and crisp, the sun shone, and we walked through Christchurch meadows before eating hot sandwiches and fries in a cosy pub by the river. In the theatre I pressed close to Gerry as he held my hand and stroked my wrist, and I thought of the wonderful evening in the summer when we had seen Graham in *Un Ballo in Maschera*, Gerry had finally, gloriously, touched and held me as I had longed. Over an early dinner we talked and laughed and basked in a sense of enormous well-being that was balm to my soul after the pain of the last weeks. As Gerry watched me drink my cappuccino, he smiled with heartaching tenderness.

'I have enjoyed today,' he said. 'No children, no deadlines, no phone messages.' He stretched out his long legs in front of him, and grinned. 'Just a beautiful, clever woman, and me.'

'Oh, I see. So any beautiful woman would have done?' I teased, kissing his hand and pressing it happily to my cheek.

'I don't think so,' he pondered. 'My preference might possibly be for you.'

'Shall I beat you up now or later?'

'Oh, later, it'll give me something to look forward to.'

We were quieter on the way home, pleasantly weary from the long winter day, but Gerry was still attentive as we travelled, and I dared to wonder if I might hope that he had made up his mind and finally wanted me to stay with them all. As we drew close to home I longed to hold back time and stay forever with him, alone in this warm, familiar car, which was so inextricably linked to the different stages of our relationship, but the landmarks of home appeared all too soon, until Gerry finally pulled up at the edge of the heath and turned off the engine. As we faced each other I moved towards him, suddenly sad and frightened.

'What is it, Madsy?' he asked gently, as he folded me in his arms.

'I love you.' It was the first time that day I had told him.

'I know. I love you, too.'

'Oh, Gerry,' I sighed, 'why don't you tell me more often?'

'I don't need to,' he said concisely. 'You should know that I love you. It's not because you tell me every day that I know you love me. It's because of everything else you do and say. When you tell me it only confirms what I know already.'

I was so moved by his words that I couldn't speak, so we kissed for a long time instead, until it wasn't just the car's heater that made me warm.

'If we carry on like this you're going to have to take me home,' I told Gerry, running my hands under his jacket.

'Hmm.'

He kissed me again and then we pulled back and looked at each other frankly.

'Thank you for a lovely day,' I said.

'Thank *you*.'

'Being with you is the most beautiful thing in the world.'

'Good.'

'It's very hard being without you.'

'I'm sorry.'

'For what?'

'That you're sad when you can't be with me,' he said. 'That you're going home now and will probably have to face Andy in a difficult mood. That you have his job to worry about.'

'Gerry?'

'Yes?'

'Did you mean what you said on Friday? That I should seriously consider the implications of Andy not going back to The Dragon because of me seeing you?'

'Yes, I did. But it's your decision to make about that, Madsy, not mine. I was just telling you that I think there is a real issue there.'

'But we've had such a nice time today.'

'Of course we have. That goes without saying. But if you decide that you have to take Andy's position seriously, and we can't see each other like this anymore, or go to bed together, or do anything that isn't strictly business, then I will accept that.'

'Just like that?'

'No, not just like that. I'd be very sorry. It's nice for you and it's nice for me, but if it's causing you problems I can't tell you to ignore them, can I?'

'Yes, you can. You can tell me to ignore them all and come to live with you and Ben and Josh.'

'I can't do that at the moment, Madison.'

We fell silent, while we toyed idly with each other's hands.

'You're very clinical about this,' I said finally.

'I'm not made of stone, Madsy; I would be very sorry if you were not part of our lives anymore, not to have any more days like this, or to see you sitting in our kitchen, serene and loving amidst all the mayhem. But I know I'm not giving you what you want, and I can't help you any more with your home situation. I can say to you that you could wait and see what happens, wait for me to get my head around all the problems I have with the idea of starting again, properly and permanently, with someone else, but if it costs you dearly to do that, I can't force you to do so. It would be incredibly selfish.'

'Just as I can't force you to take me home with you and never let me go away again,' I replied sadly.

'I will never say anything that I don't mean, Madsy, or do anything about which I can't be wholehearted.'

I nodded.

'Yes, I know that,' I told him sadly.

I gathered up my bags.

'It would be better if we didn't speak to each other for a while, I think. If I'm going to have to sacrifice my one true and perfect love on the altar of The Restless Dragon, then I don't think I can bear to see you or talk to you. Unless you change your mind and come to take me home with you, that is.'

I gave in to tears at last, burying my face in my hands, as I wept.

'Madsy,' Gerry signed, gently pulling my hands from my face. 'What can I say?'

'You don't usually have any problem,' I wept.

'I think you've said it all,' he mused.

Knowing that if I didn't leave the car now, I would take back my heartbreaking decision, I kissed him softly, drawing back quickly before I could be tempted to stay.

'Goodbye, darling. I love you forever.'

'Bye,' he answered in subdued tones.

With an enormous effort of will I left the car, closing the door without looking back. As I walked towards the front door I heard the engine rev and Gerry drove away without the slightest hesitation.

The next day, sick and exhausted, in such pain I could barely stand, I dragged myself out of my bed to speak to Andy, who was slunk before the television at three o'clock in the afternoon. I had simply told him I felt ill and he had not questioned my strange malaise.

'Andy?'

'What?'

'Listen to me a moment; please turn that off.'

He looked up ready to sneer, but my exhaustion and anguish clearly did not conceal my determination to have this conversation.

'You asked me – told me – that if I didn't see Gerry any longer then you would go back to The Dragon. I still think it was a ridiculous thing to ask of me because you should want to be at The Dragon irrespective of anything else, but you weren't prepared to look at it that way. So, for better or for worse, I've told Gerry that I'm not seeing him. If you are wise, you will take this at face value and get into that theatre on Monday morning. If you don't, and you still refuse to go back, then, as you said to me, all bets are off.'

'How do I know you're not going to see him anymore?' he asked slowly.

'Because I say so. If you're not prepared to accept my word on that, then I may as well have not done it.'

'What did you say to him?'

'That's between me and Gerry.'

'Oh, no, it's not,' he snapped. 'You tell me exactly what you said.'

'Andy, you have an excellent career at The Restless Dragon, if you want it. You also have me here, present in our home, working hard, and having accommodated exactly what you wanted me to do. I have suffered deeply, too, over these last weeks, indeed, for longer than you can possibly know, though you may consider that to be of no relevance or concern to you. But I will not be robbed now of the last shreds of whatever my friendship with Gerry has meant to either him or me. What passed between us is private and I will not talk about it anymore. I have walked away from him and I am here. Now do your part and go to see Joe and Ron, ideally today, and show them that you deserve the commitment and patience they have shown to you. Now, I'm going to make a cup of tea and take it back to bed. I have coaching tomorrow and need to be in a fit state to sing.'

I left him gazing morosely after me, and it was some time later, as I fitfully dozed that I heard Andy's murmur on the telephone and then the front door open and close again. I would discover later whether he had gone to the theatre. I idly considered my options if he hadn't done so, if he failed to return on Monday, but there were few to consider. My decision to stay away from Gerry was utterly contingent on Andy's return to The Dragon. But more than that, it was contingent on Gerry staying away from me. If he sought me out and offered me all that I longed for, then I would not reject it. I held this to my heart, and slept long into the night, hoping to find healing in oblivion.

CHAPTER 65

Andy had gone to The Dragon and he returned there three days later to resume his position as AD and in-house writer. When he came home after his first new day at the theatre, still reticent with me, but evidently more at peace with himself, I cried myself to sleep yet again, bitterly acknowledging that whilst I may not have done what felt best for me, I had done the only thing I could do to help Andy. After he left the following morning and I sat at the window gazing at the grey January skies wanting only for them to swallow me up, I knew I had to do something healing. Huddled by the radiator, I wrote to Gerry.

My dearest, beloved Gerry

Almost a week has passed since I last saw you and I write this with a heavy heart. I cannot express how deeply I love and miss you, but you already know the former, and can probably conceive of the latter. When we have been apart before, be it for days, sometimes for as long as a week, I have always known that I would see you again, and although I hated your absence I was comforted by the knowledge that soon I would be able to hold you, to hear you tease and encourage me, to see your sweet smile and feel your kisses once more. Many days and nights I cried with longing for you, but you were always there for me again and I loved the anticipation of the hours before I would see you. I would be so excited my hands would shake, and concentration on anything but the most mundane tasks was well nigh impossible! Every moment I have spent with you has been infinitely precious, even the many times (boring for you) I have cried in your patient arms. Nothing can ever take these moments from me, even as I long for you now, so crushed without the prospect of your nearness that I can barely look beyond tomorrow. But I had to learn how to live without you from day-to-day, so now I must learn to live without you every day, not only for a week or even a month, but forever.

Andy has gone back to The Dragon and I comfort myself that if he is happy perhaps I have done something right. But I will never stop loving you, and I could not walk away from you again. I am always yours and you only have to reach out for me and I will be there. You will always be my first and last waking thought.

With all my love, my darling,

Madison

Forty-eight hours later I picked up the mail from the mat with little interest – even a summons from the Met would have been hard pressed to raise a flicker from me – to be met with Gerry's distinctive script. Marvelling at the sheer good fortune that its arrival had coincided with Andy's absence, I switched on the kettle and slowly made coffee before sitting in my study armchair to open the otherwise unremarkable white envelope.

Hello Madison,

Thank you for your letter. It seems a long time since last week and I was glad to hear from you. I admit I had been worrying about you. I hope you are all right.

You have always said beautiful things to me and you said more of them in your letter. And, yes, I have missed you, too. It makes me appreciate afresh that there are different kinds of absence, as you rightly identify: the absence that marks time – sometimes happily, sometimes not – between seeing someone dear to you, and the absence which forces you to confront the fact that someone important no longer occupies the special place they held. As I write this I can hear you saying 'Gerry, you are wonderful and I do love you,' in those seductive mezzo tones, and I wish you were here with me now. But I know I have let you down. I couldn't give you the reassurance you needed that there was a bigger place in my life for you, and it is selfish of me to want you on my terms alone. For what it's worth, I think perhaps you did the right thing for Andy. Time will tell.

I do love you, Madison, although I know you are not always convinced of that. I love all the beautiful things that are you: the wonderful care you have given me, and your kindness to Ben and Josh; the special way you make love to me, always so responsive and generous. I shall miss all that very much, but perhaps we had reached the end of the particular road we have been travelling, and need to examine the signposts that confront us now.

I think of you every day, as I have done for some time now. Try to be happy. Sing wonderfully.

Love from Gerry.

I cried for many hours that day, drifting from room to room, reading Gerry's letter over again, looking through the photos, messages and sweet mementos of the last ten months, the months when I'd loved Gerry both secretly and openly, and those months when I'd lived in our amazing and strange world, holding onto a phantom of what a life with him might be. Masochistically, I replayed every detail of our time together, weeping inconsolably as *La Boheme* played in the background. '*Addio, senza rancor*', sang Mimi, and all the pain and anguish welled up from the depths of my broken heart, until I could weep no more.

I lit the bathroom with a plethora of candles, scented the bath with oils and foam, and in the flickering glow, I lay back, letting the water soothe and comfort me, sipping sedately from the largest glass of Cabernet I could pour. Later, wrapped in a fluffy robe, I grilled bacon and hash browns, cooked mushrooms and melted cheese, eating it all with crusty rolls and butter, followed by a rich helping of profiteroles in a little individual pot. I sank back, replete with unashamedly comfort eating; my newly slender frame could handle it. I faced a choice: I could live miserably without Gerry, or try to live with at least a semblance of well-being, a veneer of contentment. The second choice was clearly the better option, though a remote possibility. But my bacon and mushrooms gave me hope. I had enjoyed them, as I had the crisp hash browns, and the creamy chocolate sauce on the profiteroles. If, in deepest despair, I could find some small pleasure in the taste and texture of this simple food, then perhaps I could find it in other things – in music, in friends, in the spring sunshine that would eventually penetrate the dark winter skies, and, maybe, eventually in life again.

And so as the song moves into a new key and form, so did my life. It was a melancholy song of loss and sorrow, but I hoped there was a honourable counterpoint to it. Andy watched my every movement like a hawk, listened openly to every phone call, and though I never caught him in the act, I was sure he read my mail, looked through my bags and their contents, and rummaged amongst my papers. What he hoped or feared to find I never knew, but I made sure that my letters and messages from Gerry were safe. Perhaps one day I would find the strength to destroy them.

Gradually, Andy began to talk to me again, and as we both took up the reins of our respective careers we started to share bits of our day more easily, and about a fortnight after I'd last seen Gerry when Andy showed me the ongoing work he and Joe were doing on *Eluszka,* I detected something of a thaw in the frosty atmosphere. I went to The Dragon to hear the Polish folk songs Joe wanted me to sing in the play and they were indeed beautiful. As Andy worked front of house, Joe sat me in his office with coffee and cake and played me a tape of the simple, yet heartbreakingly sensitive, songs. He gave me an English translation as well as a phonetically spelled Polish text, and to my horror I found tears falling as I listened.

I watch the lengthening shadows
Seeking your form in them
You are gone from me as the snow melts
And the green buds form
The sun will shine but you
Are not in its beams
As spring comes to the land
Winter stays in my heart.

'Little Madsy,' said Joe in concern, 'you are crying. This song makes you sad, yes?'

I nodded, not trusting myself to speak.

'You will sing it beautifully, then. I think you understand what it is saying.'

'Yes,' I whispered, surreptitiously wiping an escaping tear.

Joe took my hands away from my face, lifting my head to look me in the eye.

'I think you have been having a very difficult time, Madsy. The Andy boy, he is not easy, is he? But I think it is more that than.'

I nodded again, longing to weep on his shoulder, but afraid that if I started I wouldn't be able to stop.

'This song, it makes you think of someone you love who is lost to you. And Andy, all is not well, not just because he is a difficult boy, but because you cry with love for another.'

'Oh, Joe,' I breathed, 'how did you know this? What has Andy said?'

'Very little, my dear, but I watch, and I think, and I draw my foolish conclusions. But this time, not so foolish, I think.'

'No, not foolish at all,' I told him. 'But please, Joe, don't say anything to Andy. I don't think I can cope with him being angry again at the moment.'

Joe nodded sagely.

'I say nothing. Now let me hear you sing this beautiful song as wonderfully as I know you will sing it, but first I speak you the Polish and you repeat after me. Yes?'

So we spent a fascinating morning as Joe taught me to pronounce the Polish text and then I sang along to the tape several times. When Andy came back to see what we were doing, Joe lifted his hands in delight.

'Ah, Andy, the lovely Madison sings with all the beauty and soul of a true Polish spirit.'

'Oh good. You're going to do it, then?' Andy asked me.

'If I'm not working when the play goes up, I'll do it live, but if I'm already on a contracted job,' I looked hard at Andy, 'then why don't we make a tape of me singing them? Do you always need to have the singer physically present?'

'Yes, of course,' Andy snapped.

At the same time Joe spoke reassuringly. 'We can work around you, Madsy. It is your voice we want in our play; if we can have your sweet face sometimes, too, all the better, but if not, we can accommodate. Yes?'

He rose, beaming at us both.

'I think today calls for a little celebration. You will both come with me for some lunch, no? Joe's treat for two of his favourite people.'

I thought Andy might refuse, but he saw Joe's kind, eager face, and nodded easily.

'That's nice of you, Joe.'

'Nothing nice about it, Andy boy,' Joe laughed. 'I just want an excuse to talk more to this lovely lady.'

'Oh, she's not short of people who want to talk to her,' Andy growled.

Only a fool would have missed the bitterness in his tone, and Joe was no fool. I winced, hoping he would not say anything to fan the embers of Andy's irritation.

'Indeed not, I'm sure,' Joe replied, smoothly leading us to the door, and in the warmth of his expansiveness, even Andy couldn't be angry for long.

CHAPTER 66

Every day when I woke it was, as in the words of Joe's song, winter in my heart, and every day it was a tussle not to email Gerry. I wanted him to know that my love for him was unchanged and my longing for him as great, but I resisted, and hoped that one day I would wake to feel the first tentative beams of spring sun warming my frozen heart back to life. I sought out Annie again, who had respected my initial bereavement by not being offended by my silence. I had phoned her the day after Gerry and I had been to Oxford, told her in brief, halting sentences what I had done, and then retreated, unable to speak to anyone of the selfish pain I was suffering. But as our first *Carmen* music calls loomed on the horizon, I began to crave her company.

'Madsy, darling, are you all right? I didn't want to intrude.'

'I'm surviving, Annie. I'll be glad to get going on *Carmen*. I need something substantial to distract me.'

'How's Andy?'

'Working, thank God, and that was the aim, so I'm grateful for that.'

'Do you want to come over? Or shall I come to you?'

'I'd love to come to you if I can. I'm practising and teaching, and I'm doing *Music Makers* finally on Saturday, but I need some company and a change of scene.'

Once again, Annie proved a true friend, uttering not one word of criticism, but every few days, as January crept along, we

371

would meet and practice together, chat, and walk over the heath or, wrapped to the gunnels, venture into Richmond Park.

'You're seeing Annie a lot,' Andy commented one evening after she'd left.

Resisting the temptation to ask whether he now thought I was having an affair with Annie, I answered easily. 'Yes, she's good company and we've been working together on *Carmen*. She's going to Robert for coaching now; she thinks he's better than her guy.'

'You're a better singer than she is,' Andy opined. 'I can't get used to her voice.'

'It's just different to mine,' I said fairly. 'We're completely different kinds of mezzos.' But I was pleased that indirectly Andy seemed to be saying he liked my singing again, albeit at Annie's expense.

So things went on until the last week in January when finally we started official *Carmen* calls and I felt I could find some strength in having my life structured by the demands of others for a while. I could have done with a production running through January, going regularly to the theatre, and immersing myself in a role onto which I could project all my pain. Another run of *Tito* would have done beautifully, or an Elvira in *Don Giovanni*. But *Carmen* would have to do, and it was wonderful to be back in a busy rehearsal studio, and to be working with focussed concentration alongside colleagues who were as pleased to be there as I was. I almost dared to be happy as I left the first music call, drinking hot chocolate with Annie and Georgina, who was playing Frasquita, and flirting mildly with Alex Johnson, our Dancairo. I hadn't met him previously, but I'd noticed him watching me as we'd sung, and when we took a break he came straight over to speak to me.

'Hi,' he said, holding out his hand. 'Clarissa Grainger told me to send you and Annie her love.'

'Oh, how nice. We were the three ladies at Glyndebourne last summer, but I expect she told you that.'

Alex nodded.

'She said you all had a great time.'

I felt such a powerful wave of nostalgia it took me a beat to answer him.

'It was perfect,' I said simply.

Later, Annie nodded at me approvingly.

'I was pleased to see you talking to Alex like a normal human being again,' she told me.

'Oh, thanks a lot,' I chided her. 'As opposed to what?'

'As opposed to a broken-hearted melancholic who's forgotten how to smile.'

'Annie, I'm not that bad!'

'Worse! You've been looking so miserable you could curdle milk. A little flirtation with an unconnected third party will do you a world of good.'

I was astonished at Annie's insensitivity, and fought unsuccessfully against the anger that rose up in me.

'No, it wouldn't, thank you. The only thing that would do any good would be to see Gerry again, and since that's not going to happen, the best I can hope for is that I can enjoy this show and that Andy won't do anything stupid at The Dragon again. I'm sorry if I look miserable, but that's because I am. I'll try harder in future.'

I promptly burst into tears, and Annie held her arms out to me contritely.

'Darling, I'm sorry. I didn't mean to be insensitive. I just want you to feel better. Gerry has caused you so much unhappiness one way or the other, I want you to leave him behind, not just physically, but emotionally, too. But I'm sorry for being so crass. I know how much you love him still.'

'Oh, Annie, I'd hoped that he would have come back to me by now, that he would have been unable to stay away, whatever I'd said to him. But every day that goes past without him contacting me, the more I have to accept that he's not going to. He's just going to wait till we do *Figaro* in the summer and by then any love he felt for me will be long gone.'

'If you really can't bear it without him you could contact him yourself,' Annie said. 'As much as I think you're ultimately better off without him messing up your head and your heart,' she added.

'But what happens if I do that, and Andy leaves The Dragon again?' I wept. 'And what if Gerry turned me away?'

'I don't think he would, Madsy.'

'If he really cared he would have come for me by now. I can't humble myself before him any more. I did that often enough and look where it got me. I'm still in such pain, Annie, I can't bear it.'

I sobbed inconsolably, and all Annie could do was wait it out, holding me tight and stroking my hair.

Later, it frightened me how badly I still missed Gerry. I was, after all, nowhere near feeling stronger, no closer to healing than I had been on the night I walked away from Gerry for the last time. But the ferocity of my reaction had shocked me and I actually feared for my mental well being. Nearly a month had passed, and still I woke in the night to feel a stone in my chest, my throat closed tight with hurt and pain, and a terrifying hopelessness. More than once as I lay awake in the early hours, I had allowed my fantasises to drift to some rose-tinted picture of suicide. The most delicious, expensive red wine I could find, a final meal of *penne* with shaved parmesan, pine kernels and broccoli florets, followed by tiramisu, and a hundred paracetamol, swallowed delicately and easily, as Mozart played on the stereo. I imagined Andy coming in late to find me dead on the settee, peaceful at last in my final, irrevocable escape from my love for Gerry. I could never quite picture Andy's reaction, but Gerry's I could see clearly, although I don't know from where my tired brain conjured it. His eyebrows raised in mocking irony, I could hear him saying, 'Silly girl, she didn't even know what real suffering is.' In my imagination, his voice was the voice of my conscience.

Who was I to be so selfishly indulgent? I had a wonderful career, a beautiful home, good friends, health, brains, and a husband who, despite the quiet anger that still simmered beneath the surface, was evidently willing to give our marriage a second chance. And my foolish fantasy was remarkably free of stomach pumping, vomiting, and the resultant guilt of facing Andy and Megan with a failed, or foiled, suicide attempt. The reality, successful or otherwise, would be grim, and revealed my fantasy for what it was – the selfish preoccupation of a woman who had not been able to manipulate real life to suit her own desires.

I had to get my life in order, and I started by phoning Megan. I had sent her emails every few days since the disaster of Christmas Day, all of which had remained unanswered, but with *Music Makers* at the Blackheath concert halls in the offing, I girded my loins and called her.

'Hi. It's me.' I sounded like Gerry.

A beat of silence hung heavy down the phone line before Megan spoke.

'Hello, Madison.'

'How are you doing?'

'Not too well.'

'Me neither,' I told her. 'Mum, all that business at Christmas.' I paused, uncertain of what to say now the moment had arrived.

'Yes?'

'I'm not seeing Gerry McFall. At all, I mean, not even for work at the moment.'

'I see.'

Megan was clearly going to make this hard work, but I wasn't going to give her more information than was necessary. I tried to stay casual.

'I thought it might be best, given Andy's reaction to it all. Things are much better for him now he's back at The Dragon.'

'I'm sure they are.'

375

I began to swallow on easy tears again.

'Please, Mum, I've been so unhappy.'

'I can hear that.'

As much as I wanted to tell her how desperately I missed Gerry, I couldn't do so, if I wanted to be reconciled.

'I'm singing *Music Makers* at the weekend. Please will you come?' I asked her.

'Is Andy going to be there?'

'Yes.'

'Very well, I'll be along.'

'Oh, good.' Relief flooded through me, but Megan did not prolong the conversation.

'Leave me a ticket at the box office. I'll see you afterwards.'

Our farewells were brief, but maybe a corner had been turned.

With the same motivation – to rebuild my shattered emotional life – I was proactive with Andy over *Elushka*, encouraging him and Joe to give me some dates and hoping that if I simulated enthusiasm for my part in the project, that I might soon begin to feel genuinely engaged and willing to be involved. Joe gave me more music and I learned it quickly, finding the melancholy shades in the music oddly comforting.

'You sound beautiful,' Andy said seriously, as I sang one of them whilst I got ready to leave for Blackheath on my concert day – my first big gig since I'd left Gerry. I looked at Andy frankly.

'Really? I wondered if my voice was too heavy for them.'

'Not at all. You suit them well. Thank you for being part of it, Madsy.'

Unbidden tears sprang to my eyes as Andy's kind words touched me. Keeping my head down I hoped he would miss them, but he was studying me too closely for concealment.

'Why are you crying?' He sounded impatient and I sighed inwardly. I couldn't face an argument today.

'I'm not,' I replied stubbornly, and indeed, the quick tears had already receded. Andy shrugged.

'Whatever you say.'

We were both silent as I resumed creaming my face. As the silence threatened to become awkward, Andy spoke again.

'You miss him, don't you?'

'Of course not.'

'Don't bother to lie, Madison. I see it in your face every day.'

I took a breath to defend myself, but Andy held up his hand.

'It doesn't matter, does it? Anyway, I meant what I said about *Elushka*. I'm really glad you agreed to sing, and Joe's over the moon, as they say.'

'Good. It'll be a lovely play, another success for The Dragon,' I nodded, and Andy said no more, but left me to my preparations.

I hadn't sung a big concert since the *Christmas Oratorio* in early December, and I enjoyed the adrenaline rush of performance, and the sheer indulgence of Elgar's score. As we rehearsed with the orchestra I tried to will myself back into my pre-Gerry incarnation, but quickly I found that I couldn't, and ultimately neither did I want to do so. Despite my sorrow, I had been utterly transformed by Gerry. I looked different, sounded different, and behaved differently. I was confident, not only in my singing, but also of my desirability as a woman. I wanted to be glamorous and energetic. My voice was more centred, spanning its range more fluently, and I gave it more freely to the music and to the audience. Whatever else had happened, Gerry had left me these legacies, gifts borne out of my love for him.

After my beloved Mozart, Elgar was one of my favourite composers, and he knew just how to write for a mezzo; *Music Makers* was a treat to sing. I sang without score, conventionally held in the hand for a work such as this, but I felt sure enough of the music to be liberated from the book, and I knew it enhanced my performance. I could communicate more openly with both audience and conductor, on this occasion a young man making his debut at the concert hall. As we immersed ourselves in the riches of Elgar's music, it was suddenly as if I stood before Gerry, singing only for him. I could see the ironic lift of his eyebrow, the intense and absolute communication with his players, the precise lift of his hand to lead me into a passage, and his smile, amused, loving, and yet, as always, self-satisfied, as we came to rest at the end of the piece. The audience applause took me by surprise. I had virtually forgotten that they were there, and yet I knew that my imaginings had only served to make my performance more vibrant. I beamed at them from the platform, glad to acknowledge their generous appreciation.

If Megan and Andy were more reserved in their praise, I was so relieved to see them standing together, having evidently survived the evening without controversy, I worried little that their old fulsomeness was restrained. But as Megan drove us home she said quietly, 'It was lovely to hear you sing today, Madison. I've missed it lately.'

'I haven't done much, Mum,' I told her. 'The next big thing is *Carmen*, and after that it all starts in earnest for the next three years: ENO, Glyndebourne again, and hopefully Europe.'

I heard Andy sigh, but mercifully Megan didn't pick it up.

'What a long way you've come, Madsy,' she said, and I didn't imagine the warmth in her hug as we parted.

CHAPTER 67

Whilst there was nothing like success to sweeten Megan, I still woke each morning to a sinking sadness. Lying awake, I recalled afresh why I felt empty and depressed, and reality would encompass me again. By the time I was up, showered, and drinking my first cup of tea of the day, I was usually feeling stronger, and on our *Carmen* rehearsal days, even pleasantly anticipatory, but I had realised by now that it would take a very long time to forget my love for Gerry, and the wonderful, yet devastating, months we had spent together. As January ended, and with it a month without seeing or hearing from Gerry, I clung to the prospect of work like a life raft, determined that whatever else happened to me, or to Andy, that I would do all in my power to ensure the success of my career. My thirty-ninth birthday passed with little ceremony, but not without a deep awareness of how very fortunate I was to have been given a chance at this privileged second career at an age when a singer would either have already been at the height of their success or have long since abandoned hope of it.

As I took a break in a music rehearsal on the Monday morning following *Music Makers*, my phone rang, forcing me to abandon another pleasant conversation with Alex.

'Excuse me,' I muttered, delving for the phone.

Alex nodded and idly flicked through the newspaper as I spoke with Sara from DCP. 'Hello, it's been a very long time,' I greeted her.

'I know how busy you are, Madison, and not really in a position to slum it with us anymore.'

'Don't be silly,' I laughed, 'I'm delighted to hear from you.'

'Can you work for us next week?' she asked. 'Two girls from St Mary's, Ascot want some ethics.'

We compared diaries and I was pleased to find I was genuinely enthusiastic at the prospect of a few hours at the college. A space away from music and the people and situations that constantly reminded me of Gerry was just what I needed. We confirmed a day and time, and as I hung up, Alex raised an eyebrow enquiringly.

'Work?' he asked.

'Yes, but not singing,' I told him, explaining about my occasional forays back into academia.

'That's really healthy,' he said approvingly. 'Too many singers have no life other than music, no other outlet; it's no wonder they get neurotic.'

He proceeded to tell me about his own passion for Renaissance art, and I was so interested that it was considerably later when I felt the familiar pang of sadness again, and I realised that I'd been pleasantly distracted for over an hour.

Just how distracted I'd been was proved when only later that day I remembered with a jolt that in going to DCP, even for a morning, I ran the risk of seeing Josh. I almost rang Sara there and then to call it all off, or at least to ask her to check that Josh's timetable precluded our meeting, but I didn't feel up to facing the questions she would legitimately ask, so I simply had to prepare for the eventuality. However many times I argued with myself that out of four hundred students in the college, the probability of seeing Josh during the five minutes it took me to get into the building and to a classroom, and five minutes to leave at the end was low, something told me that I see him I would. Eventually, I tried to persuade myself that it would be good to do so, that it would enable me to work through the demons which still haunted me, but I didn't do a very good job, and later that week, as I pushed open the door of Doddington Carter and Paine, I was sick with apprehension. A performer to the last, I concealed it effectively enough as I worked with two bright eighteen-year-olds, and by one o'clock we were good friends, laughing as we came down the stairs and said our farewells at the front door. So far, so good, I thought, deciding to risk a coffee in the office before venturing out again into the February chill.

'Was everything okay?' Sara asked as she leafed through files on her desk.

'They were lovely, and wrote pages of notes.'

'Oh good. They'll probably want to come again then, if that's all right with you.'

'If I'm free, I'd be delighted. I'm going to make a coffee. Want one?' I asked her.

'Please.'

I switched on the kettle and fiddled with mugs and coffee as staff on their lunch breaks moved in and out of the kitchen adjoining the office. I smiled with quiet pleasure. It was nice to be somewhere different with a different feel to the atmosphere and different faces to see.

'One coffee.'

I handed Sara her mug and sat on the desk beside her, casually swinging my legs and feeling suspiciously content. She babbled away about the latest DCP gossip and I sipped and nodded, putting off the moment when I had to leave. I was laughing so appreciatively at her impersonation of one of the college's more outlandish students that I wasn't aware of a surge of movement behind me until I heard a soft voice, achingly familiar. Instinctively, I looked round. Josh was standing with his back to us, talking animatedly with two other boys. One of them, a tall, squarely built young man, caught my startled gaze and the shift of his focus caused Josh and his other friend to turn to see what had attracted his attention. We met eye to eye, and my sharp intake of breath, catching in my throat, was painful with tension. I had feared this moment, and yet now it had arrived the anguished joy I felt was worth all the tears I knew I would shed later.

Josh spoke first.

'Hi, Madison.'

He looked at me under his long eyelashes, his gentle voice as sweet and sensitive as ever.

'Hi, Josh.'

We looked at each other for a moment before I edged off the desk and at the same moment Josh moved away from his friends.

'I'll see you in a minute,' he told them.

A stranger to them, I was of no interest, and they left with only the barest nod to Josh. We met in front of Sara's desk, instinctively drawing away from her earshot and towards the expansive bay window. I studied Josh closely, reaching out my hand. He took it and we stood in silence for a moment. He looked beautiful, his black hair half concealed under a fedora, half peeping out over the collar of a leopard print blouse, worn atop his customary black T-shirt. His eyes were meticulously made up, eyebrows and lashes thick and dark, lids shadowed with the hand of an artist. He had style, that was for sure.

'Have you been okay?' I asked softly.

'I guess so.' He nodded. 'And you?'

I shrugged.

'Oh, Josh, I've missed you.'

Tears welled up with their customary ease and I looked away from him, out of the window and across the garden square.

'When are you coming over to see us again?'

I couldn't speak.

'Madison?' Josh squeezed my fingers.

'I can't, darling.'

'Why not?'

'I just can't.'

We fell silent again, and a shadow closed down his open expression. He dropped my hand, reaching to pick up his bag.

'Josh,' I put out my hand to hold him back, 'I love you all very much.'

'Then you've got a funny way of showing it,' he muttered, turning away. 'Bye, Madison. Stay cool.'

And he was gone, as I stood motionless, looking after him. I watched him cross the street and the square until he was lost from my sight. Business had gone on around us as we had talked, and still it continued as students moved in and out of the office asking questions, collecting papers and delivering messages. I couldn't bear to speak to Sara again, quite unable to burden yet another set of ears with my self-inflicted woe. I waited until she caught my eye whilst in mid-conversation with a teenager. Lifting my hand in causal salutation, I mouthed a farewell and slipped away.

In the square I found a lone bench, sinking onto it gratefully, trembling with pain, and relieved to finally release it in tears. Josh's hurt, cross face was burned into my memory, and his bitter words echoed in my mind. I wondered if he would tell Gerry of our meeting, but doubted that he would do so. The secretive veil that customarily fell across Josh's life would fall across our encounter, I was sure. And with it would go the chance that Gerry would contact me, motivated by a terse word from Josh. I could ring him now, I thought impulsively, tell him how glad I had been to see his older son, how sorry that Josh had been angered by the abrupt lesson he had learned in adult inconsistency. I could ask to meet him, to see him on any terms he allowed, anything but the slow release misery of separation. My hand fiddled with the clasp of my bag, fingers running lightly over the phone's keypad, but they drew away, the call unmade. Instead I closed my eyes and, resting my head on my knee, imagined Josh's dark eyes again, his pale, intelligent face and the soft voice that uttered such profundities. The picture slowly changed into an image of Ben, all arms and legs, sighing with heavy sarcasm as he rolled his eyes in a perfect imitation of his dad. And my dear Gerry, his face sweet, resigned and exhausted, but full of tenderness, taking my hand in his and saying with ironic pleasure, 'You're looking very curvaceous today. I have noticed, you know.' And I would put my arms round him, kissing his ear, and neck, and his soft mouth, as I told him, 'Darling Gerry, I love you so much,' and I could hear his laconic response as clearly as if he sat beside me on the bench.

I let the images recede before I lifted my head, sitting for a moment to gaze around the square where the trees were just starting to put out tiny buds, little promises of what was to come. As I sat I realised that I was waiting, hoping that Josh would return, loping through the square to find me. With an effort I rose from my seat, hoisted my bag and walked with as much purpose as I could muster towards the road. If Josh did return, or if I saw him again, or Ben, or, most of all, Gerry, I would not be able to walk away. So I walked whilst I could, back towards the tube station, towards Victoria, and ultimately to The Restless Dragon.

CHAPTER 68

Annie was strangely subdued at rehearsal some days later and would not be jollied along. She sang as well as ever, always secure in her grasp of the music and intelligently thinking through how it meshed with the intense drama of the plot, but she was definitely out of sorts and more riled than usual with the posturing of our rather arrogant Escamillo. As she sighed with obvious irritation she caught my eye, but was not mollified with a wink, and when we broke for lunch she was quick to get out of the studio leaving me scuttling in her wake, hurrying to catch up.

'Annie?'

She paused fractionally to allow me to draw alongside her, but said nothing as we headed for the Rat and Parrot on West End Lane.

'Usual?' she asked me abruptly, looking around for an unoccupied table, and I nodded, grabbing a seat for us as she ordered diet Cokes and a plate of nachos.

'Sorry,' she said as she joined me again. 'I'm less than tolerant this morning. I'll be better after some food.'

'What's the matter, honey?' I asked, tapping the back of her hand lightly.

'Oh, nothing particular,' she shrugged, but a shadow passed over her face and she looked exhausted.

'Come on, I'm not going to accept that,' I chided her. 'If you don't want to tell me that's one thing, and I won't push it, but all morning you've looked so down. Tell me to shut up if you want to, but you're always looking out for me, I think I have a vested interest in doing the same for you.'

Annie smiled wryly.

'Somebody has to try to stop you getting into trouble, Madsy. Not that I've succeeded very well.'

I slapped her wrist lightly, and we giggled as our food arrived.

We tucked in silently for a while, each lost in our own thoughts until eventually Annie sat back and said quietly, 'I found a lump in my right breast three days ago. I'm having a biopsy on Friday. I've never seen a doctor move so fast, and I'm terrified.'

Tears filled her eyes as she looked down at our plate of nachos, toying idly with a tortilla chip.

'Oh, Annie, I'm sorry.' I was silent as I tried to imagine the full extent of Annie's fear. 'You acted quickly yourself. I think I'd still have been faffing around.'

'My mother died of breast cancer and so did her mother. I've been waiting for this all my life. It's a bit like having a case packed and ready to go. You don't hesitate when the call comes.'

'Annie, it'll be all right. Be positive,' I urged her.

'Maybe, maybe not,' she shrugged. 'I just want to get Friday over.' Today was Wednesday.

'Are you staying in overnight?' I asked her. 'Shall I come with you? What shall I do?'

I could see that Annie was about to shake her head, instinctively refusing any help, but she stopped short before speaking.

'You can't miss the morning call; it's bad enough that my cover will be in, but I wouldn't say no if you want to come down in the afternoon. It's at the Cromwell Hospital. They'll keep me overnight to Saturday, so I'm told.'

'And I'll be there as soon as we finish,' I assured her. 'Just text me when you're ready for me to come.'

Annie nodded wearily.

'That'll be nice, Mads. You can bring me grapes if you like.'

'I think I might find something more exciting than that,' I laughed in response, and some of the tension drained away.

I was filled with admiration for Annie as she sang with total concentration and commitment that afternoon. It was only when her determined little face was in repose that I could see the lines of anxiety around her mouth. But when she sang they were ironed out. Annie could take refuge in her music as I did, I thought. How lucky we were to be able to do so. I knew singers whose personal tragedies had devastated their voices, and I realised that perhaps there might be something worse than losing Gerry. Annie's situation, too, should surely put mine into perspective and I resolved not to bore Annie with my latest saga. The memory of seeing Josh still hurt my heart, and I would have loved to cry on her shoulder yet again, but even I knew when occasionally to be silent.

Later, as I pondered Annie's situation, I wondered what I would have done had I been in the same position. If faced with the prospect of a life-threatening illness would I be able to hold back any longer from contacting Gerry? I thought not. It would have been his arms around me that I needed, and his quiet strength encouraging and supporting me as I faced the biopsy. I was determined to give Annie the support she so richly deserved, knowing that it was the least I could do after months of her unselfish care for me.

Andy, too, was concerned when I told him.

'Poor Annie,' he said sympathetically, 'she must be feeling awful.'

'I'm going to the hospital to see her on Friday after she's had the biopsy.'

'Oh, Madsy, that's good,' Andy said warmly, taking me quite by surprise. I had expected him to immediately question if I was really going to visit Annie, or whether I was using her operation as a cover for seeing Gerry. But he didn't, and I was glad.

'I'll give her your love, shall I?' I asked him.

'Of course.'

Andy was more amenable that evening, as if Annie's news had encouraged him also to put things into perspective. We cooked a chicken and roast potatoes, served it with stir-fried vegetables in a lemon sauce, and that night the hours passed without a cross word. It didn't make me miss Gerry any the less, but it soothed me somehow.

The Cromwell Hospital, with its distinctive turquoise shielded windows, sat on the busy Cromwell Road. The building was low-rise and expensive looking and I was pleased that Annie could be in this pleasant place for her ordeal. I was glad, too, when I saw the huge bouquet that virtually concealed her diminutive frame lost against the huge white pillowcases.

'Those are lovely. Very cheering,' I said, pulling up a chair next to the bed.

'They certainly are,' she agreed with rather more energy than I expected. 'It's who they're from that cheers me most,' she grinned, but was evidently disinclined to fill me in further, looking eagerly instead to see what I'd brought her. So I regaled her with a report of the morning's rehearsal, and gave her the magazines I'd bought, together with a new book I'd found on Mozart, and some pretty toiletries to enjoy when she went home.

'How are you doing, honey?' I asked, when she began to flag.

'I'm tired,' she said, 'and I'm not happy having to wait for the biopsy results.'

'When will you get them?'

'Tomorrow morning.'

'Then you'll be able to go home?' I asked.

'It depends on the result,' she said pragmatically.

I squeezed her hand and she shrugged.

'What will be, will be. Now it's come to it, I feel oddly resigned to whatever happens. After the surgeon read my case notes he told me to 'expect the worst, but hope for the best', and to be honest, I'm more ready to hear the worst than the best now.'

'Oh, darling,' I soothed, and we smiled at each other fondly. 'We missed you this morning,' I told her, more cheerfully.

'I should bloody well hope so,' Annie retorted with spirit, 'given the nature of my substitute.'

We giggled. There was no love lost between Annie and her arrogant cover.

'Listen, Madsy,' she chuckled, 'if I have to pull out of the show, I'll tell them I demand that you take over my role, rather than Carolyn.'

'Annie, don't say that, even in jest. You'll be absolutely fine, and the best Carmen ever.'

Not only did Annie's operation soothe matters between Andy and me, but Megan, too, responded kindly. She called on Saturday morning before I was due to set out to see Annie and, without planning to do so, I found myself telling her about my friend's worries.

'She'll be fine, Madison,' Megan said encouragingly. 'She looks like the kind of girl who always beats the odds, tough and feisty. Am I right?'

'I think so,' I replied, cheered by her assessment of Annie's character and the fact that the subject seemed to genuinely stimulate some unspoken desire in us all to honour Annie's trouble with a show of good feeling between us.

To find Annie fully dressed and talking animatedly with a nurse when I arrived at the hospital gave the morning an even brighter glow. She beamed as I approached, giving me no time to ask, as she said happily, 'Madsy, I can't believe it! It's benign. I was so convinced I would be going straight back into the operating theatre I can barely take it in.'

'Well, take it in, Anastasia,' the nurse assured her. 'You're free and clear to go.'

I grinned to hear Annie called by her full name, and made a mental note to do it myself in future as often as I could get away with it.

'Let's go home and celebrate,' Annie declared enthusiastically. 'I laid in some smoked salmon just in case. I decided that if I had to stay in hospital beyond today it could rot in the fridge as a vicarious sacrifice, but if I came home I could dispose of it in the more usual way.'

Annie was buzzing all the way back to Richmond, high on the adrenaline of relief. I knew she would crash back to earth sooner or later, as her brain eventually rebelled against such a tide of emotion. It happened as she sliced a lemon for the salmon. In mid-sentence she burst into noisy tears, and I abandoned the corkscrew to hug her close. She cried freely for some time, and I didn't attempt to stop her. She needed this release after her anxious week. Finally, her tears slowed, then petered out into a sniffle.

'Sorry, Madsy,' she muttered, her voice muffled by her handkerchief.

'What about? If anyone's entitled to cry after what you've been through this week, I think you are.'

'I feel exhausted now,' she said. 'Do you mind taking over here while I collapse on the sofa?'

Annie drifted off whilst I finished preparing our lunch. It was lovely to take care of someone again. I was forcibly reminded of the few, but precious, occasions when I had cooked and cleaned for Gerry and the boys and I realised how deeply satisfying I had found it. It was a good, honest sort of caring, not holding up a flagging mast, as it so often felt with Andy, but expressing love in simple and practical ways.

We ate lunch with enthusiasm, talking of this and that, until Annie fixed me with a stare.

'Come on, then, 'fess up kid, how have you been? Are you surviving without Mr Wonderful?'

'Just,' I told her honestly, but feeling disinclined to talk about Gerry when Annie was so richly entitled to every scrap of attention.

She picked up my mood.

'You are allowed to talk, Mads,' she said wryly, 'now we know that I'm not at death's door.' We chuckled with the relief of survivors. 'Seriously, even if I was, I'd still want you to talk to me,' she said quietly. 'If you want to, that is.'

Sighing heavily, I nodded.

'I saw Josh last week. I went to DCP to do some tutoring and we bumped into each other afterwards. It was awful.'

Annie took my hand, but stayed silent.

'Actually, no, it was wonderful, but awful too. You understand what I mean, don't you?'

'Of course,' she said kindly.

'He was angry with me for not going to see them anymore. I couldn't explain it all to him, obviously, I just had to accept his anger. It was all over in a few minutes, but it took every ounce of effort not to turn around and go home with him.'

'So why didn't you?' Annie asked reasonably.

'Because I made a decision that I've got to try to stick by, and it's got to be Gerry who moves the goalposts, not me or Josh.'

'Poor Madsy, you could have done without that, it must have brought everything back so fiercely.'

I nodded sadly and we were momentarily silent.

'Francesca from *Tito* rang me yesterday after you'd gone,' Annie went on cautiously after a moment.

'Oh, yes, that was nice.'

'She asked about you and Gerry.'

Annie seemed to lose confidence, and I guessed there was a punch line coming. I waited.

'I told her that as far as I knew, you weren't seeing each other at the moment. I kept it casual, because I didn't want to encourage her to gossip.' Annie looked at me frankly. 'Madsy, she said she had wondered, because they've just started calls

391

on *Butterfly* and he's been seriously flirting with the Suzuki, and a woman came to meet him from rehearsal this week – an older, sophisticated looking woman. It sounded like that Vanessa character.' Annie finally registered my stricken face and stopped abruptly. 'Madsy, I'm sorry to be so blunt about it, but if you really want to forget about him and move on, I think you should know what Francesca told me. I appreciate it is just idle chatter, but it might help you to decide whether to forget him for good, or to rush in there and claim him back, tell these other women where to go.'

She wiped away a tear that had splashed onto my hand as I let her words sink in.

'You're committing the naturalistic fallacy, Annie.'

'What's that when it's at home?'

'Inferring an *ought* from an *is*. Gerry *is* seeing other women again, therefore I *ought* to do something about it.'

Annie looked puzzled.

'We do it all the time,' I told her. 'Gerry *is* the love of my life, therefore I *ought* to do whatever is necessary to be with him. Gerry *is* unprepared to make a commitment to me, and Andy *is* in need of my help, therefore I *ought* to drop Gerry and stick by Andy. And does *ought* mean the same as *right*? So I left Gerry and stayed with Andy because that's what I felt I *ought* to do, but was it *right*? If it was right for Andy, does that make it right for me? Or Gerry? Does the fact that Gerry so obviously doesn't give a damn mean it was right, wrong, or morally neutral? What was important, my motives? – duty to Andy, perhaps – or the consequences? – Andy's back at the Dragon, but I'm miserable. Do they cancel one another out, or is Andy's happiness (if indeed he is happy) outweigh my unhappiness? Let's do a hedonic calculus to work it all out.'

Annie was staring at me in bewilderment.

'Get a grip, Madsy, you can't turn it all into some academic debate. If you're really unhappy without Gerry then go and see him. Tell him you still love him and you want to be with him and see what happens from there. But if you're not going to do that, then just accept the decision you made and go forward, but don't try to analyse it all to death. Now let me give you a hug and then we'd better check that I can still sing, if we don't want Carolyn to muscle in on Carmen quicker than a striking cobra.'

CHAPTER 69

Annie could still sing, and very well, too, as she demonstrated most convincingly at our first production call later the following week. To everyone's great admiration she returned only four days after her operation, positively champing at the bit, and Carolyn, who had clearly been hoping for the worst, retreated glumly as the cast clustered around Annie in welcome. I was glad to see my friend so happy to be back at work. Knowing that her worst fears had been laid to rest had made her even more enthusiastic, engaging quickly with everything we had learned in her absence. To our delight, the vagaries of the schedule meant we were setting our Card Trio early in the proceedings and we took enormous pleasure in being able to work closely together on Annie's first day back in harness. It was a fascinating morning and we were delighted with the final result. Annie was needed in the afternoon to work with Don Jose, but she hugged me warmly as I left.

'Thanks for being here today, Madsy.'

'I wasn't here just to hold your hand, honey,' I joked.

'I know, but...' she trailed off. 'You know what I mean.'

I did, of course, and we hugged again as I took my leave.

'Take care down at the Violent Dragon this afternoon,' Annie told me.

'Umm.' I rolled my eyes. 'Annie?'

'Yes, lovey?'

'I think I'm going to write Gerry a formal letter withdrawing from *Figaro* this summer. I could get my agent to do it, but I don't want to be that cold. Whatever, I don't think I can sing for him. If I ever see him again I'll be total wreck, and six months hence is far too soon.'

Annie nodded thoughtfully.

'You may decide that's what you want to do, Madsy, but why don't you hold out for a few weeks yet? You're still smarting over seeing Josh and you may feel stronger come the summer and be glad of an easy job by the sea.'

'Annie, I'm not going to be able to go to the coast and see them all every day if I can't be with them.'

'Maybe so, but I just think you should give yourself a bit longer. It's up to you, I know, but, well, it's just a feeling. Indulge me, Madsy. If in a month's time you still want to write that letter, I won't say another word.'

I gave up the fight.

'All right. I'll indulge you today, Anastasia, since you're such a heroine.'

I left her to head for The Dragon. At whose instigation I knew not, but Joe and Andy had expedited work on *Elushka* and were ready for me to lay down the tracks which would be used on the nights I couldn't physically be at the theatre. Joe was touchingly pleased to see me, offering his customary coffee and cake and a big hug, before ushering us off to a small but efficient looking recording studio somewhere in the depths of Rotherhithe. The process was fascinating, and even Andy seemed to lay aside the last of his cool reserve as we worked until late into the evening. At ten o'clock we sat back with a glass of wine and a pizza, delivered to the studio at Joe's prompting, to listen to the result of our work. The technicians had done a wonderful job, patiently tolerating Joe's precise demands and Andy's blustering ones. He must have been a mind reader since both men were delighted to hear how their often conflicting suggestions had somehow meshed into perfect harmony. A soft reverberation lent the songs a haunting echo that would be much harder to achieve live, and I told Joe as much.

'You'll have to mike me on stage to get something close to that effect,' I said. 'This is quite a different technique to what I'm used to using. You might not like it so much live as on tape.'

I wish I'd bitten my tongue when I saw Andy stiffen angrily.

'That's all right, Madison,' he said tightly. 'We know you don't want to do this at the theatre, spending time with us when you could be with your opera friends or, more precisely, friend.'

Panic welled up and I tried quickly to make amends.

'Andy, I didn't mean that at all. I'm just thinking how we can get the effect you and Joe want, both live and on the recording. It would be a pity if it were inconsistent. I'm looking forward to doing it live, just because it *is* so different to what I usually do. It will be lovely.'

My raw emotions, held in check these days it seemed by the very lightest of reins, threatened to disintegrate and, mortified by the prospect of crying in front of Joe, I turned away abruptly.

'Now, children,' Joe interposed smoothly, 'don't quarrel. Madison is right, Andy, we must be very careful to get this same melancholy effect in the theatre. It is exactly what we wanted, is it not? I will speak with Eric, our sound wizard, Madsy, and perhaps you can find a moment to visit him at The Dragon and work together.'

'I'd love to do that, Joe.' I smiled at him gratefully and Andy looked faintly mollified.

Later, as we left the studio, I heard Joe mutter to Andy. 'Now, Andy boy, you should not bully our little Madsy. She is doing us a great honour to sing and you speak to her as if we do her the favour. It is not polite or nice.'

'Mind your own business, Joe,' Andy snapped, and I closed my eyes in exasperation. 'You know nothing about it.'

I felt, rather than saw, Joe's eloquent shrug before the men caught up with me at the car and said no more.

Nevertheless, work on *Elushka* served to focus Andy on more positive things, especially when I paid my promised visit to The Dragon to work with Eric. He listened to the tape we had made, and with awesome skill proceeded to tweak and slide knobs and dials until I heard the same melancholy echo floating around the empty theatre.

'That's it, Eric,' Joe cried in triumph. 'Exactly right. Now, Madsy, sing that again and we'll work on the lighting.'

So I sang, and as the oddly unfamiliar sound of my voice, amplified and technically manipulated, poured mysteriously forth from every corner of the stage, the lighting technician experimented until Joe was satisfied. The stage was now bathed in an eerie ice-blue glow, the mood perfectly matching the sound effects Eric had created. Joe practically bounced up and down in his seat, and Andy beamed with pleasure.

'Wonderful!' Joe chortled, and Andy nodded. 'Excellent, guys,' he told the techs, then turning to me, 'Beautiful, Mads. Well done.'

I saw Joe pat Andy encouragingly on the back and smile approvingly. He had clearly decided it was in everyone's best interests for Andy and I to be reconciled. Perhaps it was. Who knows? I had lost all capacity to make rational judgements as sorrow still brooded in my heart.

Nonetheless, despite my misgivings, I loved *Elushka,* and it was a fascinating counterpart to *Carmen*, which moved steadily apace. In that, too, I relished singing a role that posed few technical difficulties, and in a production that was creatively directed. Coveted though her role may be, I didn't envy Annie singing Carmen, the focus of virtually every scene in the opera, and the character whom the audience would be waiting to love or to hate. Megan, unsurprisingly, wanted to see me sing the role in a big venue, and was sceptical about Annie's ability to pull it off.

'You're so more obviously a Carmen than she is,' she said critically of my friend.

I just laughed.

'Mercedes is exactly what I want to cope with at the moment.'

Megan looked at me searchingly. 'That doesn't sound like the Madison I know,' she said with some force. 'Don't get comfortable with what you're doing, otherwise you'll find others are quick to take advantage.'

'I'm not comfortable in that sense, Mum. I've got big challenges coming up – Dorabella at the Coli in the autumn is something really important to work for. It's just now, at the moment, I need something less challenging, something I don't need to worry about.'

I hoped that Megan wouldn't push me and, thankfully, she didn't, but doubtless she drew her own conclusions. Nevertheless, as February passed, my relationship with her seemed to have been restored. I caught her studying me closely, and I wondered if she could feel my pain, and whether she actually sympathised. She would never say as much, I knew, but I recalled Gerry saying to me once, 'Parents have seen it all before, they've either been there themselves, or their friends have, or their friends' children, and they're there just to love you and support you. Perhaps you don't give Megan enough credit for being a mum. You just see her as a hardboiled city lawyer who's waiting to cut your legs from underneath you.'

'You don't know my mum, Gerry,' I had objected at the time, but as I closed my eyes and leaned against the kitchen door, I felt the faintest brush of her hand on my shoulder and I opened my eyes to see her handing me a tall wine glass.

'I've brought your favourite today, darling,' she said. 'Drink up, it's good for the blood.'

I wanted to cry and pour out my heart to her, but more than that I wanted to rebuild our strange, fragile relationship, and I could not risk shaking its foundations again. But I was glad that the icy chill of her disapproval had melted with the January frost.

After a particularly gruelling day of production, I took Annie down to The Restless Dragon and together we crashed the closing party on the outgoing play. The theatre was housing guest productions until *Elushka* opened in April so the atmosphere had something of a holiday feel about it for the regular Dragon crew. Andy had worked as ASM on the latest offering, the World War Two classic, *The Long and the Short and the Tall*, and although he had said little about it to me, I suspected that he'd actually enjoyed the relatively lowly position. He was certainly in the thick of the party, and I was struck forcibly by his obvious popularity. Everyone sought him out, and welcomed his company, and Annie and I found ourselves welcomed by association. Ron Stryker, back in London during a break in the *Lethal Desires* tours, was evidently delighted to be reunited with Andy, and they happily talked over the current fate of the play. He greeted Annie warmly and spent much of the evening with her. It was good to see my friend relaxed and smiling, fully recovered from her ordeal, and to see the spark of obvious attraction between her and Ron. She slid over to me as I talked to Joe.

'Madsy, I'm making a move. Ron's asked me to join him for supper.'

'Anastasia, you fast worker. I never knew you had it in you.'

We jousted verbally for a bit, to the amused bewilderment of Joe, and she left with a cheerful wave as Ron guided her carefully out of the theatre.

Andy and I stayed until after midnight. I ached for my bed, deeply conscious that we had a long call the next day, juggling full runs of Acts Two and Three with the children's chorus, who were going to be gradually fed in with the adults now that the opening was approaching. But I was loath to ask Andy to leave; he looked happier than he had done for weeks, in the bosom of the company he had clearly come to love, and who loved and accepted him, flaws and all. I made a superhuman effort and managed not to look tired and draggy, and was rewarded when Andy himself looked at his watch in surprise.

'Well, this is us, gentlemen. I have an early meeting tomorrow with a fellow from Alaska or Siam, and Madison will be responding to the call of her art at the crack of dawn no doubt.'

We exchanged expansive farewells with Andy's colleagues, hugged Joe, and left, Andy chattering easily about some shaggy dog story that had been shared over copious pints. His genial mood continued all the way home, lasting until I put the light out, relieved to finally close my eyes.

'Night, Mads,' he murmured. 'They loved you and Annie there tonight. You're a real superstar, *o bellissima diva*.'

I lay still, realising that Andy hadn't spoken to me in such terms for many months.

'Did you enjoy it?' he cut across my silence.

'Oh, yes, of course. They're a great bunch. I was pleased to see Annie and Ron hit it off, too.'

'Umm.' Andy was drifting off and as I buried my face deep in my pillow I pondered how relatively peaceful the day and evening had been. I actually hadn't cried. Not a single tear had escaped my eyelids – something of a record of late. Andy hadn't said a cross word, or made some barbed remark, and he had clearly enjoyed himself quite unconditionally, betraying his genuine happiness at The Dragon, despite all that had threatened it before Christmas.

I felt oddly comforted. There would always be an empty place in my heart that belonged to Gerry, Josh and Ben, but as I drifted into slumber, its raw and jagged edges felt marginally less painful, and I fancied that the first new fragile layers of healing skin might be growing over them at last.

CHAPTER 70

It felt suspiciously as if Andy and I had reached something of an understanding the next morning when I left for West Hampstead. The previous evening had been almost reminiscent of the old days, when things were at least relatively straightforward, when I didn't hanker after something I couldn't have. The trees on the heath sprouted fat green buds, bursting with promise, and the air had that clean freshness that characterises both early spring and the beginning of autumn, a sort of climatic parenthesis around the humidity of a London summer. My step was light and my heart ventured out cautiously from its prison of despondency.

On the 8.58 train to Waterloo I drank cappuccino that was hot and aromatic, with just the right amount of chocolate on top, and my almond croissant was specially sticky and sweet. On an impulse I rang Andy.

'I'm on the train,' I informed him unnecessarily. 'I've got a lovely breakfast from Puccini's.'

'Good-oh'. He sounded pleased that I'd phoned. 'Are you running today?' he asked.

'Yes. Act Two, then the children rehearse whilst we're at lunch, and Act Three this afternoon.'

'That's good – all your best bits,' Andy laughed.

'Absolutely.'

'See you later then? About sevenish?'

'Yes. Have a good day.'

'I'm almost normal again,' I murmured under my breath.

'Sorry?' The smartly dressed woman next to me looked up enquiringly.

I shook my head distractedly.

'Nothing.'

We worked hard on our Act Two run that morning. The production was coming to life and it was looking exciting. The director had set the crucial events of the act in a nightclub rather than in the usual predictably rustic inn. Frasquita, Carmen, and I sang the Gypsy Song at a microphone, karaoke style, and Escamillo entered the club like an FA cup hero on the town. Our salsa dancing was hysterical. Annie and I shimmied around each other trying not to laugh; it seemed criminal to get paid to have this much fun. The good feeling spilled over into lunch time and Annie and I wandered back from the Rat and Parrot after destroying our plate of Nachos, looking forward to the delights of Act Three.

'Deh, prendi un dolce amplesso, amico mio fedel', we harmonised as we strolled up the road, and with a shock I realised I was actually happy.

'Annie.' I stopped abruptly.

'What's up?' Annie drew to a halt beside me. 'Have you left something in the Rat?' She turned back as if to retrace our steps.

'No.' I tugged at her arm till she faced me again.

'Annie, I'm going to be okay.'

She studied me for a long moment, smiling warmly.

'Sure you are. I never doubted otherwise.'

She tucked my arm into hers and we walked again.

'How many sopranos does it take to change a light bulb?' she asked randomly.

'Tell me, mate.'

'Dahling, that's the accompanist's job.'

We were still chortling with the good, wholehearted chortle that only a mezzo can give, as we pushed open the door of the rehearsal room.

The children were just being finished off, so to speak. I saw two lines of multicoloured heads – blond, brown, and red – marching up and down, back and around, singing lustily as they went, but paid little attention as I pulled off my fleece and took out my score to quickly review Act Three. The children wrapped their rehearsal and there was a bustle as children and chaperones gathered belongings and the adult cast reassembled. I was so absorbed that I didn't realise I was being addressed till the music was forcibly removed from my hands.

'Madison, don't ignore me.'

'Sor...' The apology died in my throat as I met the eyes of my accuser. Laughing blue eyes, beaming smile, hands grasping at mine in amusement and pleasure.

'Ben.'

I could only stare as I truly felt the breath leave my lungs in a gasp. My legs shook and my arms felt too heavy for my shoulders to carry. The intensity and immediacy of my reaction shocked me almost as much as the beautiful vision before my eyes, and I could barely take in what Ben was saying.

'Dad told me I might see you today.'

'Really. Why?'

'Why what?'

'Why did he say you'd see me?'

Ben looked at me oddly.

'Because you're in *Carmen* and so am I, idiot.'

'How did he know I'd be here today?'

'He just said you would be, so I might see you.'

I realised that my pathetic questions were drawing perfectly reasonable answers from Ben, and I tried to focus properly.

'Well, darling, I didn't have any idea that I'd see you today. It's a complete surprise.' That was putting it mildly.

'Aren't you lucky?' he grinned. 'Have you missed me? You haven't been round for ages.'

The room was emptying of children and I knew we didn't have long. From the corner of my eye I saw Annie gazing in fascination at the scene Ben and I were playing out. How frighteningly normal it must have appeared, but Annie knew differently. I held my hands out.

'Ben, I've missed you very much.'

He laced his fingers between mine and we leant into each other briefly, rocking inwards on our toes.

'I'm sorry I haven't been round. It's just been a bit tricky.'

'Did you and Dad have a row?'

'Did he tell you that?'

'No. I just wondered why you don't come to see us now.'

Tears were precariously close as I squeezed his hands again.

'Darling, we didn't have a row. I just haven't been able to see you. I'm sorry if you thought I didn't want to be with you guys anymore. I really have missed you.'

'I missed you, too, Mads.'

'One less person to make fun of, eh?'

'Of course, what else?'

We laughed together, and I held out my arms. It was just so sweet to hug his wiry frame again, and to stroke his soft hair.

'I love you,' I whispered as I laid my cheek against the top of his head. How could I have kidded myself otherwise? My love was as fresh and new and vibrant as ever. The last two months rolled back like a canvas. Nothing had changed.

'Is your dad picking you up?'

'Yes. He's probably waiting downstairs now. You coming?'

'Sure. Hold on a minute.'

Annie was still staring as I released Ben and trotted over to her.

'Annie…'

'Don't say a word. I'll cover for you for ten minutes. No longer. Then you'd better be back, or you're on your own.'

'Thanks.'

'Be careful, Mads.'

Ben was tinkering with his mobile phone as I returned to him.

'You have two new messages,' he intoned, precisely mimicking the intonation of the message service.

'Come on then, I've got ten minutes.'

Ben chatted continuously as we moved on downstairs, and I was glad. I was fiercely trying not to cry as love and longing swept over me in waves.

As usual, I heard Gerry's voice before I saw him.

'I told David that since Ben's voice has got about another year, then if we don't go for *Screw* now, we never will, and he's just got to do it.'

'Hi, Dad.'

Ben threw his bag down the last three stairs, vaulted over the banister, landing at Gerry's side.

'Hello, young man. I'm telling Oli's mum here about *Screw.*'

'Yeah, Mads,' Ben turned back to me as I descended the stairs in the conventional manner, 'I'm doing *Turn of the Screw* with North in September.'

Oli's mum was still in full cry.

'Ben, that's just marvellous. Well done. Mr McFall, he's doing so well, you must be very proud of him,' she gushed insincerely. She'd lost her audience anyway.

'Well, hello, Dr Brylmer,' Gerry said calmly, 'I told the little one he might see you today.'

'So I gather.'

'It was a tough job to get this Glyndebourne star to go back into the chorus, I can tell you. But I told him everyone has to do *Carmen* at least once.'

'But Dad, I will do it at least once when I sing Don Jose at the Met. I'm only doing it to please him.' This last observation was addressed to me as Ben swung heavily on Gerry's arm.

'Well, get there quickly, and we might still be in the same cast,' I laughed, avoiding Gerry's gaze. My legs still hadn't stopped shaking.

Oli's mum knew when she wasn't wanted, and faded away murmuring, 'Well, enjoy it then, Ben. Bye, Mr McFall.'

Gerry didn't respond. He was staring at me hard, and at last I looked him in the eye.

'Hi,' I whispered.

'Hi, yourself.'

'When can I see you?'

'Am I invisible?'

'Don't be daft. You know what I mean.'

'What time do you finish here?'

'Five o'clock.'

'5.45 from Victoria? 6.15 at our place?'

'I'll be there.'

I turned quickly to run back up the stairs, not trusting myself to speak again.

'Madison.'

I paused to look back down the stairwell. Gerry smiled up at me, the same engaging grin, eyes wide and appealing.

'It's good to see you.'

I nodded wordlessly, my own smile so broad, had it been a centimetre wider it would crack my cheeks, and hurried up the staircase.

'Seven minutes and counting,' Annie muttered as I took my place beside her. The music was just starting and the assistant director glared meaningfully at me. I beamed at him in response.

'I knew it wouldn't last.'

'Annie! That's not what you said at lunchtime!'

'I lied. You were kidding yourself. I knew that; now you know it. You can't live without that wretched man.'

I was spared the need to answer. The conductor lifted his arms to give us the entry.

I raised my voice and sang.

CHAPTER 71

The friendly familiarity of the 5.45 train from Victoria was almost too much to bear. I sat by the window, glad to have claimed a seat from amongst the throng of commuters, and gazed out as the unchanged scene passed us by. The tower blocks of Pimlico, Battersea Power Station, Albert Bridge, Brixton Shopping Centre. It was as though I had been on this train every day for the last two months, so well loved were those commonplace sites. And achingly familiar too was the exquisite pain of excitement. My stomach clenched and my fingers tingled. Joy welled up from my toes and would have burst forth into undisciplined laughter, had I not gripped my bag in a tight embrace, burying my head into its soft leather. I looked up again, still smiling, wondering if anyone had observed my small convulsions. But I remembered train journeys during which I had wept copiously and no one had seen fit to even offer a tissue. I allowed a gasp of laughter to emerge, closing my eyes, savouring the sweetness of the moment. Disembarking at West Dulwich, I allowed myself to think of Andy. Coward to the end, I had left a message on his voicemail, claiming a last minute late call. I couldn't think beyond the evening ahead. Time and fate would take their own path and this time I would let them.

How ridiculously dramatic that sounded even to my foolish ears as I walked along Dulwich Common, as full of green leafy hope as its Putney counterpart had seemed this morning. I hesitated outside Gerry's house. I still had the set of keys that I had once used with such ease, but today it didn't seem right to do so. I rang the bell, waiting on the doorstep, suddenly unsure of the nature of my visit. Our brief conversation in the stairwell had constituted very little, I realised, and Gerry could already be regretting it. I'll never know if I could have turned back at that moment. The thought passed through my mind, and maybe I began to turn away, but the door opened, and the moment, if it was ever there, had passed.

'Hiya, Mads. Come in.' As usual, Ben was as full of energy as if he had just woken.

'Dad and Josh are having a fight. You need to referee.'

'Oh, Ben, what are they fighting about?'

'Clothes, make-up, body piercings.'

In the kitchen Gerry looked fraught and Josh mutinous.

'Josh, I'm being as reasonable as I can. You can't expect people to simply ignore you when you look like that. If you want to look like a troublemaker, don't be surprised if folk think you are.'

Josh was looking particularly splendid, his hair stiffly gelled into multi-spiked submission and his nails – varnished a deep purple – pulled with impotent frustration at his heavy neck chain.

'Hi, Josh, what's happening?'

I attempted to lighten the atmosphere and Gerry mimed relief at the diversion.

I was immensely gratified to see Josh's defiant face melt into a soft smile, and beneath their heavy make-up his eyes twinkled mischievously.

'Madison!'

The day was just proving far too much and tears welled again as I hugged Josh warmly.

'You look cool.'

'The police have just searched me outside MacDonald's in Lewisham.'

'What did they find?'

'Sartre.'

'Awesome.'

We laughed, one superior intellect to another; you know how it is.

'I've written so much stuff since Christmas,' Josh told me. 'Come upstairs and I'll show you.' Even after our sad little scene at DCP, Josh's forgiveness was instantly offered once I was in their midst again.

I looked inquiringly at Gerry and he nodded, glad that Josh's mutiny seemed to have passed.

'I'll bring you both some tea, but don't keep Madison to yourself all night.'

Gerry turned abruptly, busying himself with the kettle, but not before I could see the emotion on his face. I paused, hoping he'd turn again, but his back was unyielding.

'Come on, Mads.'

Josh was already halfway upstairs. I followed him, glad not to face Gerry alone just yet.

Beneath a sea of paper, books, CDs, clothes, and the other detritus of a fifteen-year-old glam rocker, Josh liberated a spiral bound notebook. His tiny handwriting filled the narrow lines – Charlotte and Emily, eat your hearts out! – and I struggled to reacquaint myself with his distinctive script.

I stand on the bridge at night
and wonder if they all know
I'm there and if they care
that I'm invisible and dead
Black water and the
decay of the dead. The
lights are the lights of Hell
And I say fuck this life
But they don't hear me
Only my mind can hear the
songs of the dead.

And so on…

'It's very evocative, Josh,' I said mildly.

We thumbed through the book, as he picked out his favourites. Death continued to feature prominently; I hoped it was a phase.

When Gerry came in with tea I saw the shutters come down over Josh's face.

'Thanks.' I took the mugs from Gerry's hands, proffering one to Josh. 'I missed GCSE mocks, didn't I?' I asked.

Josh nodded, dumb now.

'You didn't miss much,' Gerry muttered.

'There's still three months to go, aren't there? Plenty of time, in my vast experience of these things!' I laughed.

'He won't take his Ritalin.'

'Dad, I've told you. You can't make me.'

Josh was furious again, turning angrily to look out over the garden and I motioned to Gerry to leave us. Shrugging, he closed the door quietly behind him, demonstrating admirable restraint.

'Josh?'

'Madison, please tell him. I won't poison my head with that stuff. It freaks me out.'

'Darling, you need to concentrate for the exams.'

'I'll do it without it. He can't force me.'

'No, he can't, but think about it, please. Try it before the exams. Let me know what happens, and we'll talk again.'

'If you're around.'

We were silent for a moment. I'd been selfish, thinking only of my loss, my sorrow, over the last sad months.

'I hope so.' What more could I promise him? Josh was silent a moment longer, trying to read my face.

'Okay. Don't tell *him* though.'

'Sweetheart, please, Gerry loves you. He only wants what's best.'

'I know, I know. Come on. Let's go.'

I let Josh lead me downstairs again, glad, despite the adolescent angst, to feel part of it all again.

Gerry was still in the kitchen cutting bread for toast as Ben pontificated about the other boys in the chorus.

'Dad, he's such a dork.'

'Well, if you say so, it must be so,' Gerry wisely allowed. 'Are you eating with us, Madison?' Gerry was casual. 'If so, you can take over here.'

I took the knife from him, our fingers touching as he released it from his grasp. I caught his wrist, letting my fingers run down the back of his hand. Electricity surged through me, and I held myself fiercely in check. I longed to press my face into his shoulder and feel him once more, warm and yielding against me. But he stepped lightly away. The old moves were still as smooth, I thought bitterly. Only Gerry knew how to simultaneously reject me and yet not reject me, forever keeping his options open.

'How many am I cutting?' I could be smooth, too.

'Sixteen,' Ben suggested.

'Sixteen!' I feigned shock.

'That's only four each,' Ben opined.

'Sixteen it is, then.'

From the corner of my eye, I saw Gerry smile. Gerry let himself meet my glance and grin.

'Welcome back to the madhouse.'

Supper was a lively affair, and my heart brimmed with happiness as the familiar banter passed between us. I watched Gerry and the boys closely, still so good together, strong and confident. But eventually we could no longer put off the moment. Josh disappeared wordlessly to his room. Ben, more vocal, announced he was working on his computer till bedtime, and we were left facing one another across the kitchen table.

'Hello.'

'Hello.'

'Josh's going to try his Ritalin again, but you're not supposed to know.'

'Good.'

'And just chill out on the hair and make-up. I give it another six months.'

'Good.'

'Ben looks on great form. I'm so glad about *Screw.*'

'Good.'

'Gerry?'

'Madison?'

'Please say something else.'

'Something else.'

'Stop it!'

I rose angrily from the table, but he gripped my wrist firmly and held me in place.

'Sorry. Please don't get up, Madsy. Talk to me.'

I sat again, and Gerry kept hold of my hand.

'I have missed you very much,' he said seriously.

I met his soft gaze and my fear and tension drained away. Filled with utter and overwhelming love, I reached out to touch his sweet face once more.

'I thought I might die of sorrow,' I told him. 'I have never been so unhappy in my life.'

'That's not so good,' he said, raising a quirky eyebrow. 'Why didn't you ring me?'

'Why didn't you ring *me*?'

'I didn't know if that's what you wanted.'

'And neither did I know if you would want to hear from me. I was so afraid that you would reject me.'

'Of course not.'

We were silent for a moment as we took it all in.

'Gerry, I love you so much.'

'And I love you.'

Tears began to wend their familiar course down my cheeks, but at last, they were tears of joy.

'I want to be with you and the boys.'

I had known since I saw Ben in the rehearsal room that I could never leave them again, but still the decision rested with Gerry.

'Good.' I looked up sharply, but this time Gerry was smiling. 'I should think so, Dr Brylmer.'

He lifted my fingers to his lips, kissing each knuckle softly. I brought his hand back to my cheek, pressing it hard against my burning face.

'I'll tell Andy once the first night of *Carmen* is over. It's only three weeks away. Let's not put Ben in a potentially difficult position before then. Once Andy realises that Ben's in the cast, it'll be all over anyway. He must know that I couldn't stay away from you all again.'

My stomach lurched at the prospect of the unpleasant scenes ahead. I could cut and run now, but for what? To live forever with the knowledge that I had walked away not once, but twice, from the grand passion of my life. From my best friend, and from the boys who I could have loved no more had I borne them myself.

'When do I get to start decorating?'

'After you've spring cleaned?'

'I get to decorate my own music room first.'

'You get to spring clean *me* first. I need a total Madison Brylmer overhaul.'

We laughed companionably.

'How about a two month service? Will that do for now?'

'Hmm, yes... I think you'd better check all that the parts are still in working order,' Gerry smiled.

In the semi-darkness of Gerry's bedroom we made love with silent intensity. Hot tears poured down my cheeks as I held him in a tight embrace, burying my face into his neck, my hands relishing the feel of his slender frame hard against me once again. We kissed hungrily, each tracing the familiar features of the other with tender, feverish fingertips. So full of emotion was I that even had we not been compelled to silence, there were no words to convey such depth of feeling. Only as our passion grew to its height, overwhelmed by the weeks apart, could I speak again, softly murmuring against Gerry's mouth.

'*Sei il mio amor e tutto la mia vita.* I love you.'

Gerry kissed me hard, making words impossible as my body enclosed him, and I pondered that in the seven months since we had first made love on this bed, how few times Gerry had told me that he loved me, but today, for the first time I knew it for certain.

My heart was in my mouth as I let myself quietly into the house at midnight, but I needn't have worried. Andy was asleep in front of the television, and appeared to have been so for a while. I softly switched off the TV, cleared up the remnants of his supper, drew the curtains, and turned off the lights. Not for the first time, I was glad that Andy was a heavy sleeper. Although it seemed unlikely that sleep would come so easily to me, I hurried to get under the bed covers, hoping to give the impression of having been abed some hours, should Andy stir from the settee. I hugged the pillows closer to me, my body recalling with sweet pleasure the joy of our reunion just a few hours earlier. I longed to hold Gerry to me now, to wrap myself possessively around him. Soon... I drowsily pondered, as the emotional expense of the day did, after all, take its toll.

CHAPTER 72

Andy was still asleep as I left for rehearsal the next day. He didn't have to be at The Restless Dragon till the afternoon, so I felt justified in slipping out quietly before he could stir. My heart beat fast and I had no stomach for breakfast. It felt infinitely longer than twenty-four hours since I had last made this journey and it seemed impossible that this time yesterday I had thought I had got over Gerry. How deeply wrong I had been to imagine that I could lay aside the transforming, all-consuming love I had for him. I realised now that had we not met again, I may have conceivably been able to slip back into something resembling my old life, but forever my love for Gerry would have lain in my heart, calcifying like an old scar in a tree trunk.

Annie took one look at me and knew.

'Ah,' she said pointedly.

'Ah, what?'

'The lovely Mr McFall lived up to his previous publicity, I hope? Middle-aged decrepitude hasn't caught up with him since January?'

'Oh, Annie, stop it,' I blushed.

'Madsy, is he really going to make you happy this time?'

'I hope so. I love him so much.'

'I know,' she said sadly. 'What are you going to do?'

'Leave Andy.'

'Oh, Madsy,' she breathed, and turned to look at me, her face softer now with concern. 'For real?'

I nodded.

'For real.'

'When?'

'Once *Carmen* goes up.'

'Are you really sure it's the right thing to do?'

'Oh, Annie, of course it's not the *right* thing to do. It's a terrible thing to do!' I caught myself as tears began to choke me – we had to sing in five minutes. 'But it's the only thing I can do. I don't want to live without Gerry,' I concluded simply.

'Oh, sweetie,' she sighed, putting her arms round my shoulders. We leant our heads into each other, her short curly one, and my longer waves both glinting gold in the morning sun.

'Your auntie Annie will stick by you whatever you do,' she consoled.

'Thank you.'

I kissed her temple as I saw the AD indicating that our presence was required. Dancairo, Remondado, and Frasquita were standing by for our quintet, and we got to work. It felt tight and wonderfully rhythmic, the close harmonies extra scrunchy, and the feeling of unity between the girls just what I needed to strengthen me in my emotional state. I absorbed every minute of the day with a heightened sensitivity, even enjoying my final costume fittings, normally anathema to me. I wanted the day never to end, capturing in miniature a perfect day of music and work, of feeling my love for Gerry heavy in my breast, before I had to face the coming trauma. I wanted everything else to fade away and leave me with just this moment. But it had to end, and I had to face Andy, weighed down with the knowledge of my treachery. I wondered what my real motives were for postponing my flight till after the first night. Was it really concern for Ben, or simply my own need to put off the terrible scenes that would ensue? Perhaps

416

it was a combination of both, but I was honest enough to admit to my own fear and dread, even as I longed to be boarding the Dulwich-bound train and to be going home to my boys.

My phone rang as Annie and I turned into West Hampstead tube station. We stopped as I fumbled for it and as Gerry's number flashed on the display I thought with a pang that I would have to reprogram his caller ID into the memory. I remembered so well weeping bitterly as I'd deleted it two months before.

'Hello.'

'It's me.'

'I know.'

Annie wandered off to look at the magazine stand.

'What are you up to?'

'We've just finished. Can I see you?'

'What a good idea. I'm at Maida Vale.'

'Give me half an hour then.'

Annie turned back to me.

'You're not going home?'

I shook my head and she rolled her eyes at me. Before I disembarked at Baker Street to pick up the Bakerloo line Annie took my hand.

'Listen, Madsy, I know it's absolutely none of my business.'

'But...'

'But look after yourself, your career, your happiness, your peace of mind. Okay?'

I nodded.

'I mean it, Madison.' She spoke more firmly. 'You're a fabulous singer. People know you're reliable and easy to work with. Don't blow it over a man whose feet are made of clay.'

She hugged me quickly as I left the train. I knew she was right. My singing was the one thing I could depend on and I had to look after myself.

Gerry was working in the orchestra room at the studio, and I burst into tears the moment I set eyes on him.

'Madison, what's this?' he asked kindly, holding out his arms to me.

'I'm just so pleased to see you,' I sobbed.

'And I you,' he murmured softly against my hair.

We hugged tightly and kissed for a long time, and I trembled with happiness and desire.

'I love you.'

'Good.'

I laughed. Gerry's ambiguous responses didn't trouble me today.

'Is there anyone else here?' I asked, looking hungrily at the worn, but comfortable, sofa.

'I think if we give it half an hour, we might find ourselves alone,' he smiled.

And we did.

When we surfaced sometime later I said, 'Gerry, I'm going to phone a solicitor tomorrow.'

'Oh, yes.'

Gerry remained quiet, kissing my palm gently.

'Most things are in my name because I was the one with a proper job for so long, but I know I've got to make sure things are fair to Andy. Oh, Gerry, this is awful.' I looked at him in anguish.

'It's going to be tough, Madsy,' he said.

'Will you come with me? To the solicitor, I mean?' I asked.

Gerry ran his lovely fingers up and down my arm for a moment.

'I think you should go on your own,' he said. 'How you sort out that side of things is your business. You know I can give you a home, but you earn a good living and you're resourceful and independent. I'm not worried about how you decide what to do about money and so on. It's really nothing to do with me.'

I felt terribly alone as Gerry said this, although I shouldn't have expected anything else. I knew he wouldn't want to become involved in the messiness of my split with Andy. To be fair, he was probably too busy to clear time in his diary to fit in my solicitor, but it was more than that, I knew. Gerry would genuinely feel that it wasn't his business because it ultimately didn't affect him. I could make an issue of it, or let it go, and since I was, of course, perfectly capable of going on my own, and dealing alone with every last shred of bitterness, anger and sadness that would ensue over the coming months, I left it.

'Fair enough,' I said, snuggling against Gerry's shoulder. 'As long as you know I don't expect to be a kept woman.'

'I didn't occur to me that you would, ' Gerry laughed, and I enjoyed feeling him twining my hair around his fingers. I sighed and pressed closer to him.

'I still think it's grossly unfair that you've got better legs than me,' I complained.

'Well, some of us have just got what it takes,' Gerry teased, and I knew I'd done the right thing not to press him about the solicitor.

I asked him about *Butterfly* that he'd been rehearsing that day, and I was happy to lie with him on the sofa until it was quite dark outside.

CHAPTER 73

I avoided Andy as much as I could over the next week, but by the weekend it was impossible.

'Surely you haven't got *Carmen* calls all weekend,' he exclaimed. 'They're going to wear you all out before it even begins.'

We had a Sitzprobe on Sunday but evidently I would be advised to stay close to home on Saturday.

'Only on Sunday,' I replied.

'Good. Then I think it's about time we took in a movie and ate at La Scarpetta, don't you think?'

Andy sounded as if he didn't intend to negotiate.

'Yes, okay,' I acquiesced. 'You pick the film and we'll go.'

'You could sound a tad more enthusiastic, Madison,' Andy chided.

'Sorry.' I faced him squarely. 'That sounds great.'

I managed a smile, feeling like Judas. Before I'd quite moved away Andy caught my arm. I stiffened involuntarily, my mind and body recoiling at his touch. Andy felt my resistance immediately, and angrily pushed me back against the wall.

'For God's sake, Madison, when am I allowed to fucking touch you?' he shouted.

'Don't be silly,' I said, trying to salvage things quickly, 'You just took me by surprise.'

'Oh, sure,' he replied sarcastically. 'That's just today's excuse. You're my fucking wife and I'll touch you when and where I like.'

'Don't speak like that, please, Andy.'

'Don't be such a hypocrite. You spent months doing God knows what with Gerry McFall behind my back. How dare you tell me how to speak to you?'

This was so blatantly true all I could do was to keep silent.

'Just forget it. I have no interest today in going out with my wife who clearly wishes she was somewhere else. Why don't you go look up Gerry? I'm sure he'd be delighted to see you.'

Andy pushed my shoulders hard against the wall again, putting so much force into the gesture I virtually bounced back at him. He moved away sharply and I stumbled forward, putting out my hand to support myself on a bookcase. I stood in shocked silence as he grabbed his coat and angrily slammed out of the flat.

I waited till my hammering heart had slowed before I moved to the phone. Since I had reluctantly told Gerry that I ought to stay at home, I didn't expect him to be around. He was doubtless working, but answered his mobile promptly.

'Hi, it's me.' My voice sounded unfamiliar to me; small and frightened.

'Hello.' I loved Gerry's sexy, drawled greeting, and it comforted me for a moment.

'I can come over, or meet you, or something, if you like,' I told him.

'I thought you wanted to stay home?' he queried.

'It backfired. We've had a row. He's gone out.'

'What about?'

'I'll tell you later?'

'Are you all right, Madsy?'

'Nothing that a cuddle wouldn't cure,' I smiled.

'Ben's playing rugby this afternoon. I'm going to try to get over to St George's around two thirty. Why don't you join us there?'

'That sounds wonderful.'

I looked at my watch. It was now ten thirty. I hoped that Andy wouldn't come back now, and that I was safe until I left for the school around one o'clock. I hung up in relief. I ought to use the time to practice, or to go over the materials I was taking to the solicitor, but I had the heart for neither. Opening the grocery cupboard, I checked out its contents: flour, sugar, and cocoa. I had eggs and margarine. I hadn't made a cake for years, but suddenly I had an overwhelming urge to do so right now.

Two hours later I was putting the finishing touches to a not entirely unrespectable chocolate sponge sandwich, rich with thick creamy filling. It was obviously deeply psychological: sex and food; the need to protect myself from the terrors of the night by doing something earthy and nurturing. But it felt good, so I wasn't going to knock it.

I felt self-conscious as I wandered through the sprawling grounds of St George's looking for Ben's rugby team. It was a brisk March afternoon, with just a little occasional sun, and I had dressed in black jeans and a dark green fleecy. A young man in referee's kit passed me and I grabbed him before he could disappear.

'I'm looking for the under thirteen's pitch,' I asked.

'I'm heading there myself,' he replied, 'just trot along with me. You supporting the home team?' he asked as we crossed the grass.

'I'm a friend of Ben McFall,' I said, trying not to sound too proud, 'so, yes, I guess I am.'

'Ben's a great kid,' the young teacher responded enthusiastically. 'What a personality! Here we are,' he said at the same moment as I saw Gerry's tall straight back at the sidelines.

'Thanks,' I smiled as he peeled off to the left. I hesitated before joining Gerry. I had appreciated that this would be our first public outing, so to speak, the first time we were together, with Ben, in a completely non-music related setting, in a place where people knew Gerry, and would quite legitimately wonder what my connection was with the family. I had no idea how Gerry wanted me to play this one, and as much as I longed to hug and kiss him in greeting, I felt sure it would be neither prudent nor welcome. I sidled up to him.

'Hi.'

Gerry had been making some idle exchange with another dad at the sidelines, but turned to me as soon as I spoke. The warmth of his smile was worth everything.

'Hello.'

'Have I missed anything?'

'No. They're just about to come on. Did you find us okay? I realised I hadn't told you how to get to the pitch.'

'I accosted a member of staff who brought me here.'

'I should have known you would do something intelligent, Dr Brylmer,' he laughed, and I sniggered and bumped against him, enjoying a brief, warm, moment of contact.

'This is Madison Brylmer, the world's greatest mezzo,' Gerry joked, introducing me to the fellow supporter he'd been chatting with. 'And a very good friend to me and the boys.'

The man smiled in greeting and then we were distracted by the main event, as the two teams trooped on to the pitch.

St George's were playing another leading London public school, and from my vantage point of total ignorance, I think it was an exciting game, given the general enthusiasm generated around me. When he remembered that I was there, Gerry told me if something good happened, though when he jubilantly declared that Ben had scored a try, and I asked, tongue in cheek, whether that meant he needed to try harder, he looked so horrified I thought I'd better be more serious about it all. But what was truly wonderful was simply being with him, sharing his pleasure and watching Ben beavering up and down the field, his lanky frame full of energy, his shouts of pleasure or frustration louder than anyone else's. I felt curiously shy, and I hung back in the break when Ben came bouncing up to us.

'Hiya, Mads,' he greeted me, after making his usual physical assault upon Gerry. 'Did you see me make that try?'

'I certainly did,' I laughed, 'though I think I'll need some serious coaching if I'm going to understand this game.'

'That'll cost you,' Gerry joked.

'I have unlimited resources,' I grinned back at him.

'I had noticed.'

By four thirty they had a result. St George's had soundly beaten their rivals by a score which sounded bizarre to me: 131–20.

'I didn't follow,' I complained to Gerry. 'I didn't see them put the ball over that high jump thing 131 times.'

We'll explain it later, Madison,' he assured me. 'Just concentrate on figuring out the origin of the universe.'

I punched his arm, and he feigned serious injury as Ben, changed and ready to go, arrived noisily in the company of a posse of boys. I was gratified that Ben allowed me to put my arm loosely around his shoulders as we walked to the car.

'Does it always involve so much falling to the ground?' I asked.

'Of course,' he replied disparagingly, 'that's part of the fun.'

'I've obviously got a lot to learn,' I sighed. 'It looks wet, muddy, and miserable to me, but what do I know?'

In the car, Ben started singing the Toreador's aria, urging me to join in.

'Madison's coming for supper, so don't drive her crazy before we even get home,' Gerry warned him, with a smile.

'I can't drive Madison crazy,' Ben said pedantically, 'she already is. And you'd never get tired of me, would you, Mads, because I'm just so totally amazing.'

Impulsively I turned around in my seat and faced Ben. 'I still think of *Flute* so often,' I said nostalgically. 'We had such a good time.'

'Yeah,' agreed Ben causally. '*Screw* is going to be totally awesome, though. Do you know I get to die in it?'

'Yes, I do,' I laughed. 'I'm sure you'll do it very tastefully.'

'When you two stars have stopped vying with each other you may have noticed we're home,' announced Gerry, beaming at me happily. Ben had clearly accepted my reappearance with ease; it was only the adults who were likely to make things difficult. I briefly thought how different my relationship with Gerry would have been had I not loved Ben and Josh as I did. It was inconceivable; my love for them was so utterly part of my love for Gerry, but how glad I was that my heart had opened to encompass these dear boys so completely.

Josh was skulking in the kitchen as we arrived, toying in a lacklustre manner with a maths textbook. He was pleased to lay it aside to ask, more out of politeness than genuine interest I suspected, about the game, and then Gerry let Ben escape to his room whilst he surveyed the contents of the fridge.

'Oh, I've just remembered,' I said. 'Here's my contribution.' I liberated my wonderful chocolate concoction from my bag, where it didn't seem to have suffered too badly, and Gerry and Josh uttered appropriate cries of delight. Between us we cooked a huge pan of pasta with tomatoes, onions, peppers, courgettes, garlic, and herbs, which we smothered with Parmesan and ate with fat hunks of bread. I would soon be regaining all the weight I had so conveniently lost if eating like this became a habit, but tonight I just enjoyed the companionship of it all. The guys demolished most of my cake between then, squirrelling away the remnants for the next day. Gerry and Ben promptly accepted my offer to wash up, but Josh held back and, picking up a tea towel, joined me at the sink.

'How have things been going at DCP?' I asked.

'Cool,' Josh nodded. 'My mocks weren't brilliant, but I know what I've got to do, and I will take my Ritalin for the real things. I tried it again this week,' he added shyly. 'It's okay, I suppose. I did do some work.'

'That is the general idea, darling,' I laughed.

Josh smiled his infinitely sweet smile, and said slowly, 'I'm predicted at least a B in everything, and A★ in Art, English and Drama. I know I could get As in everything if I really concentrated. But I get so bored, even in the exams themselves, and then I just stop and have to get out of the room.'

I nodded.

'You need to pace yourself, then. Make sure you use the first hour of the exam time as effectively as possible, before you burn out. Do the big mark questions first.'

'Yeah, I suppose,' Josh said. 'But Madison, all I really want is to be finished with school and to do a creative writing course.'

'Oh good,' I replied. 'Then you know exactly what you're working for, then, don't you? A popular course like that is going to demand decent grades.'

'You were supposed to say that they might take me without A levels,' Josh complained.

I laughed. 'In your dreams!' I stopped clearing away to face him. 'Look, darling, I know it's what everybody else is saying, so it's not different or interesting, but you also know it's true. Do the best you can now, and you have choices in the future.'

'I know,' Josh replied disconsolately.

We resumed our work, and as we moved to join Ben and Gerry, Josh touched my arm lightly.

'Madison?'

'Josh?'

'Have you and dad made it up? You do love him, don't you?'

'Oh, Josh,' I sighed. 'Yes, I do love your dad. But things got difficult, for reasons you can probably work out for yourself, and I had to stop seeing him for a while. I missed you all dreadfully, and I'm very happy being with you again. I certainly don't intend to stay away, if that's okay with you.'

I wanted to say more, but thought it was up to Gerry to tell Ben and Josh the extent of our relationship. I held my arms out tentatively to Josh. 'I'm sorry for being inconsistent. I find that hurtful and confusing in other people and I'm truly sorry for any hurt I caused to you and Ben.'

Josh accepted my hug without hesitation. 'We knew it wouldn't be just down to you, anyway. We thought that dad must have done something to upset you.'

'We both probably have to take some responsibility,' I agreed, reluctant to criticise Gerry, 'and so we'll both have to try to look after each other a bit better now.'

We stood in silence for a moment, my arms around his bony shoulders. Why were these guys all so thin?

'I love you, Josh, and I will do my utmost always to be here for you.'

It was very special being together that evening. It was quite without ceremony, as Ben learned heavily against me whilst we watched *Casualty*, exchanging droll observations with Gerry about the plot. Even Josh stayed for a while, studying us closely with his dark eyes, doubtless drawing conclusions we hadn't even reached ourselves. Eventually the boys drifted off, and I snuggled up to Gerry.

'I'd better go,' I murmured.

He sighed and nuzzled my hair.

'You don't have to.'

I sat up and faced him.

'It's only two weeks till *Carmen* goes up, and you'd better speak to the boys soon. Josh cornered me in the kitchen; he knows something's up now, but it's not for me to tell him.'

'Really? How do you think he feels about it?'

'Well, bless his heart, I got the impression that he was quite pleased. As I think they would always have been,' I couldn't help but add.

Wisely, Gerry ignored the barb.

'I'll talk to them very soon, I promise.'

CHAPTER 74

Andy still hadn't come home when I got back to the flat. I phoned his mobile but it was turned on to voicemail.

'It's me,' I said. 'I'm at home. I assume you've stayed over with someone. See you tomorrow.'

He still hadn't returned when I was setting out for the Sitzprobe in the morning, but the phone rang as I opened the front door to leave.

'Madison. You're there.' He sounded cool.

'Oh, hello. Are you all right?'

'Yes. I stayed with Jim and Sophie.'

I could consider myself off their Christmas card list, then.

'I'm just off to the *Carmen* Sitz. Are you on your way home?'

'In due course.' He still sounded distant. 'What time do you finish?'

'Five o'clock.'

'I'll pick you up from West Hampstead at five, then.'

'Oh.'

'Any reason why not?' he asked with an edge of sarcasm.

'No, of course not. See you then.'

I hung up, calculating that the children would have finished their own call well before five o'clock and Andy was unlikely to meet Ben coming out as he came in. Nevertheless, I felt miserable all the way to West Hampstead, overwhelmed with guilt and anxiety. The sight of Ben looking aloof in the children's chorus lifted my spirits; I went straight over to him to get my hug and we chatted whilst everyone else arrived.

'You look as if all this is beneath you,' I observed.

'I've told Dad I'm not doing chorus again,' he pronounced firmly.

'I can see we're going to have to come up with some alternative methods of entertainment during this show then,' I laughed. 'Have you got *Another 150 Card Tricks* yet?'

Ben grinned, and I saw Annie watching us. She winked and I felt even better.

Some singers find Sitzprobes a bore, but I love the first time on a piece with an orchestra. The whole opera comes to life, and you are reminded of how much more you need to give. Piano rehearsals in highly reverberative studios are deceiving, and it is important to be aware of the profound difference singing with an orchestra in a house the size of the Coliseum. I managed to wangle sitting with the children for as long as possible, and once they had finished their bits they were despatched. I'd only had a brief time with Ben, but it was healing and rejuvenating.

'Bye, darling, see you tomorrow.' I kissed him quickly as he left. 'Give your dad and Josh a hug from me.'

I came down to earth with a bump when I walked out of the studio at five o'clock to find Andy waiting like a sentry guard. Annie stuck by me like glue as I greeted him.

'Hi.'

'Hello, Annie.' Andy ignored me. 'I hear you're a great Carmen.'

'Let's hope the critics think so, too,' she countered. 'Madison's singing fabulously,' she added generously.

Andy smiled tightly. 'When doesn't she?' he said without enthusiasm.

'A lot of the time,' I answered firmly, turning to Annie. 'Honey, I'll see you on Tuesday for the tech.'

'I've booked a table at La Scarpetta,' Andy informed me as we drove back to South London.

'Okay.'

We drove in silence for a while.

'How did the Sitz go?' he asked eventually.

'It was fine.' I couldn't bear this any longer. 'Andy, I was concerned when you didn't come back last night. You could have left a message on my voicemail.'

Andy shrugged.

'I'm flattered by your concern,' he said, swinging the car into a parking bay. 'Now you know what it's like to worry and wonder.'

This was something of an exaggeration, I had to admit, but I let it stand, automatically rising to my own defence.

'I have never stayed out all night without letting you know.'

'Remember Christmas Day?'

'You stayed away, too.'

'Yes, maybe. But who you were with is another matter altogether, isn't it?'

Andy had booked a table, and he exchanged cheerful banter with the waiting staff as we ordered. Once we had drinks in front of us Andy took my hand. I didn't flinch, but met his gaze boldly. He looked sad, and with his free hand he ruffled his dark curls.

'Madsy, I'm sorry I blew up yesterday. I was out of order, but I'm so afraid you're going to leave me. Whatever there was, or is, between you and Gerry, I know he can give you so much more than I can.'

I sighed unhappily. In all conscience I couldn't reassure Andy. I looked down at the tablecloth.

'I've been trying really hard, Mads,' he continued. 'But I need something from you. I know you're tied up with *Carmen*, and it's a very important time for you, but give me a bit of room, a bit of time, please.'

I grasped at the straw Andy was holding out.

'I know I've been preoccupied,' I said. 'And we've still got so much work left to do on the opera. It's going to be a tough couple of weeks.'

'I know, but don't push me aside. Not if you do want us to stay together, that is,' Andy concluded.

'Andy, you ought to know that Ben McFall is in the children's chorus.' I knew I was avoiding the real issue.

Andy looked out of the window for a moment, his face set in hard lines.

'Have you spoken to him?'

'Of course.'

Our food arrived, precluding further conversation until the waiter had left. As I lifted my cutlery, Andy spoke again.

'I don't suppose you'll see him much more anyway, since his voice will break soon.'

I toyed with my food.

'Um.'

We made desultory conversation over the rest of the meal. I had no energy and little appetite, but tried to steer Andy off dangerous topics with casual comments about *Carmen, Elushka,* and the restaurant. He went along with me, replying where appropriate, but contributing little else.

Back at home, Andy fell asleep on the far side of the bed as I clung to the opposite edge. I couldn't bear even an accidental touch. As his breathing deepened, I cried softly into my pillow: tears of longing for Gerry, of pain for Andy, and of contempt for what I was doing to him.

CHAPTER 75

Midweek, I finally saw the solicitor. I skulked into her office, shamefaced and enormously uncomfortable, anticipating her censure, only to find her businesslike, non-judgmental and pragmatic.

'Dr Brylmer, I'm not happy to hear you say that you're going to leave the home you have paid for, with no recourse to liberating even your half share in it. It just doesn't make good sense any way you look at it. I could help you to thrash out a fair and reasonable division of property and monies, one that will reflect the significant financial input you have made to your marriage. Your husband will not be destitute, if I understand you correctly, since he has a reliable source of income now, even if it was less predictable in the past.'

I shook my head.

'I appreciate your reasoning Mrs. Meredith, but I am leaving him to live with another man and his family in an enormous house off Dulwich Common. I have a very successful career, as does Gerry. So,' I continued, 'I have absolutely no moral right to force Andy to sell Exeter House and move from his home. I just want to be able to take my personal things, and my own savings, although I am more than ready to reach an agreement on a lump sum settlement.'

Sonya Meredith lifted her hands in horror.

'Absolutely not. Certainly we don't volunteer it. The value of your property should make that quite unnecessary, if you really are determined not to force a sale.'

'I am,' I told her firmly. 'This whole thing is going to be ghastly as it is. At least let me feel that I might be doing something with a shred of honour.'

So she talked me through the process of drawing up the necessary documentation, warning me that once Andy acquired his own legal representation we would have to be ready to renegotiate.

'Not that they could possibly find fault with your generous property settlement, but things can, and do, turn nasty, so we must be prepared.'

I sighed heavily, and Sonya Meredith looked at me appraisingly.

'This is hard for you, isn't it?'

'Of course. Surely it's never easy.'

'You'd be surprised just how easy some find it to dispose of people and property.'

I winced. 'I suppose you think I'm a complete bitch.'

Sonya shook her head.

'No, you're not. I can see far too much guilt and anguish for that, but like all of us, you're not perfect, whatever that might constitute. I don't expect your husband is either, or your new partner.'

'I guess not. We're all a mass of contradictions, just trying our feeble best.'

'I'd like to hear you sing,' she said, closing the file. 'What did you say you're doing next?'

'*Carmen* at ENO. I'd be delighted to get you a couple of tickets if that's your sort of thing,' I told her.

'It certainly is. That would be wonderful.'

I left Sonya's office feeling confident that she was the right person to guide me through the logistical minefield that lay ahead, but aware too that no one could help me deal with the emotional wreckage which would be strewn in my wake. Even as I thought this, I realised that I had to start trusting Gerry with my pain, and at last I felt that perhaps I could do so. We had found each other again and met on the middle ground, just as Gerry had said we might do eventually. He wanted me, maybe not as much as I wanted him, but enough to admit that his love for me had led him to the only conclusion I had ever wanted him to draw. We were to be together, along with Ben and Josh, our complementary and contradictory personalities blending and moulding into something beautiful. Whilst there could never be any moral justification for what I was doing to Andy, everything in me cried out that I was doing the only thing that offered me any hope of happiness in the future. All my philosophical training balked at such a hedonistic principle. Maybe it was essentially utilitarian, perhaps the greatest happiness of the greatest number was served if Gerry and I, Ben and Josh, were made happy by the consequences of my actions. Numerically, we outweighed Andy, yet such a method of moral calculus served only to underscore why Mill had called Bentham's theory fit for swine. And would we be happy anyway? What guarantee could either of us offer the other? I was certain that no self-respecting deontologist could find the faintest justification in my actions, no categorical imperative, no principle of universalisability, could be established on the basis of my selfish choice. It was impossible to think such thoughts and find any moral rationale and yet I could still not find it in me to change my mind, to leave Gerry once more, to limit the damage by stopping in my tracks here and now. My course was set, and I hoped deep in my heart that ultimately we could all live with it.

I wondered if Andy knew that I was seeing Gerry again. Since the evening he had picked me up from the Sitzprobe, he had been cautious and wary; not angry, as he had been before, but he studied me closely, resigned and quiet. If he had guessed, I only had myself to blame. I knew the spring was back in my step, and my eyes glowed again, despite the guilt and anxiety as the inevitable face down drew near. But still I went to The

Dragon and sang my songs as, like *Carmen*, *Elushka* approached its opening, and Andy said nothing in confirmation or denial. But my world was transformed once more and the song I sang was one of joy; yet the melancholy key of its earlier movements gave its new texture a depth and richness it would have lacked had I not known the pain of separation from Gerry, or the struggle I had fought to win his love.

Annie watched me with a wry shake of her head. She was happy, too, still energised by relief at her lucky escape, and enjoying her new friendship with Ron.

'Madsy, what shall I do?' she asked me at the tech. 'Ron suggested that we all go out together to celebrate the first night of *Carmen* – you and me, him and Andy, I mean.'

I blanched.

'Quite,' she said. 'I know you love my company, darling, but I thought you wouldn't be overjoyed at the prospect of a happy foursome.'

'Annie, can you put him off? Say that because Megan will be there, Andy and I won't be free. It's essentially true, but can you get him to hold off making another arrangement? I'm sorry. If things had been different, it would have been such fun. Why is nothing ever simple?'

'When's D Day?' she asked.

'The day after we open, if I dare.'

'You can back out, you know, Madsy.'

'No, I can't Annie. When I say I don't want to live without Gerry, I do mean it.'

Wisely, Annie did not pursue it, but patted my hand briefly.

'I hope he knows how very lucky he is,' she said, looking fierce.

'I'm the lucky one.'

'If you say so.'

'I do.'

'Madison Brylmer, you are the absolute end. Get your butt on stage fast now. Uh, oh, it's the wunderkind.'

Ben had materialised in my dressing room as if he owned it, jumping energetically onto the long make-up counter.

'Hi, Mads. Hi, Annie.'

'Hello, darling.' I held out my arms for a hug, which was patiently bestowed.

'Madison,' Ben said seriously. 'When you come to live with us, I hope you realise that you have to do my homework before you do Josh's.'

'Oh, is that so? Why should I be doing it for either of you?'

'Because Dad says if you do we'll get A grades all the time.'

'Not in maths and science, you won't,' I countered.

'It's going to be wicked,' Ben said cheerfully.

'What is?' I looked at him with mock suspicion.

'Having you living with us. Dad's in such a good mood about it.'

'Is he?'

'Yeah. He says you're going to bring order into our lives.'

Annie laughed. 'Are you sure you can stand the sheer excitement, Madsy?' She asked. 'That sounds like a euphemism for an awful lot of housework.'

'I don't mind if it is,' I told her.

'Madison!' she chided me, shocked to the core of her feminist little heart.

'You do cook better than Dad,' Ben said slyly.

'I do a lot of things better than your dad,' I told him, 'but you guys are the only people in the world who can make me truly happy.'

'Aw, shucks,' Ben smirked and as we beamed happily at each other, I heard Annie's intake of breath and thought that she probably did understand what bound me to Gerry and his boys. I looked at her questioningly and she nodded.

'Come on, children, we've got to work,' she said.

So we did.

By this time, of course, with only a few days to the opening, Gerry had told Ben and Josh of our plans. I would have loved to know exactly what had passed between them all, but he gave me only the briefest account as we cooked dinner in the spacious kitchen. Andy was at The Dragon, and I had spent the afternoon with Gerry, studying a Rossini song cycle as he worked. Now as he stirred pasta sauce, he said idly, 'I spoke with the boys last night and told them that you were going to come to live with us sometime soon.'

'Gerry! Why didn't you tell me?'

'I am telling you.'

'What did they say?'

'Josh said 'Cool,' and carried on eating baked beans, and Ben asked if you were going to sleep in my bedroom, to which Josh replied, 'Of course she is, you idiot,' and that was about the extent of it.'

'Didn't they seem shocked or upset?'

'Not at all. It was something of an anticlimax, actually.' Gerry pulled a wry face.

'Oh, darling, I'm so glad.' I sighed in relief, and held my hand out to him. He took it, kissing my palm briefly.

'That's if you still think you can bear us all, of course.'

'Umm... I think so.'

'Good.'

When Josh and Ben rolled in from their respective schools I wondered if they would behave any differently towards me, but they seemed already to take my presence for granted. As I reluctantly rose to leave after supper, longing to stay and wondering why I didn't, Ben spoke aloud my very thoughts.

'Why are you going, Mads? If you're moving in with us, why not stay now?'

'I'd like to, darling, but I can't for a week or so.'

He looked as if he was going to press me on it, but thought better of it.

'Okay,' he said easily.

'Ben?'

'Yeah.'

'Is it okay with you if I move in? I'm asking you seriously, because your opinion does matter. Josh's, too.'

437

'Of course it's okay,' he said. 'Why shouldn't it be?'

'This is your home, your space, your family, your dad. I don't want to change any of you, but my being here will change some things nevertheless.'

'I know, but it's cool.'

'I do love you, Ben,' I told him. 'You, and Josh, and Gerry. I love you all very much.'

'I know. We love you, too.'

He spoke casually, but I was so choked with emotion I couldn't speak. I held my arms out to him, and he moved easily into my embrace, which was how Gerry found us a moment later.

CHAPTER 76

That hurdle over, all that was left was for me to burn my bridges, and as much as I longed to wake up in the morning next to Gerry, I wished we could reach that point without the confrontation that had to precede it. Andy and Megan had good seats for the opening of *Carmen*, and as the day dawned I felt a pang of sadness, as I appreciated afresh that this would be the last time they came together to see me at work. Annie had made my excuses to Ron, but had arranged a seat for him, and Andy was clearly delighted that his friend would be there to dilute Megan's intense company. Opening night nerves were nothing compared to how I felt as I anticipated how I would face Andy with the news of my departure, how he would react, what Megan would say and do, what I would do if Gerry changed his mind and sent me away.

All these thoughts lurched through my brain as I dressed and did my make-up, but as the half hour call came over the tannoy, I forced myself to refocus. I imagined the hot steamy days of civil war Spain, the boredom of the soldiers guarding the cigarette factory, waiting for the girls to provide the little entertainment their day offered. I felt the pulsing excitement of the nightclub, the thrill of danger as the nationalists smuggled guns through the mountains, and of the bullfight with its macho displays of power and lust. As the moment came for me to enter the stage, I thought of nothing but the wonderful privilege of singing in this beautiful theatre to hundreds of people who were expecting the best, and I was determined to give it.

In the interval I sat with the children's chaperone, exchanging idle chat with Ben and his fellows, but not till the curtain fell and I was once again in my dressing room, preparing to face the real world, did I let the stomach churning reality of what lay ahead grip me once more. Congregating in the hallway, I saw Annie's entourage waiting to congratulate her, but as yet no sign of Andy, Megan, or Ron. Children spilled out of dressing rooms, and chorus hurried away with bags and coats to catch buses and trains. I anxiously scanned the sea of faces to glimpse Gerry before Andy appeared backstage, and there he was, grinning happily as he made his way towards me, simultaneously casting around for Ben. Instinctively I reached for him, standing on tiptoe to put my arms around his neck and hug him, as he kissed my hair and my uplifted mouth.

'Well done, little one,' he said affectionately. 'You were lovely. Where's young Benjamin?'

'On his way, I guess,' I said, kissing him in return. 'Did you recognise me, then?'

'Oh, I think so. The gorgeous one with fabulous boobs and a sexy voice?' he teased, and I hugged him again as he ran his hands over my back.

'Hi, Dad.'

Ben materialised at last, and as Gerry turned his attention to his son I slipped my hand into Gerry's and waited whilst he and Ben bantered.

I felt Andy's presence before I saw him, and as I did I realised that I had knowingly and deliberately taken this enormous risk. I could have left Gerry as soon as Ben arrived, returning to my dressing room, or taken position in the alleyway outside the stage door. If Andy had seen Gerry it would be have been by chance only, and not in my company. But I had waited with them, lingering in their presence, careless of the danger. What recklessness had come over me in this public place of work? Whatever folly had motivated me, it was too late to regret it now as Andy, standing just proud of Megan in the hall, stared at Gerry, then at Ben, finally fixing his gaze on me, his eyes cast down to my hand entwined in Gerry's. I let his hand drop, casually turning towards Megan and Andy, briefly hopeful that I could cover the moment, defer the inevitable until tomorrow. But Andy stepped forward even as Gerry turned to see what had attracted my attention. He and Andy stared at each other, their bodies still and wary, as around them singers, instrumentalists and crew moved freely, their chatter unsilenced as my life moved inexorably into its next phase.

'Hello, Andy, Megan,' Gerry said lightly, when finally somebody could speak.

'You bastard, you slimy, smirking creep.' Andy lunged forward, held back only by Ron's restraining hand.

'Easy, mate,' he soothed, 'not here.'

'Why not here?' Andy seethed, and I saw Megan turn away in distress, her features almost unrecognisable in her pain. I wanted to reach for her, but stood frozen to the spot. With a pang, I registered Ben, too, his little face shadowed with anxiety as he saw his dad straighten up before Andy. His hands firmly by his sides, Gerry looked Andy in the eye.

'If you want to speak to Madison, I'll make a move,' he said. 'It's time this young man headed for bed in any case.'

I wanted to hold him back, to ask him to stay with me, but I knew that Gerry would play this his way, and it was up to me to deal with Andy and my mother.

'Don't bother,' Andy told him furiously. 'I won't stand in the way of you both anymore. If you two want to play happy families, just get on with it. Madison, you've got your musical soulmate, so just go with him, for God's sake, and leave me out of it. Ron, I'm sorry, I'll see you tomorrow. Megan, you see what your precious daughter is made of now. She's a lying, deceiving adulterer, and the two of them are welcome to each other.'

Red-faced, I avoided the eyes of my colleagues who shuffled past us, trying to look disinterested. Andy spun on his heel and stalked stiffly away as Annie magically appeared beside me, her hand on my arm. She said nothing as Megan and I met each other's anguished gaze, and Gerry shuffled his feet.

'Mum, I'm sorry,' I said feebly.

She shook her head.

'I'm going home, Madison. I don't know what to make of this, but I have no desire to stand here and watch you bring humiliation onto my head and your own.'

She, too, left. All it needed now was for Gerry to follow her and I would be alone. Except for Annie, I thought, comforted as her arm slipped around my waist. I leant against her, with no idea of what I was supposed to do next. Gerry broke the stillness. Throwing an arm easily around Ben's shoulders, he held out his hand to me.

'Come on, guys, time to get home,' he said, and before either of us could respond he led us from the theatre into the darkened night.

I didn't break my shocked silence until we were seated in Gerry's car, Ben lolling in the back, unnaturally speechless, me shivering in the passenger seat beside Gerry. Racked with guilt, I turned to Ben.

'Darling, I'm so sorry. That was all totally unexpected. I'm very, very sorry you had to see it.'

'It's okay, Mads,' he said quietly.

'Sweetheart, I mean it…' I trailed off as Gerry took my hand to interrupt me.

'Hush now,' he said.

'Gerry, it's all my fault.'

'No, it's not. It doesn't help to attribute blame anywhere. Let's just regroup quietly and consider our options from here. A good night's sleep sounds like an excellent place to begin.'

'Okay.' I looked at him appealingly, longing for a reassuring kiss, but knowing better than to expect it now. He released my hand and started the engine. As we headed towards Dulwich I let my head rest on his shoulder, and eventually he took my hand again, holding it in his as he drove though the night, and I was mildly comforted, even as I dreaded the morning.

I was glad to let Gerry take charge when we arrived at Thurlow Park Road. He dispatched Ben to bed, issuing me with instructions to make tea, draw curtains, and lock the front door. Before Ben disappeared upstairs I hugged him tightly, horrified still by the position in which I had placed him.

'Darling, how can I apologise enough?'

'Madison, just leave it be,' Gerry urged. 'No one's dead or injured; no one's been traumatised for life. It happened, and it's over. Everyone's in one piece.'

So I let Ben escape my clutches and I boiled the kettle and set up tea until Gerry returned from seeing his son into bed.

'Gerry?'

'Madsy, just pour us some tea and sit down.'

He rubbed his hand wearily over his face, and I felt deeply sad at putting him in such an invidious position yet again. Tea poured, Gerry reached across the table and took my hand in his, idly tracing patterns across my knuckles and looking thoughtful. I looked at him from under my eyelashes, and he smiled, his familiar ironic grin only slightly dimmed by the evening's drama.

'We didn't intend for what happened tonight to happen as it did,' he began, 'but we had planned for you to move in with us sometime over the next week or so, once you had settled things with Andy in whatever way you felt was best. Things have been somewhat pre-empted now, although I suspect that Andy's reaction, and Megan's, would not have been substantially different, don't you?'

I nodded, and he continued smoothly.

'I think the first thing we need to establish is whether you're still going to live with us. Is that what we want now that events have taken over like this?'

Gerry paused and I met his eye cautiously, resisting the temptation to burst into tears and ask whether that meant he didn't want me anymore. He raised an eyebrow.

'Well? What's your feeling?'

'I haven't changed, Gerry. I would like very much to live with you and the boys. You guys are my life now.'

'Fine,' he said briskly. 'We'd like you here, but we do need to find a way to accomplish it without another scene like tonight's. It wasn't good for any of us in all kinds of ways.'

I nodded, abashed. Gerry sat back, stretching out his long legs under the table, and lacing his hands behind his head.

'Firstly, you do need to go back home fairly imminently, don't you? As far as I can see, you're here tonight with a score of *Carmen* and a make-up box. So you need to get some things, you need to see your solicitor again, I imagine, and you need to talk to Andy, and, conceivably, to Megan.'

'I'll go back tomorrow,' I said slowly. 'I don't know whether Andy's gone home, or gone to stay with Ron anyway, but I know we have to talk, and it's probably better to stay at Exeter House until we've done that.'

'That sounds smart,' he agreed.

'I have a PhD,' I said modestly, risking a little humour.

'Hmm... useful for all kinds of things,' he agreed, with a smile. 'I don't think today should be the first day of the rest of our lives,' he said, serious once more. 'Settle things with Andy, organise what you want to do, be sure that it *is* what you want to do, and then we can start on a fresh sheet, don't you think?'

I sighed.

'I'm so sorry, darling,' I told him. 'It's all my fault. I shouldn't have stayed out in the corridor with you and Ben.'

'Don't worry about it now. I was there, too, don't forget. I could have had the foresight to have just arranged to meet you tomorrow, not come to see you backstage when we knew Andy and Megan would be around.'

I smiled at him gratefully.

'You are a wonderful man,' I told him.

'You may be right about that too,' he smiled, and at last he leaned forward to kiss me across the table. 'So, let's take the next few weeks easy. After all, if we reckon that we might live to be eighty-five years old, then what's a week or two to wait to be together?'

'What indeed?'

'And I don't know about you, but it's time I went to bed. Care to join me?'

Gerry rose and held out his hand.

'What have I done to deserve you?' I asked him.

'I'm sure we'll think of something.'

CHAPTER 77

I was less sanguine the next morning when Gerry, distracted and irritable, returned from taking Ben to school and Josh to the station to make his own way up to town. I had washed up and made the beds, tidying the most obviously displaced pieces of this and that, and trying to think of how best to approach the day,

'Why does he always do it?' Gerry sighed, banging his keys down with some force.

'Do what? Who?'

'Ben. Forget the very thing he needs for the day. This morning it was his hockey stick. He'll just have to use one of the school's.'

'Do you want a coffee?' I asked soothingly.

'No. Yes. Oh, I don't know. Yes, I suppose.'

I looked at Gerry quizzically.

'Is it me? I'll get going soon, I promise.'

He sat down heavily at the table.

'No, of course it's not you. What could be nicer than having you here? It's just me. I'm in a grouchy mood this morning.'

He held his hand out to me and I joined him at the table.

'Bear with me, Madsy. We're all adjusting here.' He paused. 'I do love you.'

'Good.'

'Will you ring me tonight and tell me how it's going?'

I nodded, close to tears now I had to leave him again. Gerry looked at me knowingly.

'Come on now, don't cry. Wasn't it nice being with me last night?'

'Of course.'

'Then you've no need to cry. Ring me later, okay?'

'Okay. Have a good rehearsal.'

'And you. Now go.'

The flat was quiet when I returned and it didn't appear that Andy had spent the night there. Once again, everything was as it had been left the previous day, and I was forcibly reminded of Christmas Day and its aftermath. I showered and changed, glad that we had no call till the afternoon. With no sign of Andy by the time I had to leave I resorted to the note I'd been planning in my head all morning.

Dear Andy

To say I'm sorry about last night is inadequate, I know. I never intended for it to happen and I regret it very much. I hope you are all right. I will call The Dragon later if you have not come back here or contacted me, but we do need to talk properly now, and work out what's going to happen from here. I'll be back tonight after rehearsal.

Love, Madison

'Andy stayed with Ron last night,' Annie greeted me as soon as I walked into the studio.

'Oh, Annie, I'm sorry, that must have put paid to your plans.'

'It's no problem; there'll be other days. Are you okay? Did you go home with Gerry?'

'Yes, but we've agreed I must sort things out with Andy before I can go there permanently. I've got to see him, Annie. Do you know what his movements are today?'

She shook her head.

'I kept completely out of it.'

Andy still wasn't home in the evening. I rang Gerry, missing the sound of his voice.

'Andy stayed with Ron. If he doesn't come back here tonight I'll have to call him there or at The Dragon,' I told him dismally. 'I'm supposed to go to an *Elushka* rehearsal the day after tomorrow. I'm a bit stuck now, but at least they've got the tape.'

'You should still go to the rehearsal,' Gerry advised pragmatically, 'but perhaps you ought to try to get hold of him before that, to avoid any embarrassment with Joe.'

'I guess,' I sighed. 'Darling, I miss you.'

'I know.'

'Are the boys all right?'

'Of course.'

'I miss them too.'

'Then ring Andy, arrange to meet him, and get things straight. We can't do anything till you've done that.'

Sick with apprehension, I dialled Ron's number, half hoping that the answering machine would cut in. It didn't.

'Ron Stryker.'

'Ron, it's Madison,' I said with more confidence than I felt. 'Is Andy there? If so, could I speak with him?'

'I was wondering when you'd call,' he said mildly. 'I guessed that Annie would tell you that Andy came here last night.'

'Thanks for being there for him, Ron,' I said with genuine gratitude.

'He needed someone.'

'Yes, I know.'

We were silent for a moment.

'Is he there now?'

'I'll see if he'll come to the phone, Mads.'

I waited out the static charged silence on the line until fumbling with the receiver preceded the sound of Andy's voice.

'Yes,' he said curtly.

'Hi, it's me.'

'I know. What do you want, Madison?'

'To see that you're okay. To ask if we can talk.'

'Where are you?'

'At home.'

'With laughing boy?'

I swallowed a biting retort, and spoke quietly. 'I'm on my own, Andy. I really think we need to meet up and talk properly. We haven't done so yet, but neither of us can go forward now until we've spoken face to face.'

'Have you talked to Megan?' he asked.

'No, have you?'

'No, but she looked pretty cut up last night. You need to speak to her soon.'

'I will, but we've got to be frank with each other first. Can we meet? I'll come to The Dragon if you don't want to come here.'

Andy pondered this.

'Are you working tomorrow?' he asked.

'No, it's a rest day.'

'Okay, I'll come over at eleven. See you then.'

Andy hung up without farewells and I stared at the idle receiver for a long moment, surprised at how quickly he had agreed to the arrangement.

I phoned Gerry again to tell him what had transpired.

'Good, that's progress in the right direction,' he said seriously. 'Be wise tomorrow, be sure of what you really want. What's really best.'

'I want you. You're best for me.'

'Just take it carefully. Ring me tomorrow.'

'Or you could ring me.' I knew I sounded sulky.

'Okay, whatever,' he agreed easily, and I kicked myself for pushing him again.

'I love you.'

'I know. It's lovely.'

I giggled.

449

'What are you laughing at?'

'You. You're so funny,' I told him.

'Hmm. Go to bed, Dr Brylmer, and think of me.'

'You can be sure of that.'

I slept badly, however, my mind whirling as I pondered the hundred different routes the morning's conversation might take. Around 2 am, I gave up the effort and made tea. I tried to read, soon abandoning that as a forlorn effort. I knew Gerry would be sleeping deeply; it was one of the few things he said he could still do well at his advanced age! I suspected Andy may, too, be wakeful, but what he was thinking I could not guess. I could only wait. Sometime after three, I must have slept, for when I stirred into consciousness it was light and the sounds of the morning were already echoing outside. I used the hours before Andy's arrival to sort out my papers again: bank books and property deeds, pension plans, life insurance and wills. I stacked them logically before placing them in a filing tray out of sight. It seemed somehow tasteless to leave them in full view.

Promptly at eleven, I heard the key in the door, and I switched on the kettle yet again. It had boiled several times already in the last hour as I searched for something else to occupy my restless hands. Andy looked serious as he stood in the kitchen doorway, and I met his eye anxiously.

'Hello,' I greeted him tentatively.

'Hello.' He looked around as if the flat were suddenly unfamiliar to him.

'Did you stay here last night?' he asked.

'Yes, of course.'

'Why of course? I would have rather assumed you'd be with your friend.'

'Not yet,' I told him quietly.

'Not yet, but you will be soon?'

'Andy, shall I make us a coffee before we start? We need to talk about this properly, not rush into it as soon as you walk through the door.'

'Whatever you say, Madison,' he snapped. 'I'll be in the lounge.'

When I carried in the steaming mugs, Andy was staring gloomily out of the window, the spring sun lighting the soft greens of the heath with a radiant glow. It seemed deeply at odds with the heaviness that hung between us, and Andy looked sad as he turned from the window.

'I always loved that view.'

'It hasn't gone away.'

'Perhaps not,' he said cryptically, taking a mug. 'All right, Madison, let's talk turkey, as they say. What are your plans? I assume you do have some.'

I looked at my hands, my feet, at the mug clasped in my bone white fingers, and tried to find a voice.

'Come on, Madison. You're the one who wanted this meeting.'

'I'm going to live with Gerry,' I blurted out, my eyes still averted. 'I'm really sorry. I tried as hard as I could, maybe you think not hard enough, but I really did try, and I can't be without him. I'm so very sorry, Andy, but I simply want to spend my life with Gerry. I love him so much, and the boys, too. He's prepared to let me live with them once you and I have got things straightened, and I can't walk away from them again.'

At last I raised my eyes and met Andy's gaze. He was nodding slowly.

'Yes, I thought that was the picture. You'd already made up your mind, hadn't you? I mean, you haven't just decided this today or last night.'

'No. I stopped seeing Gerry for over two months, Andy, then at the beginning of March I met him collecting Ben from a *Carmen* rehearsal and I knew that same day what I had to do.'

'So you've been seeing him again for about a month?' he asked mildly.

'Yes. I'm sorry.'

Andy nodded again and I wondered what was passing though his mind, but I kept silent.

'You say that Gerry's prepared for you to move in with him. What do you mean, prepared? It sounds like he's doing you a favour or something.'

'Sometimes I think he is, but that's not entirely fair. It's just that his experience of all this is very different to mine, but he does love me, and I know we'll be all right.'

Andy shook his head.

'I think you've lost your marbles, Madison. You've got a lovely home here, a great career, a husband who's done everything to keep you. I know I've made a lot of mistakes over the years, but I've always loved you and been proud that you're my wife. And you're going to leave that behind for a man who's 'prepared' to have you live with him. A man with two kids and a lifestyle that I suspect leaves far less room for you than you want. He must be a great fuck, that's all I can say.'

I winced, but ignored the barb.

'I love him, Andy. That's all I can say.'

We fell silent again, and this time I did break it.

'Can we talk about the flat and suchlike?' I asked cautiously.

'I don't know what you've got in mind,' Andy said quickly, 'but I've been talking to Joe and he says that if I'd like to use the flat over The Dragon, then it's mine for as long as I want it. It's pretty basic, but then, I'm a basic sort of guy, aren't I? Not like the cultured Mr McFall.'

'But Andy,' I cried, 'this is your home. You're entitled to be here. I'm not going to make an issue of it. I'm prepared to sign it over to you, or work out some arrangement you're happy with. You don't have to move.'

He shook his head briskly.

'No, Madsy, I don't want to be here on my own. If you're moving out, then I'd rather not be here either. Do what you like with the flat for the time being. Get a lodger, live here for a while on your own. Perhaps moving in with Gerry might not be such a good idea. Keep him guessing for a bit, Mads. Shit, that bastard doesn't know when he's lucky.'

'Andy, you must know that you only have to say the word and you can come back here. The intention has never been to deprive you of your home.'

'No, just of my wife, eh?'

I looked away, abashed.

'Are you okay for money?' I asked him. 'And your things? What do you need to take? Kitchen stuff? Whatever you need.'

'I've lived off you for long enough, Madison, I've got just about enough pride not to do so now you're leaving me, and The Dragon flat has got pretty much what I need. I'll come back here one day when you're at work, or at his place, and take some things.'

'Andy, there's so much we need to decide about, I'm sure. This feels very open-ended. Should we put the flat up for sale, then?'

'Leave it, Mads. This may have been coming for months, but when it came it was still a shock. We don't need to decide these things now. For the first time in my life, I've got a real job to be proud of, and I can support myself. Just let me go away and try to do that. Stay here, don't stay here, whatever you want, but let's wait six months and see how we feel about things then.'

I drew breath to interrupt him but he held out his hand to silence me.

'I know you think that you and Gerry are going to make it together, and for what it's worth, you're probably right; the two of you are bloody made for each other. But give me time to adjust to this, Madsy. In the autumn, let's talk again about it all.'

'Okay, if that's what you want,' I agreed slowly. 'But I'm not trying to cheat you out of anything, Andy.'

'I know.'

'What about *Elushka*?' I asked him. 'I don't suppose it would be very appropriate for me to be there now, would it?' Can you use the tape?'

'I was going to talk to you about that,' Andy said. 'Joe is very keen for you still to do it. He says it depends on how I feel, and since it's so imminent, next week, in fact, well, even though we could use the tape, it seems silly not to go ahead with it on the nights you can be there.'

I looked at Andy in surprise.

'You want me to do the five shows we agreed? At the theatre?'

'Well, you could hardly do them at Heathrow Airport, could you? If you're willing, then please do them, Mads. Joe will release you from your contract if you and I can't agree on it, but for the sake of the show, especially the opening, I hope we can.'

I was stunned.

'If you're okay about it, then, yes, of course I'll do it. I don't suppose Megan will be there to see it,' I added sadly.

'Well, that's up to you, isn't it?' he opined.

'Oh, no, it's definitely up to her.'

'But, Madison, don't even think of bringing that man to see it. If I ever see his smirking face again, I'll punch it.'

'Gerry doesn't smirk,' I objected feebly, fully aware that his ironic, self-satisfied grin frequently emerged at the most inappropriate moments.

Andy let it drop.

'So we'll see you for the dress tomorrow then?' He got up in a businesslike manner. 'I'll just take one or two bits and pieces before I go.'

I heard cupboards and drawers opening and closing and Andy left with a small holdall of belongings.

'See you tomorrow,' he said without ceremony, and left.

CHAPTER 78

It was a mark of how seriously Andy had committed himself to The Dragon that he was prepared for me to sing at the opening of *Elushka* and for the remaining five performances we'd previously arranged. I felt sure, too, that it was the security offered by the theatre and his colleagues there that had enabled him not to force a confrontation over the flat, money, the future, and Gerry's part in it. I knew eventually we would have to make real decisions about practical matters, but for the time being, perhaps it was enough to concentrate on working through the emotional ones.

Gerry listened in silence as I recounted as much of the conversation *verbatim* as could recall. He contributed the occasional murmur or lift of an eyebrow, but said nothing till I'd finished.

'I think it's good you're still going to do *Elushka*,' he said finally. 'It's professionally honourable of everyone involved, and those songs are lovely. You should get a nice little crit for the opening night. It's not what I would have expected of Andy, however, and I hope you'll be all right. You don't think he'll pull some stunt on you at the theatre?'

'No, I don't. At last he values The Dragon too much to do that. He did say he'd punch you if you came to see it, though, which might be best avoided.'

'So I can't come and hear my favourite girl do her stuff? I don't think that's on, do you? I could sneak in at the back and surprise everyone.'

'It isn't funny,' I chided him. But I giggled nevertheless, knowing he was just trying to make it all easier for me. 'Gerry?'

'Madison?'

'I think it's a good idea for me to continue to stay in Putney sometimes. I know it's not what I would originally have said, but now Andy's made it possible, perhaps it might actually be best.'

'Uh-uh.' Gerry waited for me to continue.

'I could be here a good deal, but not every day; let everybody get used to it, and then we really will know when the time is right for me to settle here permanently.'

'Is that what you'd like?' he asked me seriously.

'Yes, it is. It all felt so drastic the other night. You were right to say that it was no way to begin our proper life together. We've got the chance of making time really work for us now. I know I'm usually rather more impulsive and emotional than this, but perhaps I'm learning, too.'

'Come and sit on my lap.'

Gerry shifted position on the settee so I could manoeuvre and I cuddled up to him appreciatively.

'Gerard McFall, I love you very much.'

'Hmm. I hope you're not going to stay away too much.'

'Just enough to make sure you miss me.'

Four days had passed and I had heard nothing from Megan. I resorted to email, that conveniently remote dispatcher and bearer of myriad emotions and information.

Dear Mum,

I have mentally replayed the events of Monday night many times and I cringe with shame each time I do so. I am so sorry to you and to Andy for putting you through that. It was never my intention. But it brought to a climax things that had been brewing for many months and since then I have talked at length with both Andy and Gerry and we have some idea now of the future.

Andy and I are separating, and I will, eventually, move in with Gerry and his family. I say eventually, because Andy has chosen to live at the flat over The Restless Dragon, and so for the time being I will divide my time between Exeter House and Dulwich. We don't know when I'll settle in Dulwich permanently. Not too far distant, I hope, but I think it's right to give all of us some space and time before making the final move. Only then will we decide what to do with the flat and deal with other practical matters.

I am going to fulfil my contract at the Dragon and sing for five performances of Elushka. *The tape will still be used for the shows that coincide with* Carmen, *as we had planned. Joe and Andy want me to do this and I am pleased to do so. I would love you to be there, but I understand that you may feel unable to come.*

Maybe I shouldn't say this now, but I love Gerry more than I ever believed it possible to love anyone. We share something very special, which has obviously not run an entirely smooth course for all kinds of reasons, but I feel sure we can build a future together, and with Ben and Josh. I am so sorry that all this has affected so many people. It is not what I would have planned or wished for, but my life is now bound up with Gerry's and there is no going back.

I love you, and forever owe you an enormous debt of gratitude for all that you have done for me.

Much love,

Madsy

I attended the dress rehearsal of *Elushka* distinctly apprehensive of my reception, and relieved to see Joe's cheerful smile was undimmed as I entered the theatre. He kissed me warmly.

'Little Madsy, how very glad I am that you are here,' he said simply, and left Ron to begin the rehearsal without further comment. Andy and I smiled cautiously at each other, nervous and wary until the work on stage began. Then our natural instincts took over and he treated me with exactly the same professionalism that he did the members of the cast. I relaxed and immersed myself in the lovely music, enjoying seeing how the songs fitted into the play's scheme. It was fascinating to be part of such a unique production, and gratifying to receive kind words of admiration from the members of the cast, to whom my expertise as a singer was as foreign as their highly refined acting skills were to me. Monday night's opening, exactly a week after *Carmen* had gone up, promised to be a wonderful occasion, and it felt very strange to face it with such ambivalence. Megan would not be there, I was sure; Andy, my now estranged husband, was instrumental in bringing me into the production, but our shared pleasure in it would be muted; and my dear Gerry, whom I longed to hear me sing Joe's beautiful songs just for him, was to be excluded. If I was unhappy about it, I could blame no one but myself, but it did sadden me as I said a quiet farewell to Andy.

'See you on Monday. Thank you for today. It's really going to be wonderful.'

He nodded curtly, awkward again now we were back on more personal ground.

'Let's hope the punters like it. It's a bit *avant garde*.'

'I'm sure they will,' I answered him, patting his arm instinctively. He pulled away as if stung.

'Ron wants me. See you.'

He hurried away as I gathered my things and left the theatre, freshly anxious to be with Gerry and the boys. It was time to start building our new life.

It did feel as if a new beginning had been made the next day, as Ben and I travelled up to town together to the Coli. After the *Elushka* dress, I went straight to Dulwich, and spent the evening with Josh and Ben, making supper, sharing it around the big kitchen table, looking at some of Josh's recent work, and beginning an assault on the kitchen cabinets when neither of them seemed to want my company. Josh was in his room and Ben asleep with his head on my lap as I watched a rerun of *Inspector Morse* when Gerry came in at ten thirty.

458

'He shouldn't still be up,' he reproved me, with a tilt of his eyebrows towards the recumbent Ben.

'I know, but he is in his pyjamas and he is asleep,' I said in our defence, and even as I spoke I saw the soft twinkle in Gerry's eye and I knew he wasn't really cross.

'You both look very sweet.' He sat down on the sofa next to me, whispering against my ear. 'Have you got anything on underneath that dressing gown?'

'Yes.'

'Not for long, I hope.'

'That's up to you.'

'Let's put the baby to bed, then.'

I giggled, absurdly happy.

'Where's Josh?' Gerry asked, getting up to shed his coat.

'In his room.'

'I'll go and say hello while you shift his nibs.'

It was beautiful to see Ben snuggle down in his bed, close his eyes with an incoherent murmur, only to open them again as I kissed the top of his head, looking me squarely in the eye.

'Night, Mads. Love you.'

'I love you, Ben. Every day and forever.'

'Hmm. Every day and forever,' he said sleepily as his eyes closed again.

In the bedroom, Gerry looked at me closely.

'What's up? You look dewy-eyed.'

'Ben said something really lovely.'

'Make the most of it,' he laughed wryly. 'Soon you'll see the tantrums and sulks. Now, how about you saying something really lovely to me?' He sat on the edge of the bed and pulled me onto his lap.

'I love you.'

'That's a start.' Gerry untied my dressing gown, pushing back the smooth black fabric from my shoulders.

'I find you irresistibly desirable.'

'Even better.' He slid down the thin straps of my nightdress, running his beautiful hands over my breasts.

'And I want to make love to you right now.' I began to undo his shirt buttons.

'Now that's exactly what I wanted to hear.'

As I sat on the train the following afternoon, I was thinking about precisely what had ensued.

'What are you grinning about?' Ben asked, poking me in the arm.

'Oh, nothing in particular,' I told him vaguely.

'I know what,' he said doggedly.

'Really? What's that?'

'My dad.' He fell about giggling.

'Is that so? And why would that be so funny?'

'Josh says that you're really fit and that Dad must think he's died and gone to heaven sleeping with you.'

'Ben! I don't believe for a minute that Josh said anything of the kind. You're being deliberately provocative.'

'Deliberately Provocative is my name,' he intoned. 'Hello, my world fan club, I am the global superstar, Deliberately Provocative, and this is my dad's girlfriend.'

He spoke loudly enough for our immediate neighbours to look amused, sympathetic, or irritated, depending on their particular view of precocious young boys.

'Deliberately Provocative is going to get a slap from Definitely Provoked in a minute,' I warned him.

'Too late, it's our stop.' Ben leapt up as we drew into Victoria.

'Ben, just sober down, we've a night's work ahead of us.'

'Sober down, sober down,' he crowed, doubled up with laughter.

'What's funny now?'

'Sober down,' he spluttered.

I shook my head in bewilderment. It was clearly beyond me, but I loved it.

'I'll have some of what you're having,' Annie remarked dryly as we hovered in the wings watching the children's chorus march around, singing lustily.

'What's that?'

'If my memory serves me correctly, it's less than a week since hostilities broke out before my very eyes and today you're looking radiant. Not what I was expecting even from such an indomitable spirit as you. The old McFall magic done it's work again?'

I squeezed Annie's arm in happiness.

'I can't believe it, Annie. But I'm really trying to be sensible. I'm not moving in full-time with them until it feels absolutely right.'

The children were marching back into the wings and Annie had to prepare for her own entrance.

'I'll bring you up to date later,' I told her.

'I can hardly wait.' She rolled her eyes drolly. 'What would I do without your life to bring me a little vicarious excitement?'

'So you're still doing *Elushka*?' she said in amazement as we chatted in the interval. 'That is incredible. And I must say I'm glad that you're not rushing straight into living with Gerry permanently. To be honest, you have got far more to lose than him if it all goes horribly wrong. As far as I can see it, you're the one making all the adjustments and he just has to sit back and enjoy the attention.'

'Annie, it's not that one-sided, it really isn't. I love taking care of them. I want to do it. I love sleeping with Gerry, being encouraged and supported and admired by him. He gives me everything I need, and his quirkiness and his arrogant manner are funny and sweet and just make me love him all the more.'

'I'm glad, Madsy. I know I'm cynical about it, but you might actually be starting to convince me. Not that my opinion matters, I just want you to be happy.' We smiled benevolently at each other. 'I'd like to see *Elushka*. Am I allowed, do you think?'

'Of course. I'd like Josh to come; it's his sort of thing, faintly obscure and intellectual. Would you mind him going with you?'

'I don't do children and animals, as you well know,' Annie chuckled, 'but on this occasion, I may concede.'

CHAPTER 79

Elushka opened two days later. I had stayed with Gerry after Ben and I got back from *Carmen* on Saturday night, but returned to Exeter House the following day. There had been no reply from Megan, and whilst I was not surprised, I was sad. I had gained Gerry, Ben and Josh, but the price was not only Andy's pain, but also my already ambiguous relationship with my mother. Once again, I reminded myself that I had known full well the implications of my actions, but it didn't make it any easier. I grieved for Andy that Megan would not share in his success; I had robbed him of that too.

But that it was a success was not in doubt. The audience loved Joe's and Andy's sentimental, mystical play, and I was happy that they evidently enjoyed my songs too. Ron had kindly given me my own curtain call and the warm wave of applause that greeted me was as welcome as it would have been in any international opera house. I tried to catch Andy's eye, as he watched from the wings, but he kept his gaze averted. As the cast gathered in the bar for a celebratory drink, I knew my presence would not be welcome for long. I sought out Andy, glad to find him amidst a throng of well-wishers.

'Andy, thank you for tonight. It was lovely. I'll see you on Wednesday for the next one. Annie wants to come sometime; is that okay?'

'Of course.'

We were silent.

'You were in fine voice, Mads,' he continued after a beat.

'Good.' I smiled wanly.

'Where are you off to now?' he asked.

'Home. Putney, that is.'

'Oh.'

'See you then.'

'Yes. See you.'

It felt forlorn to leave the happy cast and crew behind, but I had made my choice and I couldn't have my cake too. I looked back as I left, but Andy had already turned away, laughing again with his colleagues and there was no sign of Joe, who was entertaining the theatre's patrons. I went home alone, wishing I had asked Gerry after all if I could stay with him again that night. My consolation came when I checked my phone for messages. *Hope you had a good time. Thinking of you. See you tomorrow. Love from me,* he had written. I smiled, scrolling the message back and forth several times. It would do very nicely until the next day.

Elushka was running intermittently for just over two weeks, staging ten performances concurrently with other Polish themed events, and of which I sang at precisely half. The tape was, I learned, a perfectly adequate substitute for my physical presence, though not so perfect that my live appearances did not lend something extra to the performances. As I had anticipated, Josh showed an interest in the play and pored over the script studiously.

'Would you like to see it one night when I'm there?' I asked him, and Gerry looked up curiously.

'Would that be workable?' he asked.

'Josh could go with Annie. He won't have to come backstage. I'll just meet them both round the front afterwards. If you're happy about that.' I raised a questioning eyebrow.

'Umm, I suppose so, as long as you don't think that it will cause trouble.'

'Dad, Ben told me about what happened at *Carmen*,' Josh interrupted.

464

We looked at him in surprise; this was news to us, although on reflection it was natural for Ben to have shared the night's drama with his brother.

'You don't need to worry, you know,' he continued. 'If there was any kind of fuss I'd look after Madison.'

I was inordinately touched by Josh's protectiveness.

'Oh, darling, it's not me, it's you we're concerned about. I don't want you to face any unpleasantness.'

'I'm not worried,' he said firmly, 'and so you shouldn't be either. Dad, I really want to go. Just chill; it'll be fine.'

'I'm not sure I think it's fair that you can go and I can't,' Gerry smiled, 'but I'll give in with a good grace.'

Josh was even more enthusiastic when he read a review of *Elushka*'s first night in *The Stage*. I warranted a small but satisfying citation.

'*The atmosphere of this evocative production is richly enhanced by the skilful use of traditional Polish folk tunes, none more so than those sung by mezzo-soprano, Madison Brylmer, whose velvety tones provided a pleasing counterpoint to the action,*' Josh read aloud. 'That's cool, Mads,' he nodded in approval.

'It can't be bad,' I agreed, 'especially since I didn't even get a mention in any of the *Carmen* reviews I've seen so far. Apart from the *Evening Standard*, that is, and all they could say was something about a 'valuable supporting role.' That's what comes of playing second fiddle to Anastasia. She's getting me back for *Tito*.'

Annie, Josh and I felt highly conspiratorial as we approached The Restless Dragon for my fourth appearance there. For all Annie's show of reluctance at accompanying Josh, it was just that, and they were quite charming to each other. Annie hugged me before I disappeared backstage, and Josh fluttered his eyelashes softly.

'*Toi, toi*, girl,' Annie said cheerfully.

'Yeah, have a good time,' Josh concurred, and I left them to forge a relationship in my absence.

Andy and I exchanged few words through the evening, although when we did speak we were both careful and courteous with the other. But he wasn't within the vicinity as I packed up to leave at the end, and set off to find Annie and Josh. They were in the bar, Josh sipping a coke, and Annie breathing heavily into a glass of red wine. I was pleased to see mine waiting at her elbow.

'Hello, darlings,' I greeted them.

I was also pleased to see them happily poring over the programme together. Josh was reading aloud and didn't stop when I joined them. I enjoyed hearing his soft, intelligent voice, and I saw Annie had clearly mellowed towards him during the course of the evening. On cue she caught my eye as Josh finished, mouthing silently, 'He's gorgeous.'

I winked in agreement as Josh looked up.

'Hi, Mads. Why are you smiling at me like that?'

'I'm just thinking how much I love you,' I told him lightly, hugging his thin shoulders. 'So? What's your critical opinion?'

'It's very interesting,' he said, nodding seriously.

'You sounded beautiful, Madsy,' Annie added. 'As good as I've ever heard you.'

So we chatted about the play as I drank my wine and Josh flipped through the programme again.

'Madison Brylmer,' he said thoughtfully, as he read my biography.

'You called?'

'No, I was just thinking you should call yourself Madison Brylmer-McFall. That would sound very classy.'

I was just leaning forward to kiss his cheek, the only possible response I could muster to such a sweet suggestion, when I saw Annie stiffen slightly and her eyes flash a warning. Andy and Joe had come through the auditorium exit straight to the bar and into our sight line. Joe didn't hesitate.

'Hello, little Madsy; more lovely singing, my angel. Hello, Anastasia. I hope you enjoyed my play.'

'Yes, Joe, very much,' she smiled.

Andy hovered silently behind Joe.

'And you, young man,' Joe went on in an avuncular fashion. 'We have not met before, I think. I am Josef Budzynski. I write this play with Andy boy here. It is my story from my homeland. You look a very intelligent fellow. I am sure you enjoyed it.'

'Yeah.' Josh looked wary and his enthusiasm was muted as he weighed up the situation.

'Joe, this is my friend, Josh McFall,' I told him.

'Hello, Josh. I am pleased to meet you.' Joe held out his hand and I was relieved that Josh took it briefly, but courteously.

'Joe is the most important fringe manager in London,' I told Josh, who nodded mildly.

I dared to look up at Andy.

'I didn't have a chance to say cheerio,' I said to him. 'I couldn't find you when I came out.'

'As long as you found your friends,' he said coolly. 'Hello Annie, how are you?'

'Fine, Andy. Great play.'

'It was very Brechtian,' Josh suddenly said quietly and both Andy and Joe looked at him in surprise. 'The devices of alienation and *geste* were very well used, and Madison was like a classic Brechtian narrator, only her commentary was sung rather than spoken.'

Josh raised a perfectly pencilled eyebrow and casually ran his hand – black polished fingernails and all – through his hair. He had jettisoned gelled spikes for the occasion and his hair flopped rakishly over his forehead. He adopted a casually superior expression and, catching Annie's eye, we bit our lips to stop laughing aloud. Joe and Andy were staring vacuously at Josh. Joe recovered first.

'Well, yes, of course, that's exactly the influence we wanted to betray, but how very clever of you to see it, my young friend. That is more than many of the audience will do. You are well versed in theatre, yes?'

'I enjoy it,' Josh told him with elaborate casualness.

'Smart-arse,' Andy muttered behind me, and I decided that Josh's precocious display had gone far enough.

'I'm sorry that Tuesday will be my last show,' I told the men, 'but I've been very fortunate to have been part of it. I do appreciate it.' I looked pointedly at Andy who shrugged but looked vaguely mollified.

'Yeah, good. See you soon.' He moved to leave, as Josh spoke barely audibly.

'Bye. Cool play.'

Andy looked round again, and for a moment I thought he was going to lash out in anger at Josh, but if he was, he thought better of it. His face softened and he nodded briskly.

'Good, glad you liked it.'

He and Joe finally made their move and only then could Annie let out the laughter she had been holding back.

'Oh, Josh, that was priceless. You completely floored them.'

Josh lowered his eyelashes and smiled innocently.

'I didn't want them to think that Madison's allied herself to a bunch of ignoramuses,' he said. 'But I did enjoy it, I meant that; it was a beautiful and clever play. Thanks for letting me come, Mads.'

'It's a pleasure, darling. I'm glad you were here.'

We smiled warmly at each other, and Annie chuckled appreciatively.

'What are you laughing at, Anastasia?' I asked.

'You two,' she replied with a grin. 'You're so funny.'

'We try,' said Josh mildly, and for some silly reason we all got the giggles, and I was warm and happy with love and friendship as we left The Dragon behind for the night.

CHAPTER 80

T he next morning, Megan finally replied to my email.

Dear Madison, she wrote,

It has taken me some time to respond to your letter, but as you can imagine, it has taken a while for me to recover even a little after the appalling scene I witnessed at the opening night of Carmen. *Since then, you must have completed several performances of the opera, and of* Elushka, *too, and despite everything, I have been sorry to miss them. But you were right to say that I did not feel able to attend and I am not certain when, indeed if, the time will come when I can again see you perform without feeling deeply saddened.*

I am sure that much has gone on over the years of which I have been unaware, and I do not doubt that you have possibly borne many disappointments and unhappiness and done so with grace. You have developed your skills and talents wonderfully well, bringing pleasure to many people, myself included. But all this makes me even more unhappy about what happened three weeks ago. You have always held your head high and won the respect and love of those around you, but I consider your behaviour now to be shameful, bringing into disrepute every part of your life. I have found it impossible to come to terms with it and I cannot possibly say if and when I will do so. If your life is now bound up with Gerry McFall and his family, I can envisage no way in which we can meet together happily. My observations thus far have not led me to find anything in him to like or respect, and whilst I consider your responsibility in this affair to be considerable, he cannot be without blame. I am not confident that he will make you happy, or be the kind of partner you seem to think that he will be, but that is, of course, your decision.

This is as much as I feel able to say. In my contrariety, I hope that you will keep me in touch with your movements and I will obviously let you know if anything urgent should arise. Otherwise I have to say that your situation makes it impossible for me to continue the relationship that we have enjoyed in the past. As in all things, we might wait for time to do its work.

Megan

Megan's letter was nothing more than I had anticipated but still it left me trembling. Of all those who knew of my relationship with Gerry and the path down which it had led me, Megan alone had spoken censure. I had been astonished by the kindness and tolerance of friends and colleagues – even Joe and Ron, whose loyalty to Andy would have understandably inclined them to take a far less kindly stance towards me than they had done. And yet, I knew that Megan's voice was truly that of my conscience. I believed what she spoke and wrote far more than I believed the words of comfort and reassurance from my friends. How they were capable of holding back the condemnation that I spoke daily to myself I could not know, but Megan was not so constrained, and it was her assessment of my behaviour and my choices that I believed to be the right one. And yet I had been unable to decide in any other way. Unable to stay with Andy, or to envisage building a new future with him; unable to stay away from Gerry, who had me utterly in his thrall. That our relationship was undeniably unbalanced deterred me not in the slightest. I had lived for too long in a relationship in which the scales had been unequally weighed to know that as long as two people were prepared to live with the inequality, to use it mutually, then it need not bring failure and disappointment. Andy and I had lived with it for longer than I now believed possible and for many years we had created something that worked for us both. But when I met Gerry I could no longer live with it, and I knew that I had to accept the responsibility for that decision. I also had to accept that I was taking on another unequal pairing and this time, I was the one who kissed, and Gerry the one who proffered the cheek. He might enjoy my company, seek my support, make love to me, and welcome me into his life, entrusting to me the lives of his precious sons, but he would lose neither his head nor his heart. My heart had been lost since the day I had awoken to the realisation that I loved him; that my head had followed close behind was evident by the very position in which I now found myself. But even as I knew full well that Gerry's love for me would never be the single-minded devotion I had for him, I did know that he loved me enough to accept with humour and kindness the drama I had put us through to reach this point, and from there we could build a future.

Megan sensed the inequality, but could only evaluate it from the perspective of an outsider. She had seen my tears, Andy's anger, Gerry's self-assured aplomb as the less controlled emotions of others whirled around him, and she drew conclusions that were not entirely wrong, but she had not seen beyond them. She had not seen Gerry and I alone together, or with the boys, working and living together, free from tears and unhappiness, sharing our music, supporting each other's frailties and enhancing our strengths. She did not know how the sweet touch of his hands and mouth told me the things he did not speak aloud. I could not blame her for her scepticism. Why should she believe that Gerry could make me happy, when all she saw was an agent of destruction who had bewitched me?

I folded the letter, resisting the urge to destroy it, to hide from the reality of Megan's anger and distress. I tucked it into a drawer, filled with a new determination. One day I would prove to my mother that life with Gerry had been worth everything that we had all suffered.

CHAPTER 81

I began to find a routine of sorts as the *Carmen* run proceeded. I would stay with Gerry the day before a show and the night after it, taking Ben to and from the theatre with me on the train when Gerry didn't come with us. I would stay over at the weekend, too, going back to Putney late on Monday morning. Nearly a month had elapsed since the decisive showdown backstage, and whilst I was not a permanent member of the McFall household, it was starting to feel strange not to wake up in Gerry's bed when I stayed at home, and it felt unnaturally quiet without the boys to despatch to school.

My last performance of *Elushka* passed without incident, but I was surprised at my sadness at leaving it behind. Joe hugged me as I left the theatre after the final show.

'Little Madsy, you have made our play all the more beautiful with your voice. We will revive this many times and you will, I hope, be part of it again.'

'I'd love to Joe, as long as Andy is okay about it.'

'Andy boy will do as Josef says,' he said with confidence.

'Joe, you've been so kind to me. I really don't deserve it.' I said gratefully.

'Kind does not come into it, little one. We are all professionals, no? But Joe, he also sees and understands and I think you and the Andy are not the best suited for being married. Maybe once, for a while, but not for now, or forever. It is difficult. People will not approve, you feel guilty and sad, and Andy feels angry and sad. You have chosen a difficult course, Madison, but I understand what is in your heart, I think. I have not met your new friend. What is his name?'

'Gerry.'

'I have not met your Gerry, but I see your face light up even now as you speak his name, and I see your young friend, Joshua, who is his son, no?' I nodded. 'And I think you have found the great loves of your life.'

I nodded again, rueful and abashed.

'I have, Joe, but I shouldn't have gone to them, should I? There is no moral justification for leaving Andy because I fell in love with someone else. I could try to justify it all night, offer all kinds of reasons why I should be excused for doing so, but ultimately, none of them will satisfy Andy or my mother, or even me really. I just know that there is no life for me now without Gerry and his sons, and I have to live with the consequences. I hope we'll all be okay in the end.'

Joe took my hand in his large one.

'You look after your new family, and let Joe look out for Andy. I will see he is okay, as you say.'

I mulled over my conversation with Joe later as I made tea to drink in bed. Somehow, it had felt wrong to go to Dulwich after a performance of *Elushka*, but tonight I wondered why I was alone rather than drinking tea with Gerry as I told him about my final show, and about Joe's kindness to me. I wanted to speak to him, needing to hear his gentle, teasing tones, but I hesitated to lift the phone. It was not only the lateness of the hour that made me hold back, but an insecurity that still lingered. I couldn't be sure that Gerry would be glad to hear me call him, glad that I was thinking of him and wanting him while we were apart. And lurking deep in my heart was the fear that he may be with someone else. I felt a stab of pain as my imagination immediately conjured up a vision of Gerry making love to some faceless, but nonetheless voluptuous woman. I clutched the counter edge and closed my eyes until the picture receded. If I phoned him now, I could banish the image entirely, but still I could not lift the receiver. I would rather remain ignorant. I drank my tea and lay down to sleep, arms tight around my pillow, my face buried in its cool and comforting folds. As I drifted in to slumber, in my mind I heard myself speaking softly to Gerry – ' I love you so much' – and I felt his smile as he kissed the top of my head – 'Of course you do, you sexy thing, of course you do.'

'I missed you last night when I got back from *Elushka*,' I told Gerry the next day as I rubbed out twenty years' worth of pencil markings on orchestra parts, leaving only those made in Gerry's distinctive hand. 'I wanted to talk to you.'

'You should have phoned me,' he said, concentrating fiercely on the computer screen.

'Would that have been all right?'

'Of course.' He was still paying more attention to the monitor than to me.

'Really?'

He looked up at last.

'Yes. Why shouldn't it be?'

'Because it was late.'

Gerry laughed. 'You think with *Butterfly* opening in two days' time I would have been asleep?'

I sighed. This was another source of anxiety for me. I hated the thought of Gerry conducting fifteen performances of an opera with a perfectly good mezzo role that wasn't being sung by me.

'But I hadn't said I was going to phone, so it might not have been convenient.' I continued doggedly.

Gerry sat back in his seat, looking amused.

'Madison, there's clearly an agenda here, which I haven't seen in advance, but I'll do my best. No, it wouldn't have been too late; even if I was asleep it wouldn't have mattered – you can call me any time of the day or night – and I hardly think I need several hours' notice of your intention to call to get suitably prepared. Does that cover it?' He raised a questioning eyebrow and I wiggled with embarrassment.

'Yes, thank you,' I said humbly.

'I thought of you last night and wondered how you'd got on. It would have been nice to hear from you,' he added.

'Well, you could have rung me,' I countered.

'I didn't know you'd like me to do so. If I had done, I would,' he said simply.

We looked at each other frankly for a moment and I giggled, conscious of what a ridiculous conversation we were having. Gerry grinned and pulled a face.

'Anything else while we're at it?'

'Yes. I hate not doing *Butterfly* with you.'

'Ah, well, there's nothing we can do about that, is there? It was all organised a long time ago and I could hardly sack the Suzuki on the grounds that my girlfriend had come back to me and I wanted her to sing it instead, could I?'

'No.'

'And given that we have many years before us to work together and do lots of other wonderful things, don't you think that one opera we're not doing together isn't completely unimportant? After all, what are you going to do when you're on an ENO contract for the next three years? Tell them they've got to take me on as staff conductor or you're pulling out?'

'I would if I thought they'd go for it,' I laughed.

'I know you would, but that's not the point, is it? We're both professionals with two busy careers that occasionally overlap, and very nice it is when they do. If they hadn't done, we wouldn't be here now, sharing so much more than just our music. But we have to accept that we'll both do lots of things independently, too, and look forward to coming home and telling each other about them.'

I smiled foolishly at him, enjoying his patient pontification.

'What are you grinning at me like that for?' Gerry asked warily.

'Thinking how much I love you.'

'And I love you. Now if you've finished cleaning up my wind parts, it's time you helped Josh practice for his Italian oral exam tomorrow, and on the way you can make me a coffee.'

CHAPTER 82

Once *Elushka* had closed I heard nothing from Andy, and Megan was still silent. I sent her a short email message every few days, offering little details of my life – mostly about *Carmen*, a Mozart concert aria I'd sung at St John's Smith Square, a couple of days' teaching at The Tuition Box, and a sweet fifteen-year-old girl who had somehow ended up having singing lessons with me. It certainly widened my repertoire as we worked through the greatest hits of Whitney Houston and Celine Dion, *en route* to Pergolesi and Handel. Occasionally I would slip in the odd comment about Gerry or the boys: the opening of *Butterfly*, the start of Josh's GCSE exams, the work with Ben that Gerry had delegated to me, helping him to prepare *The Turn of the Screw* for September. I assumed that these details would be received with distaste, but still I wanted Megan to get a picture of the life I was tentatively building in the heart of a real family where what everyone did was important.

Yet as much as I loved my days and nights in Dulwich, I was surprised to find that I found some comfort still in the days I went back to Putney. Although I missed Gerry, I realised I still needed time to reflect and to resist my love for him becoming total emotional dependency. As I recognised it so vividly in myself, I knew that it would be the greatest threat to our relationship if I allowed it to spin out of control. So I really tried to grow up, tried not to become a child in the first truly adult relationship I'd had, and when I wanted nothing more than to go home to Gerry, and be seduced once again by the loving chaos of life with Josh and Ben, I would force myself to go back to Putney and put some distance between us all for a day and night. But Dulwich was beginning to feel like home, and the house seemed to take on a faintly new personality, warmer, tidier, and softer around the edges. Without impinging on the eccentricity and independence of its male occupants, it was starting to embrace me and allow me to have a little of my way with it.

Josh's sixteenth birthday fell in the middle of May.

'It's no big deal, Dad,' I heard him say to Gerry. 'I'm going to the Pathologically Abnormal gig anyway.'

'But your grandparents want to see you, nevertheless,' Gerry told him firmly, 'so they'll be coming over the next day for lunch. You can make that, I take it?'

'Yeah, I guess,' Josh mumbled. 'Mads had better cook something decent, then,' he added as I stopped eavesdropping and joined them in the kitchen. 'I'm not eating your apology for cooking.'

'Josh, that's quite uncalled for.' I leapt to Gerry's defence. 'Your dad looks after you guys brilliantly, and you know that.' Gerry said nothing, but looked pensive. Josh shrugged and left the room abruptly.

'What's his problem?' I asked Gerry, concerned that Josh seemed to have got away with being distinctly rude to his father.

'Oh, I don't know. Exams, I expect. He's right, though; my speciality cooking isn't exactly Michelin guide stuff.'

'They eat, Gerry. Anything beyond is an optional extra.'

'Having said that,' he continued, 'I hope you will be there.'

'When?'

'On Sunday when my parents come over. Any and all culinary contributions are much appreciated.'

Gerry sounded casual, but I sensed this was important.

'I'd love to. Shall I ask Josh what he'd like me to cook? After he's apologised to you, that is?'

'Okay.'

We smiled at each other for a moment, and Gerry held his arms out to me.

'I need a hug,' he said.

'Oh, good.'

'You are wonderful to us.'

'I know.'

'Is that because you love us?'

'Conceivably.'

'Splendid.'

Graham Fellowes called me the next day.

'Madison Brylmer, as I live and breathe,' he said cheerfully as I answered the phone.

'Oh, hello, Graham. How are you? Sharpless going well, I understand. You certainly sounded good at the opening.'

'Yes, fine. Haven't seen much of you lately, though, I was wondering what you're up to.'

'Still doing *Carmen* with Annie at the Coli, starting to prepare *Figaro* for July, and this and that, you know how it goes.'

'Indeed. I'm looking forward to our *Cosi* in the autumn.'

'Me, too. Graham, how did you know to ring me here?'

'Come on, Madsy, you know I keep my ear to the ground.'

'You've been listening very hard then. Only Annie knows.'

'People soon work things out for themselves, you know that,' he laughed. 'Anyway, I had you two sussed out last year.'

I hung up, chuckling. Graham was a loquacious old gossip, but engaging nonetheless.

'Did you mention me to Graham?' I asked Gerry later.

'Not in particular, I don't think. Why?'

He called me here today. I wondered how he knew where he'd find me.'

Gerry shrugged. 'Does it matter?'

'I'm just amazed at how people know things before you even know them yourself sometimes.'

''Tis the way of the world,' Gerry grinned.

'Oh, very profound.'

'Don't make fun of me, Dr Brylmer, I haven't got a PhD like some round here.'

'You do have one or two other valuable assets instead.'

'Shall we check them out?' Gerry suggested, pulling me hard against him.

'Be fools not to.'

I was very nervous as I prepared lunch for Gerry's parents. Ben and I had been singing *Carmen* the previous night, but whilst he enjoyed a leisurely lie in, I busied myself with bringing still a little more order into the McFall home and preparing vegetables. Josh appeared, bleary eyed, whilst I was mixing a port and redcurrant marinade for the lamb steaks.

'Hello, darling. Were Pathologically Awful good, if that's not an oxymoron?' I asked.

'Pathologically Abnormal,' he corrected me. 'Yes, they were cool. Your opera okay?'

'Hmm,' I nodded, crushing garlic into the mixture. 'Are you going to come to see us again before we close?'

'I guess.' Josh poured hot water onto a teabag, which he proceeded to squeeze with his fingers.

'Josh, there are spoons for that.'

'Before which fingers were made,' he countered, dropping the teabag carelessly into the bin. 'What are you making?'

'A marinade for the lamb.'

Josh dipped a finger into the liquid and tasted it appreciatively.

'That's good.'

We were silent as he slurped his tea, gazing out of the kitchen window, and I laid the steaks onto a dish and poured over the marinade. When I looked up, Josh was studying me closely.

I smiled.

'Am I doing it right?' I asked.

'I expect so,' he said, 'you do everything right.'

I laughed shortly. 'Now that would be nice, wouldn't it?'

'But you do,' he insisted. 'You're Superwoman.'

'Josh, I'm very flattered that you think so, but I'm far from it. I try to do what I do well, but that doesn't mean anything in the end. There are people – my mother in particular – who think I've done something so terrible that I'll never be able to make up for it whatever I do, and sometimes I think she's probably right.'

'Leaving your husband and coming to live with us, you mean?' Josh asked.

I nodded.

'But you did that because you love us, didn't you?'

'Yes, but it was at great cost for Andy. Whatever I feel about you and Ben and your dad, I had a commitment to Andy, which I broke. I have to acknowledge that.'

'But you are happy with us, aren't you?' Josh asked.

'Of course, but if it's at the cost of Andy's happiness, it's flawed. You're much too intelligent and thoughtful not to understand what I'm saying, darling. Being with you all is the loveliest thing that has ever happened to me, and I am very fortunate and privileged, but how it all came about was fundamentally wrong and caused great sadness for many people, including, at times, me and Gerry. So please don't think I'm perfect, because I'm not. None of us are.'

'You're perfect for us,' Josh said kindly.

I held out my arms and he sauntered over to accept a hug.

'I love you very much,' I told him.

'I love you, Madsy.'

'Then we're doing okay, aren't we?' Josh nodded and I kissed his cheek.

'Do you feel like being useful?' I asked.

'Perhaps,' he said cautiously.

'Then be an angel and put the vacuum cleaner around. You might even enjoy it.'

Later, Gerry found me, his eyes wide with amazement.

'What *is* Josh doing?'

'What does it look like?'

'Vacuuming the lounge with his headphones on.'

'There you are, you identified the activity correctly,' I laughed.

'But how did you get him to do that?'

'I asked him.'

'Then you'd better give me lessons,' Gerry marvelled, shaking his head in wonderment.

CHAPTER 83

I hung back when Gerry's parents arrived, letting their family greet them before I ventured into the hall. Ben had already dragged his grandfather upstairs to show him something on the computer, and Pauline was fussing over Josh, who looked mildly put out by it all. I said nothing, and just smiled as I moved into the lounge with a tray of mugs. Chatter continued in the hall, and left with nothing to do, I wandered back into the kitchen, wondering how to greet Gerry's mother. I had no idea how much he had told her about our arrangements or my place in their lives, and too late I realised that we should have talked about today's gathering more openly. I had been so surprised and pleased to be included I had dared not jeopardise it with questions. I sighed as I pointlessly looked into a saucepan. There were so many things we were still holding back, and I desperately wanted to deal with them all now, even as I knew that I had to let our relationship develop at Gerry's own pace. Events out of our control may force things to move faster, but I had done enough, and now I had to let time, and Gerry, control things.

My aimless reverie was broken by Gerry's voice.

'I think the kettle's just boiled. Are you ready for coffee?'

Pauline followed him into the kitchen.

'Yes, please, darling,' she said. 'Hello, Madison. How are you coping with this lot?'

I blinked, not expecting a direct question.

'Wonderfully, thank you,' I told her, as I poured water into the cafetière, hoping she would continue the conversation. I was lost for words, deeply conscious that her last sight of me was looking like an escapee from a Dickensian asylum on Christmas Day, and prior to that, a monosyllabic misery by the lake at Glyndebourne. Whatever Gerry had said to her, she must have been wondering what he had let himself in for.

'You're looking lovely,' she said, studying me closely.

Surprised, I glanced at my unremarkable black trousers and bronze top, one that did, I admit, set off my hair particularly well. In a silly moment before Pauline and Richard arrived, Josh had pencilled my eyes with gold eyeliner, and as I caught a glimpse of myself in the mirror I realised I did look good – cheeks faintly flushed and eyes bright.

'Thank you,' I said with real pleasure, and Gerry winked conspiratorially at me.

But I was still quiet and let Gerry take the lead as he chatted to Pauline and tried to encourage Josh to be forthcoming about his GCSEs. 'They're boring' was the most profound evaluation he was able to muster, but his grandmother clearly knew him well enough not to push for more.

'It's looking unnaturally tidy around here,' Pauline joked as we settled in the lounge with coffee, waiting for Ben and Richard to rejoin us.

'Madison does domestic organisation almost as well as she sings,' Gerry grinned. 'We're trying to keep things in better order in between her visits, but we like to make sure she's got something to do when she comes back. Wouldn't want her to feel she had no useful function.'

'Gerry!' Pauline scolded him. 'Poor Madison, she's not your slave.'

'Oh, I rather think she is.' Gerry gave me a meaningful look and I blushed hotly.

Josh sat down next to me on the settee, stretching out his long, black-clad legs before him, and inclining his head to rest on my shoulder.

'I'm Madison's slave,' he told his grandmother.

'I could scarcely believe my eyes,' Gerry laughed. 'I found Josh with a vacuum cleaner in his hands this morning.'

I decided it was time to clarify my position a little. 'Listen guys, I'm starting to feel like Chief Housekeeper here. I think my talents do stretch a little further.'

'Madsy, we're only teasing you,' Josh said softly.

The subject was dropped as Ben and Richard re-emerged, and soon afterwards we ate, and conversation ranged widely over the dining table. I tried to forget the fact that I was sure Gerry's parents were assessing me carefully and joined in or refrained as I would in any other gathering. Josh appeared to have appointed himself my chief protector, and sat at my side throughout lunch, dropping into the conversation so many sentences beginning 'Madison says', or 'Madison does' that it began to sound like an advertising campaign. But it certainly boosted my confidence sufficiently to slip my hand into Gerry's as we reconvened in the lounge to watch Josh open his birthday presents, and Gerry entwined his fingers around mine easily, keeping them there until events forced him to move.

'Ben, we'd love to hear you sing,' Pauline appealed to her grandson. 'Would you do that for us before we go home?'

Ben adopted a causal tone.

'If you like. Depends if Dad wants to play.'

'I imagine I might be able to summon up the energy,' Gerry answered languidly. 'What would you like to sing?'

They settled on O for the Wings of a Dove, which Ben proceeded to offer with an expression of such contrived innocence that Josh, safely obscured from his grandparents' view, made pass the sick bag gestures to me, and I had to concentrate very hard on not laughing out loud.

'It's Madison's turn now,' Ben pronounced when he'd taken his bows.

'Oh, no,' I protested. 'Pauline and Richard haven't come to hear me.'

'Please, we'd love to, if you're willing,' Pauline objected. 'It's a cheek, I know, when we should pay for tickets to the opera to hear you again, but it would be lovely.'

I looked at Gerry questioningly as he sat at the piano, fingers twitching, waiting for action.

'I'm not up to anything too dramatic after lunch,' I told them. 'Would you settle for something downmarket?'

'Oh, no, I sense Abba coming on,' Gerry moaned.

'Anything would be wonderful,' Pauline looked at me encouragingly.

So not entirely to wind up Gerry, I dug out *Someone Else's Story* from *Chess*, which my teenage voice student had been learning and sung it with gusto in what Gerry sneeringly called my pop singer's voice.

'If you want Rossini coloratura you'll have to wait till I'm warmed up and not so full of food,' I told Gerry's parents, as they clapped happily.

'Oh, that was lovely,' said Pauline, 'so natural and heartfelt, and just for us. Thank you, Madison. Do you and Ben ever sing duets?'

'No, I might show Madison up,' Ben pronounced, with a smirk.

'Our repertoire doesn't exactly overlap,' I told Pauline. 'We've messed around with Lloyd Webber's *Pie Jesu* a few times when we were kicking about backstage, but that's it, really.'

'Can we hear it now?'

'Madison only sings the second part,' Ben told them. 'It's a showpiece for the top treble.'

'Then how can we resist hearing it?' his grandmother beamed.

'Oh, all right then,' Ben agreed, clearly satisfied by this show of grandmotherly devotion. He found the music for Gerry, who looked at it with disdain.

'Another trite pastische,' he said scornfully, beginning to play.

I let Ben take centre stage in the bow of the piano, whilst I sat in the window seat behind him. His voice rang out pure and clear as I watched him with love filling my heart. I could not imagine loving a child more were he my own flesh, and even in the relatively short time I had known Gerry's wonderful sons, they had come to feel as close to me as if they were my own. I would give my life for each of them, and their happiness meant more to me than my own. I drew breath to harmonise with Ben, moderating my voice to allow him to dominate, accompanying him with my darker tones, and as we reached the final bars of the duet, my unreliable emotions got the better of me, and a single tear traced its familiar course down my cheek. I brushed it away, hoping no one had seen, but as I did, I caught Gerry's eye, only to see his also glittering with unshed tears. I was moved beyond words, and in the silence that followed Gerry's final chord, it was clear that even Josh had been touched by hearing our voices, so different in every way, blend in a unity that was not just musical, but rooted in a commitment to each other which had defied the odds. Only Gerry might know the thoughts that went through my mind in that moment, but the atmosphere was charged with an emotion that none could miss. Ben turned to me with a grin.

'Well done, Mads. I don't think I drowned you out completely, did I?'

'No, darling, I just about held my own.'

'You're not crying again, are you?' he asked disdainfully, coming over to me in the window.

'Probably.'

'You're such a girl.' He pulled at my hands, leaning back on his heels, the innocent choirboy look soon dispatched.

'Well spotted,' I smiled, kissing the back of his hand. 'I'll put the kettle on.' I got up to head for the kitchen.

'I'll help.' Pauline rose to follow and, with no good reason to refuse, I let her troop in my wake.

'Don't you think Ben's sounding on particularly good form?' I asked genially, for want of something else to say.

'Yes, I do,' she agreed, watching me fill the kettle. 'He told me that you're teaching him the Britten for later in the summer.'

'Did he? He's very casual about it, as he often is about things in general. He won't let me work on it for longer than half an hour at a go, but he's very quick, and we've got stacks of time. Do you think anybody will want cake, or will they all be full up from lunch? Silly question, of course they'll want some.'

'True,' she laughed. We sere silent for a moment as I rummaged for plates.

'Madsy?' Pauline spoke quietly. 'Sorry, is it all right to call you that?'

'Of course. I answer to a range of derivatives.' I smiled encouragingly at her, though my heart was pounding.

'Thank you for loving our boys,' she said simply, and as she looked me in the eye, I could see she was as nervous as I was. 'All three of them,' she added. 'They are very fortunate to have met you. I hope you're planning on sticking around.'

'If they'll have me, I'm planning on staying forever,' I told her.

'Oh good; I thought you might be, but I just wanted to be sure.'

'I love them all so much,' I said.

'I can see that. It's beautiful. We're so grateful to you.'

'Don't be. I'm very happy.'

Pauline held her hand out to me, and I took it gladly.

'Oh, Madison, I could see how much you loved Gerry when we met you at Glyndebourne. You barely spoke a word, and he'd clearly done something to upset you, but the love in your eyes when you looked at him made me want to cry. It was so naked, and you were in so much pain, but you were still beautiful to Ben. I wanted to slap my son, I can tell you. Here was this lovely girl, utterly devoted to him and Ben, and I thought he was going to see it all frittered away. I'm very glad he didn't, glad that you held on and didn't give up on him then and there.'

'I tried to do that at the beginning of the year, and I failed utterly,' I told her.

'Good.'

'Pauline, you should know that to all intents and purposes I'm still married. I have left my husband to be with Gerry. You may not think so kindly of me if you know all the background.'

'It's none of my business, Madison. You and Gerry, and your husband, I don't doubt, are all intelligent adults who can negotiate that without my interference. Selfishly, I'm just glad to see my son and grandsons being cared for so wonderfully by a woman who adores them. That will do for me.'

'My mother thinks rather differently,' I told her. 'She's very upset with me and has effectively withdrawn. I haven't seen her since the beginning of April, and I don't know when I'll do so again.'

Pauline nodded slowly. 'If that's her way of dealing with it, and expressing what she feels, there's nothing you can do about that, is there? You'll just have to wait for her to come round in her own time.'

'Perhaps she won't.'

'That's not likely. Speaking as a mother, I can assure you she won't hold out forever. You're her daughter and she'll want to see you.'

'I hope so.'

I held my tongue and said nothing to Gerry about my conversation with Pauline. I guessed he'd had his own with her and that in any case the day's events spoke for themselves. I decided they definitely had done when Gerry put his arms around me and pulled me close as we lay in bed, insinuating his long legs around mine.

'Hmm,' he murmured into my hair.

'Does that mean anything in particular?' I asked him.

'No, just everything in general. You are wonderful to us, beautiful, kind, sexy, and accomplished, and I love you.'

'And I you.' I sighed with happiness.

'I did have the odd inkling that you might do.'

We sang our last *Carmen* of the current season soon afterwards. It would be revived in the autumn, but in the interim I would not see Annie. She was off to Berlin for most of the summer, singing Frugola, Principessa and Zita in *Il Trittico*. After working with her so closely for over a year, and having shared so much, it was an emotional parting. She flew to Germany two days after the curtain fell on *Carmen*, and our last night on stage was the only chance we would have to say our farewells. Everyone put two hundred per cent into the final show, milking every moment of enjoyment from both music and drama, but the knowledge that we would be joining together again on the same production in less than six months' time made the final curtain less bittersweet than closings usually were. But saying goodbye to Annie till the autumn was another matter. Ben and Gerry kicked their heels as they waited for me to tear myself away.

'Darling Annie, I can't believe I won't see you for so long. How could I have got through this last year without you?'

'Oh, quite easily, I should think,' she laughed. 'After all, you never took any of my advice.'

'I'm sure I did now and then,' I objected.

'For about five minutes at a time, maybe,' she allowed. 'But if you're happy, I'm glad you didn't.'

'I am,' I told her. 'It's something of a qualified happiness, I know, but I am happy. One day, perhaps I'll wake up and be completely secure in Gerry's love, and all my guilt over Andy and Megan will be resolved, but I wouldn't change anything that's happened if it meant I couldn't be with Gerry. I know that's awful and selfish, but it's the way it is, and I can't deny it.'

'Do you remember I told you not to let Gerry have all the power?' Annie asked me.

I nodded.

'I think you still let him control you, Madsy. He may have made some kind of commitment to you, but it's on his terms.'

'Annie, it doesn't matter. I fell in love with him, I wanted to live with him and Ben and Josh, I wanted him to love me, too, and that's what I've got. What more could I ask for?'

'Not to keep looking over your shoulder to check that he's still there.'

I looked at Annie quizzically.

'Not physically, of course, but emotionally you're still doing it.'

I sighed and remained silent.

'But I've said enough on the topic,' Annie smiled. 'I'll shut up for one. Thank you for your friendship, too, Madsy. It's meant an awful lot, not least during my breast scare. Still got both of 'em, eh?'

'Absolutely, darling, even if they're not as big as mine.'

We hugged warmly, and Ben rapidly appeared to hurry me along.

'Come on, Mads. Dad wants to go.'

Annie gave me an ironic look.

'See what I mean?' she said drolly, and we laughed.

'But they're mine, Annie,' I told her.

'Then you'd better go when they call.'

We hugged again, and I was gone.

'Annie okay?' Gerry asked as we got into the car.

'Yes. I'm just going to miss her so much.'

Gerry patted my knee. 'You'll just have to make do with us then, won't you?'

'I guess,' I grinned at him.

'Good show tonight, guys,' he told us both, looking at Ben through the rear-view mirror.

'It was okay,' Ben responded nonchalantly.

I slipped my hand onto Gerry's thigh and rested my head on his shoulder.

'Hello,' I whispered.

'Hello,' he murmured back.

And as we drove through the familiar London streets, I let Ben's and Gerry's chat wash over me, until their voices, in different octaves, but alike in confident tone, blended into one, and I slept.

CHAPTER 84

I managed to speak briefly to Andy the following week. I caught him on his mobile at The Dragon, and he was reserved, but ready enough to tell me about Joe's latest job for him. He and Budzynski were visiting the provincial venues which were hosting *Puff the Magic Dragon*, making a couple of trips each week, and moves seemed to be afoot to take *Elushka* to the Donmar Warehouse for a short, but nevertheless significant, run.

'If it happens, we'll let you know,' he told me. 'With a bit of luck you may be able to sing for us again.'

'That would be nice.'

'You going to Cornwall soon?' he asked casually.

'Not till the end of July.'

'Okay.'

We were silent.

'So you're all right then?' I asked tentatively.

'Yes, not bad. And you, too?'

'Yes, I'm fine.'

There was nothing more to say, but I felt faintly reassured as I hung up. Andy was still at The Dragon; more than that, he was apparently enjoying it, and that could only be positive. I didn't expect him to forgive me, but I could hope that he could find some happiness as I had done.

I went back to the task I had been engaged in before I'd called Andy, sorting through piles of sheet music in Gerry's music room, and gradually filing and shelving them, and in so doing, actually finding some space for some of my own books. It was a long job that I tackled an hour or two at a time, finding unexpected treasures as I did so. Leafing through a copy of Scarlatti songs, an old concert programme dropped onto my knee. I'd found several already as I'd sifted through thirty years' worth of music and scores, stowing them in a box file until Gerry could allocate them a new home. Most had held my attention for a few moments as I'd read earlier biographies of Gerry, and noted with interest singers who he'd worked with long before I had come into his orbit. I expected to read nothing of greater import as I looked at the red cover that had fallen into my lap, but the words stood out boldly, and I caught my breath, heart beating heavily, as I read. 'Dominican Concerts Presents...' ran the heading, and below it three names: Morna Kingston (Soprano), Susan McFall (Flute), Gerard McFall (Piano). I opened the pages, staring with fascination at the black and white photograph of three musicians in their early thirties. I recognised Susan from a more recent photo I'd seen in Josh's bedroom. She was deeply glamorous, with masses of dark hair and huge dark eyes that gazed soulfully out of the picture. It was clear from where Josh had inherited his good looks; Ben was the image of his dad, but Josh had his mother's beauty. Gerry looked callow and youthful, not my Gerry at all. I liked how he had aged. With more hair and a smoother complexion he belonged to someone else in another era. But that was just it, of course. He had lived a long and full life before he had met me, and had shared so much with this beautiful woman who had borne his children. How could I ever catch up? How could I ever mean as much to Gerry as she must have done? I felt overwhelmed with new fears and doubts. I had chosen to leave my husband to be with Gerry, but he had not chosen me in the same way. If Susan had not died, she would still be his wife, and it would be she who slept in his arms, and who cared for Ben and Josh. Gerry would not have looked twice at me and certainly not considered making a future with me at her expense. I was here by default, and I had shaken heaven and earth to be in even this tenuous position.

Sick and trembling, I buried my face in my hands and, alone in the house, I wept aloud. My mind, whirling with desperate imaginings, was convinced that Gerry could do nothing but compare me unfavourably with Susan, that he still saw Vanessa, that he flirted and schemed with the myriad women who passed through his life each day. I cried until I was exhausted and even then remained on the floor, my head resting on my arms atop the piano stool. For a long while I sat utterly still, considering my options: to stay or to go. Only the first option had any appeal, but I wondered still whether to return to Putney, to wait and see if Gerry would come to find me. But if he didn't, what would I do? Come back of my own accord, I knew, so what was the point of going? To test Gerry and to precipitate another crisis?

I was taken aback by the sound of the front door opening and closing. I sat up hurriedly, but had no time to compose myself before Gerry's head appeared around the door.

'Hello. We finished early, so I thought I'd get home before the boys arrive.'

I kept my head averted, anxious that he should not see that I'd been crying yet again.

'That's nice, sweetheart. I'll be finished here and be out to talk to you in a minute.'

I rummaged vaguely around in the music spread out before me, my concentration completely shattered.

'Okay.' Gerry stayed in the doorway and I could feel his eyes fixed on me. I kept looking down.

'Are you all right?' he asked finally.

'Yes, of course. I'll be there shortly.'

'Madsy, look at me.'

I looked up quickly, smiling before turning back to the box file of programmes. Gerry crossed the room and I knew there was no escape. He knelt by me on the floor and turned my reluctant face towards him.

'You've been crying. What is it?'

'Nothing, it's fine,' I prevaricated.

Gerry looked at the music at my feet, trying to establish the source of my distress. His eyes alighted on the red cover of the programme still waiting to be filed. He didn't need to pick it up to know what had unaccountably upset me.

'Oh, Madsy,' he said softly.

I met his eye at last, and he took my hand, softly kissing my knuckles. I gave in to tears again, holding my arms out to be hugged.

'I can never compete, never compare, never be a real mum to Ben and Josh,' I cried.

'There is no competition and no comparison, darling,' he said tenderly. 'You and Susan couldn't be more different. She was wonderful and lovely, just as you are, but in a different way, so I don't think of her when I look at you, or make love to you, I just think of you.'

'But you must still think of her sometimes,' I objected.

'Of course I think of her. She was an enormous part of my life for many years, but I don't wish I were with her rather than you. I would never have wanted her to suffer and leave us as she did, but it happened and we had to live with it and move on. And then we met you, at just the right point: not too soon and not too late, and now it's our time, and I'm glad we didn't miss it because it took me so long to recognise it.'

I looked at Gerry incredulously.

'Is that what you really think?'

'Of course. And as for being a real mum to Ben and Josh, you're wise enough to know that unconditional love doesn't necessarily come with biological descent, any more than it depends on it. I know what you give to them and so do they.'

'They give it to me, too,' I snuffled.

'I know they do; I observe closely.'

I smiled tearily and touched his cheek. 'You weren't supposed to know I'd been crying. I wasn't expecting you yet,' I told him.

'But then I wouldn't have been able to say this to you,' Gerry said pragmatically.

'I wish I could be as secure as you are,' I sighed.

'In what way?' he asked.

'You can't possibly have a moment of doubt about me. You know I have given you my heart forever.'

'So you think I don't worry that someone might take you away from me?'

'Why should you?' I asked, puzzled.

'Because you might decide one day to go back to your husband.'

'Absolutely not.'

Gerry shrugged. 'Okay, but someone else might fall in love with you, and you might think that you're better off with them.'

'Why on earth should I think that?'

'I don't know, but that's not the point. The point is that I don't want you to leave us and so I am fearful sometimes, just as you are.'

'I would never have thought it,' I told him.

'Madison, you're so lovely and charming and cultured. You're beautiful and sexy. You have a way with men of a certain age – old crocks like me – and they want you. I see it all the time. Graham Fellowes would have you in his bed in a twinkling if he thought you'd go. I see men undress you with their eyes and lust after the special kind of loving they know they'd get from you. But you're mine and they can't have you.'

I giggled, burying my face in Gerry's shoulder.

'I don't want anyone but you, anyway,' I said.

'I hope not.'

I looked up at him, and we kissed for a gratifyingly long time, until my nerve endings began to tingle, and Gerry sighed deeply.

'I love you,' I told him.

'I love you.' Gerry ran his hands under the thin cotton fabric of my summer dress, pressing them against the warmth of my thighs. My skin burned with pleasure and anticipation.

'Oh, baby, how could I ever want anyone else, when you make me feel like this?' I asked him softly.

'Difficult to imagine, I agree,' he said, looking modest. 'Now, by my estimation, we've got about half an hour until the boys get back. Do you think we can accomplish something useful in that time?'

'You can accomplish something useful in about three minutes if you carry on like that,' I told him.

'Umm, is that so?' he murmured against my mouth, 'And then I'd miss the fun.'

'It would leave us still with twenty-seven minutes to make sure you weren't left out, so to speak.'

'Sounds like a good deal when you put it that way.'

So we proceeded to discover just how much could be achieved in thirty minutes when you really concentrate.

CHAPTER 85

One-year-old Gabrielle Swallow stared in fascination as I sang *Voi Che Sapete*. To Lizzie's delight, her little daughter had emerged from the womb with an instinctive love of music and whenever Lizzie played she was lulled immediately into enraptured silence. Fortunately, she particularly enjoyed singing and Lizzie's colleagues provided ample opportunity for Gaby to learn an extensive operatic repertoire early in life.

We were at Exeter House, working through the *Figaro* score, ensuring that Cherubino was firmly back into my brain and voice well before we started our short intensive rehearsal period in June. But we also talked a good deal between numbers, played with Gaby, and drank several cups of tea. Lizzie played the last notes of the aria and turned to check on her daughter, feeling under the piano stool to retrieve an empty box as she did so.

'Madison, why have you got a computer game called *Death Raiders in Outer Space #2*?'

'Oh, there it is.' I took it from her. 'It's Ben's. We were playing it here the other day.'

Lizzie shook her head in wonderment.

'Your life is seriously weird these days, Mads. When are you going to move in with them permanently?' she asked, idly tinkling the keys.

'Soon, I guess. I like being here part of the time, though, and staying with them other days. I'm going to have to make a decision about it, but while Andy's living at The Dragon and doesn't seem anxious to move back here, there's no immediate hurry.'

'The prospect of living with two young boys must be a real culture shock,' Lizzie laughed.

'It's pure bliss.'

We were cut short by the ringing phone. It was Andy.

'Hi, Mads.' He sounded quiet, but not particularly unhappy.

'Oh, hi. You okay?'

'I wondered if I could come over?' he asked.

'Sure. Do you want to collect something?'

'I will do, but I really wanted to talk to you. I'm about half an hour away, if that's all right.'

Lizzie was dangling a stuffed pig over Gaby's head when I went back into the music room.

'I'm sorry, Liz, we're going to have to abandon play for the day. Andy wants to come over; I didn't think I could refuse.'

We packed up all the equipment apparently necessary for taking a baby ten yards outside your own front door, and I tidied up and boiled the kettle again as I waited for Andy to arrive.

He looked better than he had at the final performance of *Elushka*. He had lost weight, but it suited his large frame, and he had made an effort with his clothes, which were smart and coordinated – a rare sight for me these days, *haute couture* not being a priority for the McFall tribe.

'How are you doing?' I asked tentatively.

'I'm okay. Joe's got me hard at work. We're off to Birmingham with *Puff* soon, and we've got projects for the autumn on the go. It's fine, Madsy. I'm enjoying it, despite, well, you know, everything.'

'Good.'

'And is the flat still okay? I mean, if you want to move back here, you only have to say. I can go to Dulwich any time.'

'It's fine. I like the company at The Dragon. There's no hurry, Mads.' He looked sad and I didn't know what else to say.

Handing Andy a mug I gestured toward the lounge, and sitting on opposite sofas we studied each other expectantly. This visit had clearly been a tremendous effort for him, but for a moment it seemed that he had lost courage. Then, taking a deep breath, he leant forward.

'It was hard for me to come here today,' he said honestly, 'but I've been doing a huge amount of thinking, as I expect you have, too.'

I nodded, but didn't move to interrupt him.

'I know I've got a long way to go until I finally come to terms with what's happened,' he continued. 'I don't imagine I'll ever be able to say that I don't regret it or that I don't wish it hadn't all worked out the way it has done, but in the last month I've started to rationalise things a little more and I need to tell you what I've been thinking and feeling.'

Andy looked as me, as if asking permission to do so.

'Okay,' I said quietly.

'I still care for you, Mads, and part of me knows very well that if you said you were giving up on Gerry and wanted us to get together again, I would be delighted, and more than prepared to give it a go. But I know that's not going to happen. I'm speaking hypothetically here because, more importantly, what I've come to realise is that I don't think it would work anyway. Not because I couldn't forgive you, because I have already.'

I felt humbled and turned my gaze from Andy's serious face.

'It's not that I wouldn't at least try to make a genuine effort, but after all these years, I think I've realised that we were in the wrong relationship with each other.'

'What do you mean?' I asked. 'That we never were right for each other?'

'In a way, yes. I looked to you to be a mother, a helper, and a friend. We fulfilled all kinds of roles for each other, but ultimately, we weren't very good at being husband and wife. I'd have made you a great brother, but I haven't been much of a husband.'

I was stunned by Andy's insight, which I recognised immediately as being absolutely correct. I moved to speak, but he hushed me quickly.

'Hold on, Mads. In the end, I don't think we could ever bring out the best in each other, because I was overly dependent on you and you allowed me to be dependent. It's not your nature to sit back and to let people make their own mistakes. You have to bail them out, and that's what you did for me. I was grateful that you did, but I know it didn't make for an equal partnership. You're so capable and independent I never really felt you needed me, not like you need Gerry.'

We were silent as Gerry's name hovered between us.

'I can see that Gerry, as much as he irritates me with his arrogant and cocky manner, is what you need. He's your muse in some way, I think, and he's done things for you that I could never do, however many years we were together. I don't mean because you work together, but what he gives you lights you up inside. I've never done that to you Mads, I know, and I can't begrudge it you if you've found it with Gerry. I only hope he's grateful for all the love you'll give to him. If he takes you for granted or hurts you, I'd want to kill him. He's so lucky to have you and I'm afraid he won't appreciate you properly. But that's the risk you've chosen to take, I guess.'

Andy stopped, staring at his hands, avoiding my astonished gaze.

'Andy, how did you come to all these conclusions?'

'They're not wrong, are they? I've had a lot of time to think, not just over the last month, but ever since you started seeing Gerry, working with him, looking after his kids. I could see it all happening and I've had as long as you had to reach the conclusion that your future lay with him and not me. It wasn't a hard conclusion to reach, Mads.'

'Andy, I'm so sorry. I don't know what happened, really. One day I woke up and everything had changed. I suddenly saw life within parameters that were defined by Gerry, and later by Josh and Ben, too. I didn't try to fight it very much, I admit, only for those couple of months earlier this year, but that simply showed me I couldn't go back to where I was – to where we were. I feel terrible. I would never have chosen for this to happen, but I can never go back either. As, incredibly, you have discovered, Gerry is the man I've needed all my life. The dynamic of my relationship with him couldn't be more different than ours; I'm not the one in charge anymore, I've got less power, less control. I think we're balancing out a bit now, but I like him being in control, anyway. He wouldn't be Gerry if he didn't dominate every situation he's in and oddly for me, I find that somehow I like that.'

Andy smiled wryly.

'You didn't get much of that with me, did you? But I'm learning, too, Mads. I'm coping better at The Dragon than I thought I would – than you thought I would, I'm sure, although you've never said as much. Even without you, now I think I can handle it. Every day when I complete a task, however small, and it goes well, when I know I've done it right, I feel good. I couldn't have done this job once, but all the years with you have finally shown me the value of self-discipline.'

I wiped away the silent tears that had fallen during Andy's speech.

'We did have some good times, didn't we?' I said.

'Oh, goodness, Madsy, we had some great times! But I know I didn't make you feel much of a woman. We were like a pair of kids in school; you were the bright, obedient one who helped the class fool with his homework and covered for him when the teacher was cross. It was a comfortable

503

relationship for me and I didn't fight it, but it's no wonder that we didn't have much interest in sex and romance and all that jazz.'

I flushed. We had never successfully addressed this issue, and I was embarrassed even now, but Andy pressed on.

'I hate to say this, but I can see that old Gerry does something for you in that department I never did, even at the beginning. I remember being backstage after *Tito* last autumn, standing with you and Megan, and he came out of his dressing room and just looked at you as if there was no one else there. There he was, fifty years old, balding, a sartorial disaster area, looking completely shattered, and you responded to him as if he was a peacock on display.'

'Oh, Andy, please.' I was mortified.

'The attraction between the pair of you was so powerful that even an oaf like me could sense it. Megan did, of course. We both knew that you and Gerry were inevitable, although even Megan didn't say it outright.'

'Andy, if you thought all this, why did you never say so at the time?'

'Because I hoped that it would all go away. I tried to underestimate its power, Mads, even though I knew I was way out of my league once Gerry had laid claim to your affections. I could see how unhappy you were in the winter, when you and he stopped seeing each other. If anything, that confirmed to me what had been happening between you. After all the time you'd spent with him, suddenly you didn't even sing a single concert for him, and you were so miserable that even Annie couldn't cheer you up. I knew the day you started seeing him again, even though it didn't all come out till that first night of *Carmen*. You'd gone out in the morning, not quite as subdued as you'd been for the previous two months, but still not your old self, and the next day you were radiant again. I fought for you in those next three weeks, you know that. I fought harder than ever before in my life, but it was no surprise to me when you couldn't pretend any longer.'

'Andy, I'm so sorry,' I said quietly.

He crossed the room to sit next to me, taking my hand in his.

'I didn't come here to make you feel bad, honestly, Madsy. I wanted you to know that, actually, I do understand. I don't like it, but I understand it. I'm letting you go today, Mads. I can do that now. Be happy with Gerry, he's the man you love and need, and who makes you blossom. Just tell me if he messes you about and I'll come and sort him out.'

'Andy, I want you to be happy, too. Happy at The Dragon, and wherever else you go; happy with someone who needs you in the way I need Gerry.'

'I'll get there, Madsy, I promise. Today is healing in itself. It's not to let you off the hook, but for me to be able to tell you to your face that I'm setting you emotionally free to be with that joker, if it is him you really want.'

I giggled despite myself.

'Just try to get him to put on a bit of bulk. Swimming might help,' Andy smiled, and we laughed with genuine warmth, and hugged each other.

'Andy, what can I say? I don't deserve this.'

'None of us get what we deserve, Mads, because essentially we don't deserve anything. I'm finally leaning to be realistic about that. I couldn't fight what happened between you and Gerry, so I've stopped trying and I feel better for it.'

A load lifted from my heart. Andy had offered me the greatest gift he could give me, not just his forgiveness and release, but the fact that he could envisage a hopeful future ahead of him, too. I realised how deeply I had underestimated him and I turned to him now in gratitude.

'Andy, I can never thank you enough for coming here today, for being able to say all this. I wish there were something I could give you in return.'

'There is,' he said decisively. 'Let's really try to be friends. I've never thought it possible when people claimed to be friends with their ex, but let's make an effort to be a couple who pull it off. You and I have been, above all, good friends, and that's perhaps what we should have stayed all those years ago. Perhaps we can have all the benefits of friendship now without the guilt of not being able to get all the other stuff right.'

'I'd like that.'

'I don't think I can be friends with the maestro, though,' he laughed, 'or with those ridiculously overconfident children.'

'You don't have to be,' I smiled, wanting to defend my lovely boys against this unfair description, but I thought it best not to push my luck.

We hugged gratefully as Andy left, promising to be in touch about the flat, and, more importantly, about our forthcoming productions. We were determined to keep supporting one another. As I watched him drive away I realised that Andy had revealed more of himself than he had done for a very long time, and he seemed more solid, more mature and purposeful than I had ever seen him. In some strange way perhaps, all three of us had been brought face to face with who we really were and what we needed to do to grow and change, and we were responding in our own way. I liked to think that there might even be a happy ending for us all.

CHAPTER 86

Andy's visit liberated me in a way I hadn't known I needed. That evening I packed four large holdalls with personal belongings and took them back to Dulwich in a cab. Gerry looked them over with interest.

'Are you staying, then?' he said, eyebrows raised.

'I'm getting a bit weary of being a nomad. It seems silly. If it's all right with you, I'll bring most of my personal stuff over this week.'

'Of course it's all right with me, Madison,' Gerry said. 'I thought the idea was that you were coming to live with us, not visit now and then. Let's take the car tomorrow and get the lot.'

I put my arms round him gratefully.

'As long as you still want me.'

'Madison Brylmer, would you like me to show you how much I want you?' He tickled me and I tried to escape his grasp but he pulled me back to him and we kissed lingeringly.

'I love you. I miss you when you're not here,' Gerry murmured.

'I miss you, too.'

'So shall we stop messing about and start being a proper family?' he asked.

'Yes, please.'

So our life in the rambling old house on Dulwich Common entered a new phase. True to his word, the next day Gerry took me over to Putney and we loaded up the estate car. I didn't just take music, clothes, books and my computer, but things that would stamp my identity on the house: candles, plants, some ceramic pieces, a favourite painting, and my show photographs and posters. Gerry said little, but offered no objection, watching me quietly as I began to turn the old storeroom at the top of the house into my study/music room. I'd need to bring my piano at some point, but I used Gerry's keyboard for the time being, and in no time the little room looked as if I had been there for years.

I even began to send out my change of address, and the first day I received a letter addressed to Dr Madison Brylmer at Thurlow Park Road, SE21, I felt a warm thrill of pleasure and wondered why I'd taken so long to make this final step. Even better, Annie, in Berlin, sent a card addressed simply to Madison and Gerry. Gerry found me crying quietly over it, a silly grin on my face.

'You okay?' He looked at me closely.

I handed him the card. 'Look.'

'It's from Annie.'

'Yes, but see who it's addressed to.'

'Us.'

'Isn't that lovely?' I sobbed happily.

Gerry smiled his lazy grin, raising his eyebrows in amusement.

'You are funny, little one,' he said, but I knew he understood my pleasure.

With fresh confidence, I thought it might be time to introduce some old friends to my new life. Thus far, the only real friends who'd kept in touch were Lizzie and Annie, but they hadn't been Andy's friends, too, and so they had no divided loyalties to trouble them. Now I made a tentative stab at inviting Sophie and Jim over to Dulwich, but I was met with a polite but firm refusal.

'Oh, hello, Mads.' Sophie sounded awkward. 'How are you?'

508

'I'm very well, Sophie. I'd love to see you both, and wondered if you and Jim would like to come for dinner. You can meet Gerry and the boys and we can catch up a bit.'

'We're tied up this week,' she said cautiously.

'Oh, well, let's make a date for a week or so ahead,' I suggested blithely.

'Can I ring you? Jim's very busy at the moment and, well, it's all rather tricky actually.'

I recognised a brush off when I heard one so I let her off the hook.

'Fine, Sophie. Call me whenever you're ready.'

I gave her my new home number and rang off despondently.

Danielle was even more blunt.

'What are you thinking of, Madison? That we can all get together as if nothing's happened? Steve and Andy are closer than ever now working at The Restless Dragon, and Andy needs all the support he can get. To see you would be like a smack in the face to him. I'll never understand what you've done; I thought you and Andy were as solid as a rock. But then you've always acted as if you were superior to him, haven't you? Now you've found someone who you think is on your level and you ditch Andy like a pair of old socks.'

'Dani, it's nothing like that at all,' I protested feebly.'

'I don't want to hear what it's like, Mads, however you've rationalised it to yourself.'

So that was another door firmly closed in my face, and Megan, too, remained silent. I hoped that she would eventually filter back into my life, but it had to be on her terms, so she would feel there was no danger of my thinking she had approved my new life.

I told Gerry about my disappointing phone calls as we lay in bed that night. I'd pulled back the covers better to admire his long, lean body, trailing my fingers absently over his arm and chest.

'I'm sorry to hear that, sweetheart,' Gerry sympathised. 'At least you tried to make the connection again. If they don't want to pursue it, there's nothing else you can do,' he added pragmatically.

I knew that whilst Gerry was genuinely sympathetic, he would see no point in labouring the point, so I just nodded silently.

'You'll meet new people,' he said, 'like you met Annie.'

'Oh, yes, Annie's worth ten of anyone else.'

'Except me, I hope,' Gerry teased.

'You're worth more than the whole world and everyone in it,' I said seriously.

I ran my hand over the flat of his stomach, his slender hips and thighs, coming to rest in the warmth between his legs, and I felt him begin to harden under my gentle palm.

'Oh, Madison,' he sighed, and I drew closer to him, sliding my leg over his hips and pulling him against me. He stroked the soft flesh of my inner thighs, gently tracing his fingers over the secret part of me that was already trembling at his touch.

'Gerard McFall, do you have any idea what you do to me?' I whispered.

'I hope it's something approximating what you do to me.'

As his fingers moved to explore further I reached to persuade him inside me.

'Hmm, just you wait,' he murmured, and proceeded to use his beautiful musician's hands to take me to levels of pleasure as only he could do.

CHAPTER 87

June was a quiet month. I had a couple of concerts but otherwise I could spend time preparing music for the summer and autumn; we would go into rehearsal for *Cosi Fan Tutte* soon after we returned from Cornwall. Gerry had some remaining performances of *Butterfly* and several corporate and church gigs, so he was pleased that I could be around for the boys in the evening. They had accepted my presence with the equanimity of youth, treating me with easy casualness, and I hoped that I would quickly understand their various moods. I knew I tended towards overprotectiveness, wanting to make everything all right for them all the time, and I tried hard to give them space to let them come to me of their own accord if they felt miserable or in need of comfort or company. As Josh's GCSE exams continued and he seemed at a loss as to how he should revise effectively, I tentatively suggested that we might work together and, to my pleasure, he seemed glad to do so. So each day we sat for an hour or so as I tested him and helped him to make fresh revision notes. His concentration and interest came in short bursts, but I was hopeful that his natural wit would see him through the exams.

Each day I woke with a fresh sense of amazement and wonder. I loved to gaze at Gerry as he lay beside me, incredulous that I slept every night beside the man who only twelve months previously I had loved with such hopeless despair. Now my love was replete with joy, and my desire for

Gerry no longer painful longing, but alight with delicious anticipation. I was coming to accept that he would never be as demonstrative as I was, forever wanting to touch and hold him, and that the words of love that fell so freely from my lips came more slowly from him. But I knew he loved me and that love was all the richer for being so hard won.

Nearly three weeks after Andy had been to see me, Josh and I were working on history revision. It was a subject of which we were both particularly fond, and we worked light-heartedly, knowing this was likely to be one of Josh's more successful examinations. We were grappling with the finer points of the Vietnam conflict when the peal of the doorbell broke the quiet afternoon. We looked at each other in irritation; Gerry's working life, and mine, too, were so rigidly scheduled that we rarely had unexpected callers – everyone made an appointment.

'I'll get it.' Josh rose from his chair. 'It's bound to be someone for dad trying to catch him on the hop.'

I studied Josh's scrappy notes as he shambled off, only faintly aware of the low murmur of conversation in the hall. I looked up in surprise as Josh appeared again, clearly alarmed.

'What is it, darling?' I asked.

My answer was in the shape of two police officers, male and female, hats in hand and grave expressions on their faces. I hurried to stand, the chair scraping back loudly.

'Can I help?'

'Dr Brylmer?' the female officer asked.

'Yes.' I was short; whatever this was about I wanted over quickly, unhappy that Josh was clearly worried.

'We understand that you are currently resident here, but that you have previously been resident at 145 Exeter House, Putney, and you are married to, but separated from, Mr Andrew Brylmer.'

'Yes.' Her formality was irritating me.

'And this is…?' She looked at Josh.

'Josh McFall. He lives here. He's my partner's son. Could you please tell us what this is about? Is Gerry all right?'

Josh blanched and I held my hand out to him reassuringly. He didn't take it, but stood rigidly at my side, looking mutinously at the police officers.

'And Gerry would be?' the male officer asked.

'My dad, for fuck's sake,' Josh replied angrily. 'What the hell do you want?'

'It's okay, darling,' I soothed, raising my eyebrows at the officers. 'Could we get on with this?'

'Dr Brylmer, you might like to sit down.' The woman officer indicated our seats at the table, glancing over Josh's books with the eye of a practised observer. History revision was probably the last thing she expected a sixteen-year-old glam rocker and his father's lover to be doing together.

'No, thank you.'

She shrugged. I was clearly irritating her, too, but she had to remain professional.

'As you wish. Dr Brylmer, I'm afraid we have some rather bad news for you.'

Josh and I instinctively drew closer.

'Are you happy for the young man to be present?' she asked. 'Or shall PC Martin...?' She gestured toward the door. I was furious.

'Does this concern Josh's father?' I asked between clenched teeth.

'No.'

'Just get on with it, then.'

'Dr Brylmer, are you aware that your estranged husband was visiting Birmingham this week?'

'Yes. He and Joe Budzynski have been there with *Puff the Magic Dragon*.'

I was glad to be able to say this with confidence. Andy and I had spoken on the phone three times since his visit to me in Putney, and our conversations had given me hope that we could be friends as we carved out new lives for ourselves.

'I'm sorry to have to tell you that Mr Brylmer and Mr Budzynski suffered a serious road traffic accident on their return journey from Birmingham last night.'

I stared at the woman blankly. This was not at all what I had been expecting.

'Oh.' I waited for more.

'I'm afraid that both men suffered fatal injuries. Mr Brylmer was killed instantly; Mr Budzynski died in hospital this morning. I'm very sorry.'

Utter silence descended on the kitchen. I played back the woman's words in my head, checking that I had understood them. I had. Andy was dead. So was Joe. I looked at Josh, he looked at me, and we both looked at the officers.

'Is there anyone you would like us to call?' the male officer asked.

I wondered whom they might have in mind: Megan? Andy's brother, rarely seen? An ancient aunt? Andy's sparse family had long since died or dissipated.

'I'll call my dad after you've gone,' Josh said, moving in to rescue me. 'I can look after Madison till he gets home.'

His sweet words brought me out of my daze.

'No. It's fine. We can sort everything out. What do I need to know now?'

The officers gave me details of the Birmingham hospital, the mortuary, the West Midlands police and the coroner's office, and gathered their hats to take their leave. As Josh moved to see them out, I motioned him back.

'Thank you for coming over.'

I was mollified to see the male officer gesture towards Josh.

'Take care, mate,' he said kindly.

Josh nodded darkly and they departed, leaving us staring after them in silence. Eventually Josh spoke again.

'Shall I ring dad?'

I looked at my watch. It was four thirty; Gerry had no evening engagement and would probably be home by eight. I shook my head.

'There's nothing he can do. It'll make no different whether we tell him now or later. It's more important that I try to contact someone in Birmingham before they close up for the night.'

'Are you okay?' Josh studied me closely.

'I think so. I'm glad you were here.' I held my hand out to him.

'I'm glad too, Mads. What can I do?'

'Pour me a glass of wine while I make some calls, and see to Ben when he gets back, would you? Is that all right?'

So, bless his heart, Josh brought me a glass of Shiraz while I rang the hospital and when Ben came slamming through the front door in a foul mood about a lost cricket match, Josh took him quickly in hand.

'Not now, Madison has enough to think about.'

His brother's sudden authority surprised Ben.

'What's going on?' he asked me.

'Andy has been killed in a car crash,' I said simply.

'Oh, Mads, what are you going to do?' He was awe-struck. 'Does it mean you're moving out?'

'Of course not.' I was suddenly tearful as the enormity of it began to strike me.

'Please don't cry, Madsy,' Ben hugged me. 'We love you. We'll look after you.'

They stayed close to me all evening as I called Andy's few relatives, and made what practical plans I could. When Gerry got home, Josh pulled Ben's arm – 'Come and watch TV with me' – leaving me to speak to Gerry alone.

'What's up with them?' he asked. 'You could cut the atmosphere with a knife.'

Through a fresh fall of tears I told him about the police visit, Andy's accident, and Josh's protective care for me. Gerry held me as I wept.

'What can I do now I'm here?' he asked.

'Exactly what you're doing now,' I said. 'I love you so much. Please be careful when you're driving. I couldn't bear anything to happen to you.'

'I'm indestructible,' he said, stroking my hair.

'No you're not, Gerry. None of us are. We can be here today and gone tomorrow.'

Wisely, he didn't pursue this and just hugged me till the boys slipped quietly back into the kitchen to check up on us.

As I kissed Ben goodnight he pulled at my hand before I could leave his side.

'You do love my dad, don't you?' he asked.

'With all my heart.'

'Cool. G'night.'

I was evidently dismissed.

'I think Ben is afraid I'm going to leave you now,' I told Gerry later.

He passed his hand wearily over his face.

'It's bringing Sue's death back to them, Madsy. It's bound to make them feel vulnerable. It may be nearly five years ago, but some days it feels like only yesterday, and this is one of them.'

Gerry looked pale and exhausted, and I sat down beside him, putting my arms around him in comfort as he so often did to me. He buried his face in the hollow of my neck, sighing heavily.

'Gerry, I'm sorry. You didn't bargain for all this when you took me on, I know.'

'Don't be silly. This is way beyond anyone's control, Madison, and we'll work through it together like anything else we'll have to face in the future. But it's knocked us a bit for six, I guess, and I understand if you feel differently about things now.'

I looked at him in amazement.

'Gerry, surely you don't think it changes how I feel about you?'

516

'No, I don't think it does. If there's one thing in this world I'm certain of, it's that you love me, even when I'm being less than loveable.'

'Especially then,' I teased.

'But take it from me, Madsy, you're going to run the gamut of emotions over the next few weeks and months: guilt, anxiety, doubt, you name it. People are going to say even more hurtful things to you than when Andy was alive to fight his corner. The sheer practicalities are going to wear you down. I've been there; I know what it's like. But for what it's worth, we're here and we love you, and I hope you'll want to stay.'

I entwined my fingers with Gerry's, taking in his brave and honest words.

'You're right that it's going to be tough, I know. I haven't absorbed it properly yet, and I know there'll be some difficult days ahead, but I don't think it will be quite as bad as it might have been.'

He looked at me enquiringly.

'I didn't tell you this at the time, but three weeks ago Andy came to see me.'

I told Gerry everything that had passed between us that day: Andy's amazing generosity and understanding, and his acceptance that Gerry and I were in some way meant to be together, despite all the heartache.

'If Andy had died without us having had that conversation I think I would have found his death very, very hard. So much unfinished business, so many words left unsaid. But he released me that day, Gerry, and set me free to love you and the boys. He was moving on, too, and it helped us both.'

'That was incredibly big hearted of him,' said Gerry in wonder.

'I know, and now it feels as if it were almost prophetic.'

We were silent, looking at each other seriously.

'I love you more than I have ever loved anyone in my life,' I said quietly.

Gerry smiled. 'Hmm. I know.'

CHAPTER 88

The days that followed took on an especially grim shape of their own. Despite our brief separation, I was, of course, still Andy's next of kin, and it was down to me to notify everyone who needed notifying and to organise his funeral. Joe's death meant that I didn't need to speak to anyone at The Dragon, however; they already knew and were reeling with shock. Joe was much loved and no one could envisage The Dragon without him at the helm. Doubtless the theatre would survive, but until his funeral it stayed dark in a gesture of respect. To my surprise, Ron Stryker telephoned me the day after the police had called.

'Madison, whatever happened between you and Andy is none of my business, but I know that you'll be feeling ghastly at the moment. I'm thinking of you, love.'

'Thank you, Ron, it's very kind of you to phone me,' I said gratefully.

'He was a good lad. We all loved him here, and he told me that coming to The Dragon was the best thing he'd ever done.'

'I know, Ron, but it's so good to hear you say it, too.'

Inevitably, of all the calls I had to make, the worst was to Megan. I picked up the phone a hundred times, replacing it again in sheer terror till Gerry made a suggestion.

'Go to see her. It may be hard facing her with the news, but ultimately I think you'll manage better than on the phone.'

I considered his words carefully. Gerry was right. A face to face encounter would give this most difficult of conversations a momentum it could quickly lose on the phone, especially if Megan hung up on me before I'd even started. I nodded slowly.

'Will you come with me?' I asked.

I stared at the phone, unable to meet Gerry's eye. I knew he hated dealing with the practicalities of my separation from Andy, and Megan had done nothing to make him feel welcome. He had every right to refuse, but I hoped he would support me in this, the hardest thing I had yet to face.

'If you'd like me to,' he said quietly.

'Very much.'

'Okay.'

He was looking at me seriously and sweetly, and I felt the power of my love for him surging through the fear and anxiety.

'Thank you,' I said.

I held out my arms and we embraced silently for a long time.

I rang Megan's secretary and made an appointment to see her at work. Clemmie had worked with Megan for nearly five years, so she knew me well. I was as frank with her as I could be.

'Clemmie, I don't know how much Megan's told you, but you've probably gathered that Mum and I are, uh, estranged.'

'I wondered, Mads,' she said tactfully.

'I need to see her urgently. I'd tell you why, but I don't think it's fair to do so before I've told her. Can I plead with you to wangle me an appointment with her tomorrow? Make up any excuse to get me in to see her, even if you have to tell her I'm someone else. I'll make sure she blames me, not you. I'm desperate Clemmie, and it can't wait any longer.'

Clemmie heard the panic in my voice and responded immediately.

'Can you come in at eight o'clock? That's when we go through the day's schedule, and she's not in court till ten. Would that give you enough time?'

'Oh, goodness, I hope so. I'm very grateful, Clemmie.'

'I won't tell her you're coming, Mads,' said Clemmie wisely. 'Just turn up and then I'll disappear. Ask for me at reception and I'll have them primed, too.'

We were both very quiet and nervous as we drove up to the city early the next morning, just beating the worst of the traffic by leaving at six thirty. Gerry squeezed my hand now and then, and let me press my face against his shoulder when he parked at the back of Megan's office, but I could see that he was feeling the pressure of this more than any of the other crises we had faced thus far. Clemmie had smoothed our way past security and we were in the lift, humming its way silently up to Megan's suite rather sooner than we'd hoped. Gripping Gerry's hand like a lifeline, I knocked on the outer door and waited as we heard a surprised murmur, and then footsteps cross the office. It seemed an eternity till Clemmie's friendly face appeared.

'Hi, Clemmie,' I stuttered.

'Madison?' she said in marvellously spontaneous surprise.

'Can we come in, please?' I asked nervously.

'Um, yes, I suppose so. Is Megan expecting you?'

I hoped this pantomime wouldn't have to go on much longer, and to my relief we were saved from further improvisation by Megan's astonished appearance at the door. She stared at us long and hard.

'I wouldn't have come if it weren't really vital. I know you don't want to see me,' I told her.

Clemmie faded away, but not before magically manoeuvring us into the office, and closing the door behind her as she left. Now Megan would have to actually throw us out if she wouldn't talk to me.

'What is it then?' she asked curtly, walking back to her desk.

I didn't know how to begin, but I knew I couldn't ask Gerry to do it for me. 'Mum.' I stopped.

'What is it Madison? I've got a busy morning.' She studiously ignored Gerry.

'Mum, Andy's been killed. He died in a car crash two days ago. I had to come to see you, to tell you in person. I couldn't do it on the phone.'

In the silence that fell as Megan took in my unexpected words, I reached for Gerry's hand again. He entwined his fingers in mine, but said nothing. It didn't matter; his presence was comfort enough.

'Where did it happen?' Megan spoke at last.

'In Birmingham. He and Joe were there with the *Puff* cast. I've arranged for his body to come back to London tomorrow. It looks as if the funeral will be next Tuesday.'

I felt an enormous wave of exhaustion wash over me. The last thirty-six hours had been a whirl of activity upon which I had no previous experience to draw and I'd no intention of asking Gerry to lend me anything but moral support. Now the effort I'd expended was catching up with me and I felt drained and weary.

Megan had wandered over to the window and was staring out over the city. I could think of nothing else to say. Eventually, she spoke again.

'This makes no difference, Madison,' she said coldly. 'I hope you didn't come here expecting me to fall into your arms. In fact, as far as I'm concerned, this makes it worse. If you think this gives you the liberty to pursue your new life free of the old, you'll soon find out to the contrary. You'll be dogged by guilt for the rest of your life, or at least you should be if you've a shred of decency left. But then, you're not the kind-hearted girl I brought up anymore, so who knows?'

Her uncompromising words left me breathless. I wanted to scream and cry, to beg her to accept me again, but I knew it would be worthless and demeaning.

'I'm sorry,' I said quietly.

'You don't know the meaning of the word,' Megan told me coldly.

'I'll let you know about the funeral.'

'Please do, I would like to be there. I hope at least you'll have the courtesy to come alone.' She glared at Gerry, who by now had had enough.

'I wouldn't dream of coming, even if Madison asked me to do so,' he said crisply. 'But I have come with her this morning because I know your response to our relationship has grieved her deeply. I am aware that it has made things difficult for you and for my part in that, I'm sorry. But I love Madison very much and I don't want her to be unhappy. It would mean a great deal to us both if you could be reconciled to her.'

I gazed at Gerry in love and gratitude, resolved to give him the hug of his life when we escaped. Megan wasn't impressed.

'I appreciate that you have Madison's best interests at heart, and I'm sure you do love each other, whatever that means, but I cannot lay aside everything I believe in so lightly. I won't go so far as to say that Madison is no daughter of mine, but I find it hard to accept that, as my daughter, she could act as she has done. I don't know how much blame I should attach to you, Gerry, but knowing my daughter as I do, I know that she does nothing she doesn't want to do, and if she chose to leave her husband to live with you, she did so of her own volition. Now, you'll have to go. I must get to work. I expect to hear about the funeral arrangements, Madison. You can leave the details with Clemmie.'

We were dismissed, so we took our leave, saying nothing till we were in the car again. Gerry reached into the back seat, retrieved the flask of coffee he'd made before we'd left home, and poured me a cup before he spoke.

'Drink some of that, sweetheart. It's sugared, but I think you need it,' he said.

I drank gratefully, then handed the empty beaker back to him, resting my head on his shoulder as he took it.

'Thank you for coming with me. I'm sorry she was rude to you.'

'I don't think she was, actually,' Gerry said thoughtfully. 'Given the circumstances, she was very restrained. After all, I am the evil seducer who has caused her little girl to stumble.'

'No, she doesn't think that,' I corrected him. 'You heard her say she knows that whatever I've done is my decision.' I put my arms round him and held him tightly. 'Darling, I love you so much. You were wonderful to me in there.'

'Hmm,' Gerry murmured cryptically, burying his face in my hair.

It was such a characteristic response that I giggled with relief, touching base with the present again. Whatever had happened, real life, present and future, lay with this beautiful man whose arms around me drove away every terror. Although he would never ask me to make the choice, at that moment I knew that Gerry had become infinitely more important to me than singing. No role, no opera house, no success, could ever take his place. A burden rolled away from me as the realisation swelled in my heart. I was free to sing, but not because it filled an empty place. Gerry had filled my emptiness and I knew, paradoxically, that in letting go of the relentless pursuit for perfection as a singer, I would grow as an artist and musician.

'I love you,' Gerry whispered.

'Good,' I murmured, adopting his inscrutable tone, and Gerry pulled my hair teasingly. I moved away to look at him, his sweet, ironic expression simultaneously tender, amused and sad. Only Gerry could look like that, and it was the face I always saw when I closed my eyes and thought of him.

'Meeting you was the most wonderful thing that could ever have happened to me,' I said, stroking his cheek.

'I'm glad you think so,' he said modestly, and it was so funny that I laughed out loud, hearty, hopeful, happy laughter.

'What did I say?' Gerry asked innocently.

'Never mind, darling, it loses something in the retelling. Let's just go home to bed. We've got to make up for that early start.'

So we did.

CHAPTER 89

Looking back to the day of Andy's funeral, with Lizzie and Annie (who had flown back from Berlin the same morning) standing loyally on either side, I felt that we did him proud. The crematorium chapel in Roehampton Vale was full to capacity and I'd had no trouble finding willing volunteers to speak about Andy. Ron and Steve were full of praise for his creativity and gift for friendship, and one of his students from the writing class he'd taught before The Dragon took over was fulsome in her gratitude to him for the inspiration he had given her. I would like to have spoken myself, but there were too many people who would have thought it unfitting, Megan, stony and unbending as she stood with Clemmie, chief amongst them. So Annie and I sang out fulsomely in the few cheerful choruses, and our voices rose together in the duet I had carefully chosen – Elgar's romantic setting of *Doubt Not Thy Father's Care*. Its sentimental religiosity may not have reflected Andy's character, but it comforted those who heard it and those who sang. The years rolled back as I let my voice fill every corner of the chapel, and I could envision Andy sitting in the front row, beaming his old proud smile, and saying, 'That's my girl, Mads. No one else stands a chance when you sing.' It was ironic, really, I mused, as Annie and I took our places again, but Gerry rarely complimented me on my singing these days. It was such an integral part of our lives that we took it for granted. Because Gerry was so closely involved in the same world he would think it redundant to tell me I was good – I wouldn't be doing it if I weren't. But Andy had been full of encouragement and praise, proud to see me making a successful career in a competitive, often intimidating, world. It didn't matter that Gerry took it for granted – his odd wry comment ('Well done, dear. Are you really going to do it like that?') meant all the more for its rarity – but I felt a wave of sadness and affection for Andy, who had so willingly given me so many years of support, even when his own career seemed to be going nowhere.

Unable to contemplate the prospect of returning to Exeter House after the funeral, I had suggested to Ron that he might like to host a small gathering at The Dragon. It had been the right decision. Andy's friends and colleagues headed off there immediately after the service, leaving Annie, Lizzie and I to finalise things at the crematorium. Desperate to speak to Megan, I grabbed her arm as she and Clemmie walked back to the Morgan. She pulled away sharply.

'Don't grab me, Madison.' She was as angry as I'd ever seen her.

'Please, Mum, don't go away like this.'

'Madison, we have no more to say to each other than we did two weeks ago,' she said coldly, climbing into the car.

Clemmie shrugged her shoulders helplessly behind Megan's back.

'Sorry, Mads,' she mouthed, and then they were gone in a rev of engine.

I sobbed as Annie and Lizzie held my hand and found me fresh tissues.

'I can't believe she's completely cut me out like this,' I cried. 'It must hurt her too.'

'I'm sure it does, Madsy,' said Lizzie wisely. 'You'll just have to wait for her to come to you in her own time.'

I was grateful to have my two friends at my side that day. Ben, bless his heart, had wanted to come with me, and I had been touched by his love and concern.

'Dad, Madison shouldn't have to go without us,' he'd complained.

'Darling, it's tough for her, I know,' Gerry agreed 'but it's just the way it's got to be.'

I longed to be back in their comforting and uncomplicated presence, but I had to make an appearance at The Dragon, feeling an outsider, but glad that in the last year of his life Andy had found a meaning and purpose and good friends. I had caused him pain, but miraculously, there had been a compensation for him in his new life at the theatre, and I was comforted again. If Joe and Andy had not taken that fatal drive, he would have been all right. He had a future that I dared to think might ultimately have brought him the happiness that lay in my life with Gerry, Ben and Josh.

My boys were beautiful to me that night. They had prepared a wonderful supper, Gerry opened a bottle of good wine, and they treated me as though I were made of Dresden china. When Ben made some crack about Josh's hair, and I giggled shakily, they decided that the best medicine was to make me laugh, each playing to the gallery in their own distinctive ways, until Gerry called time on their antics.

'Homework,' he declared in no-nonsense tones.

'Dad,' Ben wailed.

'Now.' Gerry looked pointedly at them and Josh got the message, dragging a reluctant Ben after him.

Gerry and I sat on the sofa till after dusk fell, talking softly about the past and the future, and I drew comfort from his warm, giving arms, and the knowledge that I belonged to him forever.

Figaro loomed and the next day we had to start rehearsals. I wasn't exactly in a Cherubino-type mood, but the voice took over, and I sang the familiar music with barely any conscious thought. By the end of the session I knew that Mozart would work his usual magic and be part of the healing process in the wake of Andy's death. I wasn't much fun for the boys, I knew, in those first weeks after Andy's funeral, nor for Gerry, I guessed, although he had less reason to expect me to be. We rehearsed almost every day and Gerry was also working towards a concert programme in Halifax at the beginning of July, so my subdued spirits were partly lost in the busyness. Gradually I began to feel stronger, but a lingering guilt and sadness, and the sharp pain of Megan's silence, cast a shadow over the days. I was newly grateful each day, however, for Andy's last visit to me. Without his brave and unselfish words still ringing in my head, I would have felt ten times worse.

Every few days I slipped back to Exeter House and began to put affairs there straight. I was loath to sell it, but the time had come to move everything I needed to Dulwich. It was strange how I enjoyed my quiet visits to the flat, needing time away from my new home as I truly came to terms with the dramatic events of the last year, most especially the weeks just past. But Gerry was so gentle and patient with me, I could feel sympathy emanating from him in every touch and glance, and I did my best to be the Madison he loved. I was sad that he had to go away to Halifax. He would be gone for two nights and it felt an eternity, so quickly had I become accustomed to his daily presence.

On the night before he left we lay in bed with the curtains open and watched the moon shed its light across the room.

'I'm sorry I've been rather *pianissimo* lately,' I said softly.

Gerry kissed my shoulders, running his hands over my back as he pulled me to him.

'I think it's understandable, don't you,' he replied. 'You've done brilliantly, anyway. You sat with Josh every day on his work; you're the most delicious Cherubino I've heard or seen, and you give Ben and me far more attention than we deserve at the moment. You've handled everything with dignity, and each night when you put your arms around me you remind me that I'm the luckiest man in the world. I've got my two beautiful sons, a career that many only dream of, and if that weren't enough, I've got you to share it with, and much more.'

Tears filled my eyes as Gerry smiled at me tenderly.

'You're not fed up with me then?' I asked childishly.

'I love you more every day,' he reassured me, stroking my breasts, and smiling as he watched the nipples rise to his touch.

'And I you.'

I kissed him deeply, feeling the wonderfully familiar, exciting, thrill of pleasure as our bodies responded to each other.

'My darling, if you're the luckiest man in the world, I must be the luckiest being in the whole universe. I still find it hard to believe that you love me, too, and that I'm not still gazing at you across a rehearsal studio wondering if you like me even a little bit.'

'You always were a serious distraction to me, Dr Brylmer,' he chided, 'and you knew how to take advantage of it.'

'Which I intend to do on a regular basis hereafter,' I said, pressing against him. 'Oh, Gerry, I'm going to miss you so much tomorrow – and the next day!'

'Then I'd better make sure you've got something special to remember me by,' he teased.

'As if I wouldn't.'

CHAPTER 90

I have never been made of the particular kind of female stuff that makes it possible for me to talk in even the most passing manner about what might be euphemistically dubbed 'women's troubles'. The graphic detail, fascinated and prurient interest, and sympathetic empathising that so often passed for conversation in dressing rooms throughout the land not only left me cold, but embarrassed, and I would immerse myself in my score rather than be drawn into it. One famous and talented soprano on the circuit seemed psychologically incapable of singing with anyone until they had been treated to a blow by blow account of the birth of her first child in all its gory splendour, and she wasn't the only one who seemed to think that a little female bonding could be accomplished only by a full and frank exchange on the subject of bodily functions.

So, given that I would generally rather read a good book, it took me by surprise to wake one morning two days later, and three weeks after Andy's funeral, to realise that I couldn't remember the last time I'd had a period. Such vagueness in these matters would doubtless horrify my aforementioned colleagues, but I took the same interest in the progress of my own menstrual cycle as I did in that of others: nil. This, then, was a rare, if not unique thought. I lay in bed, my hand instinctively reaching for Gerry, before remembering that he was in Halifax, and as I hugged his pillow in compensation, I tried to count back and to isolate a date. I failed utterly, wondering if I should perhaps have taken more interest in these matters before.

As I pondered, I lay so still I fancied I could hear the blood circulating in my veins. For a woman of my healthy constitution, a late period meant only one thing: I was pregnant. For a woman who was in the happy throes of a career which made peculiar physical, psychological, and chronological demands, it meant another thing: panic. I waited to start panicking. After about ten minutes I realised I wasn't, and I thought instead that perhaps I should panic about not panicking. But try as I might, all I could feel was calm, and gradually that calm was replaced by a sensation I hadn't felt since Andy's accident. An old friend was tentatively seeking new acquaintance: it was deep, consuming joy.

'Oh, Gerry,' I breathed into my pillow, and reached for the phone on the bedside table. I stopped before I lifted the receiver.

'Hold on, Madison,' I told myself severely. 'Firstly, you don't know if you *are* pregnant. Secondly, you can't possibly tell Gerry over the phone when he's two hundred miles from home. Thirdly, he may not actually be pleased, and fourthly, you don't know if *you'll* still be pleased once it's sunk in.'

I looked at the clock. I had to get Ben off to school and Josh to his new holiday job, make my way to our *Figaro* rehearsal, which was being taken by the assistant MD in Gerry's absence, and only then could I make my first ever trip to Boots for the purpose of buying a pregnancy testing kit. It was a truly incredible thought! Madison Brylmer, who up until eighteen months ago had never even wanted to spend time with a child outside a classroom or on a stage, now not only deeply loved one twelve-year-old and one sixteen-year-old, but was also, at thirty-nine years of age, contemplating with pleasure the possibility of having a baby!

I stirred reluctantly, lost in thought as I distractedly encouraged the boys to eat some breakfast, and gather together what they needed for the day. Ben complained loudly about having to take the bus to school.

'Why can't you drive, Madison?'

'Because I can't pass a driving test.' I said tersely. 'And since Gerry's got the car with him anyway, it wouldn't help if I could.'

'Dad says you've got to learn soon,' he told me.

'I know. I will.'

'Are you all right, Mads?' Josh asked. 'You're very quiet this morning.'

I looked at him tenderly.

'Yes, thank you, darling. I'm just thinking.'

'About Andy?' he asked.

'I'm ashamed to say not,' I told him, 'although he's at the back of my mind. But I'm really thinking about us.'

'Are you unhappy?' he asked, looking anxious. Ben had pricked up his ears and was listening intently to our exchange. I hastened to reassure them both, horrified that I might give them even a moment's reason to doubt that they, and their dad, were the precious centres of my life.

'Of course not.' I held out my arms. 'Come and give me a hug.'

We stood in the middle of the kitchen for a moment, our arms around each other.

'I love you both more than words can say, and being with you and Gerry makes me happier than I ever imagined I could be.'

'Cool,' Josh muttered, drawing away.

'Madison, where's my flute?' Ben asked, everything suddenly business as usual.

I was glad, and as they left the house I let myself wonder how they might receive a new sibling, so much younger than either of them that it would be virtually part of another generation. I dared to think that they were secure enough in Gerry's love to accommodate it, and I hoped that I was, too.

The prospect of a pregnant Cherubino gave me cause for some amusement that day as I bounced around with adolescent fervour. I thought the rehearsal would never end until I could eventually escape to make my purchase. Without thinking too hard about it, I went to Putney rather than Dulwich, and sat for a long time in the lounge, plucking up the courage to do the test. I gazed around the lovely flat, remembering so many things that had happened there. One day soon I would have to make a decision about it, and I knew I couldn't keep slipping back here, escaping into the peaceful solitude that it offered me. It was so quiet, ordered and beautiful. But it was not where my new life lay, and I would have to let it go at some point, even if only to allow tenants take it over for a while. Perhaps one day Ben or Josh might want it, and that would feel right and proper, it would become their new home rather than my old one.

Eventually, I did it, of course, and sat with a mug of tea whilst I waited. The fourth act of *La Bohème* played on the CD and, unable to read, I allowed the music to wash over me. The thin blue line was no surprise. I had known since I woke that morning that I was carrying Gerry's baby.

'Hello,' I whispered. 'What *is* your dad going to say?'

Gerry was at home when I finally returned.

'Where on earth have you been?' he asked, looking bewildered. 'Your mobile's turned off; I thought you'd be back ages ago. The boys didn't know where you were.'

It wasn't the most encouraging start.

'I went back to the flat for a bit,' I told him.

'Oh. Did you collect something?'

'Yes.' I held up a bag, having indeed used the opportunity to bring more personal items with me. 'Sorry, I lost track of time.'

Gerry scrutinised me closely.

'What's the matter? Has someone given you some hassle today? Megan?'

'No, darling, I'm fine. I'm sorry if I worried you. Are Josh and Ben okay?'

Gerry nodded. 'Of course. They just said they had no idea where you were and disappeared. You know what they're like. They'd do their own thing if the house fell down around them.'

'Gerry, I'm so pleased to see you.' I held my arms out to him. 'Please don't be cross with me.'

He laughed. 'I'm not cross. I was just so looking forward to seeing you, and then you weren't here. I felt cheated.'

He held me close then pushed me back against the cabinets, kissing me hard, his body firm and insistent.

'I love you,' he murmured. It was so wonderful to hear him tell me, I squirmed with pleasure.

'I love you too. Gerry?'

'Madison?'

'Oh, nothing. I missed you last night.'

'And I missed you. I intend to make up for it.'

I giggled against his chest, and we kissed until Ben slammed into the kitchen.

'Oh, boring,' he said looking us over with great patronage. 'Aren't we getting any supper tonight, Dad? Mads, I need you to do my homework.'

'You've been summoned,' Gerry said, slapping my rump. 'Go and do his Lordship's bidding. I'll cook.'

I didn't tell Gerry that night, or the next day. I hugged the news to myself, thinking and feeling thoughts and sensations I had never imagined I would ever own. I cuddled up to Gerry in bed unable to get close enough to him to express how deeply I loved and wanted him. He responded warmly and we made love with abandon that night. I woke him in the morning, stroking him to arousal and kissing him long and hard.

'Lovely, beautiful Madison,' he murmured with pleasure. 'You are insatiable, you sexy babe.'

'I can't get enough of you.'

'Good. Keep it that way.'

Nevertheless, I worried how Gerry would react when I finally told him my news. It was so early, so unexpected. We were both so old, for goodness sake. But I knew how much he adored his sons; he was the most natural and loving father I had ever seen, and that gave me hope. But still I held back, waiting for the right moment. And like all right moments, it was a long time coming.

It came when I least expected it. We were rehearsing intensively for *Figaro* all that week and the next, preparing to leave for Cornwall on the third Saturday in July. The boys were coming with us and the atmosphere in the house was one of impending holiday as well as a working week for Gerry and me.

'Thank you, God,' Gerry breathed in relief, watching Josh playing cricket in the garden with Ben. 'He went to every exam. He was there on time. He has reached the end of compulsory schooling and he actually wants to go back next term.' He turned to me, holding out his arms. 'And thank you, my darling, for everything you've done for him. For making sure my prejudices didn't prevent him going to a school that he's prepared to tolerate, and for all those hours you sat with him revising. You are a miracle, Madison.'

'Let's not get this out of proportion,' I laughed. 'I love him, and I'm good at tutoring, so it was easy. And Josh is very bright; if he does what he chooses to do he'll be fine.'

I nearly told Gerry then, but the moment passed as he dashed off to coach a visiting tenor and my courage failed me. As each day sped by, I kept testing my own responses. Was I still happy to be pregnant? What was I afraid of? It couldn't be Megan's reaction for once, since there was nothing more I could do to alienate her further than I had done already. Apart from Annie (who would be horrified, but pleased that I was happy) and Lizzie (who would envy me at least having a partner), no one else would care a jot one way or the other. It was all down to Gerry, and as I watched him, tender and loving with Ben and Josh, I couldn't work out why I was so worried.

It was over a week after I'd made my discovery and three days before we left for Cornwall when I finally gave in. We'd run *Figaro* twice that day, once with piano and once with orchestra, and we were both exhausted. Foolishly, almost dropping with weariness, and failing to notice that Ben was not in his usual good spirits, I was annoyingly pedantic with him about packing.

'But, Mads, we don't need to pack yet,' Ben declared when I suggested he considered what he wanted to take.

'No, but neither do we want to do it at 5 am on Saturday when we've a long drive ahead of us. Your dad and I are rehearsing all tomorrow and Friday. It would be helpful to do some of it now.'

A deeply boring and unnecessarily heated discussion ensued, which grew recklessly to encompass thus far unresolved topics dear to our hearts: tidiness and the lack thereof; ironing, and the failure of Mrs Tiggywinkle, or anyone else, for that matter, to manifest herself in my absence to accomplish the task; Ben's failure to take seriously my concerns about equipping himself properly for ten days away from home, and my failure to appreciate that Ben quite clearly couldn't care less if he ran out of clean clothes after three days.

I listened to myself nagging like a harpy and to Ben's mutinous outrage, thinking somewhere through my exhausted irritation, 'We must stop this', when Ben brought the ridiculous argument to a resounding halt with words that made my blood run cold.

'Anyway, what's it got to do with you?' he shouted. 'You're not my mother. We did all right before you came along. Dad doesn't need you, and Josh and I sure don't need you.'

He slammed out of the bedroom and down the stairs, venting his anger on a football lying in the hall. I heard it crash against the table, but I stood frozen to the spot. I didn't move till Gerry put his bewildered face around the door.

'What on earth was all that about?'

I burst into noisy sobs.

'Hey, hey, come on sweetheart, what is it?'

'He hates me, Gerry,' I wept, 'and I don't blame him. I was being such a miserable cow; I don't know what came over me.' I moved to get up. 'It's all right, I'm going now. I'll see you on Saturday; I'll make my own way down there.'

'Madison, stop this at once.' Gerry spoke firmly, but his arm around my shoulders was gentle. 'Whatever you said to Ben, I'm sure he gave as good as he got. We're all tired and busy, and tonight you just caught each other at the wrong moment. He'll have forgotten it in half an hour.'

'But he said that you don't need me around. If that's true, I don't want to stay.'

Gerry held me close.

'I need you very, very much. Don't ever think otherwise. And you know perfectly well that Ben and Josh adore you and would be devastated if you weren't around. We share a life now, Madison. We belong together.'

I sobbed against his chest.

'But... Oh, Gerry, they're really going to hate me now. You're going to hate me.'

'What on earth are you talking about?' Gerry sounded exasperated, and I couldn't bear it any longer.

'I'm pregnant.'

Weeping steadily, I hardly felt Gerry take my hands away from my face, and lift my head to look him in the eye.

'Are you certain?' he asked quietly.

I nodded.

'How long have you known?'

'Eight days.'

'Why didn't you tell me?'

'I was scared.'

'Of what?' Gerry looked puzzled.

'We hadn't planned it. You've already got children. We both work non-stop. We're both so old.' I sobbed again. 'And I've just proved I'll be a disaster as a mother.'

Gerry stroked my cheek softly.

'You are a beautiful mother already in every way that matters. Ben and Josh have gained a hundredfold from your love and patience and common sense.'

I rested my head on his shoulder.

'But how will we cope? We've barely been together for five minutes. I'm so sorry.'

'I was there, too,' he laughed. 'You haven't cooked this little thing up all on your own.'

I giggled damply.

'I agree it's unexpected, but perhaps that's the best way,' he continued. 'If we'd thought about it and tried to make a rational decision about whether to have a baby we'd probably have decided against it, for all the practical reasons you've outlined. But I think that would have been a great shame. Why shouldn't we? We love each other very much; we're mature and intelligent; we've both got a good sense of humour, plenty of money, a ready-made family and lots of love to give.'

I laughed more heartily this time.

'And we're not at all pleased with ourselves, are we?'

Gerry grinned. 'Darling, we'll cope. I don't know what there is not to cope about.' He looked at me happily. 'What's the time scale, then?'

'I'm not really sure yet, but I'll be all right for *Nabucco* at Glyndebourne next summer, and they can just give me a baggy costume for *Cosi*, and the *Carmen* revival.

'Well, that makes everything okay, doesn't it?' Gerry chuckled, and I knew that it would be.

'Let's tell the boys,' he said.

'Please, Gerry, can we wait? Next week perhaps, but can we keep it between us for a few days? It's so big I need to let it out bit by bit.'

538

'Okay,' he agreed, 'but don't be afraid of what they'll say. They'll be cool.'

He held his hand out to me. 'Come on, time to make peace with the little one.'

Ben was sitting in the depths of the battered settee, plucking edgily at a cushion, all the fight drained from him. He looked up anxiously.

'Hello, darling,' I said easily. 'I'm sorry I was such a bore, I think you'll have to blow a whistle when I'm being a nag, so I know when to stop.'

Ben looked immediately happier.

'I'm sorry for what I said, Mads. I didn't mean it. I don't want you to leave us.'

'I have absolutely no intention of so doing,' I said, sitting next to him. 'You'll have to try much harder than that to get rid of me.'

So we cuddled up on the settee and I'm pleased to say that I didn't mention packing once.

CHAPTER 91

Some days later I built my first sandcastle; as an adult, that is. There is photographic evidence of me having indulged in this pastime as a child, but I quickly deemed such activities demeaning and anti-intellectual. At thirty-nine I was evidently experiencing a second childhood as well as a first pregnancy, and I participated with glee in the serious task of building an especially elaborate sand structure. Even Josh clearly considered it an important enough part of the McFall family tradition to dabble a little with sand and water, looking only marginally irritated that his nail varnish was in danger of being chipped.

Figaro was going wonderfully well. We enjoyed beautiful weather, enthusiastic audiences and good reviews. I felt lush and fecund, not at all like the excitable, pubescent Cherubino, but my happiness still communicated itself in my singing, and I was so full of energy I crackled. After every performance the audience cheered as I ran down for my curtain call, untying my hair from its ponytail and shaking out my golden curls in pleasure. I didn't know how much longer I could get away with singing the role – it was a young woman's part, really – but as I looked in the mirror each evening as I did my make-up, I knew that love and happiness had taken years off me in the last twelve months.

Every day, even when we had a matinee, we went down to the beach and swam, or Gerry and I lay in the sun and talked whilst the boys did their own thing. In our rented cottage we cooked huge meals before and after the show, and slept deeply until Ben insisted we got up. One night, after Josh and Ben were asleep, Gerry and I slipped down to the cove and made love on the sand as moonlight lit the beach and the sea ran back and forth over the tiny shingle.

'When I first fell in love with you I fantasised about doing this,' I told Gerry shyly.

'I hope it's lived up to your expectations,' he joked.

'Oh, darling, it's far exceeded them,' I laughed. 'Everything's far exceeded them. I can't believe how happy we are. I certainly don't deserve it.'

'I don't care whether you deserve it or not,' Gerry replied. 'I just want to make you as happy as you make me, to keep thanking you for all the love and care you give to me and the boys.'

'I can think of a very good way of doing that right now.'

'You'd better show me,' he murmured. 'I wouldn't want to get it wrong.'

He didn't.

I'd adopted the policy that I would keep Megan in touch with where I was and what we were doing, and it was up to her if she wanted to mend the breach. I understood why she was angry with me, and I knew that however happy I was with Gerry and the life we would build with our children, I would always feel deep regret for what I had done to Andy. His death didn't make the guilt any better or worse since my part had been played long before that final chapter unfolded, but it would always be there, although I knew it would fade as time passed, and eventually I would be able to look at it with less pain. I felt sure that one day Megan would seek to be reconciled, but I was in no hurry to take the initiative. I wanted it to come from her, and for her to be ready to accept Gerry, Ben and Josh without reservation. The news that she was finally to be a grandmother could wait, too, until we had told the boys.

So it took me by surprise when Megan rang my mobile on our penultimate day in Cornwall. I had sent her a note before we left London, so she knew we would still be out of town. In previous years, of course, she would have been down to see the show, but things were different then. I hesitated as I saw her name flash on the digital display. This was sooner than I expected.

'Hello, Mum.'

'Hello.' She waited.

'Are you all right?'

'Yes. I'm fine.'

She clearly wasn't going to make this easy for me. Gerry had gone into the village to buy a newspaper and I was alone in the kitchen. It was just her and me and I had to tough it out alone.

'We're in Cornwall still,' I said. 'We've got three performances left over the next two days. The weather's been lovely.'

'I see.'

'What are you up to?'

'Working, what else?'

I didn't know where to go from here.

'Have you called for anything specific?' I asked, 'or just to chat?'

'Do I need permission to call you, then?' she asked acerbically. I sighed heavily; I'd got it wrong again.

'Of course not. It's just a surprise. You haven't called for a while.'

'Neither have you.'

'But I have written, Mum. You know where I am and what I'm doing.'

'I certainly do.'

This was ghastly. I decided to go for the big guns.

'Actually, there's something you don't know yet. I've only just found out myself.'

'Oh yes.' Megan was ice cool.

'We're expecting a baby. I think he or she will be born in February.'

There was a deathly hush at the other end of the line. Eventually, she spoke.

'I'm hanging up now, Madison.'

'Please, Mum, hold on a minute,' I said quickly. 'Isn't this a good moment to try to reconcile things?'

'I don't think so. You've chosen the life you want to lead and all I can see is the trail of disaster you've left behind you. If you ever think about it from someone else's perspective than your own, you might see that, too.'

'I know I hurt Andy, but before he died he came to see me. I didn't tell you that. He visited me and we laid some of the ghosts to rest. We were really trying to find a way to be friends still. That's what he and I always did best. Even he said that we should have been brother and sister rather than husband and wife.'

'I'm sorry, Madison, I know you think I'm hard, but I won't condone what you've done. I thought maybe we could start building our relationship again, but after what you've told me – about the baby – it's too much. I can't, not now at least.'

'Mum, this baby's going to want to know both its grandmas.'

'One day, perhaps.'

'I truly love Gerry. He's the man I was always meant to be with. He's very good to me, Mum.'

'If that's what you believe, I hope it turns out to be true.'

'What do you want?' I asked sadly. 'Do you want me to leave Gerry? Would that make everything better?'

'Do whatever your conscience tells you to do, Madison. I'm going now.'

The line went dead.

I was shaking as I put the phone down. I still didn't know whether Megan had truly been phoning in a spirit of reconciliation or not; if she was, I'd destroyed it with the news of my pregnancy, but she would have come to know at some point. Guilt weighed so heavily on my shoulders that I leaned over the table, pressing my hands flat on its surface. It was too late to mend anything that had gone before: Andy was dead, and even if he'd survived the crash I wouldn't have gone back to him. We had both accepted that; why couldn't Megan accept it too?

I needed to get out into the fresh air of the summer morning. I quickly scrawled a note, leaving it on the table for Gerry – *Gone to the cove. Back very soon. I love you* – and left the house quietly, not wanting Ben or Josh to follow me. It was still early and the path to the beach was deserted. I walked to the far side of the bay where Gerry and I had lain together earlier in the week, smiling as I sat on the warm sand and remembered the moonlight and the feel of his sweet body on mine. I sat there for a long time, not moving; not even really thinking, but just letting the lull of the sea soothe me, and the sun kiss my cheeks.

I looked out across the shining water, at the sun glittering so optimistically on its surface: yellow and blue and green, and the little puffs of white, as tiny waves occasionally broke the smooth surface. I hadn't killed Andy: I hadn't been driving the car; I hadn't tampered with the brakes; I hadn't even been a passenger; he would still have taken that fateful trip with Joe even if I hadn't left him. Neither was I responsible for Megan's unhappiness or disapproval. But I could take responsibility for myself, and for my own feelings, and it was time to claim that responsibility. I had a future of love and motherhood, if I chose to take it. I had a new life, if I chose to make it new.

I was no longer the Madison I had been; I knew that with startling clarity. Even if I walked away from this beautiful place today alone, I was still changed – the events of the last year had already determined that. But if I was irrevocably changed, if I could never again interpret my life within the parameters that had once seemed so sure, if never again could I look on the world without knowing that Gerry and Ben and

Josh were in it and that their existence made a profound difference to me, then why walk away alone?

I lifted my face to the sun and felt the warmth of its soft caress. The sun, so often my solace, comforted me now, but it seemed there was a new urgency in its touch.

'Madison, it's okay to be happy,' it seemed to say.

I smiled at my old friend, enjoying the touch of the warm rays across my cheeks.

I turned from the water to gaze idly at the cliff path winding down to the beach, watching tiny figures growing larger as they descended: children and dogs, mothers, grandfathers, brothers, people with lives so tightly interwoven that nothing could ever break the ties. And as I watched, I saw two of those figures veer away from the stream heading for the sea and move easily across the sand towards my secret corner. I could see them before they would see me, but they knew where they were going. They knew that they would find me here. Josh and Ben, their long legs matching each other stride for stride, determined, focussed. I rested my hand on my stomach, still flat and firm. 'Come on, little one,' I whispered, 'I think it's time you we introduced you to your brothers.'

I rose to meet them.

Printed in the United Kingdom
by Lightning Source UK Ltd.
101200UKS00001B/1